DEAD
WRONG

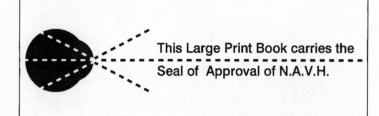
This Large Print Book carries the
Seal of Approval of N.A.V.H.

DEAD WRONG

MARIAH STEWART

WHEELER
PUBLISHING

Dead Wrong is a work of fiction. Names, places, and incidents are either a product of the author's imagination or are used fictitiously.

Published in 2004 by The Ballantine Publishing Group, a division of Random House, Inc.

Wheeler Large Print Romance.

The text of this Large Print edition is unabridged.
Other aspects of the book may vary from the original edition.

Set in 16 pt. Plantin by Myrna S. Raven.

Printed in the United States on permanent paper.

Library of Congress Cataloging-in-Publication Data

Stewart, Mariah.
    Dead wrong / Mariah Stewart.
       p. cm.
     ISBN 1-58724-804-2 (lg. print : hc : alk. paper)
     1. Government investigators — Fiction.   2. Telephone — Directories — Fiction.   3. Serial murders — Fiction.   4. Large type books.   I. Title.
PS3569.T4653D43 2004
813´.54—dc22   2004055493

DEAD
WRONG

As the Founder/CEO of NAVH, the only national health agency solely devoted to those who, although not totally blind, have an eye disease which could lead to serious visual impairment, I am pleased to recognize Thorndike Press* as one of the leading publishers in the large print field.

Founded in 1954 in San Francisco to prepare large print textbooks for partially seeing children, NAVH became the pioneer and standard setting agency in the preparation of large type.

Today, those publishers who meet our standards carry the prestigious "Seal of Approval" indicating high quality large print. We are delighted that Thorndike Press is one of the publishers whose titles meet these standards. We are also pleased to recognize the significant contribution Thorndike Press is making in this important and growing field.

Lorraine H. Marchi, L.H.D.
Founder/CEO
NAVH

* Thorndike Press encompasses the following imprints: Thorndike, Wheeler, Walker and Large Print Press.

From Pat Holsten's journal:

"Work like you don't need the money.
Dance like no one is watching.
Love like you've never been hurt."

And she did.

I think the Devil will not have me damned,
lest the oil that is in me should set Hell on fire.

— William Shakespeare
The Merry Wives of Windsor

Prologue

February 2004

Outside the courthouse, sleet hissed softly, striking the front of the old stone building at sharp angles with muffled *plunk*s. From a narrow first-floor window, Curtis Alan Channing watched water spill from partially frozen gutters to overflow in icy waterfalls onto the frosted ground below. His eyes flickered upward to a sky the color of cinders, its low clouds hovering over the naked trees that lined the main walk leading to the courthouse steps.

News vans from competing television stations were parked side by side along the one-way street. He stared for a while, hoping to see if one of the pretty young reporters might surface, but no one emerged in the face of the storm other than a cameraman who occasionally poked his head out to check the readiness of his equipment before ducking back into the shelter of the vehicle. Channing wondered idly what event could be of sufficient interest to bring all those media types out so early on such a morning.

God knows they weren't there to see him.

His eyes studied the sky as if he had nothing more immediate on his mind than the storm, but all the while he wondered how he'd managed to get himself into this mess and where it would, ultimately, lead.

It would be funny, if it had happened to someone else.

After all, to have successfully flown so low under the radar for all these years that he'd never even been fingerprinted, only to be brought in on an outstanding warrant that was a clear case of mistaken identity after he'd been stopped for blowing a stop sign, well, the irony was just killing him.

Course, now he had been fingerprinted. He'd have to keep that in mind in the future.

He shifted slightly in his seat and turned his head in the direction of the door, his ears picking up the sound of running feet. Seconds later, he heard shouts from somewhere slightly distant. Soon it became apparent that there was some sort of ruckus in the hallway beyond the small room where he'd been deposited. He hoped whatever it was wouldn't interfere with his moment in court. He wanted nothing more than to get this over with and go on his way, wherever that might lead him.

He glanced at the clock on the wall for the tenth time since he'd been shown into the anteroom off the judge's chambers to await his hearing. It was almost nine thirty in the morning. He'd been sitting there since eight forty-seven, and he was getting really, really bored.

He openly studied the young sheriff's deputy who guarded the door. Couldn't be much more than twenty-five, Channing figured. Didn't look like much of a fighter — nor much of a lover, either, he smirked inwardly. He could take this kid blindfolded and with one hand behind his back.

Which, of course, he would not be fool enough to do. He hadn't gone all these years without getting so much as a traffic ticket — well, not until Saturday morning, anyway — by being a fool. He wasn't about to start now.

No, he'd wait patiently for them to bring him before the judge, he'd explain courteously that he was not the Curtis Channing who was named in that warrant — he was Curtis *Alan* Channing, not Curtis *Andrew* Channing — and hopefully the court would check the social security numbers and physical descriptions, acknowledge the error, then see fit to let him walk out the door and go about his business. He would be gracious and charming, of course; set the arresting officers at ease by letting them know that he understood an honest mistake when he saw one and had no intention of suing them for false arrest.

A man in his position would have to be an idiot to threaten some kind of legal action.

There was more noise from the hallway, and he met the deputy's eyes momentarily.

"What's going on out there?" he asked.

The deputy smoothed his brown tie and

shrugged his disinterest, as if too cool to speak to a prisoner.

This kid is green, Channing thought.

"How long you been working for the sheriff's department?"

"Long enough."

Uh-huh.

Before he could comment aloud, the slap-slap-slap of running feet pounded past the door. This time the young deputy did react, turning nervously to the glass panes and craning his neck to see what was going on. There was shouting now, and the door opened unexpectedly. An older deputy leaned in, whispered a few words to Channing's guard, who nodded vigorously.

"We're going to have to move you," he said, motioning to his prisoner, "just into the next room."

Channing stood and shuffled past obediently, curious as to what was going down. There was much commotion in the hallway, where a great number of brown-uniformed deputy sheriffs and other law enforcement types bustled about, some with their hands on their guns.

They're on the hunt, Channing thought, and wondered if perhaps one of the other inmates who'd made the ride in with him from the prison that morning had somehow managed to slip past the guards.

"Here you go, boys," the older deputy announced as he opened the door to a room that was somewhat larger than the one Channing had occupied. "Got another roommate for you . . ."

The deputy held the door open as Channing made his entrance and nodded to the two men already within, both of whom he recognized as passengers from the van. Both were shackled like him, hands in front connected to a chain at the waist that connected to leg irons fastened at the ankles. The guard touched Channing in the middle of his back and pointed to a chair that stood against the wall. He moved toward it and sat, ignoring the indignity of being secured to the chair as were, he noticed, the other two prisoners.

"Behave yourselves, boys. No monkey business. A guard will be right outside. He's armed and he won't hesitate for one second to bring you down if you so much as move," the deputy told them, then stepped into the hallway and closed the door behind him.

"A bit heavy-handed, wouldn't you say?" Channing mused as the door snapped shut.

"He's just trying to intimidate us. There's not one deputy sheriff in this county who could hit a man from more than ten feet away. They just ain't that good," scoffed the man who sat nearest the door. His red hair was fading as it mixed with gray, his white arms and face were covered with pale freckles. He reminded Channing of an aging Woody Woodpecker.

"Ah, then you've been here before," Channing ventured.

"Lately, I been here almost as much as I been at High Meadow." Woody named the county prison.

"What d'ya suppose is going on out there?" The third occupant of the room, a baby-faced man — a kid, really — with large round eyes, frowned nervously.

"They're playing *Where's Waldo?*" Woody told him. "Waldo Scott. He rode in with us in the van this morning. He got himself free somehow and took off. Get it? *Where's Waldo?*"

"No." The young prisoner — Young Blood, Channing mentally tagged him — shook his head. "I don't get it."

"They're kids' books," Channing explained, though he couldn't remember how he knew this.

"Yeah, Waldo runs around in a red-and-white-striped hat or shirt or something, and you have to find him on each page."

"Is it hard?" Young Blood asked.

"Only for five-year-olds." Woody smirked.

"Did you know he was going to bolt?" Channing asked.

"There'd been a rumbling, you know, in the cell block." Woody leaned forward, his pale hands dangling between his legs. "But no one thought he'd be stupid enough to try it. He's going to get caught — not because these guys here" — he nodded in the direction of the hallway — "are that good. But once they put the courthouse on lockdown, like they just did,

14

there's no way to get out. There's one door in the front, and one door in the back, and they're both guarded. He can hide in here for a while — crawl around in the ductwork, find a forgotten storeroom, maybe — but they'll catch him before long. I think he's just trying to have a little fun."

"Won't be much fun if they tack on some extra time to his sentence," Channing noted.

"He's serving sixty years. I don't think he much cares about another twelve or twenty-four months."

"What'd he do?" Young Blood asked.

"Armed robbery. Hit two banks in two days out here in the county. Shot a guard. His attorney filed a motion for a new trial, but Waldo knew it wasn't going to happen. He only wanted to go through with the hearing today to see if he could get an opportunity to fly. Looks like he made it. Not that it will do him any good." He turned to Channing. "How 'bout you? What're you in for?"

"I was stopped for going through a stop sign —"

"Now, there's a manly crime," Woody muttered under his breath. "Explains the need for the leg shackles."

"— and it turned out there was an outstanding warrant for a guy with the same name," Channing continued. "You?"

"I'm in here pending appeal of a conviction." The smirk was back.

"For what?" Young Blood asked.

"A domestic dispute," Woody said dryly.

"Oh." The young man nodded warily, then volunteered, "I'm supposed to have my trial today. I hope they find Waldo in time to get started. I want to get it over with."

"What are the charges?" Channing asked.

"Well, see, they're saying I stalked this girl." His face began to cloud. "But I didn't stalk nobody. She was my girl, you know? They got the whole thing all wrong."

"She must have complained about something for them to charge you. What did she tell the police?" Channing leaned forward, interested now, wondering just what Young Blood had gotten himself into.

"She was confused. The cops made her lie." The young man grew visibly agitated. "They made her say things. Things that weren't true. I wouldn't do nothing to hurt her. . . ."

"What's your name, son?" Channing asked, changing the subject and hoping to calm the boy down. It wouldn't do to have him go off and bring in the guards, who surely had more than a little adrenaline pumping owing to the escape and the courthouse being on lockdown.

"Archer Lowell," the young man told him.

"I'm Curtis Channing. I'd shake your hand, but, well . . ." Channing held up his shackled wrists, and Lowell smiled for the first time.

Woody began to introduce himself. "Well, Archie, I'm —"

16

"Don't call me Archie. Do not ever call me Archie."

"Whoa, buddy. Chill," the red-haired man said. "No offense. No need to get all upset."

"I hate the name Archie," Lowell grumbled.

"Okay. Archer. I'm Vince Giordano. Named for my uncle, Vincenzo — maybe you heard of him? He was a singer back in the fifties. Had his own band and everything. Vinnie and the High Notes. We don't speak no more. Bastard testified against me in court. So much for blood being thicker than water."

Lowell stared at Giordano for a long minute, then said, "I know who you are. I saw you on the news when you were arrested. . . ."

"Yeah, well, I got a lot of press back then, and the trial got a lot of airtime."

Channing leaned back as far as he could in the chair and rested the back of his head upon the wall, wondering just what kind of domestic dispute had merited such coverage by the local news.

"I saw the news vans out front." Channing nodded toward the window. "I was wondering who they were here to see."

"Fame is a curse," Giordano said dryly. "Guess they're getting more of a story than they planned on."

"So how long you think they're going to leave us in here?" Lowell asked, watching Giordano with a mixture of awe and fear.

"If, as you say, the courthouse is locked

down because a prisoner escaped, we could be here for a while. At least until they find him." Channing stretched his neck so that he could peer out a nearby window. "Looks like there's lots of law enforcement activity, and lots of press around to report on it. There were only two small crews earlier. Now there are five set up, and another van just pulled in."

"Law enforcement activity," Giordano mimicked. "You mean there are lots of cops out there."

"Cops, yes, but FBI and state police, too. And if there are that many out there, you can be sure there are at least that many in here, looking for your friend."

"Hey, he's not my friend." Giordano shook his head. "Not too many got real friends inside — you know what I mean?"

Channing shook his head. He didn't know what Giordano meant, but he tried to imagine what it might be like to have a friend, in or out of prison. Except for a small dog he'd once owned, friends had pretty much eluded him.

"I don't think it's fair that I should miss my trial," Lowell whined, "just because they lost someone and can't find him."

"Yeah, well, tell it to the judge." Giordano gave him a cold stare, and the young man shrank from it. "I ain't too happy about the delay myself. We had a big day planned here. My attorney says he's going to get the judge to overturn my conviction."

"What were you convicted of?" Channing asked.

"Shooting my wife," Giordano said calmly, "among other things."

"Did you?" Channing asked, and Lowell looked appalled at the question.

Giordano merely smirked.

Channing took that as a yes. "Why would they overturn your conviction?" Channing inquired.

"Because the cop who headed the investigation — the first one at the scene — made up evidence when he couldn't find none. He lied on the witness stand, and everyone connected with the investigation knows that he lied."

"They can let you go for that?" Lowell was interested in this possibility. "If somebody lies?"

"Yup. If they lie big enough, like this guy did."

"But don't they just try you all over again?" Lowell leaned forward.

"Nope. My lawyer says they can't do it." Giordano looked smug. "First time around, the D.A. loaded the charges against me. Tried me for everything he could think of. All of those charges were supported by the evidence provided by this one cop. And none of it was good." His face lit up. "And you wanna hear the best? The cop, he's facing perjury charges. He's lost his job, he could go to prison. And they're gonna have to let me out. Ain't that a bitch?"

19

"What's the first thing you're gonna do when you get out, Vince?" Lowell tried not to look starstruck, but Channing could tell that he was fascinated by Giordano, who, apparently by virtue of his crime, was something of a local celebrity.

"Depends," Giordano shrugged, "on whether or not I'd get caught."

"What if you wouldn't? What if you could do anything — anything at all — and not get caught."

"Gotta think on that a minute . . ." Giordano rubbed his jaw thoughtfully. "I'd put a bullet through the head of my ex-mother-in-law," he said without blinking. "And then I'd do that woman — the advocate — who worked for the courts. The one who told the judge to take my kids away from me. And then the judge who said I couldn't see my kids no more. Yeah, I'd do her last. . . ."

A darkness seemed to emanate from Giordano as he spoke, spilling into the room and filling it, threatening to choke out the air around them.

No stranger to evil himself, Channing recognized it when he met it head-on. He tucked away the information and chose to ignore it, for now.

"Where are your kids?" Channing had a hunch that he knew what the answer would be, but wanted his assessment of Giordano confirmed.

20

Giordano stared at him coolly, then replied, "They're with their mother."

The three men sat in silence for a long minute.

"How 'bout you, Archer? What would you do if you could do anything when you get out and not get caught doing it?" Giordano asked.

"I don't know." Lowell's brows knit together as he pondered this. "Maybe . . . I don't know, maybe that guy, that guy that kept bothering my girl. Maybe him, if he's still around. And that neighbor of hers, that nosy bitch."

"What about your girl?" Giordano taunted. "Seems like she's the real problem here. She's the one who called the cops on you, right? Why don't you call on her when you get out? I know I would, if it was me."

"Oh, I'm gonna pay her a call, all right." Lowell narrowed his eyes, encouraged by Giordano's toughness and maybe feeling a little bit of bravado of his own. "I'm gonna call on her first thing I get out of here."

"How 'bout you, Channing? Anyone you gonna go see?" Giordano turned his attention to him.

"Never thought about it."

"Oh, that's right. You're in here because of a mistaken identity. After being picked up for a traffic violation. Guess the first guy you'd be going to see is that other Curtis Channing, right? Then maybe the cop who arrested you."

Channing laughed, and Giordano added,

21

"Hey, Curtis, we're just bullshitting here. There has to be someone, someplace, who you'd like to show a thing or two if you ever got the chance."

Channing stared out the window. Finally, he said, "Well, if I were paying visits, as you say, I guess I'd stop off at my mother's old boy-friend's."

"That's all?"

"There's a writer I wouldn't mind having a little chat with." Channing thought of a hotshot writer of true crime, including last year's block-buster *The Serial Killer Next Door.* The man had appeared on all the morning talk shows as well as *Larry King Live* and *Letterman,* and had been an insufferable know-it-all who, Channing thought, didn't really know dick about the sub-ject matter. He was itching to show him where he'd gotten it wrong.

"That's only two," Lowell reminded him. "You got one more."

Channing thought it over. There'd been that dark-haired FBI agent who'd interviewed him a few years back in Ohio, bringing a particularly satisfying run to an end. She'd seen right through him, and he'd known it. He'd wanted to reach across the table and break her pretty neck, but he had much more self-control than that. As soon as the interview was over, he'd quietly disappeared and taken his work else-where. But he'd gone with the feeling that given the chance, she'd be right on his heels.

"Well," he said with a smile, "there's a cute little FBI agent that I'd like to see again. Just to see if the chemistry is still the same."

Giordano snorted.

"Course, if we really did these things, if we really ever did go see 'em and . . . well, you know, did stuff" — Lowell grinned stupidly — "it isn't like the cops wouldn't know who to look for, you know? Like, Vince, they find your mother-in-law with a bullet in her head after you get out, the cops'll be like, *Duh. Wonder who shot her?*"

"Well, it was just talk. Didn't mean nothing." Giordano shrugged, and the three fell silent.

"Unless we like, you know, switch our people," Lowell said brightly.

Giordano frowned. "What d'ya mean, switch our people?"

"You know, like that movie. The one on the train, where these two guys meet and they each agree to whack someone that the other one wants —"

"Whoa, buddy. Watch it." Giordano glanced nervously at Channing. Who knew who this guy really was? Or Lowell, either, for that matter. "This was just idle talk. That's all. Just idle talk."

"Sure it is. I know that." Lowell nodded, eager to placate the man whom he knew to be a convicted killer. "But it doesn't hurt to pretend. We got nothing else to do in here right now. No TV, no radio. We gotta think about something."

"How old are you, Lowell?" Giordano's tone was patronizing.

"Nineteen."

"That explains it."

"Explains what?"

"Your loose mouth, that's what," Giordano snapped.

"No, come on. It's just a game. A game, that's all," Lowell hastened to assure Giordano.

"You ever kill anyone, Lowell?" Giordano asked softly.

Lowell shook his head.

"You, Channing?"

Channing merely stared.

The two older men studied each other wordlessly, as if trading secrets.

Then Lowell, oblivious to the silent exchange, said, "If we were going to play the game, then we would each have a list, and we'd each promise to do someone else's list, right?"

Giordano laughed. "Boy, you don't give up, do you, kid?"

"First, we'd have to decide how to figure out who would, you know, *do* whose people." Lowell was beginning to get into it. "I know. We could each pick a number between one and thirty and guess which number the other guy is thinking of."

Giordano laughed again.

Lowell said, "Okay, you, Channing, you go

first. Think of a number between one and thirty, and me and Vince will see if we can guess. Whoever comes closest to your number gets your names."

"Let's just keep it simple," Channing suggested. "Archer takes my list, I take yours, Giordano, and you take Archer's." Amused, Channing thought that if Lowell's hands hadn't been cuffed together, he'd be clapping like a five-year-old. Even more amusing was the thought that he needed anyone to help him find a victim. As if he'd ever needed anyone's help. Over the years, he'd done quite well all by himself.

"Cool." Lowell nodded vigorously, prompting Giordano, whose enthusiasm lagged behind that of his young companion, to remind him, "It's just a game, Archer. Just a game."

Giordano glanced around the room and appeared suddenly wary, uncertain of his companions.

"Just a game," he repeated again a bit more forcefully, his voice leaden with caution. The kid was stupid and, in Giordano's eyes, growing more stupid with each passing minute. He had half a mind to tell him just that. And he would have, had it not been for the fact that Curtis Channing appeared to be strangely entertained.

"Okay, so tell me about who's on your list, Channing," Archer Lowell, oblivious to Giordano's scorn, begged eagerly. "Tell me about who I'd be going to see."

25

"I think we should lower our voices," Giordano sighed, as if resigned to play along. "Just in case someone is listening. Even though it's just a game . . . and none of this is ever going to happen. . . ."

"Right, right. Sure." Lowell nodded intensely, his eyes shining now with excitement as he leaned forward in his chair as far as he could, considering his shackles. "Sure. None of this is ever going to really happen. It's just a game. I know that. Just a game . . ."

Chapter One

Oh, sure, I heard the little one crying. And the middle one, too. Only one I never heard was the older one, the boy. They ain't lived here long — maybe a month or so. I never saw much of them. Oh, once in a while, I'd pass the boy on the steps. He never had much to say. No, never saw the mother bring men home. Never saw her much at all, though — don't know when she came or went. Heard her sometimes, though. God knows she was loud enough, screaming at them kids the way she done. No, don't know what she was doin' to 'em to make 'em cry like that. No, never saw no social worker come around. Don't know if the kids went to school.

Did I what? No, never called nobody about it. Wasn't none of my business, what went on over there. Hey, I got troubles of my own. . . .

Mara Douglas rubbed her temples with the tips of her fingers, an unconscious gesture she made when steeped in thought or deeply upset. Reading through the notes she'd taken while interviewing the elderly, toothless, across-the-hall neighbor of the Feehan family, she was at once immersed in the children's situation and sick to her stomach. The refrain was all too familiar. The neighbors heard, the neighbors turned a deaf ear rather than get involved. It

27

was none of their business what a woman did to her children, none of their business if the kids had fallen through all the cracks. In neighborhoods as poor as this, all the tenants seemed to live in their own hell. Who could worry about someone else's?

Mara rested her elbow on the edge of the dining room table, her chin in the palm of her hand, and marveled how a child could survive such neglect and abuse and so often still defend the parent who had inflicted the physical and emotional pain.

Time after time, case after case, she'd seen the bond between parent and child tested, stretched to the very limit. Sometimes even years of the worst kind of abuse and neglect failed to fray that connection.

She turned her attention back to the case she was working on now. The mother's rights were being challenged by the paternal grandparents, who'd had custody of the three children — ages four, seven, and nine — for the past seven months. Mara was the court-appointed advocate for the children, the one who would speak on their behalf at all legal proceedings, the one whose primary interest — whose only interest — was the best interests of the children.

As their champion, Mara spent many hours reviewing the files provided by the social workers from the county Children and Youth Services department and medical reports from their physicians, and still more hours interviewing the social workers themselves, along with neighbors and teachers, emergency room personnel, family members, and family friends. All in an effort to determine what was best for the children, where their needs — all their needs — might best be met, and by whom.

Mara approached every case as a sacred trust, an opportunity to stand for that child as she would stand for her own. Tomorrow she would do exactly that, when she presented her report and her testimony to the judge who would determine whether Kelly Feehan's parental rights should be terminated and custody of her three children awarded to their deceased father's parents. It probably wouldn't be too tough a call.

Kelly, an admitted prostitute and heroin addict, had watched her world begin to close in on her after her fifth arrest for solicitation. Her nine-year-old had stayed home from school to take care of his siblings until Kelly could make bail. Unfortunately for Kelly, her former in-laws, who had been searching for the children for months while their mother had moved them from one low-rent dive to another, had finally tracked them down. The Feehans had called the police. Their next move had been to take temporary custody of the children, who were found bruised, battered, and badly malnourished.

Over time, it became apparent that Kelly wasn't doing much to rehabilitate herself. She'd shown up high on two of her last three visitation days, and the grandparents had promptly filed a petition to terminate Kelly's parental rights permanently. Total termination of parental rights was a drastic step, one never made lightly nor without a certain amount of angst and soul searching.

Mara knew all too well the torment of losing a child.

In the end, of course, the decision would rest in the hands of Judge McKettrick, whom Mara knew from experience was always reluctant to sever a parent's rights when the parent contested as vehemently as Kelly Feehan had. Much would depend on the information brought to the court in the morning. The responsibility to present everything fairly, without judgment or embellishment, was one that Mara took very seriously.

With the flick of her finger, the screen of Mara's laptop went blank, then filled with the image of a newborn snuggled up against a shoulder covered by a yellow and white hospital gown. The infant's hair was little more than pale fuzz, the eyes closed in slumber, the perfect rosebud mouth puckered just so.

Another flick of a finger, and the image was gone.

Mara's throat constricted with the pain of remembrance, the memories of the joy that had filled her every time she'd held that tiny body against her own. Abruptly she pushed back from the table and walked to the door.

"Spike," she called, and from the living room came the unmistakable sound of a little dog tail thumping on hard wood. "It's time to go for a walk."

Spike knew *walk*, but not *time*, which was just as well, since it was past one in the morning. But once the thorn of memory began to throb, Mara had to work it out of her system. Her conditioned response to emotional pain was physical. Any kind of sustained movement would do — a walk, a run, a bike ride, a trip to the gym. Anything that got her on her feet was acceptable, as long as it got her moving through the pain so that she could get past it for a while.

Mara pursued exhaustion where others might have chosen a bottle or a needle or a handful of pills, though there'd been times in the past when she'd considered those, too.

By day, Mara's neighborhood in a suburban Philadelphia college town was normally quiet, but at night, it was as silent as a tomb. She walked briskly, the soles of her walking shoes padding softly on the sidewalk, the occasional streetlamp lighting her way, Spike's little Jack Russell legs keeping pace. Four blocks down, four blocks over, and back again. That's what it usually took to clear her head. Tonight she made the loop in record time. She still had work to do, and an appointment in court at nine the next morning.

31

The evening's storm had passed through earlier, and now a full moon hung overhead and cast shadows behind her as she made her way back up the brick walk to her front door. She'd let Spike off the leash at the end of their drive and now stood watching as the dog sniffed at something in the grass.

"Spike," she whispered loudly, and the dog looked up, wagging his tail enthusiastically. "Come on, buddy. Time to go in."

With obvious reluctance, Spike left whatever it was he'd found on the lawn and followed his mistress to the front steps. Mara unlocked the front door, but did not go immediately inside. She crossed her arms and stared up at the night sky for a long moment, thinking of her own child, wondering once again where in this vast world she was at that exact moment, and who, if anyone, was standing for her.

On the television screen, the earnest five o'clock news anchor droned on and on, his delivery as flat as his crew cut. Mara turned the volume down to answer the ringing phone.

"What's for dinner?" Mara's sister, Anne Marie, dispensed with a greeting and cut to the chase.

"I was just asking myself that very thing." Mara grinned, delighted to hear Annie's voice.

"How 'bout a little Chinese?"

"You buying?"

"And delivering."

"You're back?"

"I'm on my way."

"What time will you be here?"

"Thirty minutes, give or take. I'm just leaving the airport. If you call in an order at that little place on Dover Drive, I'll swing past and pick it up."

"Perfect. What do you want?"

"Surprise me."

"Okay. See you soon."

Pleased with the unexpected prospect of Annie's company, Mara found herself whistling while she hunted up the menu. She called in the order, then set about clearing the kitchen table of all the mail that had accumulated over the past several weeks while she had worked on the Feehan case. That case having been heard just that morning, Mara could pack up the materials she'd reviewed and return them to the courthouse in the morning. She wondered where Kelly Feehan had gone that night to drown her sorrows, her parental rights having been severed by Judge McKettrick until such time as Kelly successfully completed a rehabilitation program and obtained legitimate employment, at which time she could file for visitation rights. The odds that Kelly would follow through were slim to none, but the option was there. It had been the best the judge could do for all involved.

While the decision was clearly in the best interests of the children, it still gave Mara pause to have played a part, however small, in another mother being separated from her babies, even though she knew full well that Kelly had brought her troubles upon herself. Mara had wanted to shake the young mother, shake her good and hard, for having put herself and her children in such a situation.

You had a choice, Mara had wanted to shout at the sobbing woman as her children left the courtroom with their grandparents. *We don't all get a choice. . . .*

Mara scooped dry dog food into Spike's new Scooby-Doo dish, then gave him fresh water. She turned up the volume on the television, hoping to catch the weather forecast for the morning. She'd been looking forward to her early morning twice-weekly run with several friends and was hoping that the prediction of rain had changed.

". . . and in other news, we have a somewhat bizarre story of two women who have the same name, who lived in the same town, and who met with the same fate exactly one week apart." The anchorman spoke directly into the camera. "Jason Wrigley is standing by at the Avon County courthouse with the story."

Headlights flashing through the living room window announced Annie's arrival. Mara had just begun to head for the front door when the reporter's face appeared on the television.

"This is Mary Douglas," the reporter was saying as he displayed a picture of a white-haired woman in her early sixties.

Mara watched in fascination as he held up a second photograph of another woman years younger, with dark hair and an olive complexion, and said, "And this is Mary Douglas. What do these two woman have in common besides their names?"

The reporter paused for effect, then faced the camera squarely, both photographs held in one hand, the microphone in the other.

"Both of these women lived in Lyndon. Both women were killed in their homes in that small community, in exactly the same manner, exactly one week apart. The body of the second victim was found earlier this afternoon. Local police have admitted that they are baffled as to motive."

Spike ran to the door and barked when he heard Annie's heels on the walk, but Mara's attention remained fixed on the television.

Video played of a prerecorded press conference. "Without divulging the manner in which the women were murdered, we're investigating the possibility that the first killing was an error. That the second victim may have been the intended target."

The police spokesman paused to listen to a question from the floor, then repeated the question for those who had not heard. "Do we feel it was a contract killing, was the question. I can only say at this point that anything is possible. It has been suggested that perhaps the

killer had known only the name of his victim —
no description, no address — and that after
killing the first victim and perhaps seeing some
news coverage or reading the obituary in the
newspaper, he realized that he hadn't killed the
right woman. According to friends and family
of both victims, neither Mary Douglas had an
enemy in the world. Both women were well
liked, both lived somewhat quiet lives. So with
no apparent motive, we can't rule out any scenario yet."

"Mara?" Annie called from the doorway.

The police spokesman's face was taut with
concentration as he spoke of the murders. "Yes,
we think he sought out the second Mary
Douglas and killed her, though we do not know
why either of these women would have been
targeted, for that matter. . . ."

"Mara?"

"This is bizarre." Mara shook her head.

"What is?" Annie set the bag she carried on
the coffee table.

"This news report . . ." She was still shaking
her head slowly, side to side. "Two women
named Mary Douglas were murdered one week
apart. Killed in the same way, but the police
aren't saying how they were killed."

Annie frowned.

"It's a little creepy — Mary Douglas — Mara
Douglas," Mara admitted, "and what makes it
worse is that there's a woman who works in the
D.A.'s office named Mary Douglas."

"But she wasn't . . ." Annie pointed at the television.

"No, thank God. I was holding my breath there for a minute, though. She's such a nice person — a real ray-of-sunshine type. Friendly and a good sport. Not a day goes by when we don't get at least one piece of mail meant for the other."

"You don't work in the D.A.'s office."

"Yeah, but very often the mail room will mistake Mary for Mara or vice versa, and we get each other's mail. And if something is addressed to 'M. Douglas,' it's anyone's guess whose mailbox it ends up in." Mara watched the rest of the segment, then turned off the television. "I feel sorry for the families of the two victims, but I can't help but be relieved that the Mary Douglas I know wasn't one of them."

"Odd thing, though," Annie murmured as she pulled off her short-sleeved cardigan and tossed it onto a nearby chair. "Two victims with the same name. That can't be a coincidence. . . ."

"Intrigued?"

"Hell, yes."

"Itching to know more?"

"What do you think?" Annie carried the fragrant bags of egg foo young and chicken lo mein into the kitchen.

"Maybe you'll get a call."

"Well, it's early yet. Only two victims. Have

they given out any personal information about them?"

"The first victim was a retired school librarian. Sixty-one years old, lived alone. No relatives. By all accounts a nice woman without an enemy in the world."

"And the other woman?"

"Attractive woman in her mid-fifties, two grown kids. Yoga instructor at the local YMCA. Husband died two years ago."

"Boyfriend?" Annie leaned against the door frame, her expression pensive.

"They didn't say. According to the news report, she was well liked. Active in the community, spent a lot of time doing charity work. They haven't been able to come up with a motive for either of the killings."

"There's always a motive. Sometimes it's just harder to find. They need to do a profile on the victims."

"I was waiting for that." Mara watched her sister's face, knew just what she was thinking.

As a criminal profiler for the FBI, Anne Marie McCall's experience had taught her that the more information you knew about a victim, the more likely you were to find the perpetrator of the crime.

"Can't help it. It's my nature." Annie waved Mara toward the kitchen. "Come on, dinner's going to get cold. Do I have to be hostess in your house?"

Mara got plates from the cupboard while

Annie removed the little white boxes from the bag and arranged them in a straight row along the counter.

"Buffet is good." Mara nodded approvingly and handed her sister a plate.

They chatted through dinner, but Mara could tell her sister's attention was wandering.

"Hey, I'm talking to you." Mara waved a hand in front of Annie's face.

"Sorry."

"You're thinking about those women. The Marys."

"Yeah. Sorry. Can't help it."

"You're wondering if the FBI will be called in."

Annie nodded.

"And if you'll be assigned to the case."

"Sure."

"You know where the phone is." Mara pointed to the wall.

"Maybe I should just —"

"Go."

"And actually, I have my own phone." Annie reached in her bag for her mobile phone, then paced the small kitchen while the number rang.

Somewhere deep in FBI headquarters, the call was answered.

"This is Dr. McCall. I'd like to speak with John Mancini. Is he available?"

Damn, but didn't that just beat all?

The man spread the newspaper across the

39

desk so that he could read the article that continued below the fold.

He shook his head, bewildered.

Unbelievable. He'd screwed up not once but twice!

He ran long, thin fingers across the top of his closely cropped head, laughing softly in spite of himself.

Good thing I don't work in law enforcement. Sloppy investigative work like this would've gotten me canned. And better still that I wasn't getting paid for the job.

Not that he'd ever done work for hire, of course, but even so . . .

What was I thinking?

He picked at his teeth with a wooden toothpick and considered his next move. He really needed to make this right.

He folded the paper and set it to one side of the desk. He'd have to think about this a little more. And he would. He'd think about it all day. But right now he had to get dressed and get to work.

He'd been lucky to find a job on his second day here, even if it was only washing dishes in a small diner on the highway. It was working out just fine. He got his meals for free on the shifts he worked and he made enough to pay for a rented room in a big old twin house in a run-down but relatively safe neighborhood in a small town close enough to his targets that he could come and go as he pleased.

Of course, he'd had only three targets in mind when he arrived.

The fact that he'd missed the mark — not once, but twice, he reminded himself yet again — would prolong his stay a little longer than he'd intended. His real target was still out there somewhere, and he had to find her — do it right this time — before he could move on.

And he'd have to be a little more cautious this time around, he knew. Surely the other M. Douglases — there had been several more listed in the local telephone book — might understandably be a bit edgy right about now. It was his own fault, of course. He'd gotten uncharacteristically lazy, first in assuming that the only Mary Douglas listed by full name, the kindly woman who lived alone on Fourth Avenue in Lyndon, was the *right* Mary Douglas. Then, to his great chagrin, hadn't he gone and *repeated* the same damned mistake? He'd gone to the first M. Douglas listed, and in spite of his having confirmed that she was in fact a Mary, she was *still* not the right woman.

Not that he hadn't enjoyed himself with either of them — the second Mary had been especially feisty — but still, it wasn't like him to be so careless.

He was just going to have to do better, that was all. Take the remaining M. Douglases in order and see what's what. Check them out thoroughly until he was certain that he had the right one. The next victim would have to be the right victim, else he'd look like an even greater fool than he already did.

He shuddered to think what a panic a third mistake could set off among the *other* M. Douglases, and though that could be amusing in its own way, well, he didn't really need the publicity, what with the inevitable horde of reporters who would flock to the area. After all, this wasn't supposed to be about *him*. This was all about someone else's fantasy.

Oh, he'd fully understood that it had all been a lark as far as the others — he thought of them as his buddies, blood brothers of a sort — were concerned. It was supposed to have been just a game, just a means of whiling away a few hours on a stormy winter day, locked in a forgotten room with two other strangers. But then the idea had just taken hold of him and clung on for dear life, and damn, but it had caught his imagination. What if he went through with it? What if he played it out? What would be the reaction of his buddies? Would they, each in their turn, pick up the challenge and continue the game? Would they not feel obligated to reciprocate? To continue on with the game, whether they wanted to or not?

And wasn't it a matter of principle? Sort of a new twist on the old saying, "an eye for an eye."

His fingers stretched and flexed as he remembered his Marys.

He smiled to himself, trying to imagine what

the reaction of his buddies would be when they realized what he'd done. Shock? Horror? Pleasure? Gratitude? Amusement?

It sure would be interesting to see how it all played out in the end.

As for him, well, Curtis Alan Channing wasn't about to strike out that third time.

He snapped off the light on the desk, tucked the little notebook into the pocket of his dark jacket, and headed off to work. He wanted to be early today to give himself extra time to go through the phone book and jot down a few addresses and numbers before clocking in for his shift. He needed to set up a little surveillance schedule so he could focus on the right target. This time, there would be no *uh-oh* when he turned on the TV or opened the newspaper. There simply would be the sheer satisfaction of having completed his task and completed it well, before he moved on to the next name on the list. Which he would most certainly do in short order.

After all, his honor was at stake.

Chapter Two

The first of the diners were beginning to gather in front of the hot dog cart that had served up fast food to two generations of Avon County courthouse employees. Any weekday, Maury's Doggies was set up and open for business by eleven in the morning. If the courthouse was open, Maury was there.

By eleven thirty on Friday morning, a small crowd had already arrived. All county departments housed in the courthouse — which also served as the county seat — were represented as those scheduled for the early lunch spilled onto the steps to enjoy the first really pleasant April day to follow a particularly dismal March. Local residents, drawn outside by the warmth and the opportunity to sit for a bit and bask in the sun, shared the benches around the front lawn with courthouse employees who ate sandwiches from brown paper bags or hot dogs in white cardboard boats and sipped soft drinks from cans or coffee in foam cups.

People gathered in groups, depending on whether they worked in Judicial Support or Personnel, Children and Youth or Tax Claim, and shared office gossip and weekend plans. Jurists on lunch break chatted about anything other than the case they were hearing.

A mere ten feet from the hot dog stand, a criminal defense lawyer badgered an assistant district attorney over something that had happened the previous week in court and still apparently rankled. Three employees from the D.A.'s office pretended not to notice as they passed by on their way to the queue at Maury's.

"That's Mack Thompson," Tina Gillette whispered to her companions as they approached the hot dog stand. "Sounds like he's still pissed over the verdict on the Morrison case last week."

"Thompson's a whiner," Mary Douglas responded before stepping up to place her order with the ever-cheerful Maury. An administrative assistant to several of the ADAs, Mary was familiar with many of the cases prosecuted by her office, including the one currently under discussion.

"My boss said Thompson takes loser cases that no one else wants and then whines all over town when he can't win. Bruce had a case with him last year and really whooped his butt." Joanie Fox spoke in a low voice.

"I heard about that," Tina said as she tucked her change away and gathered up her lunch. "Want to see if we can find a bench?"

"Good luck." Mary glanced around. There was not an empty seat in sight. "Why don't we just stand over there near the steps? At least we'll be in the sun for a while."

"Fine with me." Joanie nodded and fell in step with the others.

"Did you see the new ADA they hired?" Tina set her soda down near her feet in an effort to free up her hands so that she could unwrap her sandwich.

"Him or her?" Joanie asked.

"Her." Tina rolled her eyes. "She has a face like a bat."

"I can't believe you said that." Mary choked on her bite of hot dog. "That's really awful. Especially since she's so nice."

"Mary, you think everyone is nice. You even liked Annette Falcone, and we all know what a bitch she was," Tina said, recalling an especially unpopular assistant prosecutor who had worked for the county until the previous fall, when she'd left for private practice. "She was the most miserable, demanding —"

"She really wasn't," Mary protested. "She was conscientious, and okay, maybe she was a bit of a perfectionist —"

Her friends hooted.

"Boy, is that a stretch," Joanie laughed, and nudged Tina with her elbow. "We have to keep reminding ourselves that Mary takes that 'If you can't say something nice, don't say anything at all' stuff to heart."

"Yeah, well, wasn't it Eleanor Roosevelt who said, 'If you can't say something nice, come sit next to me'?" Tina grinned.

"One of the Roosevelts said it, but it wasn't

Eleanor. So, what are you doing this weekend?" Mary changed the subject. "Either of you have plans?"

"Nada." Tina shook her head. "The kids are going with their father. He's picking them up right after school and I won't see them until Sunday night. How 'bout you? You and Kevin have any plans?"

"Kevin is working night shift this weekend." Mary made a face.

"What? I thought you liked it when Kevin worked nights. Didn't you say that you liked having the house to yourself because it gave you a little time to read or watch a movie that you wanted to see?" asked Joanie.

"I did. But that was before . . ." Mary's voice trailed away.

"Before what?"

"You're going to laugh." Mary's eyes flicked back and forth between her companions.

"Maybe." Tina smirked. "Tell us anyway."

"Before the Mary Douglas murders," Mary said quietly.

"Oh, I am *so* not laughing." Tina grew solemn and shook her head. "Let me tell you, if a couple of women named Tina Gillette were found dead two weeks in a row, I'd be plenty freaked. God, I'd have myself locked away until they found him. I'd have an armed guard at my door and I'd —"

"Thanks. I no longer feel foolish," Mary said grimly. "Now I feel terrified."

"Oh, shit, I'm sorry. Me and my mouth . . ." Tina's face reddened.

"Look, how late is Kevin working tonight?" Joanie pulled a cigarette from one pocket, then searched another for matches.

"He usually leaves right after dinner, around six-thirty or so, and gets home around three in the morning."

"Would it make you feel better to have a little company? I'm not doing anything tonight. I could bring over a movie," Joanie suggested.

Before Mary could answer, Tina chimed in, "We'll make it a girls' night. I'll come, too. We can watch a movie, have a pizza break, watch another movie. . . ."

"That's so nice of both of you. Are you sure there isn't something else you'd rather do?"

"Oh, hell, what are friends for?" Tina glanced at her watch, noting that their lunch hour was just about over. "Joanie, why don't we meet up for dinner at Hugo's? We can grab a couple of movies at Chasen's next door, then shoot on over to Mary's."

"Sounds great. What do you say, Mary? Girls' night at your place?" Joanie took a few last short drags before stubbing out her cigarette. She picked up the butt and tossed it into the container at the foot of the courthouse steps.

"That would be great. More than great. Thanks. I really appreciate it." Mary breathed a sigh of relief and followed her friends back into the building, totally unaware that every move she'd made since she stepped outside forty minutes earlier had been watched oh so carefully.

As the wide glass doors closed behind Mary Douglas, the man seated on the bench diagonally across from where she'd been standing folded his newspaper, tucked the paper under his arm, and rose. Without a backward glance, he left the same way he'd come. He walked three blocks north to the side street where he'd parked his car earlier that morning after following Mary from her home to the courthouse, after which he'd walked to a local coffee shop, had a leisurely breakfast, bought a paper, and poked into a few of the shops on Main Street, just to kill a little time. Then he'd returned to the courthouse, found himself a nice bench with a clear view of the front steps, and waited. And then there she'd been, her courthouse ID pinned to the lapel of her jacket like a medal.

Employment confirmed.

Could there be any doubt that this Mary Douglas worked at the courthouse and was therefore *the* Mary Douglas involved in custody hearings? No doubt whatsoever in his mind. How many Mary Douglases could be working in there?

He'd watched her eat a hot dog and wash it down with a diet soda while she chatted with her friends. He'd momentarily lost her, early on, when she'd stepped behind the lunch truck, but he knew she'd appear again. There was only one way in or out of the courthouse, and he had a front row seat. She'd passed him twice, and he'd had ample opportunity to watch her as she walked by, ample opportunity to peer over the top of his paper with true appreciation and much anticipation at her long legs.

She was much younger, much prettier than the other two Marys.

The thought of her — of what was to come — had surged through him like an electrical charge. All the way back to his car, he fought an urge to whistle.

Just before ten on Saturday morning, Mara eased her car around the corner, searching in vain for a parking spot. As she passed by the front of the courthouse, she noted the line of news vans parked in front of the main walk. Every station in town appeared to be represented. Some reporters had already set up and were obviously preparing for live broadcasts.

Something pricked at the back of her neck. It was odd — more than odd — for there to be such activity on a Saturday.

She drove on to the next corner and made a left, hoping to find a place to park on one of the small side streets.

It was four minutes after ten a.m. when she finally found a place to park. Locking up her car, she started toward the courthouse on foot. She had an early meeting on a new case she had just inherited from one of the other attorneys in her department and she was mentally rehashing the information she'd gleaned. It was not unusual for her to come in over the weekend. What was unusual was for there to be more than a handful of people in the building with her. And never had she seen a crowd the likes of which was gathering near the front steps. Curious, she quickened her pace.

As she drew closer, Mara realized that she recognized almost everyone in the crowd as a county worker. And it was then that she realized that the majority of them were crying.

"What's happened?" Mara touched the arm of a woman she knew from the sheriff's department. "What's going on?"

"You didn't hear?" The woman was openly sobbing.

"Hear what?"

"Mary Douglas — our Mary Douglas — she was . . . she was . . ." The woman could not get the words out.

"Oh, my God, no." The blood drained from Mara's face. "When?"

"Last night. Her husband was working night shift, so two of the girls from her office went over to stay with her. She was nervous, you know, because of the other Marys —" The woman hiccuped. "They were late getting there. They'd stopped to have dinner and things ran later than they'd planned, and when they got there, they found her . . . they found . . ."

Mara felt frozen where she stood, much as those around her were frozen with shock and with sorrow.

It would be several hours before it occurred to her to feel anything more personal than grief for the loss of an acquaintance.

Mara's house phone was ringing as she unlocked her front door. She grabbed it on the third ring.

"It's me, Annie. Why is your cell phone turned off?"

"I guess I forgot to charge the battery again." Mara tossed her briefcase onto the sofa from eight feet away. "What's the matter?"

"I just got off the phone with one of our agents who's been assigned to work with your local police. She said there's been another Mary Douglas killing."

"I know. I just got in from the courthouse. This time it was the woman I told you about, the woman from the D.A.'s office." Mara sat on the sofa and accepted welcoming kisses from Spike. "I can't believe it. No one can. You can't imagine what a nice person she is. Was. There's just no rhyme or reason for anyone to want to hurt her."

"The early word on the inside track says her husband had been playing around for the past year. He was supposed to have been at work

52

last night but never showed up. They're trying to find him but he hasn't surfaced yet."

"You think her husband may have done this?"

"You know the drill: You always look at the nearest and dearest first."

"But that wouldn't explain the other Mary Douglas killings."

"Well, right now the favored theory is that he killed the other two to take suspicion away from himself. You know, make it look as if someone really did have a thing for women named Mary Douglas."

"That's a bit of a stretch, don't you think? Could anyone honestly believe that the police would go for that? That someone would be killing only women named Mary Douglas?"

"It wouldn't be the first time someone pulled something like that. Stranger things have happened." Annie paused. "But there is something I'm having checked out."

"What something?"

"It may be nothing. Listen, I have a call coming in. I should be there in . . . well, it'll depend on how long this call is."

"Doesn't matter. I'll be here. I just picked up a new case, so I'll be in all weekend."

"Do me a favor."

"Name it."

"Keep your doors locked. And don't leave the house until I get there."

"Spike needs to go out."

"Make it quick." Annie paused, then added, "And by the way, I'm bringing a friend with me."

"Friend? What friend?" Mara asked before she realized that Annie had hung up.

She held the phone in her hand for a long minute.

She located Spike's leash on the dining room floor, where he'd dragged it while she was out, and snapped the lead onto his collar. As promised, she locked the door behind her before taking the dog for a long walk around the neighborhood. The death of the latest Mary Douglas weighed heavily on her mind and in her heart. Mary had been well liked for good reason, and everyone who knew her was stunned. It was almost too terrible to be true. Every time Mara thought about that sweet young woman, she felt sick.

Mara ambled a bit farther than she'd planned and soon found herself at the tall stone gates of the local college campus. She hadn't set foot on the grounds of Miller College in years. Seven years, to be exact. Since her husband, a former mathematics professor, had disappeared and took with him everything that had given meaning to her life.

She wandered back toward her street, six blocks from the college, trying to keep her mind from going places she did not want it to go today. Mary Douglas's death was enough.

Mara could deal with only one tragedy at a time.

Annie's car was visible from the top of the street. But as Mara drew closer, she could see that there was another car parked in front of Annie's. She walked into the street and tapped on Annie's window.

"Been waiting long?" Mara asked.

Annie rolled her window all the way down. "Just pulled up."

"Who's that?" Mara asked, pointing to the shiny red Eclipse Spyder parked in front of Annie's car.

"That's the friend I said would be coming with me."

"You coming in, then?"

Annie rolled up her window and got out of her car. Immediately, the driver's side door of the sports car opened, and a tall, striking, dark-haired woman stepped out.

When the woman joined them, Annie said, "Mara, this is a friend of mine, Miranda Cahill."

"Hi. Nice to meet you."

"Good to meet you. Annie's been telling me a lot about you." Miranda offered her hand.

"Oh? Like what?" Mara said as she jangled her house keys.

"That three women whose names are way too similar to yours for comfort have been killed lately."

Mara stopped in her tracks and turned to

55

look at her sister curiously.

"Miranda's an agent with our team," Annie explained. "She was assigned to work with your local police on the Mary Douglas cases."

"And?" Mara looked from one to the other.

"Can we go inside and talk?" Annie looked around uncomfortably.

"Sure." Mara unlocked the door and pushed it open to permit the other two women to pass.

"What's going on, Annie?" Mara asked when she'd closed the door behind her.

Gesturing for Miranda to sit, Annie took a seat on the large ottoman that sat before an armchair.

"Mara . . ." Annie struggled for her opening line.

"Annie, maybe I should . . ." Miranda touched Annie's arm, and Annie nodded. Miranda looked at Mara. "As your sister told you, I've been assigned to the investigation of the Mary Douglas murders. Up until an hour ago, the theory was that this latest victim was the target all along. That her husband — who we've learned had been having an affair with a coworker — had wanted to get rid of his wife. In order to keep the light of suspicion off himself, however, he killed other women who had the same name."

"Annie and I talked about this earlier. But you said this was the theory until an hour ago?"

"An hour ago, Kevin Douglas — the husband of Mary number three — was found with a bullet through his head. Not self-inflicted."

"Oh." Mara sat on the edge of the coffee table.

Annie reached forward and took one of her sister's hands.

"Maybe the husband's mistress . . ." Mara suggested.

"She's in Cincinnati and has been since last Tuesday," replied Miranda. "It appears that Kevin Douglas was home — or arrived home — around the same time as our killer. We believe that the husband was shot and may have been transported in the killer's car, then dumped where the body was found."

"How could he have taken the body out of the house without being seen?" Mara asked. "It would have been daylight, if he did this before her friends arrived."

"The back of the Douglas property is heavily wooded, and there's a fence that runs along the drive between their house and the house next door," Miranda explained. "It would have been very easy for the killer to have carried the body out and put it into the trunk of his car. No one could have seen."

"So the Mary Douglas killer is still out there," Mara said.

"And no one has a clue to his identity or his motive." Miranda added, "Or if he's finished yet."

"What do you mean, if he's finished?" Mara stared at the FBI agent.

"Are you aware that of the three victims, only the first one was listed in the phone book as Mary Douglas? The other two were listed as M. Douglas," Miranda told her.

"No, I —"

"Annie mentioned that you are listed as M. Douglas," Miranda added.

"You and any other M. Douglas within a ten or twenty mile radius of here should be on guard. You have no idea what this man has done to these women," Annie told her. "The police have kept a very tight lid on the investigation and have not given out any information as to the manner of death, but, Mara —"

"Annie, that's enough," Miranda interjected. She turned to Mara. "Suffice it to say that we're dealing with a very . . . accomplished . . . individual. One who appears to be adept at inflicting pain on helpless women."

"I don't consider myself helpless," Mara said.

"I'm sure neither of the three Marys did either, until they were tied up and gagged," Miranda told her bluntly.

"And you're thinking I might be a potential victim?"

"I'm thinking you might even be the next victim," Miranda said.

"You want to explain how you arrived at that?" Mara's hands began to shake.

"The first victim was Mary Douglas — the only Mary Douglas listed by full name in the telephone book. The next victim — also a Mary

— is listed by initials only: M. A. Douglas. Mary Alice. The last victim was listed as M. E. Douglas. Mary Eleanor."

"You think he's going alphabetically through all of the M. Douglases?" Mara's eyes widened. "Finding his victims in the telephone book?"

"We don't know that for certain, Mara, but if he is, you're next in line," Miranda said without blinking. "M. J. Douglas. That would be you."

"But that makes no sense at all," Mara protested. "Why not all the Jane Browns, or all the Susan Smiths?"

"We have no idea why he chose that name. The only thing we know for certain at this point is that his victims have been killed in the order in which they appear in the phone book."

"And I'm the next listing." Mara bit the inside of her lip.

"Yes. We've spent the day speaking with all of the remaining M. Douglases in the phone book," Miranda noted. "There have been no threats, no strange mail or phone calls, nothing out of the ordinary, though they are, of course, understandably rattled by this."

"For God's sake." Mara stood and began to pace. "I can't imagine that anyone would do something this crazy. Kill people because of the order their names are listed in the phone book?"

"Obviously there's more to it than that," Miranda told her. "Obviously one of these M. Douglases — or someone named Mary

Douglas — has some connection to our killer. We just haven't figured out yet what that connection might be."

"So what are you going to do?" Mara asked as Annie stood and started for the kitchen. "Annie, where are you going?"

"To make a pot of coffee for you and Miranda, and to put some water on to boil for my tea. And to see if you made it to the grocery store yet this week. I'm starving."

And then, little sister, we're going to talk about the fact that I want someone to keep a close eye on you. Annie bit her lower lip while she filled the teakettle with water. *And who I think will be the best man for the job . . .*

Chapter Three

"Well, well. This is a surprise." Aidan Shields stood just inside the door of his apartment and stared at the petite blond woman with wide blue eyes who stood in the hall.

"I imagine it is." She smiled slowly. "Aren't you going to invite me in?"

He backed into the small foyer, motioning for her to follow.

He waved a hand in the direction of the small living room, which was cluttered with piles of books and magazines stacked here and there, some on the small table in front of the sofa, some on the floor, others on a chair and the windowsill.

He cleaned off a chair and gestured for her to sit.

"Still the fashion plate, I see," he noted. "Nice shirt, linen pants, not a wrinkle in sight."

"And you're still as . . . *casual* as ever." She wondered when he'd last had his hair trimmed. "Cut-off denims, moldy old tee with the sleeves ripped out."

"I don't have much cause to dress up these days."

"Your choice," she reminded him.

"Right. My choice." He pushed some newspapers aside and seated himself on the edge of the sofa. "So. What are you up to these days, Dr. McCall?"

"The usual. A kidnapping here, a serial killer there." Annie crossed her legs and rested her right elbow on the chair arm.

He stared at her blankly, wondering why she was there.

"How are you, Aidan?" Annie asked more gently than she'd meant to.

"I'm okay, Annie." He shrugged, ignoring the note of kindness. He wasn't in the mood for kind.

"Just about healed?"

"Healed?" Aidan all but spat the word. "Are you *healed?*"

"As much as I ever will be." She looked away from his eyes. They were so like Dylan's.

"Good for you."

"Good for me?" Her eyes narrowed sharply. "What's that supposed to mean?"

"It means how nice for you, Annie, that you've been able to pick up your life and just keep moving on with it."

"Instead of what? Sitting in my apartment and watching the seasons change from my window?" She glanced at the brown paper bag that sat near the door to the kitchen and over-flowed with crushed beer cans.

"Looks to me like you made a mighty quick recovery."

She bit the inside of her lip, struggling to keep from lashing out at him. "Just because I haven't brought my life to a complete stop doesn't mean I don't miss him."

He turned his head, fighting back words that would have wounded her more than he wanted.

"We all mourn in different ways, Aidan." Her voice softened. "Working helps to make the days pass for me. Being in the world helps me to get through the pain."

"I can't get past it, Annie," he said gruffly. "I'm glad for you that you've accepted that he's gone, but I —"

"I didn't say I accepted it," she snapped, her polish beginning to chip. "Dylan was my life. He was my future. There were years we should have spent together. Children we should have raised and loved. We should have grown old together. I hate it, that all those things — my love, my future — were taken from me. But there are things we cannot change, things over which I have no control."

"Ah, well, see, Annie? There's the difference." His jaw tightened. "I *had* control. And if I'd been a little more in control, the way I was supposed to have been —"

"Oh, is that what this is about?" She held out a hand as if to stop his words in their track. "Aidan, it's time to take off the hair shirt. It doesn't wear well on you."

"That's a bitchy thing to say."

"You weren't to blame for what happened."

"Of course I was."

"You know, I think you're enjoying this

martyr thing a little too much. It's giving you an excuse to hide in here and not have to face anything you don't want to ever again. It's giving you an excuse to give up." Annie rose suddenly from her chair, anger full-blown. "Dylan would hate what you're doing to yourself. He'd drop-kick your ass clear into next week."

"And if I'd been more alert that night, he'd be here to do just that, wouldn't he?"

"Stop it. It wasn't a matter of anyone not being alert. You were set up."

"He counted on me to watch his back." Aidan's eyes darkened. "He trusted me."

"And you were counting on someone else to be watching yours. It doesn't always work out the way it's supposed to — you've been in enough similar situations to know that. Sometimes the good guys lose." Annie sighed deeply, tears in her eyes. "No one holds you responsible for his death, Aidan. Please stop blaming yourself. I can't stand to see you like this."

He got up, turned his back on her, and walked from the room. Annie heard him in the kitchen, heard the refrigerator door open, then slam. When he came back in, he was taking a long draw from a bottle of beer. He didn't offer her one.

"Still out on medical leave?" she asked to change the subject. That other horse had been flogged sufficiently.

"Oh, come on, Annie. You're still active in

the Bureau." He sat back down on the sofa. "Don't act as if you haven't been checking up on me."

"Someone has to."

"No one has to." He took another long swallow.

"Any thoughts of getting back to work soon?"

"I haven't thought about it."

"Of course you have." She called him on the lie. "You think about it every day."

"What if I do?" He stood, trapped, looked as if he was about to pace, but the room was too small for his long legs to go more than three or four strides in any direction.

"What's stopping you?"

"What's stopping me?" He rubbed his chin. "Well, let's start with the fact that there's no way I will ever pass the physical."

He raised his index finger and began to count off his infirmities. "I can't run worth shit. I got enough metal in my one leg to build a small plane. I can't hold a gun in my dominant hand, and I have had blackouts. That's four. What do you think my chances are of passing the FBI's physical, Dr. McCall?"

"There are other things you can do."

"No, Anne Marie. There is nothing else I can do." His voice dropped a full octave. "I was a special agent for the FBI, just like both of my brothers, like my father. There is nothing else for me."

"Not *was*. You still *are*."

He glared at her.

"So you're just going to hide here in this apartment until you can go on active status?" Her fingers began a soft tap on the arm of the chair.

"We both know that isn't going to happen."

"We both know that you stopped going to physical therapy four months ago."

"I didn't see any point to it." He ran an impatient hand through his too-long dark hair. He needed a cut, badly.

"Just like you didn't see any point to following through with the counselor."

"Yeah. Just like that. You shrinks don't always have the answers, you know."

"It didn't occur to you that maybe talking it out . . ."

"You want me to talk it out? Okay. Let's talk it out." He crossed his arms angrily over his chest. "My brother and I were undercover to establish ourselves as major heroin dealers. Somehow, someone found out we weren't. We were ambushed. My brother was killed. I was shot up. There. I talked it out. Do I feel better?" He all but spit. "No. Not a damned bit."

Annie had watched his face etch with pain and grief. As a psychiatrist, she could assess his need to deal with emotions he'd done his best to bury. But as Dylan's lover, she understood the depth of Aidan's loss all too well. She knew just how close the brothers had been.

66

"Don't think for a minute that I don't understand. That I don't know how deeply you hurt . . ."

"Don't you miss him, Annie?" Unexpectedly, his face softened and the challenge faded from his eyes.

"Every day. I can't begin to tell you . . ." How could she explain, even to his brother, what Dylan's loss had done to her life? How she still reached for him every morning. How she fell asleep holding his pillow every night. How she often found herself weeping for no reason at all. How food had lost its flavor and how she was just beginning to learn to laugh again.

"Just tell me how you get up every day and just keep doing what you do."

"What are my choices?" she whispered.

They stared at each other for a long time, grief reaching for grief silently across the room.

Aidan sat back down on the sofa, his arms resting on his thighs, but still they did not speak.

Finally, she said, "I need a favor."

"Sure. I told you I'd always be there for you, Annie."

"Don't be so quick." She attempted a small smile. "It will require you leaving this apartment."

"To go where?" he asked warily.

"I need you to keep an eye on my sister."

He frowned, trying to remember her sister's name. "You want me to watch Mary?"

"Mara," she corrected him. "Her name is Mara. And yes, I want you to watch her. I want you to watch her like a hawk. I'm afraid someone is going to try to kill her."

Chapter Four

Aidan Shields straightened slowly as he got out of his car — the white 1963 Corvette that had been the pride and joy of his late brother, Dylan — then rolled his shoulders to work out the tension that had set in during the two-and-a-half hour drive he'd made from Rehoboth, Delaware, to the small college town of Lyndon, Pennsylvania. To say he was uncomfortable — on all fronts — would be an understatement.

For one thing, his left leg hurt like hell, having been positioned in an odd angle next to the steering wheel of the Vette. The odd angle was the result of his sitting in a manner that caused most of his weight to fall on his left hip in order to spare his bad right hip from undue pressure.

Then there was the fact that it had been close to a year since he'd been more than forty minutes from his home or spent more than an hour in the company of anyone who wasn't one of his doctors. And it had been a while since he'd been to see any of them.

Then there was the matter of Annie's sister.

Annie had waited until that morning to tell Aidan that Mara wasn't exactly expecting him.

"What does that mean, exactly?" he'd asked

pointedly into the phone. "That she's not *exactly* expecting me?"

"It means she'll be fine about it, once you get there," Annie had assured him.

"Is she not fine about it now?"

"She's just not sure that she needs to have someone living in her house, that's all."

"You never mentioned that I'd be living in her house." Aidan had frowned. He'd assumed he'd be staying in a nearby hotel. These days, he wasn't very good company. Even for himself.

"How can you possibly keep an eye on her if you aren't under the same roof?" Annie had sounded tired as well as exasperated. "Look, I'm going into a meeting right now. I'll catch up with you at Mara's later this afternoon. In the meantime, just keep in mind that my sister is the only member of my immediate family who's still living. I need to keep her that way."

Aidan locked the car door and paused at the trunk, then changed his mind about bringing his suitcase in with him. If Annie's sister was adamant about not having a live-in guest, he wasn't going to push himself on her. God knows he wouldn't appreciate a stranger moving into his apartment just because someone else thought it might be a good idea. Even if that someone was Annie.

As a matter of fact, now that he thought about it, he couldn't come up with one good reason why he would let someone else move in

70

with him, even on a temporary basis. It had been hard enough for him to leave his apartment on those rare occasions he ventured out, and most of his outings had consisted of solitary walks along long stretches of deserted beach. He was physically and emotionally uncomfortable around more than one or two people at a time these days, and lately he'd noticed that the more time he spent in his apartment, the less he wanted to leave. He didn't even try to delude himself into thinking this was a healthy thing, but at the same time, he couldn't seem to help himself. His own company was all that he could bear at times. And some days even that was pushing it.

Right now, Aidan could count on the fingers of one hand the number of people he'd welcomed — and that was a relative term — into his apartment since Dylan's death. His brother Connor — the oldest of the Shields brothers — had stayed for ten days after Aidan's release from the hospital and Dylan's funeral, which had been postponed until Aidan had recovered enough to attend. Then there'd been his boss, John Mancini, who'd driven from Virginia on several occasions to check up on him. And then, a few days ago, Annie, for the first time in several months.

If anyone other than Annie had asked this of him, he'd have told them to go to hell. But Annie would have been Aidan's sister-in-law by now if Dylan hadn't been killed, and so, as far

71

as Aidan was concerned, she was family. He was very much aware that Dylan had loved her completely. His heart and his soul, Dylan had called her one night when he and Aidan were on a stakeout on the rainy streets of D.C. If Annie needed help, Aidan would move heaven and hell to do whatever had to be done. If her sister was in danger and Annie needed someone to look out for her, well, then, Aidan was Annie's man. Whether he liked it or not.

And frankly, he didn't like it at all.

For one thing, he wished he'd had a little more notice. Just to get used to the thought of leaving the comfort of his home — such as it was — and coming to a strange place to bunk in with a strange woman. Of course, given enough time, chances were he'd have found a dozen reasons why he should have turned down Annie's request.

But then again, it was Annie who'd done the asking. And he'd promised her he'd always be there for her. . . .

Yeah, yeah, well, he was here now, and in just a peachy frame of mind.

Aidan paused and looked ahead at the house that rose from a stone and mortar foundation at the end of the brick path. The house was neat and trim — a little too neat, maybe — the front door set back into a little porch with an overhang that carefully mimicked thatch. The overall appearance was Tudor in style, the stucco a medium shade of tan and the wood

trim a darker brown. Purple and yellow prim-
roses — a bit too cheery for his taste — spilled
over the sides of a large clay pot that was set to
one side of the top step, and pewter hummingbirds danced and twirled around wind chimes
that hung from a nail on a rafter directly over
the flowers. All in all, Annie's sister's home
looked snug and homey and not at all in need
of protection.

Aidan rang the doorbell, knowing full well
that things were not always as they seemed.

He turned toward the street as he waited,
stepped back a bit when the dog on the other
side of the door began to bark. Aidan could
hear its nose tracing along the floor, sniffing
wildly, trying to register the scent as known or
unknown. Deciding the stranger was one who
needed to be frightened away, or at the very
least put in his place, the dog began to bark
and growl until Aidan stepped back off the
porch. The last thing he needed was for
someone to call the local police and report that
a strange man was trying to get into the home
of one M. Douglas.

Aidan walked across the grass and around to
the back of the property. A garage that archi-
tecturally matched the house stood at the end
of the drive. The backyard was totally fenced in
and had a large maple tree smack in the
middle. Off the rear of the house was a small
deck that held a table, four chairs, and a grill
that was still covered over from winter.

A flat of dark blue pansies sat at the foot of the deck steps as if forgotten. At the far side of the yard, alone in beds that had been lightly mulched with last year's grass clippings but neglected since, a few random red tulips bloomed as if afterthoughts. The yard had no other color, save for patches of spring grass.

"Can I help you with something?" A woman's voice came from behind, close enough to make him startle.

"You can if you're Mara Douglas." He turned to find a petite and pretty dark-haired woman in a black suit standing about ten feet away. Behind her was parked a dark blue Jetta.

"I am." She took a step backward, almost unconsciously, at the admission.

"Aidan Shields."

"Of course. Dylan's brother. Annie mentioned that you might be swinging by one day this week. I'm sorry I didn't recognize you at first."

"It's been a while. And to tell you the truth, I didn't recognize you, either."

The woman who stood before him could just as well have been a complete stranger. The last time he'd seen her had been at Dylan's funeral. Over the past few days, whenever he had tried to call up her face, the only image that appeared was that of a tired-looking, serious woman with haunted eyes.

"I suppose I should invite you in. Since you're going to be stopping by from time to

74

time, I guess you should get the lay of the land, so to speak."

Stopping by from time to time?

Apparently one of them did not have a clear understanding of what Annie had in mind. Aidan had a feeling it might be Mara.

Rather than get into that discussion there in her driveway — he was leaving that little song and dance in Annie's hands — Aidan followed Mara around the car to the front of the house and waited on the walk while she unlocked the door. The second the door opened, a small brown-and-white dog raced past Mara to stand and bark at Aidan territorially from the top step.

"Spike! It's okay. He's a friend," she called to the dog who was intent on sniffing at Aidan's shoes, all the while growling menacingly. "He'll be all right as soon as you come inside." Mara smiled weakly.

Aidan tried to ignore the dog by taking a step closer to the porch, which only caused Spike to growl more deeply.

"It's okay, Spike," she said, leaning over to pick up the dog, who continued to growl. "Sorry. He's a pit bull trapped in the body of a Jack Russell terrier. He'll be fine, really, after a bit."

Aidan stepped inside and stood to one side of the door while she closed it.

"Annie should be here momentarily." Mara put the dog on the floor. "Behave, Spike.

Aidan, please have a seat. May I offer you something to drink?"

Spike sniffed at Aidan's pants leg but the growling had ceased. Aidan wondered if it was safe to take those half dozen steps across the room to the sofa.

"Ah, well . . ."

"Tea, coffee, club soda, beer, water . . ."

"A beer would be fine. Thanks." He took a seat on the sofa.

Spike continued his busy sniffing — he was up to Aidan's knees now — and Aidan offered his open hand for the dog to investigate. Having completed his interrogation-by-nose, Spike apparently decided that their visitor was okay and jockied himself into a position where Aidan would be forced to pat his head.

Aidan heard water running in the kitchen and the sounds of cupboard doors closing lightly. He took the opportunity to look around the living room and take stock of its contents.

The slightly worn but comfortable sofa and one chair were covered in a faded blue plaid. A narrow wing chair and ottoman in coordinating floral fabrics stood near a brick fireplace. Photographs lined a short wall near a hall that lead to somewhere back in the house. Aidan wanted to get up to look at the photos at closer range but wasn't sure if any movement on his part would set off the dog again.

Mara returned with a blue-and-white mug of coffee in one hand and a bottle of beer in the other. She passed the beer to Aidan and said, "I'll just get you a glass . . ."

"Don't bother," he said as he raised the bottle to his lips.

Annie knocked on the door frame, then entered the house, frowning. "I thought we agreed that you'd keep the door locked."

"You said when I was alone in the house," Mara replied. "And as you can see, I am not alone. . . ." She gestured toward Aidan.

"Hello, pup." Annie laughed as Spike jumped straight up and down by way of greeting. "And hello, Aidan. I see you made it. The directions were okay?"

"The directions were fine, thanks."

Annie removed the jacket that matched her dress and folded it carefully over the arm of the wing chair. "I'll just pop into the kitchen and make myself a cup of tea. I've had a hellacious day."

"There's still hot water," Mara told her. "Do you want me to make it for you?"

"No, thanks. I don't mind." Annie called from the kitchen, "Was there any mail? Any good catalogs?"

"On the counter," Mara replied.

"Annie lives here now?" Aidan asked.

"She stays here when she's working in the area. She still has the apartment in Virginia, but she keeps some things here. Sometimes it's more convenient for her."

"So much nicer than a hotel, and I have the

company of my sister and her little dog, who, as you can see, clearly adores me." Annie smiled as she entered the room, Spike leaping up and down at her side like a yo-yo. She sat in the wing chair, placed her teacup on the small side table, and slipped a dog biscuit to Spike.

"Where are you living now?" Mara turned to Aidan. "Weren't you living somewhere near the beach?"

"Rehoboth, Delaware. Still."

"Are we finished with the small talk?" Annie glanced at her watch. "I'm taking a ten forty-five flight to Chicago and I still have to pack."

"I didn't know you were leaving tonight." Mara looked up at her sister.

"I wasn't aware myself until about three hours ago." Annie took a sip of tea. "Aidan, I'm grateful that you decided to come."

"I told you I'd be here," he said without emotion.

"Well, the timing is excellent, since my leaving frees up the guest room, and you can —"

"What are you talking about?" Mara's head snapped up.

"I've asked Aidan to stay here to keep an eye on things," Annie said calmly.

"You never said anything about him staying." Mara's jaw set.

"Didn't I?" Annie murmured, sipping her tea. "I was certain that I had."

"You know you did not." Mara glared at her sister, then turned to Aidan. "No offense, but I don't want . . . I don't need —"

"You *do* need, Mara," Annie said before Aidan could open his mouth. "You do need someone here with you. All three of our Mary Douglases were attacked in their home."

"I've been keeping my doors locked."

"So did Mary Douglas numbers one and two. It didn't keep him out. I'm sorry, sweetie, but Aidan stays until this is over."

"The husband of Mary number three was home when the killer arrived, and was, if you recall" — Mara was beginning to steam — "shot in the back of the head, and his body dumped by the side of the road."

"The husband of Mary number three didn't carry a Sig Sauer and wasn't trained by the FBI to use it," Annie reminded her.

"You have a gun?" Mara turned her attention to Aidan.

He nodded.

"Let me see it."

"It's in a bag in the trunk of my car."

"Fat lot of good it does there."

"I plan on bringing it in."

"I don't mean to insult you, but I don't think I want" — she paused — "anyone living here."

"Fine with me." Not one to pass up a good excuse once it was offered to him, Aidan shrugged and started to stand. He'd passed a small motel on his way into town that looked as if it would suit just fine. "So if it's all the same to you, Annie, I'll just —"

"It's not fine, and it's not all the same to me, Aidan, so sit down. You're not leaving." Annie turned to Mara. "And like it or not, he stays. Do I need to remind you that there's a man out there who's killing women — M. Douglases — in order out of the phone book —"

"And I'm next. No." Mara blew a long breath out of the corner of her mouth. "No, you don't need to remind me."

"Then act like it." Annie turned to Aidan. "And you decide right now, are you going to stay and do the job, or are you going to bolt the first time she gives you an opening?"

"I'll stay." His eyes narrowed, but he didn't argue.

"Fine. I have enough on my plate right now without worrying about my sister being raped and stabbed to death by some wacko, okay?"

"Okay, okay." Mara reached over to grab one of Annie's hands. She couldn't remember the last time she'd seen her sister this agitated. "We're on board, Annie."

"So, if we're done with the pleasantries," Aidan said dryly, "what have you got by way of a profile?"

"Not much," Annie admitted. "Oh, we know the basics. He's white — all of his victims have been white. He's in his thirties, most likely living alone. He's probably got a job where he works a shift —"

"How do you know those things?" Mara interrupted.

"Well, I don't know for certain, Mara. Profiling isn't always exact. It's merely our best educated guess. Most serial killers choose their victims from within their own ethnic group, so we feel he is white, like his victims. He's exhibited such proficiency, such meticulousness and attention to detail, I expect it's taken him several years to perfect such technique. He's probably been experimenting for a while. And he's patient. Not an amateur, not a kid." Annie sipped her tea. "All the murders occurred at the same time of the day, which speaks to routine. I think he must have conducted some sort of surveillance on his victims. He'd know what time they left in the morning, what time they arrived home later in the day. That takes planning, mobility. If you're living with someone, a wife or a girlfriend, it's more difficult to disappear for the number of hours necessary to get a handle on someone else's daily schedule."

"I'd think late at night would be a more likely time to break into someone's house if you were going to commit a murder."

"It's not uncommon for people to be a little distracted when they first arrive home at the end of the day. There's mail to be sorted through, phone messages to listen to, dogs to walk." Annie looked directly at her sister. "I've come here countless times to find the front door unlocked and you listening to the messages on your answering machine at the same

81

time you're putting the leash on Spike to take him out."

"Distractions." Mara nodded.

"Right. I think he has his victims picked out in advance, knows what time he'll find them home. Then he swings by, does his thing, then goes on home or goes to work."

"No witnesses?" Aidan asked.

"None who have come forward. But that's not so unusual. Sometimes we see things and don't realize what we've seen. We see a delivery truck, but we don't really look at the person making the delivery. We just don't notice. So yes, of course, someone may have seen our man but isn't even aware of it. Distractions, as we've said." Annie cleared her throat. "But to continue, our UNSUB — our unknown subject, the killer — is highly organized. The crime scenes were staged. There was nothing out of place, nothing to suggest that all did not go according to his plan. He brought his own tools — his rope, his duct tape, his knife — and he took everything with him when he left. There was nothing left to chance. He is physically strong — strong enough to overpower his victims with very little apparent struggle on their part. The wounds on all of the Marys were made with the same knife — each body bore exactly six stab wounds to the chest, any one of which could have been the killing blow — but other than the victims bleeding out, there was no other blood found on the premises. The women were all sexually assaulted, but all were fully dressed and seated almost primly when they were found, though that fact hasn't been released to the media."

"He raped them, then straightened out their clothing and posed them?" Aidan asked.

"Yes. The rapes were missed until the autopsies, actually. Nothing at the scene immediately indicated that there had been a sexual assault."

"Is that unusual?" Mara asked.

Annie nodded. "Very. More often than not, the rapist wants to humiliate his victim. He wants her to know that he has power over her, that he can use her and discard her because she's unimportant to him in every way except one, and he wants everyone to know that. Here, we have a rapist who not only takes care not to tear his victims' clothing, but makes sure that they are fully dressed, covered up, seated with their feet crossed neatly at the ankles. Very unusual, in my experience. Aidan? Have you seen anything like this before?"

"I've seen some highly organized crime scenes, but nothing quite that detailed."

"And here's something else that hasn't made the news," Annie continued. "The women were all blindfolded. At least, they were when the bodies were found. I'm pretty sure that they were blindfolded during the rapes. It would follow, since he made sure each woman was positioned so modestly for the police to find."

"Blindfolded?" Aidan's eyebrows rose.

"Yes. Does that mean something to you?" Annie turned to him with interest.

"A blindfold he brought with him?"

"We're assuming, since he used identical classic red-and-white bandannas on all three victims. All purchased at a national chain store."

"Available anywhere in the country."

"Yes. As were the rope and the duct tape. All so generic and commonly available, they could have been purchased in Maine or here in Lyndon." Annie was watching Aidan's face. There'd been a shadow of . . . something. . . . "Ring any bells?" she asked.

"There was a case a couple of years ago where the killer used a scarf that belonged to the victim to cover her face. Not really the same, though, as bringing something with you, something purchased for just that purpose." Aidan rubbed his chin and appeared thoughtful. "And here we have someone who breaks into his victims' homes, ties them up, blindfolds them so that they can't see what he's going to do to them, rapes them, then makes sure that their clothing is back on neatly before he goes wild with the knife."

"Almost, but not quite," Annie corrected him. "I think he goes a little wild with the knife while he's in the process of raping them, then when he's finished, he redresses them. And I don't think he blindfolds his victims to keep them from seeing what he's going to do to

84

them. I think he doesn't want them to see him. I think he knows he turns into a monster and I don't think he wants anyone to witness that transformation, however fleeting it may be. I think the only time he comes close to losing control is when he's stabbing them, and even then he controls the number of times he stabs them and the exact location where he puts the knife."

"And this is the man you think is after me?" Mara's face had drained of color.

Annie nodded.

"Okay, if I wasn't convinced before, I'm convinced now." Mara took a deep breath. "Aidan stays till this is over."

"I was hoping you'd come around." Annie's smile was grim.

"You've made a pretty compelling case."

"I just wish I could get a handle on motive." The set of Annie's jaw clearly conveyed her frustration. "No one kills without a reason, and to plot out these detailed murders, all so carefully staged, someone must have a pretty definite motive. But I just can't seem to get a focus on it. I'm missing something, and I just can't . . ."

"And you've looked carefully at the victims?" Aidan prompted.

"Of course. Know the victims, know the killer. But I can't find any connection between these women except that they shared the same name. That's the only common thread. That, and the manner in which they were killed, of course. Significant similarities, to be sure, but neither is bringing us closer to finding our killer."

"And none of the victims was an obvious target?"

"Not that we can see. These aren't high-profile women with backgrounds that would seemingly put them at risk." She shook her head slowly. "These are just . . . well, for want of a better term, average women with average lives. No domestic problems, no neighborhood feuds, no money to be fought over. The police believed that the best bet was the husband of the last victim, who was having an affair. The theory had been that he'd killed the first two to make the police think that some crazy was killing women named Mary Douglas." She wrinkled her nose. "Not a great theory, but it was the only thing they could come up with."

"And then the husband was found dead, and the mistress had been out of town when the killings took place," Mara recalled.

"And that theory — flimsy though it might have been — went out the window, leaving us with nothing." Annie stared out the window. "Except three identical crime scenes."

"Maybe there is someone killing Mary Douglases to deliberately throw off the police," Mara said. "Why would that be so crazy?"

"It's not logical to me. Not that there's always logic in murder, but most of the time things are pretty clear, once you get the focus."

She shook her head. "This time, I just can't get the focus."

"Who's working the case for the Bureau?" Aidan asked.

"We have several field agents working with the locals. Two from the Philadelphia office, two from Mancini's unit." Annie remembered that was Aidan's unit, as well. Or had been. "Miranda Cahill and Jake Domanski."

"I thought Domanski went with the terrorist unit."

"He changed his mind."

"I worked a case directly with Cahill a few years ago. One of her first cases, I think. She had a lot of promise," Aidan recalled.

"She's a good agent." Annie nodded. "She and her sister are both top-notch."

"Have you thought about a contract killing?" Aidan's thoughts returned to the crime. "Maybe the reason the killer keeps going after women named M. Douglas is because he has a name but no idea of what M. Douglas looks like."

Annie leaned her head back against the chair and looked up at the ceiling, as if in deep thought. "Most contract killings are conducted with much less emotion. A shot to the head. A slice to the throat. Strangulation. Not this . . . this *drama* . . . that he keeps playing out. I've never seen a contract killer who behaved like this. And frankly, the rape scenario is not typical of contract killings. There's something else

87

at play here. . . ." Her voice trailed off.

"The repetition of the same scene. The stabbings, the covering of the victim's face. The rearranging of the clothes, covering up the rape." Aidan repeated the facts as Annie had spelled them out for him. "The answer is in the crime scene."

"Exactly." A grim Annie turned to look at Aidan. "It all speaks to playing out a rape fantasy. The stabbings were very deliberate. Even if he killed for someone else, the rape thing, that was clearly all his own.

"But regardless of the motive, our man is no novice. He's killed before. Many times. He's too highly organized, too methodical, to be a beginner. The knife wounds on each of the victims were very specific, very precise. The wounds from victim to victim matched almost perfectly. He's honed his craft very, very well."

"And I'm assuming you put all this into the computers at the Bureau. . . ."

"Of course." Annie nodded. "We've had some limited response to certain aspects — the rearranging of the clothes, for example — but not the whole package."

"And no fingerprints that matched up with any on file."

"We have nothing. We have a killer who's obviously been practicing his trade for years but hasn't left so much as a partial print or any fluids that we could test for DNA. He wore gloves, and a condom, each time."

"You referred to him earlier as a serial killer," Mara recalled.

"Oh, no question about it. Our UNSUB — hired man or otherwise — is a serial killer." Annie turned to Mara. "And if he is going through the phone book to pick his victims, and you are next on his list, you go nowhere — I mean nowhere — without Aidan in your back pocket until this is over."

Annie stood, her hands on her hips, her face grave. "Like it or not, Mara, you've got a new housemate. And he stays until the police have made an arrest, so I suggest you get used to each other."

Chapter Five

"You might as well bring your stuff in," Annie called over her shoulder to Aidan as she began to gather her own bags.

"Can I give you a hand with those?" He reached for her suitcase.

"No, no, I'm fine. I just thought that since I was walking out, you might want to walk with me."

"She means she wants to talk to you without me there," Mara called from the kitchen, where she was finishing up the dishes from the impromptu dinner the three of them had shared.

"Oh." Aidan went to the doorway and picked up the largest of Annie's suitcases. "You could have just said so."

"She's such a smart-ass," Annie said under her breath.

"Last minute instructions, Mom?" Aidan held the front door open for her, then closed it behind them.

Annie's step slowed. "Mara's the only person I know who permits almost as few people in her personal space as you do."

"What the hell is that supposed to mean?"

"It means that she . . . she's been pretty much alone — except for me — for the past seven years."

"Why?" He frowned.

"She'll have to tell you that. If she wants to."

"Why bring it up if you're not going to tell me?"

"Because I want you to know that, well, just that she's used to being alone, that's all." Annie opened her trunk, dropped her bags in, then turned back to him with worried eyes. "Watch out for her, Aidan. Guard her with your life. She's all I have."

"I'll be here."

He stepped back onto the sidewalk and stood with his hands in his pockets, watching Annie's car until it disappeared around the corner, then retrieved his own bag, a beat-up navy blue duffel that he'd had in college and found in the front closet of his apartment. He hesitated at the rear of the Corvette. He hated to leave it out on the street where who knew what could happen to it. He glanced at the driveway. There was plenty of room behind the Jetta.

Mara was standing in the doorway, watching as he backed up the Vette and parked it behind her car.

"Do you mind?" He stopped halfway to the door. "I didn't want to leave it parked out there overnight. It could get rear-ended or side-swiped."

"No, I don't mind, but you'll have to move it before I go to work in the morning."

"Well, since I'll be following you, that won't

be a problem," he told her as he walked up the front steps.

"I don't think that's necessary, really." She stepped aside to let him in.

He didn't bother to respond. He'd do what he was going to do. There was little point in discussing it.

"So. I guess you want to get settled." Mara stood in the center of the living room, feeling awkward. It had been a very, very long time since she'd been alone in her house with a man. Any man. "Second door on the right. Annie said she made the bed up for you before she left."

"Thanks." He nodded somewhat stiffly as he went up the steps, obviously no happier with the situation than she was.

Great, she thought with a grimace. *This should be one hell of a fun time.*

Thanks, Annie.

"Annie didn't mention that you had a daughter," he was saying as he came down the stairs.

"What?"

"I said, I didn't know you had a daughter. Where is she?"

Mara appeared frozen where she stood, her face without color.

She wet her lips and turned her head away from him.

Aidan stood on the last step, confused. Her

entire demeanor had changed in the blink of an eye.

"I'm going to take Spike for a walk. I won't be long." She hurried brusquely into the kitchen and returned with the dog and leash in tow.

"I'll go with you." The mention of her daughter had obviously upset her, but he couldn't for the life of him figure out why.

"No, no need. Same walk I take every night." She was fumbling with Spike's collar. Her hands were visibly shaking, and her best efforts to hide the fact were not quite good enough.

"Wait up . . ."

"I said no need. I'll be back." She walked out the door.

Aidan followed.

"I said you didn't have to come with me. I don't want you to come with me."

"I promised Annie I'd keep an eye on you. Tough to do if I'm sitting on the sofa, playing with the remote, while you're out roaming around town in the dark."

He fell in step with her. She responded by gravitating to the far edge of the sidewalk, as if to put as much distance as possible between them.

"Look, obviously I've upset you somehow but I don't know what I've done."

"It's okay. Forget it." She brushed him off without looking at him.

They walked the entire four-block square

without speaking further, Aidan doing his best to keep up with her, but she was in far better shape than he was.

He wished she had one of those big, lumbering dogs that took their time, the ones that sort of waddled as they ambled along, instead of this speedy little thing that buzzed along the sidewalk at breakneck speed.

He wished she'd slow down.

He wished his hip wasn't bothering him. It was almost enough to make him wish that he'd finished his therapy program.

All in all, it was a pretty pathetic effort on his part.

And it was awkward, wondering just what exactly had set her off like that. Then again, with her in a huff, he wasn't pressed into making conversation, and for that he was grateful. By the time they returned to Mara's house, he was pretty much out of breath, and his left leg and his right hip were nagging at him in concert, exacting a painful duet upon him for his effort.

He tried his best not to limp.

"I'm going to close up the house," she announced as she locked the front door. "You can go on up to your room, or stay down here and watch TV. Whichever you prefer."

"I'll check the back." He started toward the back of the house.

"I said I'd do it. I'm really not helpless." She made an effort to soften her tone just a bit.

After all, he was doing her a favor by being here.

Correction. He was doing Annie a favor.

He barely glanced at her as he went down the hall to the back of the house where French doors opened onto the deck. He pulled against them, then, on his way back, pulled the slide lock shut on the basement door.

"You could use a dead bolt on those doors back there," he told her. "Did you check the kitchen windows?"

"Yes, thanks."

"Then I'll see you in the morning." He turned from her and began to climb the stairs, clearly favoring one leg, leaning heavily on the rail for support, and it was then that she realized just what his determination to keep up with her pace had cost him.

She tried to reconcile the man slowly laboring to climb the steps with all that Annie had told her over the years about the man Mara had first met at Annie and Dylan's engagement party, a meeting that Aidan apparently did not recall. She knew from Annie that both he and Dylan — along with their older brother, Connor — played at some of the Bureau's most dangerous games. The Shields brothers had moved with a sleek air of danger, of intrigue, that had fascinated and drawn the attention of all the ladies, including Mara.

That quickness, that sureness, was nowhere to be found in the man who, seconds earlier, had limped toward the stairwell without complaint, and she understood now why she hadn't immediately recognized him earlier in the driveway. The Aidan Shields on the steps was softer and twenty or so pounds heavier than the Aidan Shields who had gone undercover with his brother that one last time. The Aidan Shields who had carried his brother from an alley on a shattered leg, a bullet lodged in his hip. . . .

The brisk-paced walk around the block had clearly been too much for him. She'd been a total ass not to realize how hard-pressed he'd been to keep up. A peace offering was in order. She threw out the only thing she had that could equate his sacrifice.

"My husband and I divorced seven years ago," she said quietly. "The day after the divorce became final, he took our daughter and disappeared."

He stopped midway up the steps and turned to look down at her. This time she did not look away.

"You mean he — ?"

"Yes." She didn't wait for him to finish. "He took her and vanished and I haven't seen either of them since."

"I'm assuming that Annie . . ." He gestured helplessly with one hand, stunned by her admission.

"Yes, of course, Annie pulled out all the stops. But he's very, very smart. He's changed his name, and he's done everything that people do when they want to make certain that no one ever finds them."

"Why would he . . . How could he — ?" He spoke his thoughts aloud, understanding now why she'd been so upset by his innocent inquiry about her daughter, his mistaken entry into her room.

"He wanted to punish me" — Mara did not bother to force back her tears — "for not wanting to be married to him anymore. He knew that the only way he could really hurt me was to take her from me. And that's what he did."

"How old was she?" He lowered himself to a step and sat.

"Five. Her name is Julianne." Tears streamed down her face. She hadn't spoken aloud of her daughter to anyone except Annie in several years. She hadn't realized just how hard it would be. "At least, it was Julianne. I've often wondered if he made her change her name, too."

"I'm sorry. I had no way of knowing. Annie never told me —"

"I know. It's all right." She crossed her arms over her chest and tried to squeeze away the pain.

"You've looked for her . . . ?"

"For the first year, I did nothing else. Annie had the FBI in overdrive looking for them. Then, for almost two years, I had private detectives trying to track them down. But one thing I learned — if someone really wants to disappear, there are a million ways to do it. Once we got close, but Jules somehow knew or sensed that he was being watched, and they disappeared again. That was early on, maybe eight months or so after he left. We haven't had a good lead since then. He's kept a really low profile." She exhaled deeply. "Every couple of months, Annie runs a trace. I'm still looking for Julianne, of course. I won't stop until I find her. I'll never stop."

"If there's anything I can do . . ." He paused, thinking how stupid he sounded. He was out of shape, out of luck, out of the loop. What did he really think he could do, when all of Annie's resources — the entire FBI network — had come up empty?

"I appreciate that. Thanks." She nodded and backed away. "Well, I'm going to finish closing up. Thanks again."

Mara went into the kitchen. He heard her shut a cabinet door, heard the faucet turn on, then off. A minute later, one by one, the downstairs lights went off, and Aidan turned back to the task of climbing the steps.

Just as the clock from a nearby church tower struck two, Aidan sat straight up in the bed, prodded by dark dreams. It was not unusual for his sleep to be interrupted by nightmares. The demons had been tormenting him relentlessly for months. But tonight the old demons wore new faces. Some hunted down unsuspecting women and ravaged their bodies; some stole their children and broke their hearts. And he, Aidan Shields, was helpless, trapped in a body that betrayed him at every turn.

He lay awake until dawn, trying to make up excuses for his present condition while at the same time wondering how he'd let himself sink this low.

He'd been painfully winded just from walking around the block. Sad but true.

Okay, sure, it had been a big block, but he'd all but killed himself trying to keep up with a short woman and a little dog whose legs weren't more than eight inches long. He, who had once undergone special ops training — who had run for miles in the hot sun with a forty-pound pack on his back; who had, for six years after college, survived weeks in the desert, in the jungle, in the Arctic — couldn't walk a distance of four blocks. Hell, he'd been wheezing by the time they'd hit the corner at the end of Mara's street.

It was the little dog that really got to him the most. Spike hadn't even been breathing hard when they'd rounded the last bend for home. Pathetic.

Bested by a Jack Russell terrier. And an old one, at that.

Disgusted with himself, he shifted his weight from his throbbing bad hip.

Not much he could do about the pain, he acknowledged. And the limp . . . well, there wasn't much he could do about that, either.

It had been a hard reality to face. He'd quit physical therapy because he knew that even with the best of programs, he'd never be the same. He'd never be nearly as good. No matter what he put himself through, he'd never be able to run again without pain. He'd never work undercover, he'd never be trusted to watch someone's back. Babysitting Annie's little sister didn't count.

And on top of it all, he was out of shape in every conceivable way. Admitting that it humiliated him when he was unable to ignore the contrast between the man he was today and the man he'd once been.

He'd never be that man again. It was a hard truth to accept.

He flexed his right hand, unable to hold a gun since that terrible night, then flexed his left. He'd been trained to shoot with his nondominant hand. Surely if he worked at it, he could regain that proficiency again. . . .

The lights from a plane moved across the night sky, and he watched it for several long minutes before lying back down and closing his eyes, thinking about how hard it must be for Mara to stay in this house, to walk past that empty bedroom every day.

He recognized that, as terrible as his own tragedy had been, he, at least, had closure.

Mara had none. She had faced every new day for seven years with the same unanswered questions, the same void, the same pain. And she was handling her situation with infinitely more grace, more courage, than he was handling his. At least she kept going. He had given up.

He lay in the dark feeling pissed off at fate and life until the sun came up and spilled across the foot of the bed. Mostly, he was pissed off at himself.

When he heard the shower in the bathroom on the other side of the wall, he swung his legs over the side of the bed. Mara was up, and if he was to fulfill his promise to Annie, he needed to be up as well.

If he could do nothing else, he could at least show up.

"Could you just stay behind me so that it doesn't look like you're following me?" Mara stood next to her car, the driver's door open, keys in her hand.

"Maybe you could give me some tips on that, since I've never tailed a vehicle before." He placed his hands on his hips and stared at her. What did she think the FBI trained people to do?

Before she could respond, he went on. "Just make sure that you call me if you leave the office."

"I may have three or four appointments today. You can't spend the day running back and forth." She slid behind the wheel of the Jetta.

"Watch me." He got into the Vette, adding, "See you at lunch," as he slammed the car door.

She leaned out the window to call back to him, "What do you mean, see you at lunch?"

"I mean I'll pick you up and we'll —"

"No, we will not." She got out of her car and walked back to his. "Aidan, I don't want people in my office to think that that I'm . . . that I'm . . ."

"Dating a guy with a gimp leg?"

"Get over yourself, Aidan. That was a stupid thing to say and I'm going to ignore it." Her eyes narrowed. "I've never brought my personal business into the courthouse. I don't want to do that now."

"Well, right now we all have to do things we don't want to do."

"Look, if you don't want to be here, I don't want you to stay. God knows I don't want to hold you against your will."

"I promised your sister I'd keep you safe and alive, and that's what I'm going to do."

They stared each other down for a long minute.

"Okay." He was the first to break. "How 'bout if we compromise and I bring you lunch?"

"How 'bout if I ask someone in my office to pick up something for me when they go out?"

"As long as you're not out of that building by yourself. You have the number for my cell phone. Don't be shy about using it if for any reason you feel uncomfortable or uneasy about anything or anyone. Do not underestimate this guy."

"Do you really think he's going to come after me in the courthouse?"

"I have no idea what he's going to do. I just want to make sure I'm around when he makes his move."

"If he makes his move," she muttered as she slid behind the wheel of the Jetta.

"Just don't do anything stupid."

" 'Just don't do anything stupid,' " she muttered as she started her car. "Like I really want this guy to find me . . ."

Aidan backed out of the drive, then waited for her to pull out so that he could follow her. It was a twelve-minute ride to the courthouse, and he parked illegally while she parked in the employees' garage. It was early, early enough for her to have found a place near the gate and the Plexiglas enclosure where the attendant sat. Aidan watched her exit the garage, watched her walk across the street and along the walkway, watching all the while to see if someone else was watching her as well.

After Mara disappeared into the courthouse, he sat for another minute or so, observing the comings and goings, until a police car pulled next to him and the officer pointed to the NO

103

PARKING sign. Aidan nodded to the officer, waved, and moved on.

Back at Mara's, he parked near the garage and, using the key that Mara had given him, entered the back of the house through the French doors. Spike was there to greet him.

"You don't need to go out," Aidan said aloud. "Mara took you for a walk this morning."

Spike continued to wag his tail hopefully.

"All right, I'll tell you what. I'm going to change, and then we'll go out for a while. But you have to slow the pace down a little, understand? I'm a little out of shape right now. . . ."

Ten minutes later, a house key in one pocket of his zip-front sweatshirt, his cell phone in the other, Aidan started out with Spike.

"Slow down, would you?" He tugged lightly on Spike's leash. Miraculously, Spike responded and was immediately rewarded by finding what was apparently a noteworthy smell on a patch of grass two houses down from Mara's.

"There, see what you miss when you buzz along at that breakneck pace? This is what humans mean when they say take time to stop and smell the flowers. In your case, those would be dandelions. That other thing you were sniffing there, I don't need to know what that was."

They walked the same four-block square that Mara had followed the night before. Aidan was mildly winded by the time they returned to the house, but encouraged all the same. By slowing his pace, he had made it all the way without feeling like he needed to stop to nurse along his leg, a small victory of sorts.

He sat out on the deck steps and tried to make an honest assessment of his situation. All the exercise in the world wouldn't bring back the Aidan Shields he'd been just a short year ago. Nothing would.

But getting out of breath just walking around the block . . . well, he could do something about that.

Pathetic. He shook his head. *Just plain pathetic . . .*

The admission did little to lighten his mood. Not that he'd started out the day on a particularly chipper note. He'd slept poorly and woke in a piss-poor frame of mind. It had been all he could do not to snap at Mara. The instant coffee — instant swill had been more like it — hadn't done much for his mood. Who made instant coffee these days? He wondered if it might not be worth it to buy a coffeemaker. Would he offend Mara? Nah. Anyone who drank coffee that bad on a regular basis had to have a tougher skin than that.

He watched a wren stuff a long piece of grass through the opening of a birdhouse that hung from a low tree branch and contemplated his situation.

He couldn't even glorify what he was doing

by calling it bodyguarding.

My — he shook his head — *how the mighty have fallen.*

He called Spike and coaxed him back inside, locking the back door before moving on to the living room.

There's a book in there someplace, he told himself ruefully. *"How I Went from Feared FBI Agent to Babysitter in One Short Year." Subtitle: "Bad Coffee and Bad Gigs."*

Still, a promise was a promise. And she was Annie's sister. He'd had to keep reminding himself of the fact. Like when she'd gotten out of her car and stalked back down the driveway to the Vette to let him know in no uncertain terms that he was not coming to her office to pick her up for lunch. She'd had fire in her eyes and a purpose to her stride.

Actually, she'd looked pretty damned good.

"Forget it," he muttered aloud. "Don't even think about going there . . ."

Spike picked his head up at the sound of Aidan's voice.

"You don't want to know," Aidan told him. "And no, we're not going out again now. We just came in."

Spike sank back down with a disappointed sigh.

Mara had made it clear that she didn't want him there, didn't want to share her space with him. She'd only agreed to his staying when Annie told her about the serial killer.

Which gave Aidan an idea of just how desirable he was these days. Given the choice between his company and possibly facing a serial killer alone, Mara had reluctantly agreed to let him stay.

That pretty much said it all, didn't it? And just how much protection he'd be against a serial killer was up in the air right about then.

He wished he could go back to his little apartment where he could feel sorry for himself in peace.

Wished he could go to sleep and wake up the man he used to be.

He stretched out on the sofa, his arms folded behind his head. He usually napped around now anyway. It was something to do.

He closed his eyes, wondering just how long it would be before they got a bead on the killer. Tonight couldn't be soon enough. With luck, they'd find him before he found another victim. And then Aidan could go back to his apartment, where he could be miserable all by himself and not think about the fact that he couldn't walk around the block without wanting to pass out, where he could start off the day with good coffee, if nothing else. Eventually, he was certain, that day would come.

It was all he had to look forward to.

Chapter Six

As promised, Mara called Aidan twenty minutes before she was ready to leave the office at the end of the day. The Corvette was there, waiting to follow her home, when she emerged from the parking garage.

"I took your mail in," Aidan told her after they'd arrived at the house and she reached to open the mailbox. "It's on the kitchen counter."

"Oh. Well. Thanks." She nodded and unlocked the door. "I'll just take a quick look at it before I take Spike for his walk."

"He's been in and out all day."

"Oh. Well, then." She went to the phone and pressed the button for messages, but there were none.

"You had two calls." He handed her a slip of paper upon which he'd listed the names and numbers of the callers.

"You answered my phone?" She raised an eyebrow, mildly annoyed at this invasion of privacy.

"If someone is watching you, he might call to see if anyone picks up the phone. To see if you live alone."

"I do live alone," she reminded him somewhat tersely.

"Not this week."

"Right." She gritted her teeth. "So. What else did you do today?"

"I sweated," he said, recalling that last walk around the block.

"What?"

"Never mind."

She began to pick through her mail.

"So." She opened a bill and scanned it. "About dinner. I'm afraid I'm not much of a cook. But we have some great take-out places in town. If that's okay with you?"

He opened the refrigerator and took out a shallow pan. "Chicken cacciatore." He peeled back the foil.

"You made that?" She peered closer, then closer still, before the corners of her mouth began to turn up. "Nah, that's from Giorgio's. Nice try, though. Almost had me."

He almost smiled.

She turned the oven on and set the timer, thinking how odd it was to be sharing her home with a strange man.

"Look, you don't have to do all this. You don't have to walk my dog or answer my phone or bring in my mail or buy my food. All you're supposed to be doing is watching me so that some psycho doesn't get me. In the event that said psycho, in fact, has an interest in me. I don't want you to feel like you have to do any-thing else, except what Annie asked you to do."

"Well, let's put this into perspective, shall

we?" Aidan placed the pan on top of the stove with the same cool, precise control as his words. "I spent the day here because I had nowhere else to go. While I was here, I got bored, took a walk or two. I took Spike along. The mail was sticking out of the box when we came back from our last walk so I brought it in. I answered your phone because it was ringing, and because if the caller was the person I'm supposed to be protecting you from, I wanted him to know that I am here. I stopped and picked up something for dinner because I get hungry around six every day and had no reason to think I wouldn't be hungry tonight. End of story."

"And I appreciate it. I really do. I just don't want to impose on you any more than my sister already has."

"Fine. Maybe what we need here are a few ground rules. If you don't want me to answer the phone, or bring in the mail, or walk the dog, or —"

"No, no, it's fine. I didn't mean . . . that is, I'm grateful. Really. I am. And I do appreciate that you might get bored here during the day." She pushed a chin-length strand of dark hair back from her face and tucked it behind her ear, trying to mirror his control. "It's just that I'm used to being alone, except for those times when Annie is here. I'm not used to having . . . someone" — She'd almost said *a stranger* — "in my house. It's just going to take a little getting used to, that's all."

"I understand," Aidan told her, because he did. "Look, if you want to watch television alone tonight, or read a book, or whatever, it's okay. I can go upstairs and read, or go sit outside . . ."

"I wouldn't expect you to go sit outside while I sat in here and watched TV." The idea struck her as absurd, and she laughed out loud.

"I wouldn't mind. You have a clear overhead view from your deck. Do you ever sit out there at night and look at the stars?"

"No. Are you into stargazing?"

"It passes the time. Tonight might be a good night, if the sky stays clear. I brought my telescope with me. I think I'll set it up on the deck."

"Isn't it going to be cold?"

"That's why the jacket was invented."

"Maybe I will join you." She backed out of the kitchen, suddenly needing to escape from his presence. "But right now, I think I'd like to change. I'll just be a minute. . . ."

Mara took the steps two at a time, seeking the sanctuary of her room. Once inside, she closed the door and collapsed onto the bed, her head spinning. She hadn't expected it to be easy, having someone here with her, but she hadn't expected it to cause this level of tension, either. She was trying her best to act normal — whatever that was — but it was hard. She was used to living with ghosts, and Aidan was very much alive.

Mara closed her eyes, took several deep breaths, and tried to will away the sense of unrest that filled her. If she stayed there, in her room, she wouldn't have to talk to him, wouldn't feel compelled to make conversation that he was only pretending to be interested in.

She wanted nothing more than to stay right where she was, facedown on the bed, until the morning came and she could leave again for work.

Which, of course, she could never do. That would be inexcusably rude.

Not that he was a model of civility. The man had apparently left a good deal of his charm in Rehoboth.

Snap out of it. He's doing you a favor.

No, he's doing Annie a favor.

Did it really matter? Wasn't it was enough that he was here, that she was safer for his presence? And wasn't that the point?

She would get herself under control enough to have dinner with Aidan, do her best to be polite and genial. And if it didn't go well, then maybe she'd feign a headache so that she could retreat back up to Julianne's room, where she could pretend they were saying bedtime prayers together, just like they had every night before Julianne disappeared. Mara was aware that over the years the prayers had taken on the air of a ritual, but she couldn't help herself. In the still and darkened room, she could almost imagine Julianne's pale blond hair fanned out on the pillow, could almost hear her child's voice whispering her child's prayer, and wondered if, wherever she was, Julianne was saying her prayers and pretending that her mother was there.

Last night, Mara had waited until she felt certain that Aidan was sound asleep before she tiptoed to Julianne's room and closed the door softly behind her. She just didn't want to have to explain to a near stranger that she couldn't fall asleep until she'd tried to reach out to her daughter in the only way she could.

Mara rested for a few more minutes, then sat up, her legs dangling over the side of the bed, her toes just grazing the carpet, and marveled at the power of anxiety. Over the course of the past few years, she had faced off with some of the worst that mankind had to offer. She had seen mothers who had sent their preteen daughters out onto the streets to turn tricks or had loaned out their sons to pedophiles, fathers who had repeatedly raped their daughters and others who had sold them. She'd stood in court and recited these abominations to judges, reading aloud carefully and without emotion, wanting the facts alone to call for justice and for compassion for the children for whom she stood. And she had never blinked, never faltered. Yet here, now, in her own home, she felt unsure of herself, vulnerable.

It was just the damnedest thing.

Mara cleared her throat, forced herself off

the edge of the bed, and began to change from her office attire. Resenting Aidan's presence really wasn't fair to him at all, she reminded herself as she slipped off her skirt and panty hose. It wasn't as if he wanted to be here any more than she wanted him around. No wonder he was a little grumpy at times. Given the choice, certainly he'd rather be back at his own apartment, doing his own thing. But he hadn't been able to say no to Annie.

No one could say no to Annie.

She pulled on her jeans and searched her bottom drawer for a sweatshirt.

The thought occurred to her that it was probably as hard for Aidan to be out of his element as it was for her to have him in hers.

She tied on an old pair of running shoes and took one more deep breath, turned off the light, then opened her bedroom door and headed downstairs. They'd have dinner and try to be polite to each other, and maybe later they'd sit out back and look at the stars through his telescope. She wasn't certain it would be necessary to pretend that they were enjoying each other's company.

Wrapped in a heavy red sweater, the hood pulled over her head, Mara drew her legs up onto the chair and tried not to huddle. The night had grown unseasonably cool since she'd followed Aidan out onto the deck and watched him set up his telescope on the tripod. She hadn't wanted to go, had never had much interest in astronomy, but thought it would be impolite to send her guest outside alone.

She watched him patiently adjust the lens, then turn the scope this way and that, looking for God only knew what. Well, she'd look, she'd pretend to be interested, and then she'd go to bed. He could stay out here all night, if he wanted to. But for now, the least she could do was show some curiosity.

He was bent over the scope, moving the device ever so slowly, his face a study in concentration.

"Here," he said without taking his eyes from the lens. "Take a look."

Trying not to shiver, she stepped forward. He stood behind her and grabbed her by the elbow to lead her into position. "What am I looking at?"

She raised her hands to take hold of the scope, and he stopped her by taking her hands in his own. The sudden and unexpected intimacy of his hands trapping and holding on to hers disconcerted her, and she fought the urge to pull away.

"No, don't. You'll move it and then I'll have to adjust it again. Just . . . here . . ." He guided her to the lens. "Just look right through here."

"I'm not sure what I'm supposed to be looking at."

"What do you see?"

"A bright light — a big star, with other stars around it."

"That's Jupiter."

"Really?"

"Yes."

"It looks big. I mean, it looks small through the lens, but it looks big compared to the other stars."

"It's the largest planet in our solar system. And those little 'stars' are its moons."

"I knew that," she heard herself say. Of course she knew it. She just hadn't been thinking about it.

"Let's see what else." He leaned in next to her, one hand in the middle of her back, the side of his face momentarily close to hers. He moved the telescope slightly, adjusted the lens, then brought her back into position.

"Take a look."

"What am I looking at now?"

"That's Castor. In the constellation Gemini."

"Like the astrological sign," she said without thinking, then realized how silly that must have sounded. Laughing, she turned to him. "Sorry. That sounded incredibly stupid."

"Astronomy, astrology. All those *A* words sound alike," he said dryly.

She turned to look up at him, was surprised to find how close he still was. He smelled of soap — her soap — and just a hint of the chamomile candle that burned on the table next to the telescope.

"I didn't confuse the two. I just wasn't thinking, that's all. Of course I know the difference."

He didn't bother to reply, merely reached around her and turned the scope to his own eyes. Over the next hour, he showed her constellations, the names of which she recalled from a long-ago science class, and pointed out the stars Polaris, Sirius, Pollux.

"I'm really impressed," she said honestly. "Maybe you should have been an astronaut."

"I'd thought about it once," he admitted as he removed the telescope from the tripod.

"Are you serious?" She studied his face. Of course he was.

"When I was a kid, I used to dream about it, going into space. I wanted to be the first man to land on Mars."

For the briefest of moments, he appeared almost wistful. She'd almost caught a peek of the child he had been. Almost.

"If that was your dream, why didn't you pursue it?" She sat back in her chair. "How'd you end up in the FBI?"

"It's the family business." The phantom child she'd almost glimpsed had slipped back into hiding.

"Oh, you mean because your two brothers were agents? Why would you feel you had to follow in their footsteps?"

"It wasn't just my brothers. It was my father. An uncle. A couple of cousins."

"Oh. I can see how you'd feel . . ." She paused. Actually, she couldn't understand feeling obligated to follow a course merely because it was expected of her. "Have you ever regretted your decision?"

He looked over his shoulder, his eyes dark and guarded.

"Every day for the past year."

He slipped the telescope into the case, snapped it closed as neatly as he had closed off himself, then headed into the house, leaving Mara alone with the night sky, biting her tongue.

"Hmm, let's see . . . Esposito, Esposito . . ."

Muttering to himself, Curtis Alan Channing traced the list of names with his right index finger. He knew the address — that had been given to him — but he needed to make sure that Flora Esposito still lived at 2703 Edge Hill Road in Brownville, three small towns down the main pike from where he sat.

He found the address and dialed the number.

"Hello? Is this Mrs. Esposito?" he asked.

"Yes. Who is this?"

"Mrs. Flora Esposito?"

"Yes. Who *is* this?"

"I'm an old friend of your daughter's and I'm just back in town for a night and was thinking it would be nice to just give her a call and say hi. . . ."

The silence was long and strained. Finally,

she asked, "Who did you say you were?"

"I went to grade school with Diane, fourth through sixth grade, but then we moved to Chicago. I was just wondering how she was and, well, maybe she won't remember me at all, but I thought, hell — oh, I apologize, Mrs. Esposito — I thought maybe I'd give a call and see if you were still around, and maybe you'd give me her phone number."

"Diane is . . . Diane died almost three years ago."

"Oh, my God, no!" He was getting into it now. "Oh, I'm so sorry, Mrs. Esposito, I had no idea. . . ."

"Well, you wouldn't have, I suppose." Flora Esposito's throat began to constrict, the way it always did when Diane's name came up out of the blue like that.

"May I ask . . . how . . . what happened?" His voice dropped an octave or two.

"She . . . she was murdered." Even now, the words were so hard to speak.

"Oh, God, that's horrible! Horrible. She was such a sweet girl. I always thought she was the cutest girl in our class, you know, in sixth grade. I had such a crush on her." He pretended to be choked up for a moment before adding, "Who would do such a terrible thing to such a sweet girl?"

"Well . . . what did you say your name was?"

"Bill. Bill Callahan."

"Billy Callahan, old Dr. Callahan's nephew?"

He was tempted, but it was too risky.

"No, I'm afraid not. I was the other Billy Callahan."

"Oh. I hadn't remembered that there had been more than one."

"You were telling me about Diane." He knew, of course, that he had the right person, but some perversity in his nature wanted to hear her say it. It would help set the stage emotionally for what would come later that night.

"Her husband shot her. Her and her two boys. His own wife and his own sons, his own flesh and blood. What kind of a monster puts a gun to the head of his own children and pulls the trigger?"

"I just don't know what to say." He picked idly at a cuticle on his left thumb. "I've never been so shocked. . . . Oh, I'm so sorry to have brought this up. I can't apologize enough, Mrs. Esposito."

"It's all right, son. You wouldn't know. And it's not as if I don't think about it every day, anyway."

"I'm sure you do." He nodded absently. "I'm sure you do."

"Every day of my life, Billy, and I will until the day I die. . . ."

Billy said his kind good-byes and hung up the phone. Mrs. Esposito wouldn't be missing her Diane for much longer.

Till the day you die, indeed . . .

He'd debated over and over whether he should simply shoot her and have done with it, or take his time and do what he did best. In the end, as much as it pained him, he opted to use the gun. In the wake of the Mary Douglas killings and the resulting circus of media attention — the last one being the courthouse Mary and all that — killing Flora Esposito in the same manner could lead an investigator with some smarts directly to the county prison and to one Vince Giordano with a lot of questions. He didn't think that Giordano was the type who'd rat him out, but with one more victim to go before his part of the deal was done, why take stupid chances?

He'd enjoyed the game so far — even after his early missteps — and after tonight, there'd be only one name left on the list before he could take off for parts unknown. He was giving some serious consideration to the Outer Banks of North Carolina. Someone had been talking about it in the restaurant the other day, and it had sounded like a nice place to visit. Then again, anyplace down south was nice. He'd have to give it more thought.

He checked the gun — an old handgun he'd won in a poker game about fifteen years ago and had used only a few times. Guns were loud and had a tendency to draw attention, something he wisely avoided. He much preferred the knife, which offered so much more in the way of artistic expression.

Even now, knowing he needed to complete this task in a manner that could not be associated with his recent kills, it was with regret that he left the knife in his bag. He zipped the bag shut quickly and tucked it next to the bed, then opened the door and left the room without looking back before the knife could call to him and remind him of what they could do together.

Flora Esposito would never know just how lucky she was.

Chapter Seven

Miranda Cahill rested her chin in her hand and leaned in a bit closer to the computer screen as she scrolled down the file that had been sent, at her request, from FBI headquarters. She carefully sorted through the facts before shaking her head.

Close, but no cigar.

This latest file had outlined a series of killings that had occurred over a period of four years in western Missouri, and though the MO was somewhat similar to that of their Mary Douglas killer, she knew instinctively that the differences distinguishing them indicated two killers. All the victims in the Missouri cases had had their throats slashed. None of them had been blindfolded. Anne Marie McCall's profile had noted that both the identical knife wounds to the chest and the blindfolding of the victims were integral components of their killer's signature. Also, the Missouri killings had been disorganized, showing none of the deliberation of the killer whose identity they now sought.

Miranda pushed her hair back from her face and started on the next file. One case in Wyoming caught her attention, as did one in West Virginia. She faxed inquiries to the investigating police departments before checking the time. It was ten after seven in the morning. She'd been at her computer since four.

She answered her cell phone on the second ring.

"Miranda?" a deep male voice asked.

"Yes? Who's this?"

"I don't know if you'll remember me. My name is Aidan Shields and I —"

"Oh, for cryin' out loud, Shields." She burst out laughing. "What do you think, after a year, everyone's memory has been erased?"

"Well, it's been a while since we worked together —"

"Aidan, it's good to hear from you." She cut him off, sparing him the need to offer further excuses or to explain where he'd been. As if she didn't know. As if everyone he'd ever worked with at the Bureau didn't know. "Hey, I hear you've got a cushy new gig these days."

"Well, it's not really a —"

"Oh, come on, I hear you've been hanging out with Dr. McCall's very pretty sister," she teased. "There are a lot of guys who would have paid handsomely for that privilege, had Annie given them a chance."

"Oh, we're hanging out together, all right. I follow her to work, follow her home, make sure her doors and windows are locked at night. I walk her dog a couple of times a day and stand ready to slay any dragons that might try to slip in. All in all, it's been a pretty demanding week."

"Stop. I'm getting jealous."

"I'll bet." He paused only momentarily before getting right to the point of the call. "I hear you're involved in this case. The Mary Douglases."

"Annie told you everything, I'm sure."

"She did. Anything new?"

"Not yet. And yes, I'd tell you if there was. I mean, since you're involved and everything."

He was very quiet for a minute, causing her to wonder if he was still on the line.

"Listen, Miranda, do you remember that case we worked together about six years ago? In Ohio? Rockledge, I think, and I think it was one of your first times in the field."

"It was my first time in the field." She nodded, then realized that she wasn't so surprised to hear from him after all. "It's funny you called about that. I've been thinking about that case. The victim's name was Jenny Green. . . ."

"Yeah. There was something about the way Annie described the murder scenes here that made me think of that one. Not that the women were killed the same way, but the way the scene was set so carefully . . . the way the killer covered the faces of his victims. . . ." His voice trailed off.

"That's exactly what I was thinking, too. That something felt the same."

"Yes."

"Do you know if Jenny Green's killer was ever found?"

"No."

"Me, either. Shortly after I'd finished interviewing several suspects, I was transferred to John's unit. I never did hear, one way or the other." She tapped her pencil on the side of a half-empty cardboard coffee cup. "But I know how to find out."

"You'll fill me in?"

"Give me your number." She wrote down both his cell and Mara's home number. "I'll let you know as soon as I hear something."

Her first call was to the Rockledge, Ohio, Police Department.

Then she dialed FBI headquarters.

Sitting back in the upholstered chair next to the window, she pulled open the drapes with one hand to see what the world looked like that morning while she waited for her call to be answered. She smiled when she heard the craggy voice of Eileen Gibson, the receptionist for the unit headed by John Mancini and the woman referred to as the Little General by Mancini's staff. Strictly behind her back of course, though the woman was well aware of the nickname.

"Hi, it's Cahill."

"Which one?" Eileen asked dryly.

"Sorry. I wasn't aware that my sister was checking in through this number these days. I thought she was still out of the country on assignment."

"May I assume, then, that this is your way of identifying yourself as Agent M. Cahill rather than Agent P.?"

"You may." Miranda paused, then dropped her voice and asked, "Portia hasn't called in through this line, has she?"

"Not that I'm aware."

"Okay. Just checking. You never know when . . . well, when she'll pop up." Miranda's twin sister, Portia, had joined the terrorist unit that had expanded after 9/11 and had gone abroad. Even Miranda wasn't sure where.

"Yes, ma'am." Miranda heard a rustling sound. Eileen was rummaging in her purse for something. "Now, what can I do for you this morning, Agent Cahill?"

"I'd like to speak with Mr. Mancini, if he's in."

"He won't be in until Tuesday of next week."

"I thought he was supposed to be back from his honeymoon this past Monday."

"He's in Michigan for something or other." Eileen's shorthand for *I know but I'm not telling you.* "But Agent Snow has been back to work for three or four days now. Not a very romantic way to end a honeymoon, if you ask me, with the groom going in one direction and the bride in another."

"I'm sure they're both used to it," Miranda noted. John Mancini's new bride, Genna Snow, was a longtime agent herself. Over the past two years, Miranda figured, the couple had spent almost as much time apart as together but had somehow managed to make that work for them.

"So," Eileen said somewhat firmly, the extent of her tolerance for chitchat having been exceeded, "who did you say you wanted to speak with?"

"I didn't. I was hoping to catch up with John." Miranda thought for a moment. "How about Catherine Clark? She in this morning?"

"No. If you're looking for someone from your unit, the only one in so far is Agent Fletcher."

"Will Fletcher?"

"He's the only Fletcher we have."

And the last person Miranda felt like dealing with just then.

Will Fletcher was a loose thread that Miranda just hadn't gotten around to tying off, and wasn't sure that she'd be ready to any time soon. For now, she felt it was best to leave it that way.

"Hurry up, Cahill, my tea's getting cold."

"Could you put me into his voice mail?"

"Sure thing."

"Thanks."

"The pleasure's all mine. Now, Agent Cahill, you be sure to have a nice day."

"You, too, Eileen."

Miranda drummed impatient fingers on the desk in her hotel room and waited for the recorded message to begin.

"Fletcher."

Damn. She'd specifically asked for his voice mail.

"This is Agent Fletcher. Who's on the line?"

"Cahill," she sighed, trying not to let her annoyance show.

"Miranda?"

"Yes."

"Well, well." She could visualize him as he leaned back in his well-worn chair and rocked it slightly from side to side. "To what do I owe the honor?"

"I need a file." Might as well cut to the chase.

"Which one?"

"One from about six years ago."

"Victim? Locale?"

"Jenny Green. Southern Ohio."

He paused. She could almost hear him thumbing through his mental files. "Middle-aged blonde. Attacked in her home. Strangled. Raped . . ." He retrieved the information easily.

It had been said within the Bureau that Will Fletcher was born with a computer chip in his head and therefore never forgot anything, including the most minute details of every crime scene he'd ever worked. Miranda knew him well enough to know that it was true. She also knew that, for Will, it hadn't always been a good thing to be able to pull up all of the details so readily.

"Yes. That's the one."

"What did you need?"

"I interviewed several suspects. I'd like a

copy of the interviews and my report."

"Sure. Where do you want them sent?"

"Can you email the files to me?"

"Soon as I can pull it out of the system. Assuming it's in the system."

"Thanks."

A long, vaguely uncomfortable silence followed.

"So, how are things in Pennsylvania?"

"How do you know everything?" She'd promised herself that she wouldn't let him get to her in any way, but he never failed to exasperate her. "You're just an agent, like the rest of us. How do you know where everyone is?"

He laughed good-naturedly. "Process of elimination. Mancini's in Michigan with Clark and Moss. I'm here with Martinez and Wheeler. Stark and Jeffers are back in North Carolina. I know a team went to PA. You, Jake, and Cosmo are the only ones left, but Cosmo's wife just had a baby. A case like this, they'd only send two of you anyway."

"You're so annoying, Fletcher."

He laughed again. "You're so easy to annoy, Cahill."

Before she could respond, he asked, "So what's it look like? Are there any leads?"

"No leads. The police are interviewing all of the remaining M. Douglases in the phone book to see if they can smoke out anything. Other than that, there's been nothing."

"Forensic reports in?"

"Not all of them. There's some trace — some carpet fibers that are so totally generic that it would take several lifetimes to track down everyone who has ever purchased it. Our guy wore gloves, there's no prints, so right now, there's nothing to compare. He left nothing of himself behind that we can see. Nothing, at least, that we can trace back to him."

"So what's the connection to Jenny Green?"

"I don't know that there is one. I just wanted to check into something, that's all."

"That case is still open, last I heard."

"I'm aware." She hadn't been but didn't want to admit that to him.

"I seem to recall that we interviewed about a dozen suspects in that case."

"Yes."

"Anyone stand out in your mind?"

"Maybe." She nodded. "Maybe . . ."

"His name?"

"I don't remember." She picked at a cuticle. She hated admitting this to him. *He* would remember, if he'd done the interview.

"Then I'll send all the statements that we have to you." She heard the clicking of his keyboard. He'd be pulling up the information as they spoke. "So what about this crime scene reminded you of that one? Jenny Green was strangled, and these new killings are stabbings, right?"

"Yes. But there's a similar note, a similar feel, even beyond the obvious, that the killers cov-

131

ered the victims' faces. There's a definite methodology to both crimes, a real deliberate feel to both. . . ."

"And what stands out in your mind about this one suspect?"

"I don't know. I just had an odd feeling about him. The entire time I was interviewing him, he gave me the impression that the whole thing amused him. I felt as if he was playing with me. As if he knew something that he knew I'd never find out." She sighed. "Then again, it was my first crime scene. Maybe I just imagined —"

"Nah, your instincts have always been right on track. Trust them."

It was the closest thing to a compliment that he'd given her in a long time.

"Thanks."

"Don't let it go to your head. You going to try to track him down?"

"May not be that easy. Back then, I had wanted to bring him in for a second interview, but he had already disappeared."

"Look, I'll try to locate your interview and send it to you. Then I'll run through the system and see if we get any hits on similar unsolved murders, and I'll get in touch with the police department that investigated —"

"The system has been searched for like crimes, and I already sent them a fax. Thanks anyway."

"Oh. Then why'd you call me?"

"Because I wanted a copy of my interview

with this particular suspect now, not when the Rockledge, Ohio, PD gets around to sending it, that's why."

"I'll take care of it right away, Agent Cahill."

"Thank you, Agent Fletcher."

"Don't mention it."

She cursed to herself as another one of those silences settled in between them.

"Cahill?" His voice softened.

"Yes?"

"Take it easy, hear? Be careful."

"Not to worry, Will. My name's not Mary Douglas."

"All the same, if this turns out to be the same man you interviewed six years ago, chances are he'll remember you." He wisely chose not to annoy her by enumerating everything that a man might find memorable about Agent Miranda Cahill. "Stay in the background at the press conferences and try to keep your face out of the newspapers."

"Too late. Anne Marie and I were both asked to attend the press conference day before yesterday."

"I heard she was putting together a profile. And something about her sister . . ."

"Annie wasted no time in making sure the Bureau put this one on the front burner. Her sister is named Mara. Her married name is Douglas." She sighed. "There isn't much that doesn't get into your pipeline, is there?"

"Annie called in, early in the week. She was

concerned that the locals couldn't keep a close enough eye on her sister. She mentioned that she was going to arrange for someone to stay with Mara, someone she could trust to watch out for her."

"She has. Aidan Shields."

"Yeah, I heard."

"Of course you did," she muttered under her breath.

"Last I knew, they were still trying to put his leg back together. And I thought he was still out on medical leave."

"He is. He's doing this strictly as a favor."

"Annie couldn't have come up with anyone better than Shields."

"I agree."

He blew out a long breath. "He was right up there with the best. He and his brothers, the three of them. Damned shame about Dylan. Damned shame."

"Think Aidan will ever come back, even if he can pass the physical?"

"It would be the Bureau's loss if he doesn't. Whether he passes the physical or not," he murmured thoughtfully. Then, all business again, "Anything else I can do you for today?"

"I think we've covered everything we need to," she said, knowing that was a lie, that they had covered everything except what most needed to be said.

"Keep in touch, then."

"Sure thing. Oh, and don't forget to call me

if you get a hit on the —" But he'd already disconnected.

She hung up slowly, feeling just a little
bruised, as she always did after she'd had a
brush with him, and feeling that the air still
hadn't been cleared. That maybe they'd never
get around to saying the things that needed to
be said. That maybe the loose thread that had
been hanging between them for the past seven
or eight months was still hanging there, waiting
to be pulled . . .

That maybe it didn't matter to anyone but
her.

She called room service and ordered breakfast, then turned back to her computer and
waited for the promised file to arrive.

Chapter Eight

Under her desk, Mara's left foot tapped impatiently as she listened to the judge's law clerk recite the latest rescheduling of that afternoon's custody hearing involving five children whose mother and father were both once again incarcerated for possession with intent to deliver a hefty stash of cocaine. The judge had already granted the postponement, meaning that the children would remain in foster care for yet another three weeks at best. Three weeks they could be spending with their maternal aunt, who lived out of state but who desperately wanted to bring the children to live with her.

"Don't growl at me, Ms. Douglas," the clerk snapped. "I'm just the messenger. Take it up with Judge Fisk if you have a problem with his decision."

Mara dropped the receiver quietly into its cradle. How fortunate for the parents that they'd drawn that particular judge, one who was notoriously lenient when it came to protecting the rights of the mother and father. Other judges were not always as accommodating.

Of course, she thought as she gazed out the window on a perfectly brilliant April morning, she'd heard the judge liked a good golf game, and this was, by all accounts, the first really good golf day in weeks.

Cynic, she scolded herself and returned that afternoon's scheduled file and its reports and interviews to the folder. She wouldn't be needing it for a while. She glanced at her agenda for the following week, debating which case could most benefit from the extra time she had on her hands.

Jenner v. *Jenner* was coming up on Friday, and there were still several interviews she wanted to look over one last time. She searched through the piles on her floor until she found the file, then hoisted it onto her desk. She tugged at the inner manila folder to dislodge it from the overstuffed master, then searched for the interviews she'd conducted when she'd first been assigned to the case and settled in to refresh her memory.

When she finally glanced up to check the time, she was surprised to find it well past noon. She stood and stretched, suddenly mindful of the low rumblings from her stomach. She poked her head from her office, hoping to find someone who might be interested in running out to pick up a sandwich, but it appeared that she was alone in her section of the hall. She hesitated for a moment, then grabbed her purse and set out for the stairwell.

Of course, it occurred to her to call Aidan to join her, but it seemed, well, silly for him to drive from her house merely to accompany her

137

to the hot dog stand out front. Besides, she was hardly alone in the courthouse, the front lawn of which was filled with employees and jurors and townspeople out to enjoy the sunshine. There was no reason for her not to join them.

Standing in line at Maury's, Mara waited for her turn to order. She paid for her hot dog and soda and strolled back toward the benches that lined the wall near the front of the building. An elderly woman rose from her seat, pushing the stroller that held a sleeping infant, and started off down the sidewalk just as Mara approached. Without a second thought, she took the seat almost as soon as it was vacated, then sought to balance the soda can on the bench while she attempted to pop open the lid.

"Need a hand?" A shadow fell across her.

Mara looked up to find Aidan looking down at her. He wore a pale yellow shirt and his hands were stuck in the pockets of his worn jeans. Dark glasses shielded his eyes.

"What are you doing here?"

"Checking up on you." He took the can from her hands and popped off the tab.

"Have you been doing this every day?"

"Nope." He passed the can back to her.

"Why today?"

"I called your cell and there was no answer. I figured you'd slipped out to grab a bite." Aidan sat down next to her and leaned against the back of the bench.

Mara unwrapped her hot dog. "I wasn't

going any farther than Maury's. I really didn't think I needed to check in with you to take a fifty-yard walk from the courthouse steps to the hot dog stand." She took a bite. "You really take this watchdog thing seriously, don't you?"

"Serious as life and death."

She glanced around, her eyes darting from the small groups that gathered on the lawn to the solitary figures scattered here and there.

"You think he's here? Someone out there?" She gestured in a sweeping motion with the hand that held the soda can. "Just waiting for me to come out?"

"I would be, if I were him." His eyes scanned the crowd. "I'd want to know your every move, where you go and at what time and with whom. Then I'd know when you'd be most vulnerable."

She took another bite and chewed slowly.

"That's what he's done in the past," Aidan continued. "Watched his victims, made himself familiar with their routines."

"And you think that's what he's doing now? Watching me?"

"He's watching his next victim, sure. Studying her movements, getting to know her. We're just assuming that the next victim is going to be you."

"What about all the other M. Douglases? Is someone watching them, too?"

"That's up to the locals, but frankly, none of them are my concern."

"And I suppose that if he's watching me and he sees you around all the time, he'll cross me off his list and just go on to M. N. or M. P. or whoever is the next M. Douglas in the phone book."

"I wouldn't expect him to cross you off his list. I would expect him to come up with something a little more creative."

"Doesn't that just make things increasingly difficult for you?" One last bite finished off the hot dog. "I mean, he gets more creative, don't you have to get more creative, too?"

"You're catching on."

"Then where does it end?"

"When he finally thinks he's smarter than me."

"What if he is?"

"Then we're both fucked."

"Funny." She balled up the paper from her hot dog and tossed it into the trash can that sat five feet away. "Very funny."

"I wasn't trying to be funny."

"I don't see anyone who looks the least bit suspicious."

"You know everyone out here?"

"Well, no. Not everyone . . ."

"You know the guy three benches away, the one in the blue jacket who's been reading the same page of the newspaper since I sat down?"

She glanced over slowly and pretended to be looking past the bench in question. "No. I hadn't noticed him."

"How 'bout the guy standing about twenty feet away from us to the left, who's been sipping that same container of coffee for the past twenty minutes? You think those little cups hold that much?"

"No. I don't know him, either." Her voice softened.

"That's my point. If he's watching you, chances are you'll never notice him." From behind his dark glasses, Aidan's eyes continued to scan the crowd. "This guy is clever. He hasn't been as successful as he has by being stupid."

"Then how do you expect to catch him?"

"Sooner or later, he'll mess up."

"What if it's later than sooner?"

"Then I guess I'll be sleeping in your guest room for longer than either of us planned."

"Swell," she mumbled.

"On the other hand, maybe he'll surprise me and do something really stupid really soon," he told her. "Then I'll be on my way and out of your hair."

"Then what will you do?"

"Go back to Rehoboth."

"And . . . ?"

"And what?"

"Just that. Go back to your apartment? No other plans?"

"No." The question irritated him. What difference did it make to her what he did when he left Lyndon, as long as the killer was behind bars and she was still alive and had her home to

141

herself again once he left?

The alarm on her watch went off. She glanced at the time before turning it off.

"I have a meeting at two. I need to go." She slid her purse strap over her shoulder and stood. "Well, then. Thanks for stopping by."

"All in a day's work." He remained seated. "See you at five."

"Right." She turned toward the building. "See you at five . . ."

And he'd been there, of course, waiting across the street from the exit of the parking garage. He'd taken care of dinner, and taken in her mail, and walked her dog, all without complaint, all without fanfare. That night, again, he'd set up his telescope on the back deck and given her a lesson in stargazing. She was surprised to find she was actually starting to like it.

Walking into the courthouse the following morning, she was pondering the possibility that maybe she'd gotten used to having Aidan's company — however reluctant — and that maybe it wasn't so bad having him for a house guest. He'd certainly provided a light moment earlier that morning.

Mara grinned as she got on the elevator, remembering the looks on the faces of her morning jogging partners, Allison and Cass, when they rang the doorbell a little before seven a.m.

"Morning, ladies," Aidan had greeted them.

"Ahhhh . . ." Cass had been rendered speechless.

"We . . . ahhhh . . . we . . . w-we . . ." Allison had stuttered.

"Were you looking for Mara?" he had asked, clearly amused for the first time since he'd arrived earlier in the week.

"Oh, God, I forgot to call you." Red-faced, Mara had appeared behind Aidan.

"I meant to . . . call, that is . . . but I, um, forgot, and then when I remembered, it was . . . ah . . . too late to call and cancel. Last night, I mean . . ."

Mara had stumbled over her words almost as badly as Allison and Cass had.

"We can wait for you, if you want to get changed." Cass stared openly at Mara's nightshirt.

"Oh." Mara's face burned. She'd heard the doorbell and tried to rush down the steps before Aidan. It had never occurred to her to grab her robe. "Well . . ."

"I don't think that's a good idea, Mara," Aidan said pointedly.

"Ah, right. Not a good idea." Mara had nodded. "Sorry. I'll have to pass this week. You guys go on without me."

"Are you sure? Your . . . friend . . . is welcome to join us." Allison smiled. Mara could tell that the effort to stifle the questions she wanted to ask was just killing her.

"No, I . . . I'll catch up with you later," Mara had told them, then closed the door. She stared up at Aidan. "Why did you answer the door?"

"Because the doorbell was ringing."

"I would have gotten it."

"I wasn't sure you were up."

"I'm always up at this hour."

"I wasn't aware of that."

"You've been here for almost a week. You know I get up early."

"If you'd told me you were expecting someone at this hour, I wouldn't have answered the door."

"I forgot what day of the week it was."

"That's really not my fault."

"You could at least have put a shirt on."

"Your friends didn't seem to mind." He crossed his arms over his bare chest.

"They think you are . . . That we are . . ." Mara gestured helplessly with her hands.

"Why didn't you tell them the truth? That we think you might be the target of a serial killer."

"God." She had shook her head and headed up the steps. "I don't know which is worse. . . ."

Of course, her office phone was ringing before she even got to her desk, as she'd known it would be.

"Who was the Greek god who answered your door this morning," Cass demanded without identifying herself, "and where can I get one just like him?"

"The FBI."

"Excuse me?"

"He's with the FBI." Mara explained the situation.

"Some girls have all the luck," Cass sighed.

"Cass, having a stranger — one who is moody and somewhat terse — move into my house for a week because a serial killer may be stalking me is not lucky."

"Well, I'm sure the week has had its moments."

"Oh, it's had its moments, all right," Mara conceded. "Most of them prickly."

"Well, don't expect any sympathy from me." Cass laughed. "There are very few things I wouldn't do to have someone like that parking his shoes by my front door."

"It's because of Annie. He's only here because of Annie."

"Well, I hope you're making the most of it. God knows I would."

"Some things come more easily to some of us than to others."

"Mara, how long has it been since you've even gone on a date?"

"You can probably figure that out." Mara glanced at the clock. She had fifteen minutes before she had to leave for court.

"Well, aren't you even a teeny bit interested in . . . what's his name?"

"Aidan Shields."

"Nice. Well, aren't you at least interested?"

"I don't know."

"How can you not know?" Cass's voice lowered, and Mara suspected that Cass's officemate had arrived.

"Like I said, he's only here as a favor to my sister. That's all. He has no interest in me, other than keeping me alive."

"That's a start."

Mara laughed. "Look, we'll have to continue this later. I have to get my notes together and get downstairs. I have a hearing this morning."

"Keep in touch," Cass told her before she hung up. "And if you need any pointers, you know who to call. . . ."

"I need more than a few pointers," Mara murmured to herself as she scanned the top of her desk in search of the folder in which she kept her notes. She found it under the phone, tucked it into her briefcase, and closed the lid with a soft snap, pushing all thoughts of Aidan aside.

Later, she told herself. *I'll think this whole thing through later. . . .*

But before she knew it, the day had flown past, it was after four, and she was debating which file to take home with her that night. The Fowler case had several interviews left to be conducted before next week's hearing. She lifted the heavy folder from the shelf behind her desk and slid it onto her lap just as the phone rang.

"Mara?" Annie sounded far away.

"Annie. Where are you?" She propped up the

146

file and leaned it against the side of the desk while she opened it.

"I'm in the middle of a field outside of Lincoln, Nebraska, waiting for my turn to look at a corpse they found about two hours ago. Second one in three days."

"You're fading out."

"Then I'll talk quickly. I just got a call from Miranda Cahill. Apparently they believe they have the Mary Douglas killer in custody."

"You're kidding. I haven't heard anything. . . ." Mara's fingers stopped their searching and rested on the top of the file. "Who?"

"This is the craziest thing. Remember when we were discussing the case, and we talked about the possibility that someone was killing women named Mary Douglas to cover up the killing of a specific Mary Douglas? A possibility I thought remote at the time."

"Yes."

"Well, it looks like that might have been it after all. The guy they arrested this morning is the son of the second victim."

"He confessed?"

"No, of course not. No one confesses anymore. But the police found a bloody shirt in a bag in his closet and —"

"Why were the police looking in his closet?"

"Well, you know they're talking to everyone who knew all three of these women. The police were especially interested in this guy, Teddy Douglas, because the next-door neighbor said she'd overheard him arguing with his mother several times during the week preceding the first murder." Annie's voice faded briefly, then resumed. "They got a warrant to search the premises, found the bloody shirt. The blood type matches Mary number one. DNA results aren't back yet, but things don't look good for Teddy."

"So that's it?" Mara sat back in her chair. "It's over?"

"The police think he's the man. Seems . . . oh, I don't know, maybe a bit pat to me, but then again, I'm not privy to all the evidence that the locals have gathered. And who knows, maybe the simplest explanation is the right one." Annie paused for a moment, then said, "Anyway, I thought I'd call you before I called Aidan and let him know he is off the hook. How'd that work out this week, by the way?"

"Aidan? Oh, fine. He's been fine."

"Just fine?"

"Really. He's been . . . fine."

"Well, I'm sure you'll both be happy to have your lives back."

"You've faded again. . . . Anne Marie? Annie?"

The line dead, Mara hung up.

She knew she should be thrilled, not only that the killer had been found and arrested, but that she'd soon have her house to herself again. She could return to her own routine. Eat when she wanted, fall asleep on the sofa reading a book if she wanted . . .

So why, she asked herself, did she feel just a little let down?

Aidan was waiting for Mara outside the garage at five, just as he had been all week, and followed her home, just as he had every day since he'd arrived. She knew that when she arrived home, she'd find that her mail had been taken in, the dog had been walked, and on a pad next to the phone, in Aidan's small but neat print, her phone messages would be efficiently recorded.

"You heard the news?" he said as he got out of the Corvette in her driveway.

"Yes. It's terrific, isn't it?" She slammed the driver's side door of the Jetta and locked it with the remote. "So it looks like you're a free man. Your indenture is over."

Aidan smiled. *Rehoboth Beach, here I come.*

"I know you have better things to do with your time," she said, to make it easier for him. "You've been a good sport to stay here with a stranger and just hang out with the dog all day."

"I like your dog." Aidan followed her up the walk. "And all things considered, I guess it could have been worse."

"That's easy to say now, when you're leaving." She turned before putting the key in the front door lock. "But you're right. It hasn't been so bad. Not as bad as I thought it would be."

"Please." He held up one hand. "All these compliments are going to go right to my head."

Mara laughed, and it occurred to him that she hadn't laughed very much that week. Nor had he. They'd been pretty much all business.

A pity, it seemed now, in retrospect.

She opened the door and found his bag sitting in the middle of the living room floor, waiting to be tossed into the trunk of the Corvette. Spike danced around joyfully from Aidan to Mara.

"Oh. I see you're ready to leave."

"I figured you'd want your house to yourself again."

"Hey, at least I got a little lesson on stargazing."

"No extra charge for the instruction." He smiled.

He just doesn't do that often enough, she caught herself thinking. *He has a great smile. It goes all the way to his eyes, when he lets it.*

"Listen, if you want to stay and have dinner, I can —" She gestured in the direction of the kitchen.

"Whip up a little takeout?" Another smile.

Two smiles in less than a minute. *He must be really happy to be leaving.*

"There are several more numbers on that take-out list, you know."

"Another time, maybe." He bent over and picked up Spike. The dog's tongue aimed for Aidan's chin and struck its target. "Spike, hey, you keep guarding that front door, you hear? You never know who's going to be on the other side. The mailman, a meter reader, Mrs. West from next door . . ."

"You met Mrs. West?"

"We bonded over a couple of flats of impatiens that she brought back from the nursery this morning. She left yours on the back steps. I was thinking about helping her plant them, just for something to do, but then Annie called."

"Didn't Mrs. West wonder who you are?"

"I told her I was an old friend of Annie's in town for a few days and that you kindly offered me lodging before Annie got called away." He put Spike on the floor, then kicked his voice up an octave or two to mimic Mara's neighbor. "That Annie is always on the run. And if there's a more unseemly job for such a lovely young woman, well, I just can't imagine one."

"Not bad. Another few days and you'd have it nailed."

"I've been working on it all afternoon." He stood with his hands in his pockets.

"Aidan, I don't know how to thank you. I know that coming here, staying . . . well, I know you didn't want to be here."

"I promised Annie. I couldn't turn her down."

"I don't know too many people who can."

He lifted his bag as a means of averting his eyes. "You know, the last word that my brother

151

spoke before he died was her name. I'll always be there for her." He hesitated. Mara'd been a good sport all week, in spite of the strain.

"I appreciate your being here for me this week."

He acknowledged this with a nod, then started toward the door. He stopped suddenly and turned around, and without thinking about what he was doing, leaned over and kissed her low on her cheek, close to the corner of her mouth. "Come see me in Rehoboth sometime. Bring Spike. He'd like the beach. You have my number."

"I just might do that." She wondered if she ever would.

She walked with him to the car, Spike racing ahead, then stood back while he dropped his bag into the trunk.

"Thanks again for keeping the demons at bay."

"My specialty." He unlocked the car and slid behind the wheel.

"Spike, come here. . . ." Mara picked up the dog, then stepped back onto the grass. She smiled and waved as he backed the Vette out of the driveway, waved again when he beeped the horn as he pulled away. She stood until the car disappeared around the first corner.

She cradled the little dog in her arms and walked slowly back into the house, where the silence seemed almost overwhelming. Funny, she hadn't noticed it last week or the week before.

Or the month before, or the year before . . .

She poked through the mail and considered returning a phone call before deciding she didn't really feel like talking to anyone right then. She poured a glass of iced tea and took it and Spike out onto the deck.

She looked over the flat of red and white flowers that he'd left near the bottom step and wondered if he'd really been thinking about planting them. He hadn't struck her as the gardening type.

She sat in the same chair she'd sat in the night before. She put her feet up on the deck railing and watched Spike pounce upon a stick that was twice as long as he was.

She sipped her iced tea and, for the first time in years, felt something akin to loneliness — something apart from what she felt when she missed Julianne — settle in around her. She figured it would pass soon enough. After all, Aidan had been there for less than a week.

With the fingers of her right hand, she touched the place on her cheek where he'd kissed her. A kiss, no doubt, to celebrate his liberation.

She leaned back and looked upward, waiting for the first star to appear, and tried to recall its name.

Vince Giordano had been surprised when the guard appeared at his cell door and announced that he had visitors.

"My lawyer's not due till next week," he'd said.

"It's not your lawyer," the guard told him as he cuffed the prisoner's hands behind his back.

"Who then?"

"Don'cha wanna be surprised?" The guard grinned, showing severely crooked teeth.

"Oh, sure. I love surprises." Giordano shrugged and followed the guard through the maze of hallways.

They stopped in front of one of the visitors' rooms, and it occurred to Giordano before the door even opened that something must be up, since it wasn't visiting hours. He shuffled into the room to find two county detectives seated at the beat-up plastic table, waiting for him.

"Hello, Vincent." Evan Crosby rested his elbows on the table.

"Detective Crosby. Always a pleasure." Giordano smiled and took a seat opposite the officers. "Detective Sullivan. Good to see you again, as well."

"We're both delighted to see you, too." Evan Crosby nodded, his mouth a grim line that barely mimicked a smile.

"To what do I owe the visit, gentlemen?"

"We just thought we'd stop by and offer our condolences."

"Condolences?" Giordano raised one eyebrow. "Someone die?"

"Your mother-in-law. Former mother-in-law, I should say," Joe Sullivan told him.

"No shit. What happened? Heart attack?" Giordano looked surprised and almost concerned. Almost. "I always told her those cigarettes were no good for her."

"It wasn't cigarettes that got her, Vincent." Crosby leaned forward and dropped his voice. "She was shot through the head two nights ago."

"No shit," he said again, this time genuinely shocked. "You sure it was *Flora* Esposito?"

Detective Sullivan nodded.

"Mother of the deceased Diane Esposito Giordano. Grandmother of the late Matthew and Vincent Giordano the third." Crosby couldn't help but get a lick in. He'd been on the team that had investigated the killings of Giordano's wife and two little boys. His disgust was obvious.

"So Flora got whacked, eh? For real?" Giordano shook his head. "Who'd want to kill that miserable old bitch?"

"We thought maybe you'd have some thoughts on that."

"Nah. I can't think of anyone. . . ." He looked up at the two detectives, his eyes darting from one to the other, realizing the scrutiny he was under. "Oh, give me a fucking break, will you? You can't be serious. Yeah, right, I slipped out of here, whacked Flora, and sneaked back in."

"You could have arranged for someone to do it. It was very obvious at your trial that there was no love lost between you and the mother of

155

your murdered wife." Another dig from Crosby.

"Arranged how, through a psychic?"

"You could have contacted someone. . . ."

"I haven't had contact with anyone except for my lawyer since I got here. Early on, I had a couple of requests for interviews, but I wasn't interested. I never contacted no one about them. No one calls, no one writes, no one comes to see me. You can check with the warden. I get no mail, I send no mail. I ain't had any visitors and I ain't used the phone in months."

"Not even family members?"

"Especially not family members." He snorted. "I'm one of them . . . what do you call 'em . . . persons not grata'd."

"I can see you studied Latin," Crosby noted dryly.

"Ah, that's right. You're the funny one." Giordano's eyes went back and forth between the two men who sat across from him. "Is there anything else, now that you've delivered the sad news?"

"You don't seem as broken up as I thought you might."

"Kiss my ass, Crosby." Giordano turned toward the door and called for the guard, then stood as the door opened.

"If I find out that you had anything at all to do with the murder —"

"Good luck, Detective. I mean that. I hope you find the killer and prosecute him to the fullest extent of the law. Isn't that what the D.A. said he was gonna do to me?" He was openly sneering. "And you know where that got you, don't you? I'll be out of here before another coupla weeks have passed. Thanks to your good buddy Officer Caruso. And I do thank him. Every day. You let him know that, hear? Let him know that Vince Giordano owes him big-time for planting that evidence and then having the stones to brag about it. Tell him I remember him in my prayers every night . . . and that I'll be seeing him real soon. . . ."

Giordano was laughing as he was led away, but he still could hear the curses of the two detectives as the door closed behind him.

He walked back to the cell in silence, standing calmly while the guard removed the cuffs, let him into his cell, and locked the door behind him. Giordano sat on the edge of his mattress and covered his face with his hands and laughed until he cried.

This latest news confirmed something he had begun to suspect when he'd heard about the first Mary Douglas killing.

He did it. The crazy bastard really did it. . . .

At first, he'd thought it was some crazy coincidence. But from subsequent news reports, it began to dawn on Giordano that maybe Channing had gone through with it. That maybe he'd gotten the wrong Mary Douglas the first two times, but hey, he'd have had no way of knowing how many women there were

157

in Lyndon with the same name. What were the chances of that? It was okay. Giordano could probably have been a little more specific.

Channning, wherever you are, my man, I owe you big-time. . . .

Of course, there'd been that news report earlier that day identifying the Douglas slayer as the son of one of the victims, but Giordano seriously doubted that could be true. After hearing about Flora's untimely demise — he loved that expression, as if dying was ever timely — there was no doubt whatsoever in his mind who was behind it all.

And even better, it was obvious that the police had not made the connection between the Mary Douglas slayings and the murder of his former mother-in-law.

Channing, you slick bastard, you're a real one-man crime wave.

He wondered then if Channing remembered the name of the judge.

He fervently hoped that he did.

That bitch deserved whatever it was that Channing would do to her. Damn, but he'd give anything to be there, to watch her get what was coming to her. After all, everything was her fault. Diane and the boys would still be alive if it hadn't been for her. Who did she think she was, that bitch judge, telling him that he couldn't see his boys no more? That he couldn't so much as set foot on the property that he'd worked his ass off to buy?

Who did she think she was talking to? She was gonna tell him what he could and could not do with his own family?

He shook his head. No one told Vince Giordano what to do. No one.

As far as he was concerned, she had been the one to push Vince past his limits, forcing him to do what he'd done. Diane's blood, the blood of his children . . . it was all on her hands.

Restless anger grew within him. He got off his cot and looked up at the barred window, wondering where Her Honor was at that very moment, and if she had any idea of how little time she had left. Hours? Days? A week?

It put a smile on his face, just thinking about it.

Chapter Nine

It was cooler by the ocean than it had been in Lyndon, and Aidan dug out an old blue sweatshirt to layer over the thermal shirt he'd planned to wear during his walk. If he'd been running, the thermal would have been too much. But it had been a year since he'd run, and he doubted he'd be doing it again anytime soon, if ever. But he could walk. Over the past week, he'd walked more than he had in months. He grudgingly admitted he'd almost enjoyed it.

He'd have enjoyed the walk along the water more if he'd had that little dog with him, though. He'd forgotten how much he liked dogs. Maybe he'd pay a visit to the local SPCA and get a dog of his own. Still, that was a commitment he wasn't sure he was ready to make. He wasn't sure he was ready to be steady company for anyone, man or beast.

And then, of course, there was Mara.

When he'd promised Annie he'd keep an eye on her sister, he'd had little memory of Mara but he'd somehow expected her to look like Annie, blond and blue-eyed, soft, round, feminine to the core. He hadn't been prepared for Mara, petite and dark, with wide green eyes, her face beautiful despite its leanness. She'd been a surprise to him in every way, but he'd found that he liked her, in spite of himself. Mara was a real no-nonsense kind of woman, like her sister, and he'd appreciated that. He gave her credit for trying to make the best of the situation, for being hospitable when he knew she'd been uncomfortable with him living under her roof. Of course, he'd been uncomfortable, too. She'd just dealt with it better than he had.

In his defense, he reminded himself, it had been a long time since he'd spent any time with any woman who wasn't a nurse or a therapist, and even that contact had been months past. One might excuse him for being less than charming.

Aidan's thoughts drifted to Mara's ex-husband. The bastard. What kind of man would steal a child from her mother?

Aidan walked along the waterline, his feet sinking into the cool sand as the tide began to come in. He couldn't imagine how that must feel, to know your child was out there, somewhere, but not know where.

Hell, he thought, *after seven years, Mara doesn't even know what her daughter looks like.*

Aidan wished he could do something to help, something that would take that haunted look from those green eyes. . . .

The old Aidan Shields could have helped, he knew. He'd have moved heaven and earth to help Mara locate her daughter. After all, there had been very little that the old Aidan

Shields could not do.

He slowed his pace and fought against a wave of self-pity. Being at Mara's, with other things to occupy his mind, had taken his focus off himself and his own problems for the first time in months. As a consequence, he hadn't spent quite so much time dwelling on what he'd lost. Now that he was back home, he was going to have to try to get his life back on track. He'd never forget what had happened in the alley that night, would never stop grieving for Dylan, but over the past week, he'd come to under- stand that maybe the time had come for him to stop grieving for himself.

He would call the therapist when he got back to the apartment, he'd go every time he was supposed to, he'd do his exercises at home. He'd lose those extra pounds and he'd gain back what strength he could. He'd been a ninety-pound weakling for long enough.

Okay, make that a two-hundred-and-thirty- pound weakling, but it was all the same, wasn't it? Weak was, well, *weak,* inexcusable. And over the past five or six days, he'd realized just how tired he was of being weak.

He'd seen pity in Mara's eyes when he couldn't keep up on their walks, and he'd hated it. It had angered and embarrassed him and had kept him in a foul mood when he was around her. He hadn't wanted it to be that way, but there it was. He couldn't help but wonder if, every time she looked at him, Mara was wondering just what kind of a bodyguard this wreck of a former FBI agent could possibly be.

He hadn't wanted her to look at him that way. He'd wanted . . . hell, he didn't know what he'd wanted. As close as he came to understanding that all week was when he was leaving, and he'd kissed her. As close to her mouth as he could get without, well, kissing her on the mouth, though he'd been sorely tempted to do just that. What if she'd pushed him away? Rejection wasn't something he'd wanted to deal with right now. He had enough trouble accepting himself.

So he'd gone for the buddy kiss, the kiss on the cheek. At least she hadn't seemed offended. That was something.

He walked until his hip threatened to give out on him, then he thought about sitting for a while on the sand, but figured since he'd have difficulty getting up again, he'd just as well stand. He tried to balance his weight on both legs, tucked his hands into his pockets, and watched an osprey dive headfirst into the ocean, wings folded to its sides, only to emerge seconds later with a good-size fish in its beak. The bird flapped off toward its nest with purpose. Aidan watched it until it was no more than a dot in the sky.

Spring brought the migrating birds through the Delmarva coast, and this morning he'd seen from the deck off his apartment a flock of shorebirds. He knew that in another month or

163

so, the shoreline all along the bay would be dense with birds stopping to refuel on their way from South America to the Arctic. He'd heard about the staggering number of birds that would pass through the area, but in all the years he'd lived there, he'd never been around to witness the phenomenon himself. *Maybe this year,* he thought idly. God knows he had nothing else planned for the next few months.

His cell phone began to ring just as he was about to leave the beach.

"How's it going?" Miranda Cahill asked cheerfully.

"It's going," he responded. "What's up?"

"Remember we talked about the Jenny Green killing? I said I'd follow up?"

"You find anything?"

"Well, I'd asked to have some reports sent to me, and I just finished reviewing them. The case is still open, by the way, and the suspect I'd interviewed who'd given me the weird vibes was a guy by the name of Curt Gibbons."

"Anything on him in the computer?"

"No, nothing. I put his name through every data bank I could find, but there were no hits. I tried tracking him through the social security number he gave us — nothing. The address he gave us? He's long gone. The only thing I could find was a mention that he'd made of the school he'd graduated from. Lake Grove High in Lake Grove, Ohio. But there's no current record of him anywhere. Strange, huh?"

"Well, you know, people disappear for different reasons." He thought of Mara's husband. "I think we both know that a person who doesn't want to be found can devise any number of ways to cover his tracks."

"Most people don't just evaporate unless they are running from something, though." Miranda paused, then added, "Makes you wonder what this guy left behind, doesn't it?"

"Maybe he's dead."

"Maybe. Maybe I read way too much into him. Maybe he's off the radar because he's living a clean and quiet life someplace with a wife and a houseful of kids."

"Stranger things have happened."

"I guess. Well, I just wanted to pass that along to you. I wanted you to know that I did follow up," she told him. "Just in case you were wondering."

"I appreciate that. Thanks, Miranda."

"That's another call coming in. Gotta run. . . . Sorry I couldn't come up with something better on this guy." And she was gone.

Aidan slid his phone back into his pocket and continued to stare out at the ocean, his curiosity piqued.

He remembered Miranda talking about this suspect at the time she'd interviewed him. Curt Gibbons clearly had gotten under her skin. Funny that now he seemed to have vanished into thin air.

Aidan wandered back to his apartment,

thinking about all the ways in which a person could disappear if he wanted to badly enough, and all the reasons one might want to do so. Most of them weren't good.

He grabbed a cold bottle of beer from the refrigerator and went out onto his deck. From there he could see the ocean and the boats — fishing boats most likely, at this time of the year — and he tried to divert his attention to something other than Curt Gibbons. Finally, accepting that he wasn't going to stop thinking about it until he did something about it, he went back into the apartment and dialed information.

"Operator, I'd like the number for the Lake Grove Police Department in Lake Grove, Ohio." Aidan paced from the kitchen to the deck then back again. When the operator returned with the number, he wrote it on the back of an envelope.

"Yes, thank you," he said. "Go ahead and connect me."

The phone was answered on the second ring. "Lake Grove PD."

"Good morning. This is Special Agent Aidan Shields." Well, he was, technically, still a special agent.

"FBI?"

"Yes, sir." Always be polite with the locals, Mancini told them. You never know who is on the other end of that phone. "Is your chief available? I'd like to speak with him."

"No, I'm sorry, he's out today. But Lieutenant Forbes is here. Would you like to speak with him?"

"Yes. Thank you."

It was several long minutes until the lieutenant picked up.

"Forbes. What can I help you with?"

"Yes, Lieutenant. Shields here, FBI. We're following up on some leads on a case, and we're trying to locate an individual who once lived in Lake Grove. Guy named Curt Gibbons. Graduate of the local high school."

"Name doesn't ring a bell. How old is this Gibbons?"

"I'm not sure. Mid-thirties, maybe."

"It would help, you know, to have a little information. . . ."

"I know. I'm sorry. I just thought maybe you'd have known him."

"Me? No, I'm not from around here. I'm still getting to know the people who live here now."

"Well, maybe you can look through your records and see if the name pops up."

"Sure. I can do that."

"Let me give you a number so that you can call me back." Aidan recited the number of his mobile phone.

"We'll run it through and give you a call back as soon as we have something."

"Thanks, Lieutenant. We appreciate your help." Aidan disconnected, wondering if Lieutenant Forbes had tossed the phone message

167

into the chief's "While you were out" bin or into the trash can.

Twenty minutes later, he knew.

"Aidan Shields?" a familiar voice asked.

"Yes."

"Hold for John Mancini."

Well, at least he knew that Forbes had taken his call seriously.

"Shields," his boss greeted him pleasantly. "How are you feeling?"

"Better, thanks. How was the honeymoon?"

"Over way too soon," he replied. "Say, I just got back to the office and heard you're back on the job. I hadn't recalled that you'd reactivated."

"Ah, well . . ."

"I just got a call from the Lake Grove, Ohio, Police Department, wanting to confirm that Special Agent Aidan Shields was in fact one of the good guys. Of course, I thought I'd give you a call myself, one, to welcome you back, and two, to find out what we had going in Lake Grove, Ohio, since I don't seem to recall a case in that vicinity."

So typical of Mancini to take this approach. Throw it out there and make you explain yourself. Aidan had been here before. Everyone on Mancini's team had been there before.

Aidan explained the conversation with Miranda Cahill and his own personal curiosity about the whereabouts of Curt Gibbons.

"You think Gibbons has something to do

with the case that Cahill's on?"

"I don't really know, but Cahill and I got to talking about how that crime scene six years ago reminded us both a little of the case she's working. She mentioned this one suspect who had set off a little alarm somewhere, and when she went to follow up — just to see what he's up to today — she found that he's nowhere to be found. It just made me a little curious, that's all."

"So you called the local PD and identified yourself as an FBI agent to satisfy your curiosity?"

"Yes."

"You know it's a federal crime to pass yourself off as an FBI agent."

"Right." Aidan drained the bottle and stepped out onto the deck. Fog was closing in off the ocean. He watched it while he waited to see just where Mancini was going with this conversation.

"So as I see it, what we have here is an opportunity to let you make an honest man of yourself. Or we can send you to the federal penitentiary of your choice," Mancini offered in his typical dry manner. "Go ahead, Shields. You make the call."

"I don't know, John."

"What don't you know?"

"I won't pass the physical."

"You mean today?"

"I mean ever."

"Hmm. . . . Are you certain about that?"

"Maximum medical improvement will not be sufficient to pass the physical."

"Well, then, I guess it's jail time for you, mister."

Aidan waited, knowing that John Mancini would never deliver a real threat in so light a manner.

"Unless, of course . . ." Mancini continued.

"Unless?"

"Unless I could persuade you to do a little background work for us on this. Nothing that would put you in the line of fire while you're still medically unable to perform full duties, but there are ways in which you could serve the Bureau." Mancini paused. "You interested?"

"Keep talking."

"I'm intrigued that both you and Agent Cahill were reminded of the same crime scene. I'd like to have that followed up, but as you know, since 9/11, we've lost so many of our people to the antiterrorist unit that I just don't have the manpower to track down every one of those little things that nag at the back of your mind. But, as you also know, I greatly believe in the importance of those nagging little jolts to the memory. Intuition. Or whatever you want to call it. Many a case has been solved because an agent has followed up on his or her instincts, even when, on the surface, the connection appeared very tenuous. I've always felt that both you and Agent Cahill have very strong instincts."

"So what are you saying?"

"That I'd like you to continue along in this vein. See what you can find on this" — Mancini shuffled some papers — "Curt Gibbons. And anything else you can dig up that could relate to this case."

"Okay."

"Glad to have you back. In any capacity. We've missed you." Mancini paused. "You're a hard man to replace."

"Thanks. Oh. And about the Lake Grove PD —"

"Yes?"

"What exactly did you tell them?"

"I told them you were our guy and the Bureau would appreciate their full cooperation," Mancini said, then, before he hung up, added, "Keep in touch, Shields."

"Sure thing," Aidan said with a nod, even though he knew that the line had gone dead. "Sure thing . . ."

Sandra Styler unsnapped her black robe and hung it on a hook on the back of the door leading from her office into Courtroom B1 on the second floor of the Avon County Courthouse. She'd had a full schedule and wanted nothing more than to kick off her shoes, let down her hair, and have a drink. Or two.

It had been a really long day, and not a particularly pleasant one.

Judge Styler did not understand adults who

did things that hurt children and thus had neither patience nor sympathy nor the inclination to listen to excuses. There simply was no excuse for abusing a child. Having been a victim of abuse herself — though she'd kept this fact to herself — she was particularly single-minded when cases involving child abuse came before her. She'd had two such cases that day and as a result was leaving for home with an unrelenting headache and a bad attitude.

She took the long way home, around the lake, where she pulled over for a moment to watch a heron wading in the shallows. The large bird appeared to move in slow motion as it strode purposefully, its long neck stretched out as it searched the waters for dinner. The bird was beautiful, graceful, elegant — just observing it calmed her. There had been no beauty, grace, or elegance in her day.

Driving on past the lake, she swerved to avoid hitting a biker who had seemed to have come out of the blue. She cursed softly, her momentary calm shattered, and she stepped on the gas, anxious now to get home. Home, it appeared, was the only place she'd find any real peace that day.

The Mercedes convertible — her gift to herself on her fiftieth birthday a few years back — wound its way through the quiet neighborhood of executive-style homes. The judge's house was at the far end of the development, on the largest lot that had been available when she'd had the house built. The house was the first she'd purchased on her own, and she'd put into it everything she'd ever wanted in a home. She figured she deserved it, after her divorce from that miserable weasel she'd married less than ten years ago. The marriage hadn't lasted long, and she'd been more than happy to wash her hands of the whole thing after she'd seen her husband, Peter, seated in a cozy little booth in a nearby restaurant with one of their neighbors from the town house complex where they lived.

Within months, she was on her own and in the market for a new place to live. This time, she decided, she would please no one except herself. And the lovely red-brick house on almost an acre of rolling countryside pleased her very much.

She drove the car all the way to the end of the driveway, as was her custom, though she did not continue into the garage, and got out. She had theater tickets for that night and still hadn't decided whether or not she wanted to go.

Reaching her hand over the top of the gate, she slipped the lock and stepped into the sanctuary of her backyard. From the pool, with its spa and waterfall, to the dwarf fruit trees that grew neatly along the back fence, to the patio with its perfect furniture, all was lovely, serene, tasteful in this little world she'd created for herself. She paused for several moments, just taking it in. The view never failed to cheer her.

Sighing happily, she crossed the flagstone patio, unlocked the back door, and deactivated the alarm. The interior of the house was cool but welcoming. Her footsteps echoed softly on the Mexican tile floor of the kitchen, then faded as she passed into the dining room where her heels sunk into the plush Oriental rug. She unlocked the front door and stepped out for the mail, which she removed from the hand-painted mailbox near the front steps. Sorting through it, she separated bills from junk. She dropped all but the junk mail onto a Chippendale table in the front hall, then took the discards back into the kitchen, where she tossed them into the trash. She listened to the messages on her answering machine while she poured herself a glass of merlot and then walked back outside, debating whether she felt up to a quick swim before dinner. *Oh, what the hell*, she thought. *The pool is heated. Why not?*

She changed in the small pool house that had been built onto the side of the garage. Stepping back out into the cool of the late spring evening, she started toward the water's edge when something caught her eye. Walking to the far end of the yard, she leaned over to inspect the ground where something had dug under the back fence. That damned German shepherd of the Ryans. She gritted her teeth. Last summer it had been the landscaping in the front yard that was targeted by her across-the-street neighbor's dog. *Looks like it's time for another little chat with Paul and Celia,* she thought, and shook her head. Damned dog. She'd call them as soon as she went back inside.

The dog — and the broad hole it had dug — dismissed, she headed for the pool. The sun was beginning to set, and even though the water would be warm, in another twenty minutes or so it would begin to get dark, and the temperature of the air would start to drop faster. She shed her towel and dove into the deepest water, surfacing near the shallow end, then turned onto her back and floated, her eyes closed, listening to the gentle sound of the waterfall and thinking about how perfect her life was at that very moment.

Fifteen minutes later, she would step out of the pool and straight into the arms of a nightmare worse than anything she could ever have imagined.

Chapter Ten

". . . and we understand that the district attorney will be holding a press conference in conjunction with the police, and that is scheduled to start at any moment." The lithe blond reporter gazed directly into the camera, refraining from a smile that might make her appear shallow in the face of the day's events.

After all, it wasn't every day that a county judge — a popular, highly respected county judge — was found murdered.

So far, there'd been no details released by either the D.A.'s office or the police department, not particularly unusual under the circumstances, when one considered the status of the victim. But Candace McElroy planned to be in the front row when the conference began. With this in mind, the reporter motioned to her cameraman to follow her into the courthouse. When her cell phone began to ring, she checked the number. Jason Kerr, the rookie cop who followed her around like a puppy, had already called her twice in the past two days, both times just to talk. Candace hesitated, wondering if this was another social call or a heads-up on the judge's murder. Taking her chances that this time he was calling with a legitimate tip, she answered the phone.

She was very, very glad she had.

The press conference began ten minutes later, but by then Candace already knew everything she needed to knock every other reporter in the room off their seats. When the chief of police finished his official announcement of Judge Sandra J. Styler's death yet declined to specify the cause, Candace was the first to raise her hand with a question.

She stood, and asked in a clear voice, so that all could hear, "Is it true that Judge Styler was killed in the same manner in which the Mary Douglas victims were killed? And if so, does this mean there's a copycat killer, or does it mean that the police have arrested the wrong man?"

Standing at the side of the courthouse steps where the press and the curious had gathered, Mara leaned forward, not quite believing her ears.

"What did she say, the reporter up front?" She tapped the arm of the man slightly in front of her.

"She asked if it was true that the judge was killed the same way those Mary Douglas ladies were killed," he replied without turning around. "And if that meant the wrong guy had been arrested."

Still not certain that she'd heard correctly, Mara moved forward through the crowd, which had begun to buzz, awaiting the response of the D.A., who was in an off-the-mike powwow with the chief of police.

Judge Styler killed in the same manner as the Marys? How could that be?

It had been enough of a shock when, just as she was about to leave her office for lunch, Gil Lindquist, whose office was across the hall from hers, leaned through her doorway and asked, "Did you hear about Judge Styler?"

"No, what?" Mara had said absently.

He lowered his voice. "She was murdered."

"What?" Mara's jaw had literally dropped.

"She was murdered. They found her body in her house."

"How? What happened?" Mara couldn't believe it. She'd had a case before Judge Styler at the end of last week.

"They're being real closemouthed about that. At least, they have been so far. But I just heard on the radio that there's going to be a press conference." Gil glanced at his watch. "Just about now, actually. I was thinking about going outside to see what they had to say."

"The conference is outside?"

"On the courthouse steps. Want me to wait for you?"

"You go ahead. I'll be down in just a minute."

Mara had squeezed her eyes tightly closed as the sorrow began to build. She'd liked Sandra Styler a lot, respected her greatly for never being afraid to take a stand, for always sticking to her principles. Mara prayed that whatever had happened, however Judge Styler had lost her life, it had been a quick and painless death.

It appeared now that that may have been too much to ask.

The D.A. and Chief Donner both declined to respond to the reporter's question, citing the pending investigation, but it was obvious from their expressions that this was the last thing they'd expected when they opened for questions. When a second reporter followed up, the press conference was brought to an abrupt close.

The buzz in the crowd lasted long after the courthouse steps were cleared. Mara bought a can of soda from Maury, then sat on a bench as if in a fog, trying to put it all together. From what she had heard in the courthouse over the past few days, Teddy Douglas had freely admitted that he'd wanted to kill his mother, but he adamantly denied having killed her or the other two women. He never wavered from his insistence that he'd found the bloody shirt — the one soaked with the blood of the first Mary — in the park on the evening after she'd been killed.

Almost afraid to fully consider the consequences if Teddy was telling the truth, Mara took her cell phone from her purse and speed-dialed Annie's number. "Annie. It's me, Mara."

"Oh, I recognized the voice." Annie seemed amused that her sister had thought to identify herself. "What's up?"

Mara quickly filled her in on the news.

"Well, then, we need to know if this is an unfounded rumor or not. Because if it's true, then we run the risk of the Mary Douglas killer still being out there."

"You know I'm not one to jump to conclusions about these things, but what if . . ." Mara paused, afraid to put into words the thought that had begun to nag at her.

"What if what?"

"What if . . . oh, damn, it's sounding paranoid even to me now." She walked to the end of the sidewalk, away from the crowd.

"What does?"

"Well, when I heard about Judge Styler, the first thing I thought of was, well, we've had so many cases together, what if someone whose case we'd handled — maybe someone whose rights had been terminated, or someone whose kids had been placed in foster care . . ." She swallowed hard, then whispered, "What if that person . . . if he . . ."

"What if the killer has been after you from the beginning? What if you're the M. Douglas he's been looking for all along, because of a recommendation you may have made to the court? To Judge Styler. Is that what you're thinking?"

"Is that totally crazy? That maybe the killer was after me because of something that happened on one of my cases, and that maybe he just made a mistake about my name? Am I

180

starting to get paranoid?"

"No. And no, it doesn't sound crazy. We both know that you must have pissed off a lot of people over the past several years. I think we need to take a closer look at the cases you had in common with Judge Styler. Let me make a call or two, then I'll get back to you. Go back to your office and stay there until you hear from me."

Mara rose on legs that shook just slightly. She didn't want to make any assumptions, didn't want to be melodramatic about this, but it was unsettling that Judge Styler would be murdered so soon after the Mary Douglas murders. And if it was the same MO as the other three women, stranger still. . . .

Mara's cell phone began to ring just as she returned to her office.

Annie bypassed a greeting. "I think we need to go to plan B."

"What?"

"Well, let's start with this kid they locked up. According to Miranda Cahill, he's said all along that he'd found that shirt in the park, and it's beginning to look like he could be telling the truth. Now, he has confessed that he's been wanting to kill his mother for several years. By the way, do you know why?"

"No, I hadn't heard the motive."

"Teddy Douglas told the police — as for years he has been telling anyone who will listen to him — that his father was an alien from the planet Targ."

"I've never heard of the planet Targ."

"Nor has anyone else. Apparently it exists only in Teddy's mind. Anyway, his father being an ET makes Teddy half-alien. He believes that a shuttle is coming to take him to Targ on the first of May —"

"Oh, boy . . ."

"— and that the only person who knows where the shuttle is supposed to pick him up is his mother, and that she had refused to tell him."

"So if he misses his flight, it will be her fault, and he would have to kill her."

"That was his plan."

"Why'd he keep the bloody shirt?"

"He thought it was a sign, because the victim's name had been Mary Douglas, just like his mother's. He thought the shirt had some power he could tap into if he needed to kill Mom."

"So, what you're saying is that you don't believe Teddy Douglas is the killer."

"In view of the fact that the judge was murdered while Teddy was locked up, it hardly matters, but just to make certain, I asked Miranda to fax a copy of his statement to me. It's very clear, after reading it, that while Teddy Douglas is delusional — among other things — he's not the man the police are looking for. He needs help, but he's not a serial killer. He belongs in therapy — intensive, preferably inpatient therapy — not in a prison cell."

"Have you told the FBI and the Lyndon police department this?"

"I've spoken with Miranda, and I've got a call in to my boss. I'm not really involved in the investigation at this point."

"So what do I do now?" Mara asked softly.

"Right now you wait there in your office until someone from your PD arrives."

"You called them?"

"Miranda did. Look, it may very well be that the real killer is someone connected to a case that you and the judge had in common, and that he's still out there somewhere. Frankly, the more I think about it, the more it makes sense. There's a logic to this, and besides, it would explain a lot about the case."

"Like what?"

"Like the possibility that this is a contract killing. Someone who faced you in court wouldn't be fumbling around, picking off women from the phone book. He'd know what you look like. Unless he hired someone else to do the job."

"Someone who doesn't know what I look like." Mara chewed on her bottom lip. "Someone who doesn't realize that my name is Mara, not Mary."

"Let me get on this. If you don't hear from anyone in your PD within the next twenty minutes, I want you to call me back."

"Okay."

"And while you wait, think about maybe

183

taking a little vacation until someone gets a handle on this thing. There's the cabin, you know. You could go up there."

"I'll think about it. I will," Mara promised.

"One more thing . . ."

"What?"

"We may want to call Aidan back."

After she hung up, Mara sat at her desk, both hands in her lap. She stared out the window, trying to put it all into focus, but she simply could not. She couldn't begin to believe that three women may have died terrible deaths because someone had been searching for her and repeatedly missed. But there was Judge Styler. . . .

Mara turned to her computer and searched the files for the cases she and the judge had had in common. There had been quite a few, but several stood out.

Birney v. *Birney.*

Anderson v. *Anderson.*

Giordano v. *Giordano.*

Walsh v. *Walsh.*

All four cases had been fraught with violence; all four had left ugly legacies. But the Giordano case had been by far the worst. After years of abuse at the hands of her husband, Diane Giordano had finally obtained a protection order and had filed for divorce from her husband, Vince. She also filed for sole custody of their two sons, but her husband fought her tooth and nail on this. The hearings had been

184

horrid affairs, and Mara recalled quite clearly how Vincent Giordano had glared at her from across the room as she read her recommendations to the court, and how he had cursed Judge Styler when she announced her decision to award custody of the boys to their mother.

"Who are you?" He had angrily approached the bench. *"Who are you to tell me that I cannot see my sons? You think you can stop me from seeing my sons? Watch me. Yeah. You just watch me. . . ."*

Vince Giordano's jaw had tightened and his eyes had narrowed to dark slits. He had been fined for contempt for the threats he had made against the judge that day almost three years ago and forcibly removed from the courtroom.

And less than twenty-four hours later, Vince Giordano had entered the home he had once shared with his family and calmly placed one bullet into the back of each of his sleeping sons' heads before shooting his wife.

Oh, yes. Mara remembered Vince Giordano all too well.

The soft knock caused her to turn around. Two men in khakis and tweed sport jackets stood in her doorway.

"Detective Crosby. Good to see you again." She swung her chair toward the door.

"Mara." He offered his hand, and she rose to take it. "Guess you know why we're here . . ."

Mara glanced at her watch. "That was fast. I just got off the phone with my sister."

"FBI lady. Profiler, I heard." Detective Joe

185

Sullivan dug his hands into his jacket pockets.

"Right." Mara nodded.

"Works with that team who came up here from Virginia to give us a hand," Sullivan continued. "Show us how it's done."

Ignoring his sarcasm, Mara turned back to her computer and hit Print. As the reports slid from the printer, she handed a copy to each of her visitors.

"The list of cases common to both Judge Styler and me."

"Didn't waste much time," Sullivan noted.

"We — my sister and I — thought you should know."

"It's hard to not go back to Giordano." Evan Crosby sat on the edge of Mara's desk and scanned the names on the list. "It's just too good a fit. I wouldn't put anything past that bastard."

"Strange, the judge being murdered so soon after Giordano's ex-mother-in-law is found dead." Sullivan exchanged a glance with Crosby.

"Oh, my God." Mara sat back down. "Was she killed the same way as the Marys?"

"Bullet to the head, just like her daughter," Sullivan explained. "Awfully coincidental, if you ask me."

Evan Crosby continued to look over Mara's list, weighing each name. "These others, well, Kevin Birney was a junkie, but once he got out of prison that last time, he went back into

186

rehab, really straightened himself out. I'd bet everything I have that he's not our man."

"I wasn't aware that he'd cleaned himself up," Mara said. "Good for him."

"And Tommy Anderson, he left town about a year ago, is said to be living out in Seattle. I don't see him coming back here. He was just as happy to leave."

"That leaves Walsh and Giordano," Mara noted. "And of the two of them, I don't think there's any contest. Without question, Giordano is the more likely of the two."

"Gotta be him." Sullivan nodded. "I just don't know how he's doing it."

"I know you must remember how he went off in court at his criminal trial. I seem to remember hearing that he'd mouthed off at Styler, too, after she'd granted custody to the wife," Detective Crosby told her. "You were there for that, right?"

"Yes."

"How did he strike you that day?"

"Like a vicious, macho thug." The words were out of Mara's mouth before she even realized she'd spoken. "Like a man who was incensed that anyone had the nerve to come between him and what was his. The only emotion he exhibited was anger."

"That's how he struck me at the criminal trial, too." Crosby nodded.

"Boy, the thought of that animal getting out of prison . . ." Sullivan shook his head.

"What are the chances of that?" Mara asked. "I've heard some rumors."

"The chances are better than anyone would like them to be. He had a hearing that had been postponed for some reason, but it's been rescheduled. If he can prove that all the evidence used to convict him was corrupt and the officer upon whose testimony the case was built had lied, the convictions go out the window."

"And you think that's likely?"

"I hate to say it, but yes, I do." Crosby shook his head to show his disgust. "Joe and I stopped by for a little chat with Vince about two weeks ago, right after his former mother-in-law was found dead. We haven't been able to tie him to it. But suddenly it seems that everyone who pissed him off is dying."

"Maybe he hired someone," Mara said.

"Well, if he did, he arranged it on the psychic hotline." Sullivan rubbed the back of his neck. "He's had no visitors other than his lawyer, no phone calls other than to his lawyer, and no mail. And God only knows how he'd pay off the contract — the guy is broke. No open bank accounts. His defense took every penny that he had. We've checked out every angle, believe me."

"Maybe his lawyer brought something in. . . ." Mara suggested.

"He swears he didn't."

"And you believe him?" She raised an eyebrow.

"Harry Matusek is a lot of things, but he's not a liar. I've known him for years. I don't always like his clients, but I think if something was going on, he might hedge — you know, client privilege and all that. But he didn't. He just flat out said no, he's passed on no messages to Giordano. Delivered no mail, no packages. But it's tough to imagine that Vince doesn't have a hand in this. The judge, the mother-in-law — too much of a coincidence. And those women all named Mary Douglas . . ." Evan Crosby shook his head. "Mara, Mary . . . way too close to be a coincidence. And you were the advocate for his boys. I think we need to proceed as if you were the target all along. And I think we need to determine whether Giordano knows — whether the killer knows — that the advocate is still alive."

There was silence in the small office.

"My sister thinks I should take a little vacation," Mara said quietly.

"Well, that may not be a bad idea," Sullivan told her. "But then again, unless someone tells him otherwise, he might think he's already gotten to you."

"Right, I'm safe as long as he believes that he's already killed the right person," Mara agreed. "He must have thought the last Mary Douglas was me, because she worked here in the courthouse. But isn't there a chance that Vince Giordano has realized the mistake and that he'll get the word out to the killer somehow? Her picture was in the paper. If Vince had seen that — and if he's behind this — he'd know that I'm still alive. If in fact I was intended to be his victim."

Crosby said, "We're having him watched twenty-four/seven. If he so much as speaks to someone in the hallway, we'll know about it. So even if he's figured out that you're still alive, we'll know if he tries to convey that to someone else."

"All the same, maybe we should have someone watch Ms. Douglas's house until we have a better feel for what's going on," Joe Sullivan said.

"I think Joe's right. Someone should be keeping an eye on you," Crosby agreed. "I'll see what we can arrange."

"That would be appreciated."

"And if you decide to take that vacation, you'll let us know, right?"

"I will, Detective Crosby. I haven't made up my mind about that yet, but yes, I'll let you know."

Aidan toyed with the telephone. It had been almost forty-eight hours since he'd called the Lake Grove PD. You'd have thought that someone would return a call from the FBI — particularly since someone had seen fit to actually check his credentials. Of course, that had led to the call from John Mancini.

That call had led Aidan to spending the last

two days working out with his therapist — who'd greeted him with a hearty, "Knew you'd be back, Mr. Shields" — and taking walks along the beach.

This morning he would walk down to that new condo complex that stood at the edge of the sand. Later, this afternoon, he'd repeat the walk.

Digging his bare heels into the damp, cold sand along the water's edge had been therapeutic, and every day he added to the distance he walked to build his endurance. But it had also given him time to clear his head, time to think as he walked along the shoreline, the waves pounding at his feet, froth swirling around him as he walked purposefully. It seemed that lately, there was so much to think about.

For the past several months, he'd thought about little other than himself. His injuries. His pain. His loss. His future, or lack of one.

And then there had been that visit from Annie, and somehow his priorities had begun to shift. He'd been reminded of how much pain, how much loss there was in this world that had nothing to do with him.

He stopped to pick up a piece of sea glass that the tide had tossed upon the sand. It was green, as green, he thought, as Mara's eyes. Without thinking, he tucked it into the pocket of his shorts and continued on his way. It occurred to him then that he'd been thinking an awful lot about Mara lately.

Not that that was a bad thing.

It was just . . . different. It had been a long time since he'd found his thoughts turning to the same woman over and over again.

He reached the jetty and stood for a moment, looking out beyond the breakers, where several small boats rocked in the wake of a large fishing vessel, then turned back the way he came, recalling again his conversation with John Mancini.

He never thought it could happen, but he was back with the Bureau. Even in his present condition, they wanted him back. He'd make certain that John never had cause to doubt or regret his decision.

Maybe tomorrow he'd drive out to that shooting range off Route 1 and he'd see what his nondominant left hand remembered about holding a gun. If Curt Gibbons was still out there, he would find him, find out just what it was that had set off Miranda Cahill's bells a few years back.

The minute he returned to his apartment, Aidan went directly for the pocket of the shirt he'd worn the day before, his fingers searching for the slip of paper he'd tucked in there. Smoothing out the wrinkles, he dialed the number. He'd given the Lake Grove Police Department two days to call him back. He wasn't giving them any more.

To his surprise, the call was answered by

Chief Lanigan himself.

"Oh, yes, Agent Shields. There was a message from you here someplace," the chief began. "Something about someone who used to live in Lake Grove . . ."

"Curt Gibbons," Aidan reminded him.

"Right, right. Gibbons . . ." Chief Lanigan paused, then said, "Can't say that the name rings a bell with me, but I've only been here for about four years. Now, maybe Chief Tanner might know the name."

"Chief Tanner?"

"The chief before me. I replaced him when he retired."

"Is he still around?"

"Oh, yeah, sure. Lives out by the lake now."

"Could you give me his number?"

"Phone number?"

"Yes."

"Nope."

"Excuse me?"

"Chief Tanner has no phone. Said for the last fifty years of his life, his life was ruled by the telephone, that it never rang when it wasn't something he had to tend to, and now that he didn't have to tend to it anymore, he didn't want to hear a phone ring ever again. So he doesn't have one. He loves company, loves to talk about the old days. But you want to talk to him, you'll have to do it in person."

"Well, then, I guess that's what I'll have to do."

"If I happen to see him in town, I'll let him know that you called."

"Great. I appreciate that." Aidan paused, then asked, "Chief Lanigan, are there any unsolved murders there in Lake Grove?"

"Unsolved murders? No, not out here. Lake Grove is a real small, quiet town. The last murder out here was maybe five, six years ago. Man killed his brother with a hunting rifle. Other than that, we've had a few domestics over the years. The last big murder case I recall hearing about happened a long time ago, twenty-five, thirty years maybe, but I don't know the details. That was long before my time."

"And it was solved?"

"Yes. I imagine Chief Tanner can fill you in on that one. He would have been on the force at the time, though probably not as chief back then. Now, you planning on maybe taking a trip out here?"

"I think so, yes."

"What's going on that the FBI is interested in?"

"Just following up on a loose end, that's all. Thanks for your help, Chief."

"Yeah, well, you want to see Tanner, you stop in here when you get to Lake Grove and I'll give you directions. I'm in my office every day by nine."

"Thanks, Chief. I'll be sure to do that."

Aidan hung up the phone and went to the refrigerator, hoping to find a cold beer.

"Well, the cupboard certainly is bare, isn't it?" he muttered to himself as he moved several bottles of water out of the way in his search. Finding nothing hiding behind the bottles of Deer Park, he had to content himself with one of those.

"Just as well. Should drink more water anyway. Healthier."

He took the bottle of water out onto the small balcony and sat on a folding chair. He rested his legs on the railing, crossing his feet at the ankles, and from there contemplated how he'd spend the next few days. A trip to Ohio where he'd sit and talk with an oldtime cop who may or may not know something about Curt Gibbons.

Judging by Gibbons's date of birth on the statement he'd given Miranda, Aidan knew that, if alive, he would be in his late thirties. If Lake Grove was as small a town as Lanigan had said, wouldn't the police know just about every family in town? Maybe Tanner could point Aidan to some of Gibbons's family who might have remained in the area. It was well worth the effort, if for no other reason than to see what Gibbons was up to these days. Scratch that itch in the back of his mind.

Aidan went inside and grabbed the phone book. If he was going on a road trip, he'd be driving something other than Dylan's Corvette. While beloved, the old Vette wasn't the car to take on a long trip. He'd thought that even the drive to Lyndon might have been pushing it. It would be better off left in the garage here at home.

Maybe something with a great sound system, he thought as he scanned the names of the rental car agencies. Something fast and sleek.

Smiling, Aidan dialed the number. He was back in the game, albeit in a very limited capacity, and it felt great.

It was a start.

Chapter Eleven

Mara started dialing the number, then disconnected, for the third time in a row.

She chided herself for her apparent lack of
nerve. *This shouldn't be difficult. He said call him
if I needed him. Well, I need him.*

*He'll say yes, or he'll say no. And this time, it
won't be Annie asking. He can say no to me, if he
has something better to do for the next week or so,
or if he just doesn't feel like it. He'd never say no to
Annie.*

*And if he says yes, it won't be because he feels ob-
ligated, as if it's part of his penance. He doesn't
owe me a thing.*

Her fingers dialed the number, and she
walked away from the telephone base before
she could hang up again.

"Hello?"

"Aidan? It's Mara. Mara Douglas."

"Hey, how are you?"

"I'm okay. You?"

"Good."

Her pause was just a little too long.

"So what's up, Mara?" he asked somewhat
cautiously.

"Oh, well . . ." She was finding this a wee
more difficult than she'd thought it would be.

"Out with it."

She told him about Judge Styler's death, the connection between her and the judge, Vince Giordano, the death of his ex-mother-in-law, and Mara's visit from the local detectives.

"Doesn't sound good," he told her, his mind trying to fit those pieces together without benefit of having been involved in the investigation and without knowing any of the parties.

"Annie thinks I should take a vacation."

"Not a bad idea, to leave town for a while. Anyplace in mind?"

"Well, actually, we have a cabin. Annie and I do. Our grandparents built it back in the fifties. It's in the mountains here, in Pennsylvania. Up beyond Scranton."

"I don't think I know the area."

"You've never heard of the Poconos?"

"Oh, wait. That's the place with the heart-shaped bathtubs in the hotel rooms?"

Mara laughed. "Well, Annie did put in a hot tub a few years back, but I don't recall that it was heart-shaped. But yes, the area is known as the honeymoon capital of the east. Or maybe it's the world. Lots of what we used to call honeymoon hostelries."

"You're planning on going there?"

"I'm thinking about it, yes."

"How isolated is this cabin?"

"The closest town is about two miles away. We're off a main road, but there are a few other

198

cabins in the area. The closest is at the end of our road."

"Weapons?"

"What?"

"Are you taking any weapons?"

"I don't own any." She paused. "Though I think there are some old hunting rifles up there. My granddad was a collector as well as a sportsman. My dad, who was more of a scholar than a hunter, held on to them. As far as I know, Grampa's old gun collection is still up there. Annie and I have talked about selling it but we've never gotten around to it."

He walked out onto the balcony and watched a young gull circle overhead in a blue, blue sky. He was postponing the inevitable. He knew what he had to do, and like a good soldier, he'd do it. He just wished he'd gotten his trip to Ohio in first.

"What time can you be ready?"

"What?"

"I asked what time you can be ready. I'll have to pick you up today, because I'll be leaving for Ohio in about an hour. But you're going to have to put off your trip for a few days."

"What are you talking about?"

"You really don't think I'd let you go off alone, do you?" He paused for a moment, then asked somewhat hopefully, "Unless someone's going with you?"

"No. No, there's no one else. Actually, I was

calling to see if maybe you could . . . if you weren't doing anything else this week, that is . . ."

"You're not used to asking for help, are you?"

"No." She exhaled. "No, I'm not. But I am asking now. If this would interfere with what you have to do, though . . ."

"As long as you don't mind tagging along." *Damn. Damn damn damn . . .*

"No, no. Whatever you have to do." She paused, not deaf to the hesitation in his voice. His plans — now that he actually *had* plans — hadn't included her. "But, you know, maybe we're overreacting. I'd probably be fine at the cabin for a few days. As far as I know, no one else even knows that we have it. So there's no way for anyone — Giordano, if in fact he's involved in all this, or anyone else — to find out about it."

"This Giordano — you said he's still in prison?"

"Yes, but apparently he could be released at any time." She explained about the grounds for appeal. "I think the district attorney's office is going to do everything they can to delay his release for as long as possible, but I don't think they can keep him much longer without running into other legal problems."

"And you're sure — you are absolutely certain — that no one knows where this cabin is?"

"Positive."

He mentally debated, weighing her arguments.

There was no way around it. He couldn't take the chance. If something happened to her because he just hadn't felt like taking her along on his trip to Ohio . . .

"Well, all of your rationalizations aside, there's no way you're going to go off into the mountains alone. And the fact is that I do have this assignment —"

"Assignment?" she asked, puzzled. Hadn't he said he was no longer able to work?

"Craziest thing," he told her, starting with the story of Miranda's brush with Curt Gibbons six years ago, and leading to the fact that the Mary Douglas crime scenes had held a wisp of familiarity for both Aidan and Miranda.

"That's amazing," she said. "That you both had the same feeling, that your boss is willing to let you follow through."

"Yeah." He began to pull a few items from a dresser drawer and tossed them into his duffel bag.

"Congratulations. I'm really happy for you. But if you're supposed to be working on something, I'll just be in the way."

"I'm just following up on some information. Your going with me isn't going to compromise some big investigation." He glanced at his watch. "Look, the day's marching on here. Go pack a bag."

"Aidan, if you don't want to do this, I'll understand. I swear I will. It'll be okay."

"Hey, I promised Annie that I'd stick until

this was over. It obviously isn't over. I'll see you in a few hours."

Mara returned the phone to the base.

I promised Annie. . . .

She hung up the phone, feeling more than a little disappointed. Of course he still felt obligated.

He'd promised Annie.

It had taken Aidan longer than he'd estimated to go through the rental car process. He'd had to settle for a Ford Explorer instead of the sleek Lexus he'd asked for, and by the time he'd gotten through all the paperwork and on the road, he was running an hour behind. It was nearly three p.m. when he arrived at Mara's house.

"I ran into a lot of traffic on I-95 around Wilmington," he explained when she answered the door.

"It's always a mess there." She stepped aside to let him in. At the sound of Aidan's voice, Spike had flown down the stairwell from his perch on the top step and had danced joyfully on Aidan's behalf.

"I think he's glad to see me." Aidan leaned over to pat Spike on the head.

"I forgot to ask you if we could bring him along."

"I don't think he'll be a problem. Does he need stuff — dog food and things?"

"Sure." Mara lifted a canvas tote bag. "Food,

treats, his pull rope, a tennis ball, his bowl, his little dog bed, and his blankey."

"Spike has a blankey?"

"Can't sleep without it."

"Well, then, let's get all this stuff out into the car." Aidan grabbed her bag along with the one holding Spike's essentials. "Annie knows where you're going? Anyone else you need to tell?"

"I spoke with Annie after you and I chatted. She said . . ."

Mara hesitated long enough for Aidan to ask, "She said what?"

"That she owes you another one."

"No, she doesn't," Aidan said very deliberately. "She doesn't owe me a thing. This is between you and me."

Mara nodded, feeling her face flush and hoping he meant it. The last thing she wanted was to be repayment of someone else's debt.

He went out the front door, her bag and the dog bag under his arm, Spike trotting next to him on the leash. Mara checked the French doors one last time, then started out, stopping to lock the front door. She paused, the key in her hand, then pushed the door open and went back inside.

She ran up the steps to Julianne's room. Standing in the doorway, she glanced around, then walked to the little white armoire upon which Mara herself had painted the little violets. She swung the door open all the way so that she could better survey the contents.

Making her selection, she tucked the item into her shoulder bag and left the room.

"Forget something?" Aidan asked as she crossed the lawn.

"I just wanted to make sure all the windows were locked, that's all." She waved to Mrs. West, her elderly neighbor, who was emptying her trunk of that day's purchases from the nursery. "Give me just one more minute. . . ."

Mara walked across the strip of grass that separated her driveway from her neighbor's.

"Mrs. West, I can't believe you have room for one more plant in that garden of yours," Mara teased as she scooped up a flat of some red, feathery plant from the trunk of the car.

"Oh, there's always room for another plant or two" — the old woman smiled, showing off her dimples — "or forty-eight. Now, when I go back tomorrow, I'm going to pick up another flat of those celosia for you. I think they'd be nice in a bed along your garage."

Mara paused and looked over her shoulder. "There is no bed along the garage."

"There will be by the time I finish." She brushed her hands together, palm to palm, a satisfied grin on her face.

"Mrs. West, you really don't need to plant things in my yard. As much as I appreciate it."

Her neighbor waved her off. "As you pointed out, I'm running out of room in my own yard. And I love to make new flower beds. It makes me feel so creative."

"I don't know what to say, except thank you." Mara knew when to give up. "Would you like these out back near your porch?"

"Yes, thank you." Mrs. West placed the pot of pink impatiens she carried next to the flat on the porch. "Now, do I see that nice young man is visiting you again?"

"Oh . . . yes. He's really a friend of Annie's —"

"So he said." Mrs. West's eyes twinkled. Any fool could see that Annie was nowhere in sight.

"And actually, we're . . . we're taking a little trip. A business trip, you see —"

"You and Annie's friend?"

"Yes. And I was wondering if you wouldn't mind taking in my mail for the next few days."

"I wouldn't mind at all, dear. You just go on and have a nice 'business' trip with Annie's friend. You and Spike both. I see he's there in the backseat. You could leave him with me, you know. He's no trouble. If you think he'd interfere with . . . whatever business you need to tend to."

Mara burst out laughing. "You are not very subtle, Mrs. West. And Aidan is very much a friend. To Annie and to me."

"Just a friend?" The woman frowned. "Nothing more?"

"Nothing more," Mara assured her.

"Pity . . ." She shook her head slowly. "He's quite a hunk."

They stopped at a market on the other side

of Lancaster, two hours into their trip. Aidan went inside and, finding the deli counter still open, picked up two containers of soup, a few sandwiches, and several bottles of soda and water. They ate in rapidly fading daylight at a picnic table set up in a grassy area adjacent to the store and made small talk. Mara walked Spike on the leash before they set off again. When she returned to the car, Aidan was checking the map.

"How do we get to where we're going?" she asked as she lifted Spike into his little dog bed, which Aidan had placed on the floor behind the driver's seat.

"We're going to swing out to Harrisburg and pick up Route 76. Take that clear across the state and into Ohio." He turned the key in the ignition and watched her buckle her seat belt. "Ready?"

"All set." She smiled at him, and in spite of himself, it occurred to him that bringing her along on this trip might not have been such a bad idea after all.

"Feel free to look for another station on the radio."

"What, you don't like hip-hop?"

He rolled his eyes.

Mara leaned forward and scanned for something a little more to Aidan's liking. She found a pop station and stayed with that.

They rode in silence for nearly twenty minutes before Aidan asked, "Do you hear something? An odd noise?"

"It's Spike. He snores."

"He snores, he can't sleep without his blankey, and he travels with his own little bed. It's like having a little person along."

"He thinks he is a little person." She rested her head against the headrest and gazed out the window. The sun had set behind the rolling hills, but the last fingers of light stretched upward from the horizon. Lavender and orange, set in a gray-blue sky.

"Were you planning on stopping somewhere?" she asked after they had moved onto the highway and were headed west.

"You mean, stop somewhere for the night?"

"Yes."

"I was planning on driving straight through." He gestured with a nod of his head toward the backseat. "There's a blanket there if you're cold. You can tilt the seat back and sleep if you get tired."

"That's fine." She reached behind her and grabbed the blanket. It was soft and down-filled and fit around her nicely. She searched for the mechanism that would allow the seat to recline. Finding it, she lowered her seat halfway. "And you know, I can drive, if you want to rest for a while."

"I'll be fine. Thanks anyway."

"What's the name of the town we're going to?"

"Lake Grove."

"Am I allowed to ask what's there?"

"Sure. This is not a secret FBI mission. It's really just a sort of follow-up. No big deal." He checked his rearview mirror before pulling into the left lane to pass a pickup.

"How do you do that sort of thing? How do you know where to start?"

"You find someone in the area who might still have connections to the person you're looking for. In this case, that person is Curt Gibbons. I'm hoping that Chief Tanner —"

"Who's Chief Tanner?"

"He was with the Lake Grove PD for fifty years or so. Retired several years ago after a long career as chief."

"He must know a lot about what happened over the years. Why didn't you just call him?"

"Tanner doesn't have a phone. Figured that after having been its slave for so long, he'd had enough."

"I can understand that." She closed her eyes, and the slight rocking motion of the car lulled her. "Are you sure you want to keep driving straight through? Really, we could take turns. I don't mind."

"No, I'm anxious to get there."

And besides, he acknowledged to himself, after all this time, it felt good — damn good — to have a destination again.

For the second time in less than two weeks, Curtis Channing was getting ready to leave town. The map was spread out over the single bed, his eyes tracing the route south. His work here was done, and he was anxious to move on now. While he felt reasonably certain there was no way the events of the past month could lead to his door, he was restless without a plan.

He wondered how long it would take to drive to Louisiana. He'd heard there was a serial killer spreading chaos along the bayous. He thought it might be fun to go on down there and share his special kind of mayhem. That would really shake up those southern boys, wouldn't it, when they realized there were two serial killers in the neighborhood?

Louisiana it was.

He began to hum as he finished his packing. He'd already quit his job and called his land-lord to let him know he'd be leaving town to-morrow. It was already ten p.m., but he didn't have anything to hold him here in town.

Like he said, his work here was done. . . .

He turned off the light on the small desk and looked around to make certain that he was leaving nothing behind. Placing the duffel bag near the door, he looked under the bed. The only thing there was a toothpick that he'd dropped a few days earlier and hadn't been able to find. He flicked it into the small trash can near the desk and checked the closet one last time. Content that he had everything, he started down the steps.

He was just at the second floor landing when a door opened.

"Hey, Curt, man, where you goin'?" The drunk who lived in the room two from Curtis's stuck his head out. "Where you goin'?"

"Moving on, Buddy. Moving on." Curtis barely paused.

"Well, you wouldn't be leaving without a good-bye, would you? Come in and havva beer. Drink to your safe journey."

"Thanks, Buddy, but I don't have time —"

"Sure ya do. Everybody got time for one beer." Buddy swayed a little in the doorway. " 'Sides, I just hadda pizza delivered. Have a slice, you won't have to stop for dinner. . . ."

The smell of the cheese and pepperoni wafting through the doorway made Curtis's mouth water. He hesitated, then decided a quick bite now would save him time later.

"Sure, Buddy. Thanks. I think I will join you after all."

Curtis swung his duffel through the doorway and left it near the door. Buddy's room was considerably larger than his own and boasted an alcove that held two chairs and an ottoman, upon which rested a box from the pizzeria around the corner.

His host motioned for Channing to take a seat while he rustled around in a brown paper bag for paper plates and a package of napkins.

"Here. Help yourself," Buddy told him. "I'll get you a beer. Get myself one while I'm at it."

Buddy had clearly had plenty, but there was no point in mentioning it.

"Feel free to turn on the television there, Curt. I always watch the news this time of the day. You watch the news?" More rustling of the bag.

"Once in a while."

"You ever watch Channel Five? See that girl, Candy what's 'er name? She is hot, don'cha think?" Buddy popped open a can and passed it to his guest, then popped the second for himself. "I knew a guy once, worked at the station, said she's a real snob, though. Don't talk to no one."

The room may have been slightly shabby, but the television was top of the line. The reporter appeared almost life-size.

". . . the bizarre developments in this case," Candace McElroy was saying. "Channel Five has learned — exclusively — that it appears the Mary Douglas killer may have missed his true target after all."

Channing's hand gripped the can in a reflex action. What was she saying?

". . . also looking at a possible connection between Judge Styler and a woman who worked within the family court system, but official police sources will not confirm or deny that rumor . . ."

Channing stared at the screen. Next to him, Buddy was still babbling on about how hot that Candace McElroy was and how he'd seen her in the park one day wearing short-shorts.

"However, the attorney for Teddy Douglas, who had been arrested for the murder of the three Mary Douglases, has told me that his client will be released from custody within the hour."

"Candace, have the police confirmed that Judge Styler and the Mary Douglas victims were killed in the same manner, as we reported here this morning?" The anchor back at the station cut into Candace's broadcast from the front of the police station.

"Burt, neither the police nor the D.A. will officially confirm *anything* on this case right now. Now, my source tells me that a press conference may be scheduled for tomorrow morning. Perhaps some of this will be cleared up then."

"Thanks, Candace, for that exclusive report. Now, in other news . . ."

The anchor faded away, just as Buddy's chatter faded away, and Channing was left to contemplate this most unwelcome — this most *unexpected* — news.

He exhaled softly and reached for another slice of pizza. Well, at least he hadn't turned in his key, and he had the room until the next morning.

Bayou country would just have to wait.

Chapter Twelve

Mara yawned and opened her eyes slowly, then realized that the car had stopped moving. She turned toward the driver's seat, but it was empty, as was Spike's little dog bed.

Unbuckling her seat belt, she opened the door and stepped out into a cool and foggy morning. She had absolutely no idea where she was. There was movement off to her left, and she called softly, "Aidan?"

"Over here." He stepped through the parting mist following Spike, who took off for Mara.

She scooped him up. "Bugged Aidan for a walk, did you?"

"We both needed to stretch our legs. Hungry?"

"Very. Where are we? Is this a rest stop?"

"It's a park. If you want a ladies' room, there's a wooden structure back near the entrance that has rest rooms. It's not far. I just changed down there. Figured if I'm going to meet with the local police, I should look like an FBI agent."

"Well, you look nice." She smiled. He did look nice in his light gray tweed jacket. "But I thought you all went for that Men in Black look."

"We field agents don't have to do the MIB

thing all the time. Mostly we save it for when we're trying to impress someone. I do have the dark glasses, though. Somewhere . . ." He looked almost amused.

Mara smiled. She liked this Aidan. He seemed more relaxed, less moody than the man who'd stayed with her in Lyndon. It was a nice change.

"The building's right down this path. Just follow it to the end."

The building was clearly marked, and though less than luxurious, it was clean and well-kept and contained all the necessary equipment. Mara used the toilet, then washed her face at the sink. She brushed her hair, then rummaged in her purse for makeup, but a small compact containing loose powder and some lip gloss were all she had at hand. She fussed for a moment, wishing she had a little blush and maybe a little mascara, then smiled to herself, trying to recall the last time she had fussed over makeup. It had been a while. She knew without even thinking about it that the effort was for Aidan's benefit. Something to think about, to be sure . . .

When she came outside, the Explorer had been pulled up close to the building to wait for her.

"Thanks, but I could have walked back," she said as she climbed into the SUV.

"Spike was anxious to get on the road."

"Spike seems to have taken a liking to your

214

lap. Can you drive with him sitting there?"

"I drove the last hundred or so miles with him on my lap."

"You're spoiling him."

"We're buds."

"You found your glasses," she noted. "Nice touch."

"Thanks."

"Do you really think you need them now? The sun is barely up."

"Just trying to get back into the groove."

"By the way, where are we?" Mara asked as they drove from the park. "And how much farther to Lake Grove."

"We're there."

"We're there? Already?"

"Yup."

"Where to now?"

He glanced at his watch. They had close to two hours before Aidan figured the chief would be at his desk.

"We have time to stop for breakfast before we check in with Chief Lanigan. I planned to chat with him for a while, then get directions to Tanner's place."

Ignoring Spike's indignant sigh at being left in the car, Mara and Aidan stopped at an all-night diner whose sign declared that it served breakfast twenty-four hours a day. They took their time, because they had so much time to kill. And even so, they arrived at the police station a full forty minutes before the chief checked in. Mara took Spike for a walk around town while Aidan met with the chief.

"Agent Shields." Chief Martin Lanigan met Aidan at the front desk with a handshake and an uncertain smile.

"Thanks for taking time from your schedule to meet with me. I appreciate it." Aidan recognized a wary local when he saw one. He'd do his best to set Lanigan at ease.

"Come on back to my office. Mary Rose," the chief called over his shoulder to the young receptionist, "if you'd be kind enough to bring us some of that good coffee of yours . . ."

Aidan followed the chief down a short hallway that had two doors on each side. Judging by what he'd already seen of Lake Grove that morning, he figured they didn't need too large a force.

"So remind me again why you're here. . . ." Lanigan walked around his desk to a large leather chair with a well-worn seat.

"Just a follow-up on an old case," Aidan told him casually.

"Now, which old case would that be?"

"Actually, it wasn't a case here in Lake Grove."

"Oh?"

"It was a case we handled about six years ago, down in Rockledge," Aidan told him.

"Rockledge?" The chief frowned. "What would that have to do with Lake Grove?"

"Not sure it does." Aidan rolled his chair out

of the way of the receptionist, who entered the room carrying a tray with two mugs of coffee and a cardboard carton of creamer.

"Rockledge is almost seventy miles from here. What's the connection?" the chief asked as he passed a mug to Aidan.

"There's a current case in Pennsylvania in which several women have been killed in a very methodical fashion." Aidan rested his forearms on his thighs and leaned forward slightly. "The scene was very carefully staged."

"We got a bulletin on that case. Woman's name . . ."

"Mary Douglas."

"Right. Asked us to search our records, see if we had anything like that on our computer. I can assure you that I found nothing even similar, and those computer records go back twenty years. And yes, before you ask, I searched the computer myself and so responded." Lanigan looked slightly offended.

"I'm sure you did, sir. I'm not here to follow up on your response." Aidan sipped at his coffee. It was too hot and burned his tongue. He reached for the cream, hoping to cool the coffee just a bit. "The case in Rockledge had a similarly crafted scene. Now, the MO was different, but that crafting, the staging, could be a signature. That case has not been solved, and we're following up on several of the potential suspects who were interviewed at that time. One of them gave his home address as Lake Grove."

"Ah, I see. You're looking to interview this suspect again."

"Exactly. Only he seems to have disappeared. We were hoping to find someone here who knew him or knew his family —"

"Got it. That's why you want to speak with Chief Tanner. Well, anyone who'd lived in Lake Grove just about anytime over the past seventy years, Tanner would know about it." Understanding now that the visit from the federal agent had nothing to do with him or the running of his department, Lanigan's entire demeanor changed.

"Yes, sir. That was the plan."

"Easy enough to get to his place. Go straight out here past the station and go three miles until you hit the lake. Take a right, go about a mile and a half till the paved road ends, then go about another three-quarters of a mile on the dirt road to the end. Tanner's house is right there. Overlooks the lake." Lanigan glanced up at the wall clock. "He ought to be sitting on his deck right about now, watching the ducks feed. You want to get off on the right foot, you'll take him a large cup of coffee from the convenience store across the street, a loaf of bread for the ducks, and a bag of birdseed for his feeders. Oh, and a box of dog biscuits wouldn't hurt. He's got himself two or three old dogs he picked up at the pound."

"Thanks, Chief. I appreciate the tip."

"Welcome. Now, all I ask is that if you find

something that I should know about, you let me know. I don't want to be reading about it in some memo coming over the fax machine."

"Did you get directions?" Mara asked when Aidan approached the car.

"Yes." He leaned into her open window. "I have to make a run to that store across the way. Can I bring you something?"

"Coffee would be good. Cream and whatever form of artificial sweetener they have on hand."

Aidan returned in under ten minutes, a large bag in one hand, a smaller bag and a cardboard tray holding three paper cups of coffee in the other.

"What's in the bag?" Mara asked.

"My bribe's in the big one. The little one's for us."

She peered into the larger of the two. "Bird-seed, a loaf of bread, and a box of dog biscuits. Who are you bribing, Doctor Dolittle?"

"Chief Tanner. We'll know in about five minutes whether or not Lanigan knew what he was talking about."

Mara opened the smaller bag.

"Doughnuts." She grinned. "Flip you for the jelly."

"It's yours. I'm more of the chocolate-frosted type myself."

The retired chief was exactly where Chief Lanigan had said he would be, sitting on his deck overlooking peaceful Lake Grove, from which the town took its name. Three dogs of questionable age and breed lay near his feet, and bird feeders were everywhere. A dozen or more ducks swam just off a makeshift dock.

Lanigan knew his man, all right.

"Think it would be okay if I took Spike for a walk while you're visiting?"

"I don't see why not." Aidan got out of the car and slammed the door. "Would you hand me the big bag and that last cup of coffee there? Might as well make the most of what I've got."

Aidan had barely taken five steps from the car when he was surrounded by the dogs.

"They're okay, they don't mean any harm. Unless you do." The man raised himself slowly from the chair in which he sat.

"No, no," Aidan assured him. "I'm just here to meet Chief Tanner and have a little chat."

Aidan introduced himself, then asked, "Would you be Chief Tanner?" knowing full well that the man was.

"Depends on what your business is, son. Never had an FBI agent stop in when it wasn't bad news."

"No bad news." Aidan smiled. "How'd you know I was FBI?"

Tanner just smiled.

"Like I told Lanigan, we're just following up on a loose end. I just wanted to test your memory."

"Well, then. You're in luck." Elwood Tanner

stood on his top step and gestured for Aidan to come up onto the deck. "I have a memory today. Some days, it's not so sharp. But today, well, I'm feeling spunky today."

"Then I am in luck." Aidan handed him the cup of coffee along with the bag. "Chief Lanigan said you liked your coffee black."

The old man threw his head back and laughed.

"Coffee from Parker's in town, ah, that's the best. And let's just see what's in that bag. . . ." He peered inside. "Birdseed . . . oh, the good kind, too. Lots of thistle. Good, good . . ."

He looked up at Aidan and said, "Is the bread for me or for the ducks?"

"The ducks."

"And I see some biscuits for the boys." He called the dogs to him and they sat obediently at his feet. "Manny, Moe, and Jack, meet Agent Shields."

Three dog tails thumped in unison.

"That your girl out there in the car?"

Aidan hesitated, then, rather than explain that he was more bodyguard than anything else, said, "Yes, sir. It is."

"Is she ugly?"

"No." Aidan stared at the man. Was he kidding? "No, she's not ugly. She's beautiful."

"Then why are you leaving her locked up in the car? Tell her to come on up and join us."

Aidan rose and took the steps two at a time.

"And is that a little dog I see there, too?

Bring the girl and the dog."

Mara leaned out the window as Aidan approached.

"Let me guess," she said. "He took the bribe then told you to beat it."

"No. He took the bribe and told me to get the girl and the dog out of the car and have you join us on the deck."

"Oh. Okay. Come on, Spike. Wait, are you sure he said the dog, too? I decided against walking him. Those are some pretty large pups he has there. I'd hate to see Spike being used in a tug of war."

"His dogs are old and seem to be pretty calm. I think it will be fine. Just grab his leash."

Mara did, along with the remaining two cups of coffee, and Aidan opened the door for her. "Oh, and he thinks you're my girlfriend."

"Why does he think that?" Mara slammed the car door behind her.

"He assumed. I figured it was let him believe that or tell him the truth. And I didn't know if you'd want me to go into all that."

She fell into step next to him, not commenting.

"I'm Mara. This is Spike," she told Chief Tanner when they arrived at the foot of the deck. "I've heard a lot about you."

"Name one thing."

"I heard that if you didn't know about it, it didn't happen in Lake Grove."

Tanner laughed again and pointed to the

chair beside him. "You'll sit next to me, I think."

Mara moved the indicated rocking chair closer to the railing and looked out at the lake. "You have a spectacular view," she told him. "I'll bet it's beautiful in the fall."

"All year round, it's beautiful." He nodded. "Every season has its moments."

Aidan took the seat on Mara's other side so he could keep an eye on Spike, who was busily trying to decide which of Tanner's dogs to bully first.

"So, Mr. Shields, special agent with the FBI, we still haven't established what brings you to my door." Tanner rocked gently and gazed out at the lake.

Aidan paused, then said, "You know, somehow I expected that Chief Lanigan would have paid you a visit after I spoke with him on the phone yesterday."

"Actually, he did. Mentioned that you asked about old murders in Lake Grove. We've had our share over the years, God knows, mostly jealous husbands or stupid kids."

"I was particularly interested in any unsolved murders, Chief."

"Sorry, son. I can't think of a one that we didn't make an arrest on, some easier than others, of course. I remember them all. Some were worse, naturally — if one death can be considered worse than another."

"Some deaths are harder than others. If

you're looking at a homicide, chances are the death wasn't a gentle one," Aidan agreed. "And some cases are just tougher, all the way around, than others."

"Well, ironically, the nastiest death I ever saw was my easiest arrest. Guy called in and told us what he'd done and asked us to send a car out for him — imagine that? Course, that was one for the books, any way you looked at it. You get one case like that, you don't need to see another. Plenty to talk about, a scene like that one." Tanner shook his head. "Gruesome, what he did to that woman. Yessir, that was a case to remember."

"What case was that, sir?" Aidan asked, more out of politeness. He'd come seeking information on Curt Gibbons, but if the way to Gibbons was through Tanner's war stories, so be it. He wasn't in a hurry.

"I remember it like it was yesterday, though it has to be a good thirty years past. . . ." He shook his head slowly and gazed out toward the lake. "Never seen anything like it, before or since. The call came in from Al Unger that he'd just killed his woman. I was out on the street in my patrol car and heard the call, went over to Unger's place. He was sitting on the front steps wearing just his boxers. You could tell he'd been drinking, but he wasn't drunk. He didn't even look up when I got out of the car. 'She's in there,' he told me. 'I done it. I killed her.' "

You could hear a pin drop right about now, Mara

224

thought as she watched memory take Tanner by the hand and lead him back in time.

"So I go on in — never thought to wait for backup, you know — and there she was. Blood everywhere."

"What was the cause of death?"

"Multiple stab wounds. It was the damnedest thing I'd ever seen. She was lying there on the floor, her skirt all neat around her legs — didn't even know she'd been raped until the autopsy —"

Aidan's ears began to ring.

"— and that cloth over her face —"

"There was a cloth over her face?"

"Yeah. Like one of them linen towels from the kitchen."

"Six stab wounds?" Aidan said without realizing he'd spoken aloud.

"Now how in the world would you know that?" Tanner stopped rocking and turned to Aidan.

Aidan told Tanner about the Mary Douglas killings in eastern Pennsylvania.

"Now that beats all." Tanner shook his head. "That just beats all."

"Where is this guy, this Unger, now?"

"He served his thirty years — heard he did get a little time off for good behavior when he came up for parole. Been out about ten months now."

"He's *out?*" Aidan's jaw dropped.

"Yes. Served his time and they released him.

Said he was a model prisoner, never caused a bit of trouble in prison."

"How do we find this man?"

"Chief Lanigan can probably get in touch with his parole officer." Tanner leaned forward, looking around Mara to Aidan. "You can't possibly think for one minute that Albert Unger had anything to do with these other killings."

"You have to admit, it's pretty suspicious. The MO is pretty distinctive."

"Well, hell. He's gotta be near as old as I am. And the chances of him running back and forth to Pennsylvania to kill . . . how many women did this guy kill?"

"Four that we know of."

"I just don't see it happening, but you ask Lanigan to give a call to the parole officer. See what's what."

"I'll do that, sir."

"Yep, worth a follow-up, I'd say. You'll stop back after you see him? Let me know if there's any smoke behind that fire?"

"We will, yes." Aidan stood and held out his hand for Mara, thinking that he'd want to make a trip back anyway. He hadn't gotten around to asking about Curt Gibbons. "Thanks again, Chief. We'll be in touch."

Tanner began to rock again, more slowly. "Yes, sir, that was the worst thing I ever seen, that woman lying dead there on the floor. . . ."

Less than two hours later, thanks to the quick work of Chief Lanigan, Mara and Aidan were on their way to Telford, several towns over, where they would try to locate Albert Unger. Aidan went first to the small motel where, the parole officer had told the chief, Unger rented a room by the week.

The motel parking lot was littered with fast-food wrappers and cigarette butts, but few cars were parked on the faded black asphalt that appeared, like the rest of the motel, to need a serious overhaul. Aidan went into the office and cleared his throat to get the attention of the thin balding man who sat behind the counter, trimming his nails with a pocket knife and watching a daytime soap on a small TV.

"Excuse me," Aidan said. "I'm looking for Al Unger. I understand he's living here."

"Yeah, he has a room," the man responded without looking up. "Whatcha want with Al?"

"Just need to talk to him."

"Al's at work."

"What time do you expect him back?"

"After midnight, most nights, by the time he gets back."

"From?"

"What's it worth to you?"

Aidan slid a twenty-dollar bill across the worn wooden counter. The man finally looked up, examined the bill, then shrugged.

"He works at the movie theater downtown. Right on Main Street. Can't miss it. Only one there."

"Thanks."

Aidan left the office and walked back to the car.

"He's not here?" Mara asked as he got behind the wheel.

"No. But I know where he is. Let's see if we can get him to talk to us."

"Us?"

"He might be more at ease with you present. Do you mind?"

She shook her head. "Of course not."

By the time they arrived at the theater, the early matinee had twenty minutes left on its run. Aidan bought two tickets from the young girl in the booth, and as he pocketed his change, asked, "Do you know where I can find Al Unger?"

"You can ask the manager." She pointed across the lobby to a man in a white shirt, the sleeves rolled up to his elbows.

"Is Al Unger in yet?" Aidan asked as they approached the manager, who looked from Aidan to Mara, then back again.

"What he do? He's not in any trouble, is he? I hired him on the provision that he keep it clean."

"No, no. No trouble," Aidan assured him. "I just need to ask him a question or two."

"And who are you?"

"I'm with the FBI." Aidan offered his credentials. "But Mr. Unger hasn't done anything wrong. We're just following up on something routine."

228

"You sure? Because if he broke his parole —"

"Nothing like that. Just a follow-up on something."

"Unger cleans up after the shows. Sweeps the floors, collects the trash left behind, that sort of thing. The movie that's showing now has less than a half hour to run."

"That's what the tickets say," Mara noted.

"You bought tickets? Give 'em to me. I'll get you a refund." He held out his hand. "You're not even gonna watch the show. Here, give me the tickets."

"Thanks anyway, but that's not necessary." Aidan declined the offer.

"Hey, you sure? We like to cooperate here, you know?"

"I'm sure you do," Aidan said, but did not hand over the tickets.

"All right, let me know if you change your mind. Now, why don't you just slip into the back here, take a seat — plenty of those, we're not crowded at the weekday afternoon matinees. You just wait around till the show is over and everyone leaves, and Al will be along to clean up."

"Thanks. We appreciate it." Aidan nodded and opened one of the doors into the theater for Mara.

They sat in the back, in the dark, and watched the action film near its climax.

"Want some popcorn?" Aidan whispered.

"Sure."

"I'll be right back."

He was back in less than five minutes, a jumbo box of buttered popcorn tucked in the crook of his elbow and a large drink in each hand.

"I hope you like a lot of butter," he said as he handed her one of the drinks and held out the box of popcorn.

"What is the movie theater experience without hot buttered fingers?" she whispered as she dug in.

The movie ended with the hero single-handedly dispatching the villain and a dozen or more of his cronies. The few moviegoers who still remained when the lights came on moved slowly up the aisle. Soon the theater was empty except for Mara and Aidan, who sat in the back row munching on popcorn while they waited for Albert Unger.

They heard him before they saw him. The vacuum cleaner whirred from down near the front row, and Aidan leaned forward to observe.

Albert Unger was, as Chief Tanner had told him, well into his seventies.

"He looks awfully old," Mara noted, "and not very strong."

"No way he's our man. Unless he knows he's being watched. Look how he has to stoop over with the vacuum, how frail he appears to be. There is no way he'd have the physical strength to kill those women."

"Well, his parole officer did tell Lanigan that

Unger hasn't left town since he got out. Are you still going to talk to him?"

Aidan nodded.

He had his chance when the old man reached the back row and realized that not all of the theater's patrons had left when the lights went on.

" 'Scuse me, folks. I'm going to have to vacuum here. But if you want to still chat some, you can move on down to where I cleaned. I won't tell the manager. . . ."

"Thanks." Aidan smiled. "But we actually would like to talk with you. If you have a minute."

"With me?" Unger's wary pale blue eyes flickered from Aidan, to Mara, then back to Aidan again. He knew law when he saw it. "What would you want with me?"

"I was just wondering if you'd be willing to —"

"I ain't done a thing, I swear." The old man's hands began to shake. "Swear to God. Done one thing in all my days, and I done my time for it."

"We know that, Mr. Unger. Look, what time are you finished here? Do you get a break? Could we buy you a cup of coffee and just sit and talk for a few minutes?"

"Who are you?"

Aidan told him.

"You want to know about what I done . . . back then?"

"Yes."

"You writin' a book or something?"

"No, sir. Just trying to find a needle in a hay-stack. Thought maybe you could help us look."

"I go on break soon as I finish up here. Usually go next door and have my dinner when the matinee cleanup is done."

"How about if we meet you there?" Aidan offered.

"Dinner on you?" Unger asked slyly.

"Sure."

"Fifteen, twenty minutes, tops." Unger turned the vacuum cleaner back on and went back to work.

"You really think he'll show?" Mara asked after they'd been seated for almost twenty minutes at the small luncheonette-style eatery.

"I think so. I think he's curious."

"What do you think you'll learn from him? He's obviously not the Mary Douglas killer."

"I don't know. Maybe just a glimpse into the mind of someone who does that sort of thing. Kills a woman like that, then tries to tidy up the scene."

The door opened and Unger shuffled in.

Mara smiled as the man approached the table. "Mr. Unger."

"Miss." He stood in front of the table, apparently not knowing what to do next, whether to sit next to Mara or to Aidan.

She motioned to him to take the seat next to hers, which would, she figured, allow Aidan to

232

make eye contact with Unger. This was, after all, Aidan's show. She was only along for the ride.

The waitress took their orders, teasing Unger by saying, "So, Albie, looks like you won't be dining alone today, eh?"

Unger nodded and blushed.

"You're a cop, I know you told me that, but tell me again what kind." Unger took slow sips from the coffee the waitress had left for him.

"I'm with the FBI. My name is Aidan Shields. This is Mara Douglas."

He watched Unger's face to see if there was any reaction whatsoever when he mentioned Mara's name. There was none.

"I didn't do nothin' that the FBI needs to know about." Unger looked as if he was about to panic.

"We know that. We just want you to tell us, if you wouldn't mind, what happened between you and your wife."

"She weren't my wife, though I loved her like she was and tried to be a father to her boy. That's the truth. That's the one thing you have to understand. I loved Joanie. I did."

He paused when he saw the waitress approach with his soup and did not resume speaking until she was out of hearing range. He lowered his voice, though, just to make certain that he wasn't overheard. It would serve no good cause for the people he dealt with every day to know that he had served almost thirty years in prison for murder.

"We'd been living together for almost two years. Oh, I knew she wasn't gonna be around forever, she being almost fifteen years younger than me. But I gave her a home, took in her and her boy too, tried to get her off the drugs, tried to get her to stay away from the drink. I was doing pretty good there for a while, too. Then I screwed up and went to prison for ten months. Well . . ." He sipped his soup from his spoon, as if he needed the sustenance to go on.

"Well, I come out when my time is up, first thing I do is go to the house we had out there on Railroad Avenue, not sure she would still be there. The prison was about a hundred eighty miles from Lake Grove, you know. She didn't have no car and unless she could get someone to bring her out, she couldn't visit much." He turned his attention back to the soup, stirring it and looking into the cup intently.

"Was she still there?" Aidan asked.

Unger finished the soup, then sat back while the waitress took his empty cup, and served his dinner and the salads ordered by Mara and Aidan.

"Enjoy," she said brightly as she walked away.

"She was still there, all right." Unger's face hardened. "Strung out on heroin and drunk as a skunk. I left the house and went down to Eagle's, the bar at the corner. I look back on that day now, and I think, if I hadn't gone, I wouldn't have known. . . ."

"Known what, Mr. Unger?" Mara heard herself ask.

"She'd been turning tricks from just about the day I left. In my house. In my bed. And other things, things worse than whorin'. Things no decent person would even think of doing." He looked at Aidan. "I was drunk, I admit it, and it ain't no excuse, and I never said it was. But I came back home and threw her to the floor and I . . . forced her. Next thing I know, the knife was in my hand and I don't know what took over me but I started stabbing her and I couldn't stop. All's I remember thinking is that after what she done, she deserved it. Had it coming to her, not even so much for what she done to me, but for what she done to that boy. Animals got more respect for their young than she did."

Unger's head shook slowly, side to side. "She — Joanie — she had no business putting that boy out."

"Putting the boy out?" Aidan put his fork down.

"Some of her boyfriends liked little boys as best they liked women."

"You mean she — ?" Mara found the words too distasteful.

"Traded her son for drugs, yeah."

"How old was he at the time, do you remember?" Aidan asked.

"Seven, eight, nine, somewhere thereabouts."

"What happened to him? Where is he now,

do you know?" Aidan asked as the first hint of understanding began to hum in his brain.

"No idea." Unger shrugged. "They put him into foster care. I never heard what became of him."

"What was Joanie's last name, Mr. Unger?" Aidan stared at his plate. Knowing.

"It was Gibbons. Joanie Gibbons . . ."

Chapter Thirteen

Curtis Channing had lain awake most of the night, staring at the dark smudge in the center of the ceiling that was the overhead light fixture. Too exasperated with himself to even be annoyed, he focused on a game plan. As he saw it, he had two choices. He could forget the whole thing and move on. Or he could finish the job and *then* move on.

By morning he'd decided that it was times like this that proved the mettle of a man. And he, Curtis Alan Channing, whatever else he might be, was a man of his word. He'd heard someone famous once — he couldn't remember who it was, but it was someone really big — say that a man's word had to be his bond. Well, okay then. He'd find a way to make it right.

He crossed his legs at the ankles under the light blanket and closed his eyes. Sometimes it helped to visualize the task at hand. No problem there. Once he found his quarry, he knew exactly what he'd do. If he could get close enough, that is.

It was a given that the police would be watching the home of every M. Douglas from here to Harrisburg and back. How could he narrow the field if he couldn't get close enough to take a look? Some of those M. Douglases would be men, right? Once he identified who was who, he could cross off those right away and concentrate on the others.

He shifted on the old mattress and sighed. This would have been so much easier if he hadn't been so careless the first two times and so cocky the third. Following Mary number three to the courthouse hadn't been enough, he realized now, but *damn,* what were the chances of two women with identical names working in the same place?

He'd asked himself that same question many times.

It was a greater challenge now, with greater risks. That was the only way to look at it.

And if the risks were greater, so then would be the rewards.

He just had to figure out how to get close enough to find his own M. Douglas.

In the end, it had been way too easy. The police had all but stretched a banner over the front of the house:

KILLER TAKE NOTE: THIS IS THE ONE.

Channing had set out first thing in the morning to buy a Walkman and some new running shoes. Returning to his room, he called his landlord and feigned illness, asking if he could keep the room for another few days, then pulled on a pair of sweatpants. He laced up the running shoes, then went out to his car. Armed with the page he'd ripped from the *D* section of the local phone book, and thinking that starting at the top of the list had gotten him nowhere, he drove to the neighborhood where the last M. Douglas on the list lived. He parked four blocks away, then set out on his run. By the time he passed the house, he was already starting to glisten with sweat, which he thought made him look all the more authentic. Jogging past the home, he pretended not to notice the police car parked out front.

1145 Green Avenue. One down.

On to the second name on the list and 821 Forrest.

And then the third: 2232 Oak.

1757 Baker. The fourth.

Each house had a police car parked in front or across the street.

And then, bingo.

1733 Hillcrest.

A house with not one, not two, but three police cars on the street. Of course, they'd want to make certain that no one got near the real M. Douglas, and if one cop was good, three cops were better.

Thank you, Lyndon PD.

He observed as much as he could while jogging past, pretending to notice nothing.

The house next door was a bungalow. An old woman stood at the end of the driveway, directing the delivery of several bags of mulch and several flats of flowers from a nursery truck.

Walsh's Nursery.

The name on the mailbox was Helena West.

Now all he had to do was figure out how to use this information to get past the police and close enough to his M. Douglas to take care of business.

He returned to his room, and by the time he was showered and dressed, he had a plan.

At three-thirty that afternoon, Channing parked his car in Helena West's driveway. On the way over, he'd stopped at Walsh's and picked up several more flats of the same flowers he'd seen being delivered to the West home that morning.

He pretended not to notice the police officer who stood near the back gate of the house next door as he walked up the path that ran alongside the West house.

"Mrs. West?" he called from end of the path. "Mrs. West?"

The elderly woman poked her head out the back door. "Yes?"

"I'm from Walsh's. The truck that came over earlier didn't bring your entire order."

"They didn't?"

"No. They forgot a few flats. Where would you like me to put them?"

"Oh." She frowned, looking just slightly confused for a moment. "Are you certain? I thought I had all of my flowers."

She came through the back door and onto the porch, where she peered over the back railing. "Yes, see, there. There they are. Three flats. That's what I bought." She pointed to the flowers on the ground below.

"I don't know, ma'am. I just deliver where they tell me to."

"Well, I know what I bought and I know what I paid for. You'll have to take them back."

"Are you sure? They were pretty sure these went to you." He searched his pocket for the paper on which he'd written her address. "To 1735 Hillcrest. Mrs. West."

"That's me, but the flowers are not mine. I bought those three flats this morning, and the only reason I had them delivered was I bought some mulch, too, and couldn't fit it into the back of my car. Now, sometimes I do buy a little extra for my neighbor — your prices there at Walsh's are so low, you know — but today, I didn't bother because —" She stopped, deciding she shouldn't say another word. She might be old, but she wasn't stupid.

She'd seen the news, knew that Mara worked for the court system, knew even from past conversations that Mara had had several cases with Judge Styler. After seeing that newscast the night before, she had figured out in a flash why Mara had been whisked away by that good-looking Aidan fellow.

She could put two and two together and get four every time.

Of course, none of this was the business of the delivery man from Walsh's Nursery.

"I didn't bother because she's finished planting for the season," she told him. "In any event, those flowers are not mine. You're going to have to take them back."

"Sure thing." He started to lift the first flat, then pretended to notice the police presence next door.

"Say, what's going on? They have a robbery over there?"

"No, no, we've never had a robbery in this neighborhood."

"Then what's with the cops?"

"I don't know." She shrugged. "Maybe a problem with her alarm system."

She bent over to pick up the second flat of flowers, and it occurred to him how very easy it would be to reach down and break her neck. It could be done quietly, discreetly. He wouldn't have to worry that she would remember him later, would be able to describe him. And he could stay in her house, keep an eye on the police. No one would know he was there.

He started to lean forward just slightly.

All he had to do was reach down. . . .

"Let me carry this out to your car for you." She smiled at him as she lifted the flat. "Then let me give you a bottle of water and a little something for your trouble."

"No, no, that's all right, Mrs. West. No need."

"It's not a problem, son."

She set the flat in the trunk of his car and he followed with the second.

"I'll be right back with your water. Can't have too many fluids on a warm day like this one."

He put the third flat into the car, then returned to the yard. She stood on the top of the steps, looking down, holding a quart bottle of water.

"This is the only size I have," she said as she offered it to him.

"This is very kind of you. Thank you." He opened it and took a long drink. He hadn't realized how thirsty he was. "Thank you. It just hit the spot."

He looked around her yard as if admiring her flower beds while he scoped out the yards that bordered hers. "You have a really beautiful garden, Mrs. West."

"Why, thank you. The beds all look best in the late spring, though. You'll have to stop back in about a month."

"Maybe I'll do that."

His eyes rested on the grape arbor and the tangle of vines that ran along the back of her garage. He stared at it for a long minute, remembering . . .

"Son? Are you all right?" she asked, real concern in her voice.

"What? Oh, just the heat, as you said. Guess I didn't realize just how dehydrated I was." He looked back at the arbor and said, "We had one of those, in the house where I grew up."

"And did your mother make jam from the grapes?"

"Actually, she did. Every summer. When I was in high school, I used to pick the ones from the top vines for her. She was a little lady, much like you, and she couldn't reach."

"That was nice of you." Mrs. West nodded. "I wish I'd had a boy like you. My husband and I never did have children."

He wasn't sure she'd have wanted a boy like him, he thought as he finished the bottle of water.

From inside, her phone began to ring.

"Well, you run along and get that phone. I'll take these back and I just won't mention that someone made a mistake. I'm sure Mr. Walsh would be upset if he knew we messed up where such a good customer was concerned."

She reached for the empty water bottle, and he handed it over. "My lips are sealed." She waved and retreated into her house, dropping the bottle into a small trash container that stood near the back door.

For a moment he stood there in the shade cast by the end of the garage, thinking how vaguely familiar the scene was. The vines twisted around the old grape arbor, the colorful flower beds, the crisply painted black shutters on white clapboard. The pots of house plants set outside the back door to catch the late afternoon sun . . .

He closed his eyes, his nostrils recalling the scent of the overripened fruit that clung to the topmost vines at the end of summer.

"Leave them for the birds," she'd tell him. *"We won't be making any more jam this summer."*

And then she'd ask him to sit with her on the back porch, deep in the shade, and watch the blue jays steal those last grapes from the arbor. . . .

He inhaled deeply, wanting to take the scent of it with him. Remembering that time — that only time — when life was good and someone had honestly cared for him and he had almost believed that he could be just like everyone else . . .

The recollection had caught him unaware. He almost never permitted himself to think of those days anymore. There was so much pain, so much he'd had to leave behind. . . .

Silently he saluted Mrs. West.

He whistled on his way to the car, glad that he hadn't broken her neck when he had the chance.

Back in his room, he sat on the bed, the remnants of his dinner in a bag on the desk. His mind was too busy to watch television, and it was too early for sleep. He had figured out what he needed to do — he needed to get inside the house of the M. Douglas who lived next door to Mrs. West and do what had to be done. How to get the police to vacate the premises so that he could take care of business?

When it came to him, the solution was so simple he was almost embarrassed that it had taken him so long to figure it out. He dressed quickly and left the room, heading for a bar across town he'd gone to one night after work with one of the kitchen crew. The clientele had been a questionable crowd — most of the friends of his friend seemed more than a little shady — and that was just what the doctor ordered for the job at hand.

He entered the bar through the back door from the parking lot, and stood for a long moment looking around the room. Three or four tired-looking couples sat at tables here and there along one side, and two men were playing a loud game of pool at a table that had clearly seen better days. Most of the bar stools were filled. He studied the patrons sitting at the bar for a while before walking through the thick veil of cigarette smoke to take a place beside a short balding man wearing a shabby blue sweater and dirty jeans.

"Say, aren't you Carl's friend?" Channing slid onto the bar stool, the seat of which had once been red leather but now was worn down in places to the tan backing. "Give me a minute, I'll remember your name."

Not bothering to turn his head, the man

shook his head. "Don't have no friend named Carl."

"Sure you do. Wait, now, it'll come to me." Channing signaled to the bartender. "I'll have a draft. And pour another one for my friend here."

"Maybe I do remember a Carl. He stay in one of the shelters?" The man turned his attention to the newcomer. Anyone who was willing to buy him a beer, well, it was worth a little white lie.

"Yeah. You seen him lately?"

"No. I ain't been up to the shelters in a while."

"Where you been staying?"

"Got a room over on Twenty-third Street. Just till I get on my feet, you know how it is."

"I sure do."

"What you say your name was?" the man asked as the bartender delivered their beers and turned to ring up the sale from the twenty Channing had laid on the bar.

"Calvin," Channing told him, taking his cue from the label on the back of the bartender's jeans.

"Right, right, I remember now." The man sipped at his beer. "So what have you been up to since I last seen you, Calvin?"

"Well, a little of this, a little of that. Moved last weekend — that was a bitch. Had to, though. The wife kicked me out, didn't have much choice."

"Say, I'm sorry to hear that."

"Yeah, it's really been hard on me." Channing caught the bartender's eye. "Can I have a shot here? And one for my friend."

"Say, thanks, Calvin."

"Hey, don't mention it. I hate to drink alone."

"I know what you mean."

The bartender served the shots, and Channing's new buddy raised his glass. "To you, Calvin."

"And to you . . . damn, but I can't remember your name."

"Tommy Mulholland."

"Of course. Tommy Mulholland. I did know that." Channing tipped the shot glass in Tommy's direction. "Here's to better days for both of us, eh?"

Tommy happily downed the shot, knowing instinctively that if he played his cards right with his generous friend, there'd be another — and a few more beers — before the night was over.

"Yeah, the wife wanted me out." Channing shook his head slowly. "And the thing of it is, I know we could have worked things out. We were this close, you know?"

"What happened? 'Nother guy moving in?"

"Worse." Channing made a sour face. "Her mother."

"Oh, boy." Mulholland nodded knowingly. "I know all about that."

"Woman is miserable in her own life, she has to ruin everyone else's." Channing forced a tear to form. "And it's too late, you know what I mean? She's got Lisa — that's my wife — convinced that she's better off without me."

"Jeez, that's tough, Calvin."

Channing waved to the bartender to refill Mulholland's glass.

"Another round of shots, gentlemen?" the bartender asked.

"Sure, sure." Channing nodded.

"Thanks, Cal. 'Preciate it." Mulholland threw back the shot.

"I wish I could —"

"You wish you could what, buddy?" Mulholland draped a friendly arm around Channing's shoulder.

"Aw, it's stupid."

"What's that?"

"I just wish I could do something to sort of get back at her."

"Your wife?"

"My mother-in-law. I know it's dumb, it's childish. But I just wish I could do something that would . . . shit, even just something that would scare her bad, you know?"

"Don't blame you." Mulholland nodded. "No one would blame you."

"I'd pay someone to do it, you know, not to hurt her, but maybe just to do something that would give her a scare."

"Like what are you thinking?"

"Like . . . oh, I don't know, maybe just break into her house and make some noise. Just to scare her into thinking that something bad was going to happen to her."

Mulholland started to laugh. "That'd be really funny, you know?"

Channing joined in the laughter. "Yeah, it's harmless, but still, I'd love to see the look on her face when she first hears the noise. Just try to picture it. First she won't be sure she's really hearing anything, that maybe it isn't just her imagination. She'll keep listening, and then she'll hear a little something more. . . . Scare the shit out of her, that's what it would do. She'd be thinking there's some bad dude in her house."

"Calvin, you sure you ain't a writer? You got some imagination."

"Oh, I've thought about it often enough. What to do that could scare her, I mean. Not hurt her — I'd never hurt nobody, even her." Channing took a long, slow sip of beer. "Man, I'd pay a hundred bucks, I could get someone to do that for me."

"A hundred bucks just to scare an old lady?"

"Yeah. Definitely. Be worth every penny."

"Why don't you do it yourself?"

"Man, I'd be the first person she'd accuse. But if I was someplace else at the time — like here, for instance, in plain view of the bartender — well, then, she couldn't very well blame me, could she?"

"Yeah, yeah. That's good, Calvin. Smart."

"Yeah, I thought so. And I'm gonna do it. I'm gonna find someone and I'm gonna pay 'em —" Channing dug his hand into his pocket and pulled out a roll of bills. He pretended to count them. "— one hundred dollars. I got it right here. Bet one of those boys back there at the pool table would jump at the chance."

A dim light went on behind Mulholland's dull brown eyes. "Hey, Calvin, you know what? You been a buddy to me tonight. I'll do it."

"Are you serious? You'd do that for me?"

"Sure, man. Sure." Mulholland's eyes never left the roll of bills that Channing held in his hand. "But what if she calls 911?"

"You don't need to worry about that. See, what you do is you pick the lock on the back door. The lock is loose anyway — she's too cheap to get a new one. Then you go inside. Knock a few things over, make a little noise. Then you go right out the back door, leave it open. She won't find anyone when she comes looking, but the back door will be open and she'll know that someone was there. She will be scared shitless, I'm telling you, just thinking about some stranger creeping around in her house."

"She live alone? I mean, no dogs or nothin'?"

"No. She's alone."

"Well, sure, what the hell. Why not? Where's she live?"

"At 2232 Oak Avenue."

251

"Oak? That's just about three blocks down from here, over a block . . ." Mulholland began to think about the logistics. "Well, hell, I could walk over there, do this little favor for you, be back here on this stool by midnight."

"With another shot lined up waiting for you and a hundred dollars in your pocket."

"She turn in early?"

"It's going on eleven. She's been in bed for about an hour already."

"What if someone sees me?"

"There's an alley that runs behind the houses. You can go right through the back-yard."

"How do I know you'll be here when I get back?" Mulholland paused to consider this possibility.

"How do I know you won't just be going home from here?" Channing's eyes narrowed, then he smiled. "Here, you want the hundred now?"

"Nah, we're buddies. Payment on delivery, as my old man used to say." Mulholland leaned over and said in a low voice, "And don't you worry. I'll give the old lady a scare she'll never forget."

"I'm counting on it, Tommy." Channing slapped him on the back. "I'm counting on it."

Less than three minutes after Tommy Mulholland left the bar by the front door, Curtis Channing slipped out the back. He

252

drove slowly, taking side streets, watching for Mulholland. One block away from Oak, Channing spotted him. He pulled over to one side of the road and watched his new best friend disappear into the poorly lit alley where he would, undoubtedly, walk right into the arms of the police. Satisfied that within less than fifteen minutes, most of the Lyndon Police Department would be converging on the home of M. T. Douglas — Martha Teresa Douglas, he'd learned in his surveillence — he smiled and took off in the direction of Hillcrest.

Leaving his car near the entrance to the college, Channing walked down Bellevue, the street that ran directly behind Hillcrest. He counted the houses until he found the one that, earlier in the day, he'd figured out backed up to Mrs. West's. Keeping to the shadows, he sought the silhouette of the grape arbor and, finding it, crawled through a row of hedges until he reached Mrs. West's garage. He studied the house and was relieved to find that no lights were on. He'd have hated it if the old woman had heard him and come outside to investigate. He really would not want to hurt her.

But he'd been lucky so far.

He lay flat on his stomach and watched the house next door. One police officer sat in his car on the opposite side of the street. Two others stood near the back gate, talking softly.

He wondered how long before they'd get the

call that there'd been an attempted break-in at the home of an M. Douglas across town. He glanced at his watch. Given the fact that the house on Oak was still under police watch, it shouldn't be more than another few minutes before his good buddy Tommy Mulholland would be facedown in the dirt, a gun to his head and his wrists neatly cuffed.

There. Here we go. . . .

The door of the patrol car across the street swung open suddenly, and the young officer ran toward the house.

"Rhodes! Walker! We got a break-in at one of the other houses. All units respond."

"But I thought this one was the —" The officer nearest the gate pointed to the Douglas house.

"Apparently our perp hasn't figured that out. Let's go."

"Shouldn't one of us stay?"

"Why? The guy's already made his move. They're calling in all units."

The officer closest to the gate muttered something under his breath as he hurried to his patrol car. Within seconds, all three patrol cars were speeding down Hillcrest.

Channing crouched in the dark, watching the taillights of the last of the cars disappear down the street.

And knew immediately that she wasn't there.

This may be the right house, his M. Douglas's house, but if she had actually been inside, they'd have left at least one officer there with her.

Might as well make the most of the opportunity to get to know her a little better. Who knew when he'd have a chance like this again, or how long it would take for Mulholland to convince the police that he'd been set up?

Keeping to the darkened area around the garage, Channing made his way to the house and through the unlatched gate. The lock on the French doors was new, but it was still easy pickings for someone with his skill. He slipped on thin rubber gloves, went to work, then opened the door and stepped quickly inside. He stood for a moment to get his bearings before proceeding deeper into the house. A hallway, a laundry room. Den. Living room. Dining room into the kitchen that was, unexpectedly, at the front of the house.

He moved quietly, just in case he'd been wrong and someone was here. Maybe not her, but someone else. He'd learned the hard way the perils of taking anything for granted. It would be stupid for the police to have left the house unguarded if anyone was there, but on the other hand, it had been pretty stupid for them to have three cars parked in plain sight here, when all the others had only one.

He crept up the stairs to the second floor, fingering the handle of the knife that hung from the scabbard at his waist, his breath coming a little faster with each step forward.

There were four doors, and he peeked into the first as he passed. A room with a double bed, a chair, a dresser. Didn't look occupied, like maybe it was the spare room.

He ducked into the room across the hall.

A child's room.

Channing frowned. He hadn't thought about there being a child, didn't like it that there was.

He did not do children.

He stared at the bed, with its pink spread and mound of stuffed animals on the pillow. Curious, he stepped closer.

Where was the child?

Anywhere but here, apparently. The bed was empty.

He left the room and proceeded straight to the room at the end of the hall. That would have to be the room. The only other being the bathroom, and he'd just passed that.

His excitement building, he pushed open the door, no longer taking pains to be quiet. He went straight to the bed, his hands moving right to where her head would be on the pillow.

Nothing.

He searched the house from top to bottom, just in case, but found that his instincts had been correct. She wasn't here.

Well. He was here, in her house, he told himself. He might as well take advantage of the opportunity.

Let's see what we can find out about Ms. Douglas . . .

256

She drinks a lot of bottled water, he realized as he stared into her refrigerator, *and eats a lot of yogurt.*

Not a lot of food, though. He frowned. *She either expects to be out of town for a while, or else she doesn't eat many meals at home.*

In one of the drawers, he found a stack of menus from local restaurants, but he found nothing else of interest there.

In the living room, next to the sofa, he found a chewed-up tennis ball and a chew bone.

He hadn't known there'd be a dog, either. She must have taken the child and the dog someplace. He hoped she left them there. He didn't want to deal with a child. Or a dog.

He did have his standards.

From the living room he went into the den near the back of the house. He drew the blinds tightly and switched on the small lamp on the desk. A stack of bills stood in a gray metal holder, and he thumbed through them. Department store credit card, American Express, the electric bill, the phone bill.

All addressed to Mara Douglas.

I'll be a son of bitch. He shook his head. *Mara. Not Mary, but Mara.*

He could've sworn that Giordano had said Mary, but hey, the names were that close.

A drawer on the left side of the desk held files, and he scanned the headers. Insurance. Bank statements. Car. Property taxes. Mountain cabin.

Mountain cabin?

Hel-lo . . .

Channing pulled out the file and studied the contents. Mostly tax receipts for a property in a place called Little Falls, Pennsylvania. He folded one and put it into his pocket.

A car door slammed somewhere outside, and he peered out through the blinds. A neighbor's kid coming home from a late night with his buddies. He watched the young man stumble from his car to the front walk.

He turned off the light, headed back out the way he'd come in, and closed the door behind him. He eased through the gate and along Mrs. West's backyard, following the path he'd taken earlier. Within minutes, he was in his car and on his way home, though of course he had to swing as close to Oak as he could get, which wasn't too close at all, since a mass of police cars had blocked off the alley as well as the street. He tried to feel sorry for what had befallen Tommy Mulholland but couldn't feel badly about the outcome.

Channing smiled and began to whistle a happy tune. On his way back to his room, he'd stop at that convenience store on the corner and buy a map of Pennsylvania, see if he could figure out where Little Falls was. He figured that by the time the police realized they'd been had, he'd be halfway there.

Chapter Fourteen

"Well, looks like we'll have a little time to kill," Aidan said as they left Chief Lanigan's office. "Want to grab a bite while we wait? That salad hasn't stayed with me."

"I think you're optimistic if you think we'll hear back from him any time soon." Mara followed him down the hallway to the back door that led to the parking lot behind the police station. "I expect it will take a while to check foster records going back thirty years."

"Well, the county social worker told Lanigan all those records are on microfiche. If we're lucky enough to find the name of the Gibbons boy's foster family —"

"And if they're still alive and still living in the area," she added.

"Right. All that." Aidan unlocked the car doors.

"It's a long shot, you know."

"I know," he said as he slid behind the wheel, moving Spike out of the way as he did so. He handed the dog to Mara. "John Mancini said if the county couldn't come up with the name of the foster parents, he'd send someone down to give them a hand."

"Can he do that?"

"He can find a way to do pretty much anything. He agrees that we're on to something here. We don't know exactly what it is yet, but there's something here, all right."

Mara watched his face as he backed out the car. He looked pleased: pleased with the developments, pleased with himself. She said so.

"I am pleased with myself, I have to admit." He nodded. "It feels damned good to be involved again. To be doing something useful again. It's been a long time, since . . ."

He hesitated, long enough for her to see the shadow move across his face. She wanted to reach out and push it away.

"Aidan, there's a deli across the street." She touched his arm. "Let's get a bite there and take it out to that park we were at this morning."

He looked up at the sky, where dark clouds had begun to gather. "It looks like it's going to rain."

"There was a pavilion there, remember? Maybe there are picnic tables. I'll walk over and pick up something for us to eat if you'll stay here with Spike. I think he's starting to feel abandoned."

"Okay," he said, and drove back into the parking space he'd just left.

"Any requests?"

"I could really go for a roast beef on rye with horseradish, maybe some chips. Anything cold to drink."

"My treat this time." She hopped out of the

car. "I'll be back in a flash."

Angelo's Delicatessen was all but empty when she walked in, the lunch hour long past. She ordered sandwiches from a grandfatherly type who'd been sitting at a small table reading a newspaper. She surveyed the drinks in the cooler before moving to the counter with an iced tea in each hand, then sorted through the selection of chips and wondered which Aidan preferred. Sour cream and onion? Barbecue? Old Bay? Salt and vinegar?

Way too many choices.

She grabbed a bag of plain chips and placed them on the counter next to the drinks.

"You like brownies?" the man asked as he brought the sandwiches to the cash register. "We got some nice brownies — cream cheese or peanut butter. My wife made them. You'll like them."

"Are you Angelo?"

"I am." He nodded and rang up her tab, packing the bag as he went along. He smiled when she added a few brownies to the pile, noting, "You won't be disappointed in these, trust me. You don't think these are the best brownies you ever ate, you come back and tell me and I'll give you back your money."

"You're on." She smiled as she paid him, then gathered up her bag.

She walked back to the car, then slowed her step. Aidan and Spike were in the driver's seat, Spike leaning out the side window, Aidan gazing out the front.

He has a great profile — not classically hand-some, but rugged and solid. He may well be the nicest man I ever met, in spite of his occasional crustiness, she thought as she approached the car. *And very possibly the sexiest . . .*

There was no point in trying to overlook that any longer. She wondered, as she opened the car door, if Dylan had been much like Aidan. She hadn't known Dylan very well, something she now regretted. She'd always thought there'd be plenty of time to get to know Annie's guy. Sadly, she'd been so wrong.

And if she hadn't taken this trip with Aidan, she wouldn't have gotten to know the man beyond that terse facade of his. She liked this Aidan so much more than she'd liked the man who'd moved into her house and invaded her privacy. This man was more relaxed, more easygoing. And, she was beginning to suspect, he might even have a sense of humor.

"Something smells really good." Aidan reached for the bag and held it while she fastened her seat belt. "I didn't realize how hungry I was until I was sitting here, just thinking about food."

"Fortunately, we're not that far from the park," she said as he started the engine. "I didn't realize how hungry I was, either, until I went into that deli and found an amazing array of meats and cheeses —"

"Stop. Not another word about food until after we've eaten."

"Deal. Come here, Spike." She patted her lap, and the dog jumped from Aidan's to hers. She lowered the window so that he could lean out, holding on to the little body as he pushed his face into the air.

They discovered the park was crowded, with several games being played at once. A boys' baseball game was in progress on one field, girls' lacrosse on another, the players glancing at the ever-darkening sky at every deep rumble from the distance. Mara found a picnic table not far from the lacrosse game, and they watched the girls on the field as they ate.

"You ever play?" Aidan nodded in the direction of the game.

"No. I played soccer. You?"

"I played in college, mostly to keep in shape for football. It's a great game, fast, tough. I really liked it." He took a long drink from the bottle of iced tea she'd bought him. "Connor was really good. College All-American. Unfortunately, my dad didn't get the whole lacrosse thing, thought it was a strange game. He thought it was a fad that would pass out of popularity very quickly. Lacrosse and hockey. He never really got either of them."

"Did Dylan play, too?"

"Dylan played baseball, and only baseball. He could have played with the pros." Aidan's eyes flickered slightly.

"I was just thinking how sorry I am that I didn't get to know him as well as I'd have liked to."

He continued to stare at the girls running by, their sticks in the air, yelling to the teammate who cradled the bright yellow ball in the tiny net at the end of her stick.

"I'm sorry," she said at last.

"For what?"

"For . . . I don't know, asking about your brother. I didn't mean to . . ." She struggled with her words.

"It's okay," he told her, his eyes never leaving the game. "I think about him every day. I just haven't had much occasion to talk about him. Except once in a while with Annie."

"I'm sorry," she repeated, because she didn't know what else to say. She understood his sense of loss and wanted to be respectful of it. At the same time, it seemed so much a part of him, it was hard to ignore.

They watched the rest of the game in silence, the red team winning handily over the white. Cars loaded up with grinning girls and equipment, and soon everyone had departed except a young boy who chased a big sheepdog-type beast across the field. Spike whined, agitated, wanting to join in the chase. Aidan got off the bench and picked up the dog.

"Soon as they leave, we'll play fetch, okay, Spike?" He sat back down on the bench next to

Mara, the dog on his lap. "What made you think of Dylan?"

"What?"

"Before. You said you were thinking about Dylan."

"I was wondering if he was anything like you."

He shook his head. "Dylan was the golden boy. The best of us three. The best student, the best athlete. The best all around."

He spoke easily, without envy.

"He was probably the best guy I ever knew. I was always in awe of him, for as long as I can remember. He was my idol." He took a deep breath, then turned to look at her. "I love Connor — always will — but he's six years older than me, and I never related to him the way I did Dylan."

"What was the difference in your ages?"

"Dylan was two years older than me. We shared a lot, growing up." His smile held a touch of sadness. "More than just a room."

"Are you and Connor close?"

"In our way, we are. He keeps pretty busy. It seems they always have him running off some-place." He smiled and shrugged. "We've never known exactly where he goes or what he does when he gets there. He's up a few levels from the rest of us, I'd guess. A real mystery man."

"What Annie calls a super-agent?"

He laughed, and the solemn moment broke and faded. "I guess. I know there are a few units that exist almost as separate entities. The government doesn't always acknowledge them, but they're there, and the rest of us all know it. Since Connor never talks about his work, Dylan and I always suspected he was part of that, but you don't ask."

"I'd ask. If it was Annie, my curiosity would get the better of me and I'd have to ask."

Spooked apparently by the thunder that was moving closer, the boy and the big floppy dog left the field.

"Here's our chance, boy. Let's go find a nice stick." Aidan put a hand on Mara's shoulder and gave it a gentle squeeze. "You're welcome to play, too. But I gotta warn you. He's not one to give up the stick easily."

"He's all yours." Mara smiled. "You two go right ahead."

Aidan found a stick that he thought would make a good fetch stick, but Spike had already found one he liked better, so they used it.

Mara gathered up the trash from the deli and deposited it in one of the large containers at the edge of the pavilion, then returned to the table and sat on it, to better view the man who tossed the stick into the air and the dog who leapt to catch it. Then the chase began, Spike running, slowing to let Aidan almost catch up before racing off with the stick again. For Aidan, it was painfully slow running, granted, but it was running all the same, and she wondered how uncomfortable that leg must be, how sore that hip. When Aidan gave up the chase and stood in one spot, Spike brought the stick to him and dropped it at his feet. Aidan picked it up and threw it again, and the game resumed.

They didn't play long, but they had played hard, and it wasn't long before Aidan returned to the pavilion with Spike trotting along behind him, the cherished stick still in the dog's mouth. Lightning flashed ominously nearby. Winded, Aidan sat next to Mara on the table-top.

"Out of shape," he said. "I started working out again, but I have a long way to go. I took a lot of time off. Too much time, I guess."

"You mean after the accident?"

His face froze. "It wasn't an accident, Mara."

"Then what would you call it?" she asked softly.

"A major fuck-up. And I'm the one who fucked up."

"I guess you knew that those men — the ones who shot at you and Dylan — I guess you knew that they were there, behind you —"

"Don't." He held up a hand as if to ward off her words. "Don't, because you don't know what you're talking about."

"I know what Annie told me, Aidan," she said, her voice still low.

"And what was that?"

"That you and Dylan were to go to a ware-house to meet with some guys the Bureau had

267

been watching for months and who thought you were major drug suppliers. That you were sent around to a side door, and as soon as you did, cars pulled up and blocked off the entrance to the alley. That someone started shooting and that by the time the other agents in the area arrived, you and Dylan were both badly shot up."

"I was supposed to be watching his back."

She reached up and put her hand on the back of his head, as if feeling around.

"What are you doing?" he asked.

"Looking for the eyes you must have in the back of your head."

"Not funny."

"Not trying to be. How could you have seen what was behind you? Wasn't someone else supposed to be watching you two? Annie said that someone was supposed to be in the building across the alley, watching out for you both." Her hand lingered on the nape of his neck. "Who was supposed to be watching your back, Aidan?"

"It all happened too fast. They didn't have enough time to react."

"If you can be that forgiving of them — whoever they are — why can't you be as forgiving of yourself?"

She didn't wait for an answer, knew there wouldn't be one. She called Spike, and he followed her to the car, where she filled his water dish from a bottle of spring water and his food dish with dry food from a bag, setting both bowls on the ground. She sat on the car seat, watching the dog eat, occasionally glancing over at the pavilion where Aidan still sat on the table, his feet on the bench below, his elbows resting on his knees, staring straight ahead.

They stayed in their places as the storm closed in and the afternoon turned to early evening, but the rain held off. To give Aidan some space, Mara took Spike on a leisurely walk on the bike path that wound around the park. The first fat drops of rain began to fall and spatter against the asphalt as they were returning to the pavilion.

"Did you hear from Chief Lanigan while we were gone?" she asked.

"No."

"I wonder if he'll find them, the people who took in Joanie Gibbons's little boy."

"He'll find them. It just may take a little time. Let's go," he said, shaking his head. "Sometimes the most obvious is right under your nose. . . ."

"Come on, Spike," she called to the dog, who'd drifted away, following a scent. He trotted back as she was spilling the remaining water in the bowl onto the ground. She gathered up the bowls and carried them to the car, Spike dancing at her heels.

Aidan opened the door for her, but before she could get in, he pulled her to him. He touched the side of her face, smoothed back

269

her hair, and rubbed his thumb slowly over her bottom lip as if he were fixated on it.

"You know, when I told Annie I'd keep her sister company, it was the last thing in the world I wanted to do," he told her softly. "But I have to admit, I definitely got the best of the bargain."

He lowered his mouth to hers and kissed her, tentatively at first, then deeper, as if he meant it. Mara rose up on her toes slightly, kissing him back and meaning it, shifting closer to him without even realizing that she'd moved. It seemed the most natural thing in the world to be doing at that moment, standing in the rain and kissing Aidan, and hoping he'd kiss her again. He did.

He drew away from her, looking down into her eyes, as if debating with himself. He leaned down and kissed her one more time, a promise of something more, then tucked her into the car.

"Let's go see what our friend Tanner has to say." He slammed the car door and walked around to the driver's side, his head buzzing, wondering what had possessed him to do what he'd done, but damned glad that he had.

The lights were on in one room of Tanner's house, but they found the old man sitting on his porch in the same chair they'd left him in that morning, watching the last of the storm blow over.

"Hey!" he called to them as they walked up the path. "Whatcha find out?"

"What makes you think we found out anything?" Aidan grinned and climbed the steps, hand in hand with Mara.

"You're back. You said you'd come back if you found out anything. Here you are." He rocked a little faster, anticipating something of interest. "Take a seat. Tell me what you know."

Aidan filled him in on their visit with Al Unger.

"So, you saw him, eh?" The rocking slowed. "How's he look, old Albert?"

"He looked tired. Worn out," Aidan said, then added, "Of course, he could have looked like that before the murder, too."

Tanner shook his head. "He was a strong enough man back then. Prison does that other to you — makes you weary of being a man." He looked at Mara and added, "That's just from personal observation, not personal experience, you understand. But every man I ever knew who went into prison for any substantial amount of time came out looking like half his old self. Expect Unger would be the same. Shame about him was he wasn't a violent man by nature, had no priors for anything that ever hurt anyone. She just brought out the worst in him, I guess. Some women do that."

"He mentioned that Joanie Gibbons had had a son."

"Yeah, poor kid." Tanner shook his head

271

slowly. "I never saw him at all, you know? Not at the house. Saw him later. They brought him down to the station — didn't know what else to do with him. He was hiding in that closet all the time his mother was being killed. Stayed in that closet, till someone found him after the body was removed and the premises were being searched."

The information was staggering. Aidan didn't dare look at Mara. Who could imagine what such horror could do to a young mind? "Unger said the little boy went into foster care."

"Seems that would be right." Tanner nodded.

"You wouldn't happen to remember where he went or with whom, would you?" Aidan asked. "Who the foster family was?"

"Seems to me it was someone — a couple, that is — out near Clark Road somewhere." He stopped rocking altogether, his brows knitting close together. "Damn. What was their name?"

Tanner stared out at the lake, where, the clouds having lifted, moonlight spread quietly across the surface of the water.

"Give me a bit. It'll come to me. . . ." Chief Tanner absently scratched behind the ear of whichever of his dogs sat next to him. "Sooner or later, it'll come. . . ."

He began to rock silently, his hand still on the dog's head.

"If I'd known we'd have been sitting here to-night, with this open sky overhead, I'd have brought a telescope," Aidan said.

"You like that?" Tanner asked. "Star watching?"

"Sure."

"Never had no time for it." Tanner looked out at the sky beyond the porch roof. "Though sometimes now I think about it. What's out there. Who, maybe." He turned to Aidan. "You think there's anyone out there?"

"Can't think of any reason why there wouldn't be." Aidan's chair rocked in concert with Tanner's. "I think it's a little arrogant to believe that out of all that's out there in space, this planet would be the only one to have intelligent life."

He paused, then added, "Assuming that you believe mankind represents intelligent life . . ."

Tanner snorted. "Don't start me there, boy. I've seen too much in my day. I've fought in wars and I've spent fifty good years in law enforcement. You don't want to get into a debate with me on what represents intelligent life."

Aidan laughed softly. "Tell you what, Chief Tanner. If I get out this way again, I'll be sure to bring my telescope. You can take a good look around the universe and tell me what you think."

"Fair enough." He nodded, visibly pleased. "I'll hold you to that, you ever get back out this way."

Some night creature screamed from across

the lake, and the dogs stirred restlessly.

"Do you think we should start back to Lake Grove? We're going to have to look for a place to stay tonight," Mara asked. She'd been mostly quiet up until now, letting the old, retired chief of police and the young FBI agent share their thoughts. She'd felt apart from them, but she was all right with that. She had never walked in their world.

"Good point." Reluctantly, Aidan stopped rocking. He'd been soothed by it. "There was that motel on the highway driving in."

"You're not going to be staying in a place like that," Tanner said.

"Why not?"

"The place has a reputation — well earned, I might add — as a —" He glanced at Mara. "A trysting place."

In the dark, Mara smiled.

"Not suitable for the young lady," he continued. "Or for a man of the law, for that matter."

"I see." Aidan nodded and tried to hide his amusement. "Perhaps you could recommend someplace else?"

"Catherine Paisley's place is being repainted, I heard. Doubt she's open yet."

"Once we start driving, we'll find something," Aidan assured Mara.

"Or you could stay here," Tanner offered. "I only have one spare room, but if you're bunking together —"

"No," Mara and Aidan said simultaneously. "We're not."

"Oh. Sorry. I just thought . . . ." Tanner grinned sheepishly. "Well, then, Miss Mara here can have the spare room, and you, sir, may sleep on the sofa, if you don't mind."

"I wouldn't mind." Aidan turned to Mara. "What do you think? Shall we take Chief Tanner up on his generous offer?"

"This is very kind of you, and not at all expected. Are you sure you want us invading your solitude?"

"Missy, I have solitude three hundred and sixty-five nights each year. A little company now and then does a man good."

"Then I'd love to stay. Thank you very much for your offer."

"I'll go in and get your linens and things," Tanner said as he stood. "You'll have to make up your own bed . . . and the little dog should probably stay upstairs with you."

Tanner stopped on his way to the door and asked, "He is housebroken, isn't he?"

"Oh, yes." Mara patted Aidan on the arm. "So's the dog."

"Very funny," Aidan said from the corner of his mouth.

Chief Tanner chuckled and disappeared into the house.

Lights went on in several rooms as he walked through the downstairs.

"This really is sweet of him," Mara said.

"It is." Aidan reached over and took Mara's hand. "Nice and peaceful here, isn't it?"

"Um-hmmm." She nodded.

"No wonder Tanner doesn't want a telephone out here. I don't think I'd want the bother either, in a place like this. You could get addicted to it, you know?" He closed his eyes, holding her hand in the dark, feeling the silence around him. He felt warm, quieted inside for the first time in almost a year.

The door opened and the chief stuck his head out. "Aidan, I left bedding on the sofa for you, and bedding on the steps going upstairs for the lady. There's only one room; you can't miss it. Now, I'm going to be turning in soon, but you're free to relax out here for a spell if you want. Just bring the dogs in with you, if you don't mind. I never leave them out at night."

"Thanks, Chief. I'll bring them in," Aidan told him.

"Actually," Mara said, glancing at her watch, "I think I'm ready to turn in, too. It's been a really, really long day."

She squeezed Aidan's hand. "You must be exhausted after all the driving you did, going straight through the night."

"I think it is starting to catch up with me," he admitted.

He brought her hand to his lips, held it there for a long minute before releasing it.

"Sweet dreams, Mara."

"You too, Aidan." She looked about her for Spike and found him near Aidan's feet. "Come on, Spike. Time to turn in."

Roused from sleep, the little dog rose slowly, then followed her to the door.

"Would you rather I sat here with you for a while?" she asked uncertainly from the doorway.

"No, no. I'll be going in, in just a few. You go on to bed."

"Okay, then. I'll see you in the morning."

The screen door closed behind her, and he sat motionless in the chair, listening to the dark world of night unfold around him. A few moments later, he began to rock slowly, as the old man had done, trying the rhythm on for size. It was a comfortable fit, and he continued to rock just so for close to a half hour, his mind filled with images that flashed past at a breathtaking speed. He closed his eyes and gave in to the visions, as he always did.

A warehouse loomed before him, dark on dark. Too late, the sound of footsteps behind him, the sound of tires squealing and doors slamming. A shout from someplace, those first bullets whizzing past his head. Him ducking to avoid their path, calling for Dylan, and getting no response.

Who was supposed to be watching your back? Mara had asked.

His mind went back to the others, the ones who had been in the building opposite the warehouse that night, the ones whose job it had been to cover him and Dylan. Where had they been when the cars had sped into the alley, when the shots had ripped through the night? Where had they been?

He'd understood how quickly it had all happened, offered understanding and excuses to them, but none to himself.

If you can be that forgiving of them, why can't you be as forgiving of yourself?

He thought, *Because Dylan was my flesh and blood, not theirs. My hero. My idol. My brother . . .*

For the first time in months, when the sadness came and washed over him, it was without the soul-searing guilt that generally accompanied it. He wasn't sure why it spared him that night, but he was grateful. He eased deeper into the chair, feeling just a little lighter than he had in a long, long time.

Overhead, clouds began to shift across the moon, changing shape as they drifted. An owl called faintly, his whoooooooooooooooo a muffled echo in the night. At the edge of the lake, cattails, tall and thin, stirred along the bank, sending their hushed whispers on the breeze.

Aidan closed his eyes and felt peace, just ever so tentatively, settle around him. Not enough to chase away all the demons, but for tonight it was enough.

He wished Mara had stayed for a while. He wanted to kiss her again. Bringing her along had done more than just keep her out of harm's way. Her company had been good for him. *She* was good for him. He sat on the porch and thought about her for a long time.

From somewhere inside, a clock struck midnight, long past the time for sleep. He pushed himself from the chair and called softly to Manny, Moe, and Jack. The three dogs followed him into the house as if they'd been doing so for years, then plunked in their respective places around the large front room as Aidan prepared the sofa.

Later, after he'd been sleeping for some hours, he awoke to find Chief Tanner seated in one of the high-back wing chairs near the fireplace.

"Their name was Channing," the chief said when he sensed that Aidan had awakened. "Marshall and Claire Channing. They were the ones who took the boy in."

Chapter Fifteen

The road to Little Falls had taken Channing up the Northeast Extension of the Pennsylvania Turnpike, then dumped him just this side of I-80 in search of a two-lane road that wound through state game land.

Why in the world anyone would want to own property up in this neck of the woods — with a cabin or otherwise — was beyond him. The forests here were deep, like those in fairy tales, dense and rising tall on both sides of the road. Some might call it scenic. He thought it was downright creepy.

He stopped at an old general store outside some little town whose name he never did figure out, and bought staples — milk, bread, eggs, bacon, peanut butter — then threw in a couple of Hershey's bars to appease his sweet tooth. On his way to the register he saw a box of wooden toothpicks — the flat old-fashioned kind he preferred — and he tossed those onto the counter along with the box of tea bags he held in the crook of his arm.

A small man of indeterminable age shuffled from the office to the counter, smiling at Channing as he did so.

"Son's on vacation with his family," the man explained. "Can't get him back here soon enough to suit me. Hate dealing with these vendors online, you know what I mean?" He shook his head. "Bring back the days when the suppliers came right on into the store and showed you what they had and you bought what you needed and they took away what you didn't." The man shook his head again. "Ah, well. Whatcha gonna do?" He began to ring up Channing's order somewhat absently.

Channing paid for his purchases and headed back through the door. A couple in their mid-fifties nodded and held the door for him as he went to the car. He got behind the wheel and took the map out, trying to get his bearings.

It was almost impossible to figure out exactly where he was.

A few minutes later, the couple he'd passed in the doorway emerged from the store.

Seeing Channing studying the map, the man called to him, "Where you headed? Need some help there?"

Hesitating to broadcast his destination, lest there be cause in the days to come for them to recall having met him, Channing glanced at the map and gave the name of a town that appeared to be several miles beyond Little Falls.

"Oh, you want to go through Darien and Little Falls, then about eight miles north on Route 231."

"I'm just not sure how to get there from here," Channing said.

"Let me see that map." The man walked to

the car and peered in. "Oh, that's not right." He shook his head. "This must be an old map. Look, what you want to do is to go up here" — he pointed past the general store — "till you come to a fork in the road. Take the left fork and just go straight till you come to Little Falls. It's not marked well. You blink and you'll miss it."

Channing's head was beginning to ache. How to find the road mentioned on the tax bill without coming right out and asking for directions specifically to that spot? He knew how this could play out. Sooner or later, the police would start to believe Mulholland's story. After that, they'd call in a compositor who'd do a sketch, and if it was good enough, there were people who would recognize him. People he worked with. People in the rooming house.

Maybe even this couple right here could remember him, might recall that he'd asked for directions to Mara's road.

He needed to be careful, but he needed directions if he was ever to find Mara's cabin.

"I was here once before," he said casually. "Seems to me I went out on a road called Poor House Road or something like that."

"You mean Poor Farm Road? No, no, that road dead-ends about a mile or so back into the woods, and there are only one or two houses back there." The man shook his head. "No, you want to take Little Falls Road straight on through —"

"Oh, right. Right. I remember now. Straight through Little Falls . . ." Channing nodded.

"You ever seen the falls out there?" the man asked.

"No, I've only passed through," Channing told him, anxious to be on his way, knowing that the more time he spent in conversation with them, the more likely they were to remember him.

"You get a chance, you don't want to miss those falls. There's a clearing right after the turn for Poor Farm Road. You park there and walk on back maybe three-quarters of a mile or so. Real pretty this time of year."

"Thanks. I might just do that." Channing put the car into reverse, but the man didn't take the hint.

"Think nothing of it. Now, you do any hiking, you take care of the bears. Lots of caves out there, might be cubs in some of them. Mountain lions been sighted out there too this past week."

"Thanks for the tip." Channing waved and backed the car out of the small parking lot.

Too much chatter, he berated himself. Way too much chatter. Chances were they would remember him if the newscasts carried his picture at some time in the coming week or so. Would they broadcast that story way up here? he wondered.

Why would they? Who would think to look up here for him? No one knew he'd be coming this way. Oh, sure, the story might make the evening news, but probably not the sketch, if they did one. Wouldn't they only show the sketch in the general area where they would expect him to be? That's what the police had done in Wyoming last year, where he'd been for a few months.

He smiled at the memory. He'd enjoyed Wyoming. Nothing like those wide open spaces to make a man feel free.

Well, he wasn't going to waste time worrying about it.

He'd gambled that Mara — he still couldn't get over the name, still wanted to think of her as Mary — had taken refuge up here at this mountain cabin, and figured that this was his best bet to find her. And if she wasn't here, well, at least he had a place to hide out for a time while he collected his thoughts. He wanted to finish what he'd started, wanted to hold true to his word, do Giordano's deeds, but not at the expense of his own neck. He'd do what he could — do his best — but he didn't want to be stupid about it. He couldn't be anywhere near Lyndon — anywhere near the Philadelphia area, for that matter — when the police started to catch on.

Poor Farm Road was easy enough to find, and he turned onto the narrow dirt road and followed it slowly. He passed one small cabin that sat half an acre off the road. It looked to be no more than a four-room shack, though he noted that electric lines did extend off the main road to it. He stopped the car and studied the tiny structure for a time. It just didn't feel right for some reason. He kept going until he was almost to the dead end. A contemporary two-story log home rose off to his left. Steps rose from the ground level to the second-story deck that wrapped around two sides of the house and gave a view out over the hills that rose gently beyond a slight ridge. There were lots of windows, lots of glass.

This is it. This is her place.

He turned the car around, looking for some sign of life, but there was none. He cut the engine and opened the door, stepped out of the car and stood stock still, listening. Nothing but the occasional birdsong from the thicket across the road. Not another sound.

Tentatively he walked across the road to the house and studied it. The ground level appeared to be mostly garage. He rubbed at the dusty glass of one windowpane with the sleeve of his shirt and peered inside. Sleds, a toboggan, and several pairs of skis and snowshoes were hanging on the walls. A workbench ran along the inner wall, and he noted a variety of garden tools — pruning shears, a few shovels, a wheelbarrow. But no car.

He turned back to the road and checked the dirt for tire marks. He found none but his own.

If she was coming here, she's yet to arrive, he thought.

He went up the steps, taking care to make as little noise as possible, just in case. He tried to look through the windows, but the drapes inside had been closed. He tried the door, but of course it was locked. Dead bolt. He could pop it, but if she showed up later, it would be a dead giveaway that someone had been here. He went back to the garage and looked for a way in.

He found it. A small door in the back wall was locked, but not securely enough to keep out someone with his talents. It was embarrassingly easy for him to gain entry to the garage and, from there, easier still to pick the lock on the door that led into the house.

A flight of stairs took him into a service area that held a washer and dryer and a small pantry. A hall led into a galley-type kitchen that opened onto a great room where a sectional sofa wrapped in front of a stone fireplace that took up all of one wall. A farmhouse-style table with six chairs stood along the windows across the back, and he stood there for a moment and gazed out at the spectacular view.

Nice, he thought, nodding to himself. *Very, very nice.*

Another hall led to bedrooms — he counted three, one of which had its own bath — and several large closets that held linens — bedding and towels and such — packed in clear plastic bags. Missy Mara was apparently quite organized. But her house in Lyndon hadn't appeared to be quite as neat as this place, he thought as he looked around, and he wondered for the first time if possibly he'd made a mistake. He began to look for something that had a name on it. In a basket of magazines near the fireplace, he found a year-old issue of *Psychology Today*. The name on the label was Anne Marie McCall.

Shit. It wasn't her place after all. Damn. Hers must have been that tiny place closer to the main road. Funny, that place just hadn't looked right, but there you go. That's what happened when you made assumptions. Well, he'd go down there and scope it out, but he'd come back here to sleep the night. Those beds looked pretty comfortable, and he doubted anyone would be coming along anytime soon. Maybe she was on her way; maybe she wasn't coming here at all. But he had a nice place — a really nice place — to stay in for a while, and that was okay, too.

He continued to look around the house, and downstairs found behind the garage another room, a den with an old leather chair and a worn leather sofa and lots of bookshelves on the walls. He turned on the overhead light, then whistled long and low.

"Holy shit, would you look at that?"

Gun racks covered one whole wall, from roughly shoulder height to the ceiling. He went straight to them, his eyes glancing from one shelf to the other. Mostly rifles, some old.

Some very old, he realized. He lifted one with a fancy handle and held it, sighted it.

"Damn, you're a beauty, aren't you? Bet you're worth a pretty penny, too, with all that fancy carving. . . ."

He returned it respectfully to the brackets that held it and inspected each firearm on the racks until he'd seen them all.

He knew one thing. However long he stayed, he'd be taking as many of those guns with him as he could fit in his car.

His stomach reminded him that he hadn't eaten in hours. He'd bring in his groceries and make himself a sandwich. He started to the door, but a book on the shelf nearest him caught his eye. *An Encyclopedia of Firearms: 1800–1899.* He took it with him and snapped off the light, pulling the door closed tightly behind him.

He flipped through the pages of the book as he ate at the table in the great room, then took it with him to the sofa, where he sat and read for an hour or so. He began to feel sleepy and just a little chilled, now that the day had begun to cloud up. He'd seen a stack of firewood outside but was afraid that smoke from the chimney might be noticed. He'd have to make do. One of the closets had several shelves of blankets, and he sorted through them until he found a knitted afghan. He took it and a pillow from one of the beds and made himself cozy on the sofa. He leaned back against the pillow and decided he didn't care if he was in the wrong house. He was relaxed and comfortable and warm. He had this nice book about guns to read, and he could probably stay right here for a while.

He liked this place. He liked it a lot. He hoped Anne Marie McCall wouldn't be coming around anytime soon. He'd hate to have to hurt her, after she'd provided him with such perfect shelter.

He felt his eyes closing, but he forced himself to sit up, remembering the car. He'd have to move it. Just in case someone came along and stopped to investigate. He got up and unlocked the front door, stepped out onto the deck. He took in a deep breath of mountain air and exhaled slowly.

Oh, yes, this was the life.

He drove back down Poor Farm Road, looking for a place to leave the car where it wouldn't be seen, but found nothing that suited. He turned the car around, thinking perhaps he should just leave it in the garage, when he drove past the little log cabin. He stepped on the brake, pausing, then pulled in front of the cabin and stopped again. Getting out, he walked up to the cabin and looked around. No one was there, and from all appearances, no one had been there in quite some time. He drove the car to the rear of the cabin and parked it there, then picked the lock on the back door and went inside. Several pieces of old mail on the wooden mantel in the large front room were addressed to Roger Keppler. He looked through the drawers in the kitchen, found a hunting license in the same name.

Was Roger Keppler somehow related to Mara Douglas?

Or was Mara Douglas maybe related to the McCall woman?

Maybe he had gotten the house right the first time.

Well, perhaps time would tell. He went out the way he came in, then walked back around front. Satisfied that his car was well hidden from view, he hiked back up the road to his temporary lodgings. He climbed the stairs to the deck, then leaned against the railing, admiring the view, pretending that this place was his. For now, it was.

Tomorrow, he'd take a walk. He'd explore his newfound paradise, see if he could find those falls. He'd take it day by day. He still believed that Mara Douglas would show up. After all, isn't that what a woman would do, if she knew someone was after her? Wouldn't she go someplace where she felt safe, where she wouldn't be found? He figured if it were him, and he needed a safe haven for a time, this is where he'd come, if he had such a place. He felt strongly that sooner or later, Mara would, too.

He'd be here waiting for her.

Chapter Sixteen

Mara awoke in a sweat, her knees pulled up to her chest, her heart pounding, her fingers clutched around the little fabric bunny puppet she'd snatched from her daughter's room on her way out of the house two days ago. In the hour before dawn, the room was still in darkness, the first thin threads of light not yet on the horizon. Long minutes ticked away on the clock on the small table to the right of the narrow bed in the strange room. One hand flew to the space next to the pillow, searching for the telephone, and not finding it, she panicked.

What if Julianne had tried to call her — to call home — and she hadn't been there to get the call?

She turned onto her back, the fabric bunny held close under her chin in both hands, and fought against the panic by taking deep breaths and pushing it away, pushing it down, down through her body, and out through the soles of her feet, the way her psychiatrist had taught her.

It was better, once she could feel the fear leave and her heart rate return to normal. Better, but not good. Mornings were never very good. Another night without her child, another night when the phone had not rung. Despite the fact that Julianne knew the number, in seven years, the call had never come.

Before she turned four, Julianne could recite her full name, address, and telephone number, just as the nursery school teacher had suggested. On that terrible day when Mara arrived at kindergarten to find that Jules had picked Julianne up early, Mara had waited for her daughter to call, as she always did when she was with her father, to tell her when she'd be home. The hours had passed slowly that night, Mara jumping every time the phone rang. Finally, Mara began calling Jules's home phone and his car phone, even his office phone, all night. Listening to each of those phones ring and ring, leaving message after message.

"Jules, this isn't funny. Please call me and let me know where you are and when you'll be bringing her home. Please call me. . . ."

Her emotions going from anger to fear. Had there been an accident? Were both her child and her exhusband lying unconscious in a hospital someplace? At ten p.m. she'd started calling all the hospitals in the area. Then she called Jules's neighbors. His coworkers. His friends.

And finally, she called Annie, who, seeing the situation more clearly than Mara had, told Mara to call the police.

Annie called the local FBI field office and started a statewide search for Jules. His car was found in the parking garage at Philadelphia International Airport the following afternoon, but there was no trace of Jules or their daughter.

Annie had kept the search active longer than usual through her contacts, but to no avail. Father and daughter had disappeared literally into thin air. Mara had held together for the first long, agonizing weeks, dealing with the tangled issues of betrayal and loss and abject terror at not knowing where her child was and when she'd see her again, but firm in her belief that the FBI would pull through, if not for her, then for Annie.

After a month had passed, however — every day beginning with hope that today would be the day, and every night ending with prayers and sobbing attempts to bargain with God for the safe return of her daughter — the sickening fear that she might never again see Julianne filled her completely, and Mara's strength began to crumble. Annie had called on a friend, a classmate and colleague, to talk to Mara, to help see her through the terrible days and terrible nights. It had taken almost a year before Mara had begun to accept the truth that Julianne was gone and might not be coming back, and another year before she could begin to get her life in order again.

After her daughter's disappearance, Mara had taken a leave from her job with a large plaintiff-oriented law firm in the city. When she was finally ready to face working every day again, she found she needed to refocus her career. Personal injury cases just didn't seem as important to her anymore. She applied for a job as a child advocate with the courts in several of the outlying counties and accepted the first position that was offered to her. The pay cut was significant, but in speaking to the court for those who could not speak for themselves, she found an outlet for her pain. To every child she interviewed, every case she reviewed, she offered her single-minded desire to realize what was best for that child and to bring that recommendation before the court. In her heart, Mara understood that it was her way of honoring her daughter, her way of making right for someone else what she could not make right for herself. It was the only thing that kept her going.

In the seven years since Julianne had been taken, there had been only a handful of nights when Mara had not fallen asleep with the telephone next to her pillow. If her daughter reached out for her, she wanted to be there. Those few nights when she had not slept at home had been difficult. Her intellect knew that after all this time, Julianne was not likely to call in the middle of the night. Her heart, however, would not give up the hope that some night the phone might ring.

She lay awake now, in this lakeside cabin, wondering if the phone at home had rung during the night. Knowing that it hadn't, but wondering all the same. It had been a long time since she'd spent more than two nights away from home. If they went to the mountain cabin from here, that would be another night or two — maybe more, if they didn't find the killer soon. The thought of staying away — staying out of her daughter's reach for days on end — caused her pulse to begin pounding again.

She sat up and looked out the window. The sun was up now, though just barely, the first glow warming the lake and waking the birds that nested in the trees that lined the banks on the opposite side. Already the ducks had left their nests and taken to the water, keeping their babies close and near to the shore, warily watching the great blue heron that at this early hour was fishing for his breakfast, no doubt watching with one eye the momma duck and her tiny ducklings and hoping that one might stray.

Plumping the pillow behind her, Mara settled back, the bunny resting on her abdomen. The small house had its creaks and groans, but otherwise all was quiet in spite of the activity of the new day outside. It was strange being here, in this strange house, two strangers sleeping downstairs. Well, one of them not so much a stranger. Not anymore, anyway.

She'd begun to recognize Aidan as a man whose strength lay in many levels, a man who understood kindness and who understood pain. A man who understood what it was like to live with ghosts, because he lived with his own.

Of course, there had been a time when she

believed that Jules was a man worthy of trust, of respect, too. A man who embodied only the finest qualities. Until she walked into his office one night and found him in a compromising situation with one of the assistant professors in his department, a woman who had dined at their home just the weekend before.

Despite Jules's assurances that his affair didn't really mean anything, Mara consulted an attorney by the end of the week. For Julianne's sake, she agreed to joint custody. For Julianne's sake, she'd remained friendly with Jules and never — never — let their daughter know what had happened to cause the split. And Jules had repaid her by stealing her child.

She'd never seen it coming. She believed that whatever else Jules Douglas might be, his love for their daughter was genuine. She'd believed him when he'd agreed that it was Julianne's right to grow up strong and secure in the love of both parents. She'd spent the last seven years paying for that error in judgment.

Mara sighed and looked over the edge of the bed for Spike.

"Spike?" she whispered. "Spike?"

No dog.

The door to her room was slightly ajar, the way she'd left it the night before to allow a little bit of light into the room. She got out of bed, tiptoed to the door, and opened it just enough to step out into the open loft area that over-looked the living room of Chief Tanner's cabin.

She crept to the rail and looked down.

Aidan was stretched out on the sofa below, his hands behind his head, a small bundle of brown and white fur alongside him.

"That little traitor," Mara muttered.

"What was that?" Aidan asked.

"I said Spike is a little traitor. He's supposed to be up here keeping me company."

"I could come up there and keep you company," he said, his eyes still closed, a smile crossing his face.

"Thanks. I think I'll get dressed and come down there."

"Spoilsport." He pretended to frown.

Mara changed quickly into jeans and looked through her bag for a sweatshirt, since the air drifting in through the window was cool, and realized she was still smiling.

This new Aidan was worth smiling about.

It seemed clear to her that he grew more at ease with her as he grew more at ease with himself. Having his job back had gone a long way to bringing that about, she suspected. He was clearly a man who loved his work, and from what she had seen, he was good at it.

It had been a long time since any man had gotten close enough to kiss her. But Aidan, she recognized, wasn't just any man. She had known that the night he'd come to her house with an offer to stay. She remembered him pushing himself to keep up with her and Spike on their nightly walk, in spite of the pain the exertion had caused.

Galahad with a bum hip and a pound of metal in his leg and no grip in his sword hand. But he'd come and stayed with her, all the same. And when she'd called him, he'd come for her to keep her from harm's way.

There'd never been a hero in her life before. It was something to think about.

She pulled the sweatshirt over her head, recalling that Annie had once said that Dylan had swept her off her feet the first time she met him. Mara had teased her sister, never having understood the whole swept-off-the-feet thing. Now she was beginning to wonder if there wasn't something to it after all.

Aidan stopped the Explorer in front of the neat ranch home with the wide front lawn and the trimmed hedge across the front. Bright yellow daffodils grew around the base of the mailbox that announced the street number of the house — 459 — and the name of the occupant — Channing. Aidan knew from Chief Tanner that Mr. Channing had died several years earlier, and that the missus now lived there alone.

"Do you think she'll talk to you?" Mara asked.

"Don't know. She might feel intimidated if I go in alone. Having a woman with me might make her more comfortable. Feel like risking a federal prison term by impersonating an FBI agent?"

"My sister's with the FBI. Does that make me a Fed by blood?"

"Close enough." Aidan nodded. "Let's go."

A long brick walk led from the mailbox to a small covered front porch where a newspaper wrapped in a clear tube of plastic lay on the top step. Aidan picked it up and tucked it under his arm. He rang the doorbell, and they waited until they heard the door unlatch from the inside.

A small woman who appeared to be in her early seventies opened the inner door slowly. Glancing from Aidan to Mara, she frowned slightly.

"Yes?" she asked tentatively.

"Mrs. Channing?" Aidan asked. "My name is Aidan Shields. I'm with the FBI —"

"The FBI? Oh, my . . ." She appeared taken aback.

"— and this is Ms. Douglas," he continued, not identifying Mara other than by name. "May we speak with you for a moment?"

"What is this about?"

"It's about a foster child whom we believe once lived with you," Aidan told her as he handed her the newspaper.

"Oh. Curtis? You have news of Curtis?" Her eyes lit up, and she smiled just briefly, before the smile froze. "If you're from the FBI, then it can't be good, can it? Has something terrible happened to Curtis?"

"May we come in, please?" Aidan showed her

his credentials. He hoped she would be focused enough on those to not realize Mara had offered neither ID nor badge.

"It's been so long since I've seen him." Mrs. Channing motioned for them to come inside. "Please. Sit down."

"Do you hear from him often?" Aidan asked as he and Mara took seats on the sofa.

"No, not in years. He just . . . he just disappeared out of our lives. I didn't even know how to contact him when my husband died, and I think Curtis would have liked to have known about that." She shook her head and drew her cardigan sweater around her as if to warm herself. "I just didn't have any way to get in touch to let him know."

"Mrs. Channing, what can you tell us about Curtis?" Aidan asked softly.

"Well, I don't know what all you want to know."

"Why don't you start at the beginning, when you first took him in as a foster child?" Aidan suggested.

"Oh, that was a time." She shook her head. "Marshall and I had tried for so long to have children and we just finally gave up. We started going through the adoption process here in the county, met with the social workers and all. We told them we would take any child, any child who needed us. Well, no sooner than we'd met with them that we got a call. Not to adopt, but to take in this boy. They wanted to place him right away, immediately, didn't want him to go into a group home."

"Why was that?"

"Because of what he'd gone through, they knew he'd have . . . troubles." Claire Channing looked at Mara, who had not spoken since they'd entered the house. "He'd had a terrible start in life, that boy did."

"We know about his mother, Mrs. Channing," Mara told her.

"Then you know how damaged that poor child was. We were determined, Marshall and I were, to make it up to him as best we could. To give him as normal a home as we could. But nothing we could do for him would ever make right what had happened to him. I think we both understood that." She smiled sadly at Mara. "I used to tell the social worker, it's just a matter of time before it all catches up with him. Oh, we sent him for therapy — he was in therapy for years — but in my heart I knew that no amount of therapy could undo what had been done to that boy. All he'd been through, all he'd seen . . ."

Tears had formed in her eyes. "He was such a good boy, Agent Shields. Studied hard and helped around the house . . ." Her eyes wandered to the window, and she looked outside as if searching for something lost long ago. "We had a little garden together out there, him and me. He helped Marshall with all the yard work. Helped him build a grape arbor out back,

301

planted the grapes." She smiled even as the tears fell over her cheeks. "We used to make grape jam together. Curtis would help me pick, and we'd get out the canning equipment. . . ."

She rose and pulled a tissue from the top of a nearby box. "But all the same, we knew that he'd never gotten over it. How could he have? All the things that had happened to him. All he'd seen . . ."

It was the second time in less than two minutes that she'd used that expression. *All he'd seen . . .*

"What are you referring to, Mrs. Channing? What had he seen?" Aidan asked.

The woman lowered herself slowly onto an ottoman close to Mara's chair and leaned forward slightly.

"Didn't you know?" Her voice dropped as if she were about to speak the unspeakable. "All the while that man was raping Curtis's mother, while he was stabbing her to death . . . Curtis was watching from the closet."

Mara and Aidan exchanged a long look.

"Chief Tanner told us that Curtis had been found hiding in the closet —" Aidan began.

"He saw the whole thing. Can you imagine what that did to that child?" The tissue twisted in her hands. "The police told us that when they found him there on the closet floor, he was covered with blood. That he must have touched her, maybe to see if she was still alive. As best we could piece together, he'd probably watched from the closet, then when the man who killed her — that man, Unger — you believe they've let him out of prison? — left the house to wait for the police, Curtis crept out and went to her." She shuddered. "They said he had her blood on his clothes, on his face . . . his hands. . . ."

Claire Channing held her hands up in front of her. "I just couldn't imagine that sweet little boy having to watch that terrible thing. We thought if we gave him a good home . . ."

"I'm sure that you did, Mrs. Channing. I'm sure that you and Mr. Channing were the best thing that ever happened to Curtis." Mara tried to comfort the woman who now wept openly.

"But you have no idea where he is now?" Aidan asked.

Mrs. Channing shook her head. "No. As I told you, I haven't heard from him in years. After he graduated from high school, he came to us, thanked us for giving him a home. Thanked us for all we did for him. But he said he had to go. He said it would be for the best."

"And there's been no word since?"

"None. I would tell you if —" She paused to search their faces. "Has he done something bad?"

"We don't know, Mrs. Channing. We're just trying to follow up on something that's come to our attention."

"I've always feared that someday . . ." She didn't finish the sentence. It hung in the air. It wasn't difficult to figure out what she feared

303

would eventually happen.

"Do you know if he had any friends in the area, any family, someone who would be in contact with him?"

"No. There's no one. Curtis didn't have many friends. He wasn't very outgoing."

"Do you have any pictures of him?" Aidan asked.

"Only from years ago. I think the last would be his high school graduation picture."

"May we see?"

"Certainly." She opened the drawer of a chest that stood against the front wall and pulled out a box. "There are some in here, I think."

She sat back on the ottoman and crossed her legs to balance the box while she sorted through a stack of photos.

"This was the first year that he was with us." She passed a photo to Mara, who was seated closest to her.

Mara glanced at it before passing it to Aidan. The face in the photo was that of a sad, solemn little boy with dark, haunted eyes.

"And these are a few years later." Mrs. Channing handed Mara a whole stack.

"He looks happier in these," Mara murmured aloud as she gave the photos to Aidan.

"Oh, thank you." Mrs. Channing teared up again. "We like to think . . . well, he seemed happy, after a time. Here, here's a few more."

Mara shuffled briefly through the pile, then

paused. She held up one photo and asked, "You had a Jack Russell terrier?"

"Oh, yes. Curtis's dog. We got it for him for Christmas the second year he was here. Oh, how he loved that dog."

"They are wonderful dogs," Mara agreed. "I have one."

"Do you?"

Mara nodded, about to mention that Spike was right out in the car, but Aidan picked up the questioning.

"He liked animals?" he asked, well aware that the typical profile for serial killers often included cruelty to animals from a young age.

"Oh, yes," Mrs. Channing assured him.

"There were never any incidents of abusing animals or . . ."

"Oh, no." Her eyes widened at the thought. "No, no. Curtis loved animals. He was very good with them."

Aidan proceeded through the usual serial killer profile while he had the chance. "Was he a bed wetter?"

"Well, yes. He was. Marshall and me, we decided not to make a big deal out of it, you know, after all the boy had been through."

"How about fire, Mrs. Channing? Did Curtis like fire, like to start fires?"

"He and my husband used to burn brush out back, years ago. Burn leaves and such, but that's all I can recall . . ."

"What happened to the dog?" Mara asked.

"Oh, poor little Jake. He died the year Curtis was a junior in high school."

"Did the dog have . . . an accident?" Aidan asked cautiously.

"No, no. Cancer. And Curtis just cried and cried. Only time I ever saw that boy cry was when his dog died. He never even cried, they said, when they found him in the closet. If he ever cried for his mother, I never saw it. But he sure did cry over that dog."

"Do you have anything that belonged to him?" A hairbrush or hat that would have DNA on it would be too much to ask, Aidan knew, but maybe there was something. . . .

"No, no, not anymore." She shook her head.

"May I take this with me?" Aidan held up Curtis's senior year photograph by one corner. He turned it over. *Curtis Alan Channing* was written in pencil across the back.

"Of course." Mrs. Channing nodded. "Can you tell me what you think he might have done, Agent Shields?"

"Not at this time, I'm sorry." Aidan took her hands in his. "If we're wrong, you'd have been upset for no reason, and I know that just having us here, asking after him, has upset you enough."

Claire Channing smiled. "Agent Shields, I've been upset for Curtis's sake every day since the day we brought him home." She rose, understanding that there were no more questions. "I still pray for him every morning, every evening."

"You just keep on doing that, Mrs. Channing." Aidan squeezed her hands gently. "You just keep on praying for him. . . ."

Aidan was on the phone with John Mancini almost before they got back to the car.

"Sounds like you struck gold, Shields," John exclaimed after Aidan laid out the entire story.

"It's actually Cahill's gold," Aidan reminded him. "She was the one who remembered the Ohio case and gave us that lead."

"You know, I always say to trust your intuition. Follow your gut. Good work, Shields. We'll get this out on the wires. Now, if we can get a good description of what he looks like . . ."

"We were able to get one of his high school graduation photos. I think a good compositor could probably do a fairly accurate projection on what he'd look like now."

"We have one of the best. Get that photo to me as quickly as you can, and we'll get it to her immediately."

"I'll take it to Chief Lanigan at the Lake Grove PD and ask him to fax it to you."

"Excellent. With any luck, we'll be able to get that sketch completed and out within twenty-four hours. Do I understand that Ms. Douglas is still with you?"

"Yes. She's here."

"Stay with her, Shields." Mancini related the details of what had happened the night before in Lyndon. "It looks like someone — Channing or otherwise — may have tried to get to her last night, but we don't have the details yet. Keep her out of sight, if you can, while we try to piece this whole thing together."

"Yes, sir. I'll do my best."

Aidan returned the phone to his jacket pocket while he filled Mara in on the attempted break-in.

"So the boss thinks I should stick with you for a while," Aidan said.

"And what do you think?"

"I think I'm sticking, regardless." He leaned across the console and kissed her. "If that's okay with you . . ."

"It's more than okay." She drew closer, meeting him halfway, kissing him back.

"It may be a while. . . ." he told her, his lips brushing against hers.

"It just so happens I have some time on my hands right now. . . ."

"Then maybe we should make the best of it." He kissed her again, and her head began to swim.

How long had it been, she asked herself, since she'd felt this rush of heat and pleasure and anticipation at the mere touch of lips?

She couldn't recall, gave up trying to remember, and gave in to what he offered her.

Until her cell phone began to ring.

She sighed and dug the phone out of her purse and checked the caller ID. It was Annie.

"Hey," Mara said as she answered the phone.

"Hey, yourself. What's doing?"

"Aidan and I are in Ohio."

"So John tells me. He says you might have identified our killer."

"Looks like we might have."

"They're bringing in the best sketch artist we have to try to age the photo that Aidan is sending us."

"I thought that was all done digitally these days."

"It can be, yes. And they'll do that, no doubt, as well, but John likes the human touch. And once we get a bead on this guy, the sketch can be updated with hard facts so it can be released to the media. I'm also going to take a good look at this guy Channing from a psychological standpoint, see if he fits the profile."

"He's had a horrific background."

"So I understand. Listen, John told me that he asked you to hang with Aidan for a while. Is that all right with you?"

"Perfectly fine."

"Oh? Perfectly fine?"

"Um-hmm."

"Oh, my," Annie laughed softly. "From 'perfectly fine' to 'um-hmm' in under ten seconds. Are you *fraternizing* with my almost brother-in-law?"

"Somewhat."

"Somewhat fraternizing. Well, well, well. Who'd have ever . . ."

Mara could all but see her sister shaking her

head and smiling while she did so.

"Mara, are you still there?" Annie asked.

"Yes, I'm here. It's this damned phone." Mara frowned as the connection grew fuzzy.

"Look, I'll talk fast. I don't think you should come back to Lyndon until we find Channing. Can you find something to do for a while until we get a handle on all this out here?"

"Sure. We can find something to do."

The line fuzzed up again.

"Leave the phone on," Annie told her. "I'll give you a call when I reach Lyndon."

"Okay." Mara disconnected the call. "Annie's on her way to Lyndon. They're going to try to get a sketch artist to update the photo that you're sending in. They're going to release the picture in the hope of finding someone who recognizes Channing. Annie's going to call back after she gets there. She doesn't think we should go back just yet, though."

"I agree with her." Aidan nodded. "Keep a good distance between you and our Mary Douglas killer."

"Do you think it's Channing?"

"I think it would be an incredible coincidence if it were anyone else." He turned the key in the ignition. "Let's help them get the ball rolling by getting this photograph of young Curtis Channing over to Chief Lanigan so that they can work on the sketch, see if anyone steps forward to identify him, to confirm that he's been seen around Lyndon. That's the starting gate. Has Curtis Channing been in Lyndon? If we get a positive ID, one that places him there over the past month, then I'd say it's damned likely that Curtis Alan Channing is our Mary Douglas killer."

Chapter Seventeen

Evan Crosby chewed on the end of his pen and stared at the computer screen in front of him. The call from Agent Cahill had been short and sweet and to the point. She would be in his office within the hour, accompanied by the FBI profiler, to help him break the Mary Douglas case. Even after he'd told her they had a suspect in custody, she'd insisted that unless their suspect was one Curtis Alan Channing, aka Curt Gibbons, the Lyndon PD had the wrong man.

Having spent the better part of the night interviewing the suspect, Crosby had to admit that he wasn't convinced that Tom Mulholland was their killer, not by a long shot. Nothing about him — from his disheveled appearance to the disorganized mess of his small rented room — suggested that he was a man who could so coolly, so methodically, stage a crime scene. He just didn't strike Crosby as a man who planned that far ahead for anything. And there was nothing neat or tidy about him. It was Crosby's personal opinion that if Tom Mulholland ever killed anyone, it would be spur-of-the-moment, the scene would be utter chaos, and he'd be caught within hours because he'd leave his fingerprints everywhere and would, most likely, drop his wallet on his way out the door.

And Mulholland had sworn he'd never heard of Mara Douglas and never met a man named Vincent Giordano.

Crosby'd spent the past forty minutes going over his notes from the night before, trying to reconcile what he knew about Mulholland with what he knew of the killings, hoping to find the key before they arrived. Cahill had been just a little too cocky, a little too sure of herself.

He sighed and turned away from the screen, admitted that he wasn't any closer to finding the truth than he was when this whole mess started. He bounced the pen off the partition on the opposite side of the room in disgust. Maybe Agent Cahill was right. Maybe she could help them to break it. Part of him hoped she could. The other part wanted to break it himself.

It was one thirty in the afternoon when tall, leggy Miranda Cahill walked into his tiny cubicle accompanied by Anne Marie McCall.

"I think you may have met Dr. McCall," Cahill said by way of greeting Crosby, before cutting right to the chase. "We think we have a very strong lead."

"Dr. McCall." Crosby nodded to acknowledge the pretty blond psychiatrist. "How strong?"

"How strong would a name and a face be?"

"As you already know, Agent Cahill, we have

a name and a face. In custody, at this very minute. What do you have that can convince me that we have the wrong man?"

Miranda dropped an envelope atop the pile of mail, papers, and files that littered the desk. From it she took a sketch that she passed to Crosby. "This is, we believe, your Mary Douglas killer. His name is Curtis Alan Channing. Our paths first crossed six years ago. I was part of a team that was investigating a string of murders along the Ohio–Kentucky border."

Crosby studied the sketch. "Who did this sketch?"

"This was digitally enhanced from an old photo, aged to what the computer thinks he might look like now. The FBI is having a sketch artist work on a drawing, which we think will be more true to life, but we wanted something in hand quickly, and the computer gave us this."

"Let me get my partner in here." He punched the three numbers into the intercom. "Joe. Come in here."

Joe Sullivan appeared in the doorway almost instantaneously. "What's up?"

"You remember Agent Cahill? Dr. McCall? FBI?" Crosby nodded to the two women who were crowded into the small space. "They're here to discuss the Mary Douglas killer."

"What's to discuss?" Sullivan shrugged. "The case is solved. Or didn't anyone think to inform the FBI that we have a man in custody?"

"Agent Cahill thinks that Mulholland is telling the truth."

Sullivan snorted. "And how did Agent Cahill come to that conclusion?"

She filled him in, ignoring his defensive attitude and relating what she'd already told Evan Crosby.

"These murders in Ohio, they were the same MO as ours?" Sullivan asked.

"No, but the same feel as yours," she told him.

"The same *feel?*" The detective scoffed. "How did they *feel?*"

"Controlled. Organized." Miranda took the high road and disregarded his sarcasm. This time. "Planned down to the last detail."

"Victims stabbed to death?" Crosby asked.

"No, they were strangled."

"Then where's the connection?" Sullivan turned on her. "Serial killers stab or they shoot or they strangle, but they don't change their MO. Everybody knows that."

"That's not exactly correct, Detective." Anne Marie spoke up for the first time.

"Then why don't you set me straight, Dr. McCall?" Sullivan's tone was condescending.

"I think that Agent Cahill is right on target. Serial killers don't always follow the exact MO — although it might appear that way on the surface. If they're active long enough, they often evolve over time, as the killer moves

315

closer and closer to the ideal fantasy."

"Fantasy? You think this is about fantasy?"

"It almost always is, Detective Sullivan. He's following a script, as most serial killers do. But the script changes as he moves closer and closer to his goal." Anne Marie turned her attention to Detective Crosby, who struck her as being the more receptive of the two. "His early attempts might include some aspects of his later, perfected work, but he won't start out achieving perfection."

"So what you're saying is that his early killings might only exhibit part of what drives him, maybe his need for controlling the scene, but his method of killing might be different from what he does later on?" Crosby asked.

"Exactly." Annie nodded.

"Explain to me why you think this guy is our guy." Sullivan nodded toward the sketch.

Miranda took over. "When I interviewed him six years ago, I had felt very strongly that he might have been connected to the murders we were investigating, but we didn't have anything to hold him with. When we tried to locate him for a second interview, he'd disappeared. Recently, when I viewed the scenes of your Mary Douglas slayings, the details — the face covered by the cloths, the clothing pulled down as if to hide the fact of the rape — I was reminded of that scene. We dug up that old interview and sent an agent out to check around his home town."

316

"And you found him, just like that." Sullivan snapped his fingers. "Gee, the FBI is swell."

Miranda leaned into his face, a wicked grin on hers. "Oh, you don't know the half of it," she whispered. "I'm about to show you just how swell we really are."

She turned back to the desk and picked up the photo. "This is the man I interviewed six years ago. Curt Gibbons, whom we now know as Curtis Alan Channing. Through some truly swell investigative work" — she glanced at Sullivan — "we've learned that as a young boy Curtis had the very unfortunate experience of watching his mother raped and murdered. Stabbed to death."

She looked from one detective to the other, then asked, "Either of you want to guess how many times Momma had been stabbed?"

"I'm gonna go out on a limb here and guess six," Crosby said.

"Can't put anything over on you, Crosby. Want to hear it all?"

He nodded. "Shoot."

Miranda repeated the entire story as she'd heard it from Aidan Shields just hours earlier.

When she finished, the room was totally silent.

"Well, you could hear a pin drop in here right about now," she noted with grim satisfaction. "Nothing to say, Detective Sullivan?"

"We already have a suspect in custody, and that" — Sullivan pointed to the sketch — "ain't him. What do you have that says this guy has ever set foot in Lyndon?"

"That's something we were hoping you could assist us in establishing."

"Use the locals to do the dirty work?"

"Joe, that's enough." Crosby shot him a look.

Ignoring the rude remark, Anne Marie touched Crosby's arm and asked, "What happened after the suspect was caught last night, Detective? Was the surveillance on the Mary Douglas homes terminated?"

Sullivan jumped in. "And why wouldn't it be? Any fool could see that this guy — Mulholland — was lying. What's the first thing anyone says when they're picked up? 'I didn't do it, you got the wrong guy.'" Sullivan laughed darkly, then added, "But in Mulholland's case, it was, 'Oh, some guy I met in a bar paid me to break into this house. I wasn't going to hurt her, I was just supposed to scare her.' And her name just happened to be Mary Douglas? Right, pal. We got our man, Agent Cahill. If you think otherwise, you can track this guy — this Channing — all by yourself."

"Joe, I think you have other cases that need your attention," Crosby told him. "Go work on them."

"Gladly." He rose to leave the cubicle. "You're wasting your time, Evan. She" — he pointed at Miranda — "obviously has her own agenda here. You know the Feds can't stand not being the ones to make the bust. . . ."

"Joe." Crosby's face grew dark.

"Aw, they're all yours," he muttered as he walked away.

"Where did the Lyndon PD find him?" Anne Marie shook her head as Joe Sullivan's footsteps faded down the hall. "He's like a stereotype of every narrow-minded small-town cop I ever met. I honestly thought they stopped making them like that years ago."

"Hey, he's a good cop, but you just pushed a button." Detective Crosby shrugged. "Sorry about that."

"Accepted." Miranda dismissed the departed detective.

"If this guy Channing is a serial killer . . ." Crosby swung slowly, side to side, in his beat-up chair, weighing what he knew against what he suspected. "What connects him to our victims? To Mara Douglas? To Giordano? I never heard of a serial killer who took contracts."

"I don't know how he became involved," Annie admitted. "But I think the killings are right on target — in terms of escalation — with where Channing would be if he'd started out with strangulations. He watched the rape and murder of his mother. Now, he may have hated his mother for the terrible things she did to him — but she was still his mother. The police say that when they found him in the closet, he was covered with her blood. He'd been alone in the house with her body. According to the police report, the killer admitted raping her, admitted stabbing her to death, but he denied that he pulled her skirt down, denied having covered her face."

"You're thinking the boy came out of the closet and did that." Crosby nodded slowly. "Covered her up . . ."

"I do. And years later, he's repeating that scene over and over and over."

"Why?"

"One, I think because the image was so strong in his head, and two, because I think he wished he'd done it himself, to end the abuse. It's no accident that all Channing's victims had six stab wounds in the exact same locations. I'm positive that when we get our hands on a sketch or a photo of his mother's body, we'll find that the placement of the stab wounds match up with those found on your vics. I think he watched the whole thing from the closet, watched the knife go up and down. He saw the wounds. He remembered exactly where they were."

"But you said his early victims were strangled," the detective reminded her.

"He wasn't ready then to deal with everything as he remembered it. He repeated the rapes because that gave him control, power, allowed him to humiliate his victims, who were unfortunate substitutes for his mother."

"Then why cover her face when it's over? Why pull her clothes together, if intimidation was a goal?" Crosby asked. "Wouldn't the exposure be humiliating?"

"Yes, but she was still his *mother*. He doesn't want anyone else to see her exposed like that," Annie said.

"And maybe he doesn't want her watching him while he's doing his thing," Miranda suggested.

"That's part of it, too," Annie agreed. "I think he's had this need to re-create his mother's death, but it's been a fantasy for years. It's taken him a while to build up to the real deal. As he grew stronger, more comfortable acting out the scenario, he was able to recreate the stabbings. But I think it took him years to get to that point."

"So let's assume that Channing was hired by Giordano to dispose of several people in his life who had been major sources of irritation," Crosby thought aloud. "But the actual murders —"

"Were Channing's own fantasies." Annie nodded. "I'd bet a bundle that Giordano had no idea of what he was getting."

Miranda sat on the edge of her chair. "So, what we need from the Lyndon PD is, first and foremost, assistance in finding this man, this Curtis Alan Channing."

"Where is your suspect now?" Annie asked.

"He's meeting with his public defender."

"Here? In the building?"

"Yes. I see where you're going. And I agree.

Let's start with the suspect we have, see if Mulholland recognizes this man." Crosby picked up the sketch. "We'll give him a set of different composites. If he identifies your Channing as the man he met in the bar last night . . . well, we'll take it from there. Agent Cahill, Dr. McCall, this way, please."

Anne Marie and Miranda followed Detective Crosby to the room where a weeping Tom Mulholland was meeting with his attorney. From behind the glass, the women watched as Crosby laid the sketch of Curtis Channing, along with four or five sketches of other faces, on the table in front of the suspect.

"He knows," Miranda murmured. "Crosby knows that Mulholland isn't the killer. He barely even argued with us. . . ."

"Watch." Annie pointed at the glass. "Watch Mulholland's face."

"That's him," Mulholland exclaimed without hesitation and before Crosby could say a word. He pounded a fist on Curtis Alan Channing's face. "That's Calvin. He looked a little different, a little older, and his hair was different, shorter, like a crew cut, and he had these dark glasses on, but that's him, that son of a bitch. He set me up for this. He set me up."

Crosby glanced at the glass wall and smiled. Still without having said a word, he picked up the sketches and left the room.

"Convinced, Detective?" Miranda asked.

"Mulholland went right to the sketch of

Channing — did not hesitate, did not deliberate, as I'm sure you saw. I think we need to meet with our chief of police and the head of our county CID. We may want to get an artist in to speak with Mulholland, get a more current sketch."

"The FBI is having a sketch artist update the photo."

"Let's get it, then, so that we can get it out right away, send it to all the local stations. If he was here in the area, someone would have seen him. If we move now, we should be able to get a sketch on the early news. We'll show it on all the subsequent broadcasts until we find him."

"Find him quickly, Detective Crosby," Annie said softly, thinking of Mara.

"First things first. That means convincing Chief Donner that we still have a killer on the loose. And after we've tackled that formidable task, we're going to take a drive, the three of us. . . ."

"I can't help it, Giordano, I keep coming back to you. We all keep coming back to you."

Evan Crosby loosened his tie and scratched behind one ear. Across the ugly table with the marred Formica top, Vince Giordano smirked even as he ogled the two women who had accompanied the detective on his trip to the county prison.

"When you're bringing along the eye candy,

you can come back as often as you like." The prisoner winked at Miranda Cahill.

"You're not my type, Vinnie." She rested both arms on the table and stared into his face with as little emotion as she could muster. "May I call you Vinnie?"

"You can call me anything you want, doll-face. You could start with 'lover' —"

"Vinnie, there's just something about men who kill kids. . . . I don't know, it's just a real turn-off for me."

"I'm gonna be released, you wait and see," he told her, even as the red flush spread from his neck to his face. "My lawyer called this morning. He's petitioned the court for an emergency hearing because I been in here so long on a bad conviction. Could be as soon as tomorrow, day after. Thirty-six hours from now, I could be a free man."

"And that would mean that you didn't pull the trigger?" She continued to stare at him. "Sorry." She lowered her voice. "You have sleaze written all over you."

"Maybe I'll come see you when I get out, Miss Mouth. Maybe we'll find out we have a lot in common."

"Actually, we do have something in common. Thanks for reminding me." She turned to Crosby. "You have that sketch?"

The detective opened his briefcase and passed the file to her.

"This man." She held up the picture of

Channing. "I believe we've both made his acquaintance."

"Never saw him before." Giordano's smirk was back.

"Oh, come on, Vinnie, take another look." Miranda moved the drawing closer. "Now, when I met him, he called himself Curt Gibbons. Did he use that name when you met him, or did he use Curt Channing?"

"I told you, I never saw him before."

"You buying that, Detective Crosby? You think Vinnie sounds sincere?"

"Nah. Now, here's what we have, Vince." Crosby took over. "We have a really odd set of coincidences. We have three women named Mary Douglas dead, all three murdered by the same person. Why? There's nothing to connect them except their names. Then we find your ex-mother-in-law dead, a bullet between the eyes. And then, on top of that, we find Judge Styler — the judge who officiated at your custody hearing, the same judge who denied you visitation with your sons — murdered. In exactly the same way that the Mary Douglases were killed."

"Hey, I heard about Styler. A tragedy," Giordano deadpanned. "I don't see what all this has to do with me. I never knew any of those women, those Mary Douglas women."

"Ah, but you knew Mara Douglas. *Mara,*" Crosby emphasized. "The child advocate who recommended to Judge Styler that you not be

325

permitted to see your sons because you couldn't have a conversation with either one of them without beating the crap out of him."

The corners of Giordano's mouth twitched, but he said nothing.

"We figure that Channing misunderstood you. That he thought you said *Mary* instead of *Mara,* and didn't do his homework before he did the deed."

"We talked about this before, Crosby. I told you I've had no contact with anyone except my lawyer. I've had no mail, no phone calls, no visitors except you and your buddy Sullivan. So when would I have met this guy, this Channing?" Giordano smiled slyly. "And where? I've been locked up since the day after that hearing, and I haven't been out of here except to go to court."

Crosby stared at the inmate. Those were the very questions he'd been asking himself.

"And supposing I did meet this guy and asked him to do these terrible things you're accusing me of. What incentive do I have to offer? I can't pay him — my lawyer owns every dime I'll make for the next forty fucking years. What could I possibly do to make someone — a complete stranger — want to kill three people for me?" Giordano sat back in his seat, the irons clanging softly. "Tell me that, Detective Crosby. Why would this man be willing to kill for me, even assuming that I wanted him to?"

"I don't know." Crosby shook his head. "I don't know. That's the missing piece of the puzzle."

"That's a pretty big piece, wouldn't you say?" Giordano turned his attention to the two women who sat on the opposite side of the table. "You don't have much to say, do you, blondie?"

"My job is just to observe," Anne Marie said coolly. *Blondie* clearly rankled.

"Observe what?"

"You."

"You came here just to watch me?" He snickered. "Baby, you come see me when I get out, I'll give you something to look at."

When she didn't so much as blink, he said, "Well, it's nice to see that the Lyndon Police Department finally hired some good-looking cops. I'm tired of looking at your ugly face all the time, Crosby."

"We're not Lyndon PD," Miranda told him.

"Oh? Then what are you?"

"FBI."

"Oh, hey, this must be something really special, the FBI is in town." He made a silly face. "You an agent, gorgeous? What's your name?"

"Agent Miranda Cahill."

"Cahill." He repeated the name softly to himself once, then again. "Cahill . . ." He studied her face. "We meet before?"

"No."

"No. Guess not. I'd remember you, all right.

I'd remember your face. I'd remember your body. . . ."

"Okay, that's it for today." Crosby pushed back from the table and signaled for the guard. "Guess there's no point in me saying, 'So when you're ready to talk about Curtis Channing, give me a call,' huh?"

Giordano laughed in his face. "Never heard of him till today."

The guard stepped in to lead Giordano back to his cell. The prisoner stopped and turned to look at Miranda one more time, stared at her for a long minute before turning away and shuffling from the room.

"Well, that was enlightening," Miranda said as they walked from the prison into the parking lot.

"Actually, it was," Annie told her. "He was clearly lying through his teeth."

"I agree. But how do we prove that? And how do we connect Giordano to Channing?"

"Find Channing," Crosby said simply.

"That's your job, Detective," Annie replied as she got into the police car. "Do it before the son of a bitch finds my sister, will you?"

"And before Giordano gets out of here," Miranda added, looking back at the gray stone building.

"Unfortunately, I have no control over that," Crosby told her. "The state won't deny his appeal because we think he has a connection to Channing. Who has not yet been confirmed as the murderer, Agent Cahill."

"Then we're going to have to connect the dots quickly, Detective. The good news is that we will then be able to kill two birds with one stone. We'll have Channing, and we'll have Giordano."

"Sure. No problem," he muttered as he got behind the wheel. "All we have to do is figure out where those two intersect. Giordano and Channing. Once we find someone who can actually place Channing in Lyndon, then maybe we can figure out what he did while he was here. Where he went, what he did. Besides kill five women, that is . . ."

Alone in his cell, Giordano was still smiling. The temptation had been so great. He'd had to bite his tongue to keep from asking, "So, Detective Crosby, how's your little sister doin' these days?"

But he wasn't stupid. And asking about Crosby's sister, when he was so close to the game, would be just too stupid for words. There'd be time enough, once he got out of here. . . .

He turned his attention to the matter that had been puzzling him all afternoon: Why did the name Miranda Cahill ring so loud a bell?

It came to him later that night as he lay awake on his cot.

Channing. He'd named his three for Archer, and Giordano had committed them to memory along with the names he'd been given by Archer Lowell.

Channing had named his old lady's boyfriend, Albert Unger.

That writer, Joshua Manning, who'd done some books about serial killers.

And an FBI agent named Miranda Cahill.

Well, he could certainly see why she'd be memorable, and he could think of plenty of things he'd love to do to her, but killing her would be the least of them.

Though there was some appeal, he conceded, to have her on her knees, begging for his mercy. . . .

But that little number would fall to Archer.

Damn, didn't that boy have the luck?

Damn if he didn't . . .

Chapter Eighteen

"Are you sure I can't do some of the driving?" Mara asked as she threw her bag into the cargo area of the Explorer. "I really don't mind."

"Positive." Aidan threw his duffel in next to hers and slammed the door. "Come on, Spike. Time's up."

The dog took one last sniff of the shrub he'd been investigating before taking the long way to the car.

Aidan turned the key in the ignition, then waved a last good-bye to Chief Tanner, who stood on the end of his deck, arms folded across his chest, watching his guests depart. Aidan and Mara had stopped by late on the previous afternoon to bring Tanner up to date, as they'd promised. They'd also come armed with a couple of steaks and a bottle of wine and a proposal to test out that new grill on the chief's deck. In return, the chief had offered another night's lodging, which they'd gratefully accepted.

"Are you sure we can't stop in Lyndon just for a minute?" she asked as they drove back toward town.

"Was there something you needed?"

"The weather's turned warm again. I could use some lighter clothes."

"I think you're just going to have to make do with what you brought. I don't think we should push our luck. Channing's proven himself to be a pretty canny fellow, and we have no idea where he is right now."

"I guess. Maybe Annie left some things at the cabin."

"How long has it been since you've been to this place, anyway?"

"Oh, maybe two years." She frowned, trying to remember exactly how long. "It was really —"

She stopped in midsentence, remembering, then shot him a guilty glance out of the corner of her eye.

"It was really what?"

"It was really Annie's place. Hers and Dylan's. It's where they used to go to get away."

"He'd mentioned that."

"Does that change . . . well, your wanting to go there?"

"You mean, do I not want to go because Dylan used to visit there?" Aidan eased the Explorer onto the highway. She could not read his face. "Now, that would be silly, wouldn't it?"

"Aidan, he didn't just visit there. They more or less lived there those last six or seven months."

"That's nice, that he and Annie had that time together."

"That's why I haven't been there in a while. It just was, well . . . their place. It didn't feel like mine anymore." She quickly added, "But that was okay with me. I didn't like to be away from home much these past few years."

"Were you afraid she'd come back and you wouldn't be there?" No need to explain who *she* was.

"No. I was afraid she'd call in the middle of the night and I wouldn't be there to answer." She looked out the window. "Do you think that's stupid?"

"Not at all. I don't think it's unreasonable to hope that your daughter would try to contact you at some time." He stole a glance in her direction, choosing his words carefully. "Although, you know, there's a good chance that might not happen until she's older. . . ."

"What do you mean? Why would you say that?" She frowned.

"You don't know what your ex has told her. He might very well have told her that you died and that's why you're not with them." There was really no way to soften the words.

Mara rested her head against the back of the seat and stared straight ahead.

"Well, that would explain it, wouldn't it? Why all these years, she's made no attempt to get in touch with me. None that I know of, anyway," she said thoughtfully. "Early on, after it first happened — oh, maybe four or five months after — Annie had suggested that very thing and I totally freaked out on her. Back then, I really believed that my daughter would *know* that I was alive, would *know* that I was

333

waiting for her right there at home."

"And now?"

"And now I don't know what to believe." She chewed on the end of a finger and watched the scenery go by in a blur.

They rode in silence for several miles.

"When I think of Julianne, I think of her as a small child. In my mind, I still see her as a five-year-old, even though I know she isn't a little girl anymore," she said, her voice tired and confessional. "I don't even know what she looks like, Aidan."

He reached out and took her hand in his and let her hold on.

"My daughter's almost a teenager, and I don't know what she looks like. What music she listens to. What kind of clothes she wears or what books she reads. Is she athletic? Did she go to dancing school? Did she dye her hair purple and get her nose pierced?" Mara shook her head slowly, pain etched into every line in her face. "I don't know anything about her. I don't know who she is. She's the most precious thing in the world to me, but I don't even know her."

Aidan wished he could think of something clever to say, but there were no words that could soothe or comfort. So he merely continued to hold her hand to offer that small bit of human contact as consolation. It was inadequate, he knew, but at that moment, it was all he had to give her.

Mara closed her eyes, fighting back the sting. She hated that this gloom hung over her, followed her everywhere she went, and as much as she wanted her child back, she wished that she could shake some of that ache, once in a while, and have a day not colored by loss. She knew there was beauty and joy in the world, and more and more she found herself longing for a glimpse of it.

She opened her eyes and turned her head to watch Aidan as he flicked on the radio and began to search for a station. The only good reception seemed to be of country music.

"Is this all right with you?" he asked her, breaking the silence. "Can you handle a little country?"

"Sure."

"Ah, this is classic stuff. Patsy Cline. My mom was a big Patsy Cline fan. I used to know the words to all of her songs." He turned up the volume and began singing along, delivering his own somewhat off-key version of "I Fall to Pieces."

Four hours later, they stopped for lunch outside Harrisburg. On the final leg of the journey, as they sped along on Route 78, Mara happened to glance out the window as they passed a sign that announced the exit for Hamburg was right ahead.

"Hamburg!" she exclaimed. "I remember Hamburg!"

"One of your old haunts?" Aidan laughed.

She'd been so quiet for most of the drive, and her outburst had been so unexpected.

"My mother used to take Annie and me there." She craned her neck to look out at the southeast stretch of Allegheny Mountains known as the Kittatinny ridge. "There's a place out there, out beyond the town. It's called Hawk Mountain. Mom used to pack Annie and me up and drag us there to watch the raptor migrations in the fall."

"How far from here, do you remember?"

"No, I was too little. I just remember the name of the town because it made me think of hamburgers, which were, back then, one of my favorite foods."

He pulled smoothly into the exit lane, his turn signal blinking away.

"What are you doing? Are you getting off here?"

"I am." He checked the rearview mirror.

"Why?"

"Anything that can cause your face to light up like that must be pretty special. It can't be all that far. It's worth a look. And it's not like we're punching a clock. We have plenty of time."

"Thank you." She smiled, remembering. "You know, back then, people used to come from everywhere to sit on the rocks and watch the hawks and the eagles and the falcons. I used to complain and whine and grumble be-cause she made us go, but I look back on those times now and just cherish that I had that part of her, that she shared so much of herself with us."

"Well, let's see if it's all as you remembered it."

"I'm sure it's changed a lot. I read in the paper not long ago that there are new lookouts up there, new parking lots, and that they now attract thousands of visitors every year. When I was little, there'd only be a handful of watchers up there with us."

"Guess bird-watching's big out here," Aidan noted, looking out at the mountains to their left.

"Well, it was set up as a sanctuary. I think it might have been the first one in this country. Years ago, hunters used to go there to shoot the hawks and the eagles when they migrated through every fall. They'd slaughter them by the thousands for sport. Then, about forty years ago, when it became apparent that the populations were way down — some species all but extinct — the sanctuary was established. It was my mother's favorite place. We saw some awesome sights up there, the three of us."

"It's nice that you have such good memories of her."

"Oh, she was such a nature enthusiast. She grew up in the country, out near State College, but when she and my dad married and he got the teaching position at Drexel, they moved to the city. I don't remember her ever saying that

337

she hated it, but we all knew she did. Every chance she got, she packed us into the car and drove us out into the country. Annie and I still laugh about Mom's little nature moments. We'd be driving along the road and she'd slam on the brakes and point out the window with great excitement. Hawk in the tree! Herd of deer! Momma fox and kits! Swans in the pond!"

Mara laughed out loud, remembering her mother's enthusiastic pronouncements. "And when we went up to the cabin, she never gave us a minute's peace. There were times we'd be sound asleep, and she'd wake us up to see the hummingbirds at the feeder or a baby owl on the deck railing. And hike, omigod, did that woman like to hike. She drove us crazy, making us walk with her when we were little, but when we got old enough to protest, she didn't force us. She'd just go off by herself. Annie and I just didn't get it, you know, that she'd want to walk the same trails and see the same trees and the same caves over and over. But somehow she saw something new every day."

"How old were you when she died?"

"Eleven." Her voice softened. "When she realized that she wasn't going to get any better, she couldn't decide whether she wanted to die at home or at the cabin. By the time she decided on the cabin, it was too late, she was too sick to travel. In the end she said it was just as well. She knew that Dad would eventually sell the house in the city, but he'd never sell the cabin. And at least when we went there, we wouldn't be thinking about her having died there."

"And your father?"

"He and my stepmother moved to Las Vegas about nine years ago, after he retired. He died four years ago. And Mom was right about him never selling the cabin. He gave it to Annie and me outright. He didn't set a foot in it after Mom died. We think he just couldn't bear to be there without her, her presence is so strong."

She paused, remembering.

"She used to bring us things from her walks. An eagle feather, a stone arrowhead, a pretty flower, something. I used to love those little gifts. I wish I'd told her — just one time — how much it meant to me that she always brought me those little surprises."

"I'll bet she knew."

"I hope so. Sometimes it hurts so much to think about that time before she got sick. Sometimes I just wish I could reach across time and pull those moments into the present. . . ."

"You can," he said as he pulled into the gas station. "That's what memories are."

He got out and filled the tank while Mara went into the station and bought two cans of soda from the machine and got directions to Hawk Mountain from the teenage boy who was manning the cash register.

They were just getting into the car when

Aidan's phone rang.

"Shields . . . Oh, hi." He stopped at the side of the station's lot and put the car into park. "What's up?"

Mara watched his face crease, watched him bite the inside of his lower lip as he listened attentively to the caller.

"I don't know." He turned to Mara. "How far are we from Lyndon?"

"Maybe an hour and a half, a little more. Depends on traffic."

He glanced at his watch. "We can probably be there by four." He hung up the phone and shifted into drive, then turned onto the roadway, heading back toward the highway, his face solemn, his comments limited to brief questions that gave Mara no real clue as to what was going on.

"I take it we're on our way back home?" she asked as he stopped at a red light.

"We are. There's been an odd development." He watched the light, rolled up toward the intersection slightly, eager to move. "It looks as if there's been a break-in at your house."

"How could that happen?" She frowned. "I thought the police were watching my house."

"They were. However, while the police were swarming to apprehend the suspect who was caught breaking into the home of one of the other Douglases under surveillance — that was the arrest that John called about yesterday — someone slipped the lock on your back door.

Your presence is requested in Lyndon so you can go through the house and see if anything was taken."

"But I thought there were supposed to be extra guards on my house."

"Looks like our boy is much smarter than anyone gave him credit for. The guy they arrested turned out to have been set up by Channing to lure the police to another address while he broke into your home." Aidan accelerated to pass an eighteen wheeler. "But the big news is that Channing has been positively identified as having been in the Lyndon area for the past month. Mancini tells me that not only have his employer and his landlord identified him, but Mrs. West claims he was at her house the other day."

"Holy Mother," Mara exclaimed. "Is she all right?"

"She's fine."

"But I thought the police were supposed to be watching for anyone who looked suspicious."

"Well, that's the thing. He probably didn't act in any way that set off anyone's alarms."

"What was he doing there?" she wondered aloud.

"You'll be able to ask her yourself, soon as we get to Lyndon. I'm sure she'll have a story to tell."

Mara fell silent again.

"You know, you're awfully calm about all

this," Aidan remarked. "Most people would be a little more nervous or upset, knowing that a serial killer has their name on his hit list."

She continued to stare out the window.

"After all, it's a pretty scary thing," he continued. "I'd be scared. It's okay if you are. I mean, most people would be hard-pressed to think of something worse than having a serial killer on their trail."

"Of course I'm scared. I'd be an idiot not to be afraid of Channing, knowing what he's capable of. But is this the worst thing that could happen to me?" She appeared to ponder the question.

"Actually, the worst thing that could happen to me already did." She turned toward him. "Seven years ago. If I survived that, I can survive this."

"Assuming that we can keep you alive until he's caught," Aidan replied solemnly.

"That's your job," she said softly. "And I'd trust you with my life."

It was on the tip of his tongue to remind her what had happened to the last person who had so trusted him, but the words stuck in his throat.

He gunned the engine and sped toward the highway that would take them to Lyndon, determined that history would not repeat itself.

Mrs. West had a story, all right, and Mara wasn't even out of the car before the woman set off across the driveway to tell her all about it.

". . . telling me that the delivery from Walsh's was light by a few flats. He brought them on back for me just as nice as you please," Mrs. West was saying as Mara opened her car door. "Now, I know what I buy, and I knew that I hadn't bought those extra flats that he was bringing by, for all he insisted that I had."

"He didn't hurt you or scare you, though, did he?" Mara gave her neighbor a hug.

"Oh, my, no. He was a perfect gentleman. I gave him a bottle of water. It was hot and he was sweating quite a bit. Hard to believe he's a cold-blooded serial killer." Mrs. West shuddered. "He seemed like such a nice young man. But that was him. I saw the sketch on television and I called the police to tell them that he'd been here just a few days ago. He was asking about the police being over at your place, but I didn't tell him why, nope. I wasn't born yesterday, you know. I figured it was no accident that you were going out of town with that friend of Annie's who anyone with eyes in their head could see has *federal law enforcement* written all over him. Oh, there's that nice Detective Crosby. He's the one I talked to when I called the police station. He's been here all afternoon."

"Hello, Mara." Evan Crosby walked up the driveway.

"Evan." She nodded. "I understand someone's been in my house?"

"Looks that way. Come on around back." He motioned to her to follow him, paused, and took a long look at Aidan.

"Detective Crosby, Special Agent Shields." Mara made the introductions without breaking stride across the drive. The two men nodded to each other and followed her.

"Has anyone brought you up to date on what happened here the night before last?" Crosby asked.

"Only bits and pieces from Agent Shields. Why don't you give me a quick rundown?"

He did.

"So you arrested this man, Mulholland, thinking he was the Mary Douglas killer —"

"Just as the real killer wanted us to do. We think he'd somehow managed to figure out that you were his real target, and that you lived here, so he had to draw attention away from this house."

"He would had to have known that if Mara had been the target, the police never would have left her unguarded," Aidan noted as they walked into the back hallway.

"I think he figured out real fast when all three patrol cars left at the same time that she wasn't here," Crosby said dryly. "But I think up until that time, he hadn't been certain, and figured that maybe two of the guards would have left, and he'd have been able to take out the third one. I'm thinking that once he realized that Mara wasn't here, he decided to take advantage of the situation and let himself in."

Mara snapped on one of the lamps in the living room. She walked through to the kitchen, not touching anything, her hands clasped behind her back.

"There's nothing out of place," she told Crosby. "Even the mail is right where I left it."

She pointed to the counter, where a stack of mail sat, topped by an open magazine.

"I was thumbing through my college alumni magazine when Aidan — Agent Shields — rang the doorbell the other day. That's the article I was reading, and that's right where I left it."

She walked back through the living room. "Nothing out of place here," she said, and walked up the steps.

Five minutes later, she came back downstairs.

"It doesn't appear that anyone was up there, either." She walked back down the hall to her den. "Only one other place to look . . ."

She turned on the light and looked around the small room. This month's bills were still in their neat pile. She sorted through them, found them all there.

"I don't see that anything has been touched, but I'm sure you'll be dusting for fingerprints."

"We were waiting for you before we moved anything." Crosby nodded. "We were able to lift some prints off a bottle of water Mrs. West had given him to drink. Luckily the trash had not been picked up. We'll be comparing them to prints we took from the rooming house where he's been staying."

"You have no idea where he is now?" Mara asked.

"No. Chances are he hasn't gone too far. He's gone through all this to get to you. I doubt he's going to back off now."

"You still think he's connected to Vince Giordano somehow?"

"I do. I just can't piece it together."

"You haven't been able to place them together yet?" Aidan asked. "Haven't been able to put them at the same place at the same time?"

"Actually, we did do that." Evan Crosby looked pained. "They were both incarcerated at the county prison for an overlapping period of forty-eight hours, but we haven't been able to determine when they could have met. They were housed in different wings, they were not on the same meal or exercise schedule, they were not in the library at the same time. In short, if their paths ever crossed, we can't figure out where or how. But we are still looking at that. If these two have met, it was sometime during those forty-eight hours."

"If he was at the prison, that means he . . ." Mara turned toward the detective.

"Right." Crosby nodded with no small amount of embarrassment. "It means he'd been arrested. And yes, it was our department that picked him up. He'd been stopped for a traffic violation, and it turned out there was a warrant outstanding for someone else with the same name. He was held from the time of the arrest until Monday morning, when he had his moment in court. He was apparently able to prove to the judge that he wasn't the man described in the warrant, and he was released after paying the traffic fine. Don't think for one second that I haven't been kicking myself in the ass ever since I realized we'd had him, right in our lockup."

Crosby stopped and appeared to be thinking something over.

"Shit," he muttered under his breath. He took out his cell phone and placed a call, still cursing softly. "It's Crosby. Check the roster of prisoners who were transported to the courthouse in the van with Channing. Well, then, get someone back there to open the office. I need to see that list."

Curtis woke up from an unplanned nap on the sofa and, momentarily disoriented, blinked a time or two until he got his bearings. Ah, yes. Mara's cabin. At least, he hoped it was Mara's.

He stretched, arms over his head, and repositioned himself lazily. A rumble from his stomach reminded him that it had been several hours since he'd eaten. A glance at the clock told him that an afternoon snack was the way to go. He sat up, rolled his shoulders to work out a kink, and was just about to get up and head for the kitchen when the telephone rang, jolting him as its ring battered the silence.

After the third ring, the answering machine picked up.

"Hey, are you there yet? Guess not. I tried to call your cell phone, but sweetie, you have to remember to recharge that battery every once in a while for the phone to work. Anyway, I'm on my way up there now, should be there in less than an hour. I'll stop at the market and pick up something for dinner. See you soon. Love you . . ."

Channing sat still as a stone, listening to the voice. Who was the woman who had left the message, and who had she left it for? The only thing he knew for certain was that someone was on their way and would be there soon.

He rose and began to pace, his mind racing. Was it Mara? Or this other woman, this Anne Marie McCall whose name had been on the magazine label?

Either way, he could expect company within the hour.

He'd be waiting.

Chapter Nineteen

Annie drove along the Northeast Extension of the Pennsylvania Turnpike, thinking about food, the music on the radio, the scenery. Anything other than being at the cabin. Without Dylan.

She'd forced herself to make the drive several times since Dylan's death, but those times, she'd had the house to herself. She'd slept in the bed they'd shared, clutching one of the flannel shirts he'd left in the closet, broke out the envelopes full of photographs, drank too much wine, and did what she had to do to work some of her grief out of her system. Little by little she'd done that. But she'd done it alone. Tonight she would share the cabin with her sister, and his brother. She wasn't certain she was ready to do that.

On the other hand, she was intrigued, dying to know what exactly had been going on between Mara and Aidan over the past few days, though she had to remind herself not to hope for too much. After all, they'd known each other for only a few weeks. But Mara's noncommittal comments had been real teasers.

Wouldn't it be nice, she thought as she exited the highway, *if the two of them found each other. God knows Aidan's punished himself long enough over Dylan's death, and Mara, well, she's shown little or no interest in anyone or anything since that despicable excuse of a husband of hers slunk off into the night and disappeared with her child.* Annie's blood pressure began to rise just thinking about it. A man like Jules could turn any woman off men permanently.

Bastard.

Annie adjusted the volume on the radio and scanned for something she felt like listening to. Finding nothing, she slipped in a CD and hit Play. Clannad. Sweet and sad and soothing. Just the thing.

She was still wondering if something was developing between Aidan and Mara, and thinking how pleased Dylan would have been if it were, when she turned onto Poor Farm Road. She passed old Mr. Keppler's place down near the main road, noted that it was dark, as she'd expected. Two years ago he'd moved to Florida, leaving the cabin in the care of his grandson. Annie wondered idly if the grandson — he was in his thirties and owned a gas station someplace in New Jersey — ever visited the cabin. It would be a shame for it to just sit, unoccupied, year after year. It was a cute place, she was thinking, if somewhat small.

There was no sign of Mara or anyone else when Annie reached the McCall cabin. Maybe they got a late start, or maybe they stopped for dinner, Annie thought as she parked near the mailbox, upon the side of which was neatly painted the number of the cabin. Two. It had been a joke between her and Mara, since mail was never delivered here. One went to the local post office to pick up mail. She and Mara used to leave little messages to each other in the box. Annie opened the box and looked in, but of course there was no message from her sister. Looking around, she spotted a dandelion in the grass. She picked it and put it in the box. If, on a whim, Mara should look, as Annie had just done, there'd be something inside.

Swinging her overnight bag onto her shoulder, Annie picked her way over the stones to the steps leading to the deck. The late afternoon sun had dropped down behind the house, casting shadows from the tall oaks that grew along the ridge out back. She paused, looking up at the cabin. Funny, but she'd never studied it in this light before. It looked dark, and maybe just a little foreboding.

Ridiculous. She shook her head as she began to climb the steps. *Of course it looks dark. It's late in the day, the sun is beginning to set, the place is empty, there are no lights on, and the drapes are all drawn. Tough to look cheery with all that going on.*

Well, she thought as she unlocked the front door, *I'll pull back the drapes and turn on a few lights, maybe set a fire in the fireplace, so that at least this place won't look so gloomy by the time Mara arrives. Whenever that will be . . .*

She paused in the doorway, thinking that something, somehow, was different. From where she was standing she could see that all was as it had been the last time she had been there. Still, there was something in the air. . . .

Exactly.

Someone had been cooking with onions.

Frowning, she dropped her bag, preparing to go straight into the kitchen. She turned to close the door and found herself face-to-face with the last person in the world she'd expected to see.

"Oh!" She backed up quickly, one hand behind her searching for the doorknob.

"Don't," he said calmly. "Just . . . don't. There's nowhere for you to go, no one to hear you if you scream, and all you're going to accomplish is to aggravate me, which you do not want to do. So . . . don't."

Annie's mind all but froze. How could this be possible? How could he have known about this place?

"I want you to move over there, to the sofa, and sit." He took her elbow to guide her, as if it were his home and she were his visitor. "Sit right here."

He led her to the sofa and turned on the lamp that stood on the end table. The light glinted off the tip of the knife that he held in his right hand.

"Who are you?" she asked.

"The more important question is, who are you?" He gently pushed her onto the cushion and stood above her, looking down.

When she did not answer, he chuckled and with the knife, cut the strap of her shoulder bag. He reached in and took out her wallet.

"Anne Marie McCall," he read aloud from her driver's license. "There are magazines here with your name on them. You left the message on the answering machine. Was the message for Mara?"

Annie merely stared at him.

"Now, we're going to establish a few rules here." He leaned a little closer. "If I ask you a question, you answer. For one thing, it's the polite thing to do." Closer still, his harsh whisper raising the hairs on her forearms. "For another, I'll cut off one of your fingers every time I have to repeat myself. Understand?"

"Yes. I understand." She nodded, shaken.

"Good. Now I will ask you one more time, with the reminder that this is the only time you will ever get a second chance. Did you leave a message on the answering machine, and was the message for Mara Douglas?"

"Yes. To both."

"Is she on her way?"

"I believe she is."

"You believe. You don't know for certain?"

"I was under the impression that she was driving up here today." No need, Annie reasoned, to mention that Aidan would be accompanying Mara. There could be an advantage if her captor was unaware that Mara would not be arriving alone.

"But that wasn't confirmed?"

"No. I couldn't get through to her on her mobile phone. She sometimes forgets to recharge her battery. But I believe she will be along. Maybe tonight, maybe tomorrow."

"What are you to her?"

"I'm her sister."

"Oh." He nodded, a smile slowly crossing his face. "I've never had sisters before. Well, not at the same time, at least. Could be interesting . . . oh, now, don't give me that look. You might enjoy it. Well, then again, maybe not . . ."

"How did you find this place?" she asked.

"The information was in a file in a desk drawer at your sister's house. I figured if she was going to be lying low for a few days, she might come here. Good guess on my part, huh?"

"What do you want with her?"

"Let's just say our paths were destined to cross."

"Why?"

"Why?" He pondered the question. "Because I gave my word. And what is a man if he doesn't keep his word?"

"Who did you give your word to?" she asked quietly.

"What difference does it make?" He glanced at her. "A deal is a deal, no matter who you make it with, right?"

"They know who you are, you know."

"Oh?" He pulled over an ottoman and sat in

front of her. "And how might they have figured that out?"

"I don't know."

"I'll bet you do know, Miss McCall." He opened her wallet again and flipped through it. Something caught his eye, and he smiled, holding up a credit card. "Or should I say Dr. McCall? What kind of a doctor are you, Dr. McCall?"

"I'm a psychiatrist."

"Oh, well, shit, doesn't that just figure?" Laughing, he snapped the wallet closed and tossed it back into her purse. "I finally get my own doctor to play doctor with, and here you're a goddammed shrink. Well, shit, don't that just beat all?"

"What do you have against psychiatrists?"

"Well, let's put it this way. Over the course of my life, I've probably spent more time talking to your colleagues than you have."

"And did it help?" she asked dryly.

Surprised at the remark, he looked at her for a long moment before laughing out loud.

"Well, apparently not, since . . . well, just look at your own circumstances." He stood up and seemed to be considering something.

"Maybe you didn't talk to the right person," she said, still outwardly calm, though inside she was fighting back panic. How to get the knife from him? How to escape? Did he have a gun? How to warn Mara?

"I talked to more shrinks . . . I wasn't kidding

when I said that over the years, I probably knew more shrinks than you. There was the kiddie shrink, then the shrink the courts assigned. Then there was the school shrink, then the one my —" He paused, his face clouding over for a brief moment.

"The one your parents hired?" Annie tried to recall everything she had been told about Channing's foster parents.

"It doesn't matter," he cut her off.

"Of course it does. They cared about you. And you cared enough about them to take their name." She was going to have to gamble here.

He stared at her. "Now, how would you know all that?" He leaned down into her face. "How would you know about them?"

"Because my employer — that would be the Federal Bureau of Investigation — has developed a deep interest in you. As a matter of fact, they've been trying to learn everything there is to know about you."

"You're FBI?"

"Yes." She squared her shoulders. In for a dime, in for a dollar. She'd find out soon enough whether full disclosure had been a good idea.

"Well, well. What do you know? The surprises just keep coming fast and furious here, that's a fact." He laughed, a short, mirthless snort. "My luck just keeps getting better and better. Now, if worse came to worst, what do you think the FBI

356

would give up for your safety?"

"I have no idea."

"Well, maybe I'll just have to hold on to you for a while in case I need to find out. But it wasn't nice of you to lie to me. To pretend that you didn't know me. Lying isn't nice." He ran the knife along her jawline. "I think I'll save your punishment for later. I want to think about it for a while."

He gestured for her to stand. "But right now, I need you to come with me."

"Where?"

"Downstairs. Come on. And please do not make this difficult for me. I'm just not in the mood to get pissed off right now." He grabbed her arm and turned her around so that she was in front of him. He leaned into her body and whispered in her ear. "You give me a hard time, you'll make it that much worse for her and for you, understand me? I'm bigger than you and much stronger. You will not overpower me. Unless, of course, you have a gun. Does the FBI give their shrinks guns, lady shrink?"

His hands roamed her body, top to bottom, groping and searching her pockets, her waistband, his breathing coming more and more unevenly.

"I don't carry weapons," she told him. "I'm a profiler."

His hands stopped where they were. "A profiler? Like you see on TV?"

"Yes."

357

"Well, hot damn. How 'bout that?" He gripped her upper arms and steered her in the direction of the basement steps. "Well, we can have some fun, you and I. I can tell you a secret or two from my past, and you can profile me."

"Sounds like my idea of a good time."

He opened the basement door and turned on the light, then forced her down the steps. At the bottom, he nodded at the room where he'd found the guns.

"Those your guns in there?" he asked, one hand on the door that lead into the garage.

"My grandfather's," she told him.

"He a hunter?"

"He was, when he was younger. Later in his life he did more collecting than shooting. When he died, my dad inherited the property, and he moved all the guns down here. He didn't want them around us kids, didn't want to look at them."

"Oh, a real peace-i-fist, eh?"

"My dad was an academic, a math professor. He had no interest in hunting or in guns. He kept them because they had belonged to his father, but he never used any of them."

"Worth a lot of money, some of 'em, you know that?"

"No," she replied, though of course she did. She knew exactly what the collection was worth. She'd had a dealer offer her an impressive sum just two years ago, but had declined because Dylan had been delighted with the guns. She'd planned on giving the collection to him as a wedding present.

On their last long stay here, Dylan had spent days cleaning selected firearms, and had even purchased new ammunition for several of the old handguns that he'd had retrofitted. She wished she'd paid closer attention to which ones. She tried to remember which ones he'd taken out for target practice and where he'd left the newly purchased ammo.

"Here." He motioned to her to precede him into the garage.

"Where are we going?"

"Just here, in the garage. I saw something down here that I need . . . yeah, there." He took a length of coiled rope down from its hook on the wall and slid it onto his arm, up to the shoulder. "We can go on back upstairs now. You first."

She eyed the rope and felt her knees weaken. Whatever he planned to do with it, it wasn't going to be good for her.

"Go." He nudged her. "And don't try any of those FBI tricks. Remember that I still have a knife at your back."

Once upstairs, he turned off the downstairs light and closed the door behind them.

"Into the living room," he told her. "Stop. Stop there."

He grabbed first one arm, then the other, and tied her wrists together behind her.

"Sit. There on the sofa, where you were

before," he instructed.

She sat, awkwardly, while he tied her feet at the ankle, sorely tempted to take her chances and kick him in the head. But he was, as he'd pointed out, bigger and stronger than she, and he was armed. By the time she'd decided that discretion was in truth the better part of valor, the point was moot. Channing was on his feet and her ankles were crossed and tied into that position.

"Just so that I can go about my business without wondering what you're doing," he told her as he cut away the unused portion of the rope with the knife.

"And what business would that be?"

"Waiting for your sister." He went to the window and looked out. It was still light, but darkness would soon enough descend.

He needed a revised plan.

"Does she know that you're here? That you were coming here?" he asked.

"No. I told you. I wasn't able to contact her to let her know. I thought she was here, or on her way here. That's why I left the message on the answering machine."

"So you don't know where she is now?"

"No."

"What could have delayed her?"

"I have no idea."

He paced for a moment in front of the fireplace. "Where are your car keys?"

"In my bag."

He picked up the tan leather bag and sorted through it until he found the key ring. He tossed the keys back and forth in his hands for a minute, then, without a word, left the cabin, closing the door behind him.

Swell, she thought. *He's stealing my car and leaving me tied up here.*

Nah. That's not his style, she told herself. *He's looking for the upper hand. He's hiding the car so Mara doesn't know I'm here. So that she'll walk into the dark house and he'll grab her, just like he grabbed me. And there's no way I can warn her.*

But there's Aidan. He doesn't know about Aidan. . . .

She tried to stand, but with her arms behind her back and her ankles tied, she had difficulty getting up from the too-soft seat cushions. By the time she'd gotten herself to the edge of the sofa, his footsteps were on the stairs. She eased back into the position she was in when he left.

"Where'd you hide my car?" she asked casually. "I'm guessing down in that deep ravine. That's where I'd leave it."

"Smart, aren't you?"

"I get by."

He laughed. "You're something, you know that? I don't usually care much for blondes, but you're something."

"Your mother was blond, wasn't she?" Annie couldn't resist.

"Don't go there, Dr. McCall." His voice held a quiet threat. "You do not want to go there."

"Sorry. Didn't mean to bring up unpleasant memories."

"You are pushing your luck, and you know it." He went into the kitchen, and she heard him banging around.

Better to bang on a few pots than bang something off my head, she rationalized.

"I've made us some soup," he said from the kitchen doorway, which was behind her, so she could not see him.

"Then you're going to have to untie me if I'm going to eat." *And then maybe I can talk him into letting me go into the bathroom, and I can look in the closet and see if there's anything there I can use as a weapon. I can break off a toothbrush so that it has a sharp end —*

"If you're hungry, I'll feed you. But I won't untie you." He stood in front of her now. "You've had too much time to yourself, too much time to think of what you might do if you get a chance."

"You're pretty smart yourself," she said wryly.

"Thanks," he said as he pulled her to her feet. "See if you can hop on over to the table here . . ."

He pulled out the closest chair for her, and she fell into it awkwardly.

"Not my usual graceful self," she told him.

"I'll bet you are graceful." He looked down at her. "Did you dance when you were little?"

"What?"

"When you were a little girl, did you take dancing lessons?"

"Yes."

"Thought so. You remind me of a girl who lived near us when I was in high school. She took dancing lessons. She was the first person I ever knew who I'd call graceful. Even when she walked, she . . . flowed." His eyes clouded, remembering. "She was beautiful."

"I guess you never hurt her, did you, Curtis?"

"Of course not," he snapped back. "How could you even suggest such a thing?"

He pushed himself away from the table and went into the kitchen, leaving her alone, wondering if she should try to push his buttons. If she rattled him, would it prove to be advantageous or detrimental?

"Well, since we're here, alone, with all of this time to kill, maybe we should use it to get to know each other," Annie said when he came back holding a loaf of bread and a butter knife.

"Like what would you like to know, lady shrink?" He buttered a piece of bread and offered her a bite.

She shook her head. "Thanks, but I seem to have lost my appetite."

"You might be sorry later. Never know where your next meal might be coming from, but, hey, suit yourself." He grinned and took a bite of the bread. "Now, what were you going to ask me?"

"Was it your idea to change your name from

363

Gibbons to Channing?"

He stopped chewing momentarily, then resumed, slowly, until the bread was paste and he
finally swallowed.

"My foster parents suggested it. They wanted
me to take their name."

"No doubt to help you to put the past behind
you. Very kind of them, very caring. They must
be wonderful people."

"Nicest people I ever met." He nodded.

"I guess that's why you left when you did."
Annie sat back to watch his face. "You must
have felt all that churning inside and wanted to
get away from them before it exploded. Were
you afraid of hurting them?"

"I never would have lifted a finger against either one of them."

"Then you just were afraid that they'd see
what was inside you. Afraid that they'd recognize what you were becoming."

He knocked the knife off the side of his plate.
"It was just time to go, that's all."

"How old were you when you knew that
something was growing inside you, Channing?
How old were you when you realized that you
were not like other people?" Her voice
dropped, and she prayed he wouldn't respond
by slicing her throat. If she could keep him
talking, keep him absorbed, she could keep his
focus off Mara's arrival, maybe take away a bit
of his advantage.

He bit off another piece of bread, again

chewing slowly, as if debating whether to respond or to discontinue the conversation altogether.

"I was always different, and I always knew it. I don't remember a time when I didn't feel different from everyone else. But you being a shrink, you probably figured that out."

She nodded as he spoke, as if to affirm his statement. "Did it start when Unger went to prison?"

"Nah." He stirred his soup with his spoon. "Long before that. She started trading me to her johns for drugs . . . shit, for as far back as I can remember. The only time it stopped was when we lived with Al. He gave her whatever she wanted, so there was no need for her to put me out. That was the only time I was safe, when we lived with Al."

"And then he went to prison. . . ."

"You know a lot, don't you, lady shrink?" he said without looking at her. "Yeah, Al went off to prison. I have tried, all my life, to forgive him, but I just never could."

"Forgive him for what? I thought you said you were safe with him."

"For being so goddamn stupid to get sent up for some stupid piddling thing like stealing, and leaving me alone with her. He had a gun in his pocket when he walked into that little Mom and Pop. He never took it out, but it was on him, and they said that made it armed robbery." His face darkened. "Just plain stupid . . ."

"And as soon as he was gone . . ."

"She started taking men in again. Some of them liked little boys. She didn't care, didn't give a shit, long as she got what she needed."

"And there was never anyone you could tell . . . no one you could trust? A teacher? Your minister?"

"We weren't exactly a churchgoing family. And at school, well, I was just a poor, transient kid. Way behind everyone else in the class, always, 'cause we'd moved around so much. Then there were days when I was in no shape to go to school . . ."

His eyes darkened, and his voice dropped.

"And then Al came back . . ." Annie prompted.

"Yeah. She'd been too high to remember he was coming home that day, and she was having herself a party with some guy she'd picked up. Al came in and started looking around the house for her. When he found her, boy oh boy, you should have heard the two of them."

"Big fireworks, eh?"

"Screaming, both of them." He shook his head, remembering. "He left the house, and she finished up what she was doing with this other guy, then sent him packing right before Al came back. He'd been drinking, I could tell that, and when he started in on her, I just snuck into the closet and closed the door. I stayed in there, hiding, but then I heard all the commotion in the living room and I opened the door just a bit. He had her on the floor, with her skirt up . . . and then that knife was in his hand. Up and down, up and down, up and down . . ."

"Six times."

"Yes. Six times. She started screaming when she saw that knife — never made a peep the whole time he was raping her, but she saw that knife and, oooweee, she was screaming bloody murder. Which was exactly what Al had in mind, I suppose. . . ."

"I am so sorry," she whispered. "No child should ever have to see —"

"Don't." He squeezed his eyes closed tightly. "Don't think you can win me over by pretending to sympathize —"

"I'm not pretending. No child should ever have to go through what you went through."

He stood abruptly, then began to clear his place, carrying the bowl and plate into the kitchen. She heard the sound of running water. A few minutes later, he came back into the room and sat next to her.

"Sorry. I was taught to clean up after myself. Where were we? Oh, right, Unger was killing my mother and I was watching from the closet." For all the emotion he displayed, they could have been talking about the weather.

"Anyway, in the long run, it worked in my favor. They took me out of there and sent me to live with the Channings. That was the first real home I ever had."

"But you thought you didn't deserve it."

"Wouldn't be much of a shrink if you didn't see that, would you?"

"Wouldn't be much of a shrink if I didn't see that everything that happened to you by the time you were four or five made you what you are. Then, later, seeing your mother raped, watching her murdered, just gave you a visual blueprint for your anger and —"

"Yeah, yeah, my anger and my pain." He laughed hoarsely. "I'll tell you what took away some of the pain, lady shrink. When I came out of that closet and saw that she was dead and I picked up that knife and slid it into the places where he'd cut her —"

He raised his right hand and began to plunge it down slowly, stabbing an invisible knife into an invisible body.

"— and made believe that I had been the one to kill her" — his face took on a dreamy look — "I had been the one who'd made her bleed like that. . . ."

"So that she couldn't let you be hurt again."

He nodded. "I used to fall asleep at night praying that I'd wake up in the morning and be big enough, strong enough, to hurt her so that she could never hurt me again. I was grateful to Al for doing it, and at the same time I hated him, because I wanted to be the one. He took that from me."

"But you pulled her skirt down and covered her face," she reminded him. "You tried to hide the fact of the rape, and you shielded her eyes."

"Yeah, well," he mumbled, "she was still my mother."

Outside, a car door slammed. He sat up like a shot.

"Shit. She's here." He ran to the window and looked out, watching two figures move through the light from the car's headlights. "Who's that with her? Who is it?"

He turned to Annie, furious.

"I don't know." She shrugged.

"You tell me." He crossed the room and grabbed her by the arm. Cutting the ropes that tied her ankles together, he pulled her roughly to the window and held the drape back by less than half an inch so that the lamplight would not be visible from outside the cabin. "He looks like law. Is he one of your buddies from the FBI?"

"Yes."

"Swell. Just fucking swell." He pulled her away from the window. "You knew she wouldn't be alone. You knew. That's why you're so calm — you thought the FBI would come storming in here to save you. Fuck that. *Fuck* that."

He turned off the lamp and dragged her through the kitchen, where he grabbed a dish towel and stuffed it partially into her mouth.

"Just in case you were thinking about warning her . . ." He opened the basement door and shoved her down the steps brusquely,

369

holding on to her so that she did not fall. Once downstairs, he searched for the side entrance and unlocked it, pulling her along with him into the cool air of early evening.

The presence of the FBI agent changed everything. He'd have to regroup, he thought as he dragged Annie through the brush just below the ridge behind the cabin. He'd need a place to stow her while he came back for Mara, and he had just the place in mind.

Tightening his grip on her arm, he quickened his pace, hoping he could find his way back to the cabin at the top of the road in the dark. After a quick stop at his car, he'd come back to rid himself of the FBI.

Then, finally, he'd claim his prize, and the first part of the game would have played out.

Chapter Twenty

"Boy, you weren't kidding when you said this place was quiet. And *dark*."

Aidan paused next to the car and searched the darkness for a recognizable form. Other than a few trees silhouetted against the sky, there was little to be seen in the inky darkness. "This would be the perfect place to watch the stars. There's no competing light for . . . how many miles are we from civilization, would you say?"

Mara laughed. "We're a few miles outside of town, but since town doesn't consist of much, I guess you can reasonably assume that we're pretty much out there."

His hands on his hips, Aidan took a deep breath. "Makes you think about the days when people built cabins like this in the wilderness, you know? Nothing around them, no lights anywhere. They'd step outside and stand, looking up, just like we are right now. Infinite night. The difference for them was that it would never change, night to night. It would always be wilderness, always be isolated. Talk about a lonely existence."

"Most nights there'd be no lights inside, either, except maybe an oil lamp, if they could afford that. Otherwise, there'd be just the fire in the fireplace."

"No *Sex in the City*. No MTV." He nudged her. "*Survivor* had a whole different meaning back then."

A screech shattered the silence, and Mara jumped, then laughed nervously.

"For some, surviving the night out here is still a challenge." She tilted her head upward and scanned the treetops, looking for the owl that had just shattered the silence.

She looked around the darkened road. "Which leads to the obvious question, where is Spike?"

"He jumped out when I opened the door."

"Spike!" she called. "Spike!"

From behind her, the dog barked and she turned in his direction.

"Guess I need to remind you of the rules, buddy. You can't take off on your own around here. Didn't you hear that owl?" she scolded. "You'd make a pretty tempting target."

Spike barked again and moved toward the house.

"You don't let him run loose up here?"

"No." She shook her head and walked to the back of the car with Aidan, who opened the cargo space. "It's just plain dangerous to let your pet go off on his own. He'd be no match for a bear or a hungry cat. And we have raptors up here with wingspans you wouldn't believe. Everything from bald eagles to hawks, any one of which could pick up and take off with a dog

372

the size of Spike. It's a pain to have to keep the dog on a leash, but you have to remember, we're invading the space of the wild animals that live here. We have to play on their terms."

She fished in her pockets for the key, then reached for her bag.

"I have it," Aidan told her. "Why don't you just go ahead and unlock the door and turn some lights on."

"Okay." Mara called again for Spike, who, sensing she meant business this time, bounded out from some shrubs off the path to the cabin. "Watch your step here, Aidan. The stones are a little uneven."

She felt in the darkness for the stair railing, then grabbed hold. "And it's ten steps to the top," she called back to him. "Count them on your way up, or you could misjudge in the dark and trip."

"Wait, let me turn the car around so that the lights shine on the house." He did so. "There. That should help."

"Wonderful. I don't know why I didn't think of that."

The stairs illuminated, she found her way to the front door, then searched for the lock. The headlights from Aidan's car did not reach the door, and after it took her a few tries to get the key into the lock, she reminded herself that the last time she'd been there, she'd promised herself a key ring with a small flashlight. "Next time I'm out, I will definitely buy one of those."

"What?" Aidan said, reaching the top of the steps.

"I said, I need to buy one of those key rings that have a little flashlight."

"Or maybe a sensor light that goes on automatically."

"You mean the kind that turns a light on when someone walks within a certain distance of the house?" She pushed the door open and felt along the inside wall for the light switches. Finding them, she illuminated not only the deck, but the small inside entry area.

"Right. Easy to install and relatively inexpensive."

"Sounds like a simple solution to the problem." She snapped on the lamp on one of the tables in the living room area.

Aidan dropped their bags just inside the door. "We can run into that home supply place we passed about twenty miles back and pick one up tomorrow. I can put it up for you."

"Thanks, but I really didn't mean to put you to work while we're here. I'm sure I can find an electrician —"

"What, and deprive me of a chance to show you what a talented guy I am? Not on your life," he said, and grinned as he went back out the door and to the car.

"Spike, come back here," she called as the dog followed Aidan. "We'll go for a walk later."

She went into the kitchen and turned on the water to fill the dog's water dish, then spilled half of it as she attempted to put it down on the floor. She mopped the water up with paper towels, then opened the trash can to toss them in. The lid had dropped quickly, but not before she thought she saw something.

She opened the lid again and looked into the trash. An empty can of condensed soup lay amidst the discarded towels. She was still staring down at it when Aidan came in, carrying the bags of groceries they'd picked up on their way.

"I hope you don't mind, but I opened those drapes in the living room partway. There's a nice view of the sky . . ." He paused in the doorway. "What's the matter?"

"Probably nothing."

"Why are you staring into the trash?"

"There's an empty soup can."

"Hmmm. No wonder you're suspicious. Someone having eaten soup in a mountain cabin . . ."

"Annie's the only person that I know of who's been here. She doesn't like tomato soup. Never did."

"Maybe she had a friend with her one weekend, and the friend brought some food up. Much like we did."

"Oh. Right. That's probably it." Mara dropped the lid. "Odd she forgot to take the trash with her, though . . ."

"Hey, I'll bet even Annie forgets things once in a while."

"That would be a first, but I suppose anything is possible."

Mara began to unpack the bags and put the groceries away.

"Hey, I see there's some wood stacked up in here," Aidan called from the next room. "How about if I make a fire?"

"Great idea. Thanks." Mara smiled as she placed the bottle of wine on the counter and searched the cupboards for a couple of wineglasses.

The sound of music filled the cabin. Aidan had found the stereo.

Perfect. A little music, a little wine, a cozy fire . . .

Mara began to hum as she opened the freezer. Annie always kept an assortment of frozen goodies for just such times. There, just as she suspected, she found a frozen pizza. She'd just pop it in the oven while Aidan got the fire going, then they could snack on the floor in front of the hearth, sip wine, and . . . well, who knew where that could lead?

She poured wine into the glasses and carried them into the living room. She handed one to Aidan, who sat on the floor, leaning back against the sofa, watching the flames.

"The fire looks great," she noted.

"Sit with me" — he patted the floor next to him — "and we'll enjoy it together."

"Let me just get Spike situated first." She set her glass on the brick mantel and walked to the entry. Opening the inside door, she leaned down to adjust a latch on the screen door.

"What are you doing?" Aidan asked.

"Opening the pet port," she replied, "so that Spike can go in and out as he pleases, which is pretty much constantly."

"I thought you didn't let him run loose up here."

"Oh, I don't. There's a kiddie gate at the top of the steps. I'll latch that over so he can't leave the deck. I'll be right back. . . ."

Once outside, Mara closed the expandable gate and locked it, then called Spike outside. He came right through the pet door and, happily wagging his tail, began his inspection of the deck.

"Okay, Spike, you know the drill. You can come and go, but there will be none of this let-dog-in, let-dog-out nonsense, understand? You can just do your little doggy thing." She lifted the dog and whispered in his ear, "But try to do it mostly out here for a while, all right? Momma's got plans for Aidan. . . ."

She set the dog back onto the deck, picked up his leash, and draped it over the railing. She went back inside and returned with a fuzzy stuffed toy that looked like an oversized baseball, which she rolled across the deck. Spike pounced on it and happily lay down with his head resting on it.

"That's the idea." Mara grinned. "Good doggie."

"The timer just went off in the kitchen."

Aidan started to stand up.

"Oh, I was heating the oven. I thought I'd throw in a pizza."

"Great idea." He lowered himself to the floor again and stretched out his left leg. He was tired from all the driving. His eyes closed, he rested his head against the sofa and prayed that his bad leg would settle down. There were definite romantic vibes in the air, but a fat lot of good it would do if he couldn't get the *bam bam bam* of pain to ease up.

Maybe the wine would help. He lifted his glass and was just about to take a sip when Mara sat down next to him. He put an arm around her and drew her close. She leaned against his shoulder, feeling secure and calm in spite of everything that had been happening.

"It's so peaceful here," he said, as if reading her mind. "You could almost forget about Channing for a while."

"I want to forget about him. I want to forget about what he is and what he's done, if only for a few hours. Just for a while, I want to think about something besides the killing and I want to stop thinking about the fact that he's intending to add my name to his list of victims." She sat silent for a moment, then added, "Of course, you, being FBI, could probably not forget for too long."

"Probably not," he said with a nod. "But maybe we could, just for a few hours, focus on something good. Something . . ."

He drew her close and traced the outline of her mouth with his tongue before parting her lips and kissing her, lightly at first, then more deeply. Mara pulled away momentarily to put their wineglasses on the table next to the sofa before sinking back into his arms. She did feel safe, did feel secure, wanted that feeling to last. It had been so very long since she'd felt anything other than dead inside. It was nice to discover that it wasn't a permanent state.

How long had it been since she craved the sensation of someone's mouth on hers, of kisses that started on the side of her face and trailed down her throat? How long since she'd wanted to feel a man's hands on her body, the sensation of warmth that was beginning to spread through her with no sign of stopping?

Stop thinking, she chastised herself. *Just feel . . .*

She did just that, lowering herself to the rough carpet and pulling Aidan with her, her head spinning as heat began to build as his hands slid under her shirt and found her breasts.

Damn sports bra . . .

"Wait," she whispered, and partially sat up to remove the offending article, then eased back down again, bringing him with her. Her mouth opened for his kiss and her hands fisted in his hair, dragging his mouth back to hers. She arched her back, offering herself to him, and he took, his hands everywhere at once, his mouth everywhere at once, and she fought back tiny cries, so clever were his fingers and his tongue. . . .

"What was that?" He froze in her arms.

"What?" She opened her eyes, feeling slightly dazed. "I didn't hear anything."

"I thought I heard Spike bark." Aidan frowned and raised himself up to look toward the window that opened to the deck.

"You must have super hearing." She shook her head. "I guess that's a requirement for being a special agent."

"I want to take a look." He got up and walked to the window and looked out.

Spike stood on the deck, still as a stone. When Aidan tapped on the window, the dog turned, then wagged his tail tentatively.

"What did you see, buddy?" Aidan asked.

Spike continued to look up at the house, wagging his tail.

"I don't see anything." Aidan turned back to Mara.

"He could have seen a raccoon or an opossum down on the ground." Mara leaned on one elbow. "Or a leaf could have blown across the deck. Any distraction is pretty much the same to Spike."

"I guess." He sat on the edge of the sofa, rubbing his throbbing thigh, reaching for the wine and wondering if it would help.

"Are you all right?" Mara asked.

"Sure." He tossed back the wine.

"You look like you're in pain."

"It will pass."

She reached up for him and he lay alongside her.

"You know, I'm not really prepared for this," he said softly. "I mean for us."

"Neither am I." She leaned back and looked into his eyes.

"But I'm wondering if Dylan . . . if he left something here. In the bathroom . . ."

"Or maybe in their room. In Annie's room," she corrected herself. "Maybe in the bedside table."

"Now would be a good time to look." He kissed her on the tip of the nose.

"Second door on the right," Mara told him as he got up.

She sat back against the sofa and closed her eyes. The last thing she'd expected when Aidan showed up at her door was for him to be more than a companion, a bodyguard. The past week with him had reawakened yearnings she'd forgotten she could feel, and her feelings toward him had grown into something that went way beyond friendship. Still, they'd known each other for only a few weeks. . . .

"Look what I found," Aidan said as he emerged from the hallway.

"Something wrapped in foil?"

"Yes," he laughed, "but look here." He held up a handgun with a fancy handle. "Dylan told me there was a collection of old guns here."

She nodded. "In my dad's study, downstairs."

"He said Annie'd let him go through them, and he'd cleaned them up and even had a few refitted to hold modern ammo." He sat down beside her, admiring the handgun.

"Is it loaded?"

"No, no." He shook his head. "But there's a box of small-caliber bullets in there, so I'm guessing he shot this one a time or two."

"Maybe tomorrow you can shoot it." She took the gun from his hands and placed it on the table. "Right now, I think I'm more interested in picking up where we left off."

"Well, then, how about I put another log on the fire" — he placed a split piece of oak on the fading embers — "and maybe a little more music . . ." He hit replay, then, following her to the floor, whispered, "I think we were right about here. . . ."

Channing cursed under his breath almost continuously until he reached the cabin steps. He'd lost count of the number of times he'd tripped on his way up here. Everything from loose stones to small branches to God knew what else lay in his path. It was really hard, he thought wryly, to sneak up on the cabin when every other step he took was punctuated with a grunt or some other automatic reaction to tripping.

"Shit," he muttered softly as he missed the bottom step.

382

From the top of the deck, there was a low rumbling. Channing looked up, and in the dim light he could make out the outline of a small dog.

"Hey, pup," he whispered.

Spike growled again.

"Hey, you're a Jack Russell," Channing exclaimed. "I used to have a doggie just like you. Jake, his name was."

He climbed the rest of the steps, his caution now secondary to wanting to see the dog a little closer.

"Yep, you look just like my Jake." He nodded. "He was the best little dog in the world. My best friend. The best friend I ever had."

Spike took several steps back from the gate as Channing slipped the latch and sat on the top step, holding out his hand for Spike to sniff.

"There, see? I won't hurt you. I would never hurt you," Channing crooned. "I like dogs."

He sat still as a stone while Spike investigated him. Slowly, Channing began to stroke the back of the little dog's head.

"You're a real sweet dog, aren't you?" Channing smiled, captivated, his mission, for the moment, put aside. "My dog was a sweet dog, too. I missed him for a long time."

Soothed by the gentle tone, Spike sat next to Channing, who continued to pet him. Channing almost forgot what he was there for.

Almost. But not quite.

He reached into his pocket and pulled out a granola bar.

"You want a little snack?" he whispered. "This is all I have, but I'll share. Let's see if you like strawberry."

Spike's tail wagged eagerly as Channing broke off a small piece and offered it to his canine companion, who sniffed it once before accepting the tidbit. Over the next few minutes, Channing fed most of the remaining bar to Spike.

Believing that the dog would not bark to announce the presence of the stranger, now that they had made friends, Channing stood and crept up to the window. Inside he could see that both the lights and the fire were low and he could hear soft music playing. The table at the end of the sofa held two glasses, each partly filled with wine, and a gun. A step closer to the window, and he could see the shadowy bodies, entwined on the floor. He couldn't see what they were doing, but he could guess.

Looks like they weren't expecting company. He chuckled to himself, thinking that now might be the best time to take out the FBI guy, while his full attention was elsewhere. Then again, if his reflexes were good, he'd be on that gun in a flash.

He started toward the door, thinking he might take his chances, but the dog began to bark. A quick glance inside the house indicated that the man had heard and was getting up to investigate. Channing flattened himself into the shadows alongside the bay window, hoping that the man wouldn't look to the end of the deck.

He didn't. He opened the door, and stepped out onto the deck, but the dog held his attention, as it had held Channing's.

"What are you barking at, Spike? Oh, your baseball is caught in the doggie door, is that it?" The man bent over and released the large, fuzzy, stuffed blue-and-white ball and rolled it across the deck.

The dog pounced on it and dragged it back to the door.

"We'll play later." The man stooped to pat the dog on the head. "Go lie down, Spike."

The dog wagged his tail slowly, watching the man disappear back into the house. He'd been much bigger — taller and better built — than Channing had originally thought. Might be a tough takedown.

"Hey, Spike," Channing whispered. "Bring it here. I'll play with you."

Spike's tail began to wag a little faster. He jumped at the ball, pushing it across the deck. Channing stopped it with one foot, then gave it a gentle kick, sending the ball to the opposite side of the deck. Spike returned the ball eagerly, happy to play. Grinning now and pleased with the game, Channing gave it another kick, a little harder this time. It rolled to the edge of the deck and rolled off.

"Oh, damn," Channing sighed.

In the game now, Spike ran to his new playmate, his little tail wagging merrily.

"I suppose you want me to go get that, don't you?"

Spike wagged a little faster.

"Tell you what I'm going to do, little buddy." He knelt down and scooped up the dog, who swiped a pink tongue to lick at Channing's chin. "I'm going to take you for a walk. Yeah, you and me."

He reached for the leash that hung over the side of the deck and snapped it onto Spike's collar. He took one last furtive look inside the cabin and decided that the couple in there were likely to be there for a while. While the element of surprise was his, the gun and the physical advantage went to Mara's lover.

Besides, right now, he realized, he wanted the dog. It took him back to the only good time in his life, when there had been people who had cared about him. It had been too late to have made a difference in the long run, but for a time there'd been no pain and nothing to fear. For a time, he had the kind of life he'd dreamed about. A mother like the ones on the television, the kind who made you breakfast and sat with you while you did your homework. A father who taught you things, who took you fishing, and who put a basketball net on the side of the garage and taught you how to shoot the ball so that you wouldn't be embarrassed again in gym class when everyone knew how but you. Parents who bought you presents for your birthday and for Christmas and gave you little gifts just because they cared. Parents who never hurt you — not one time — and who had asked nothing of you but that you love them.

And he had. God knows, he had loved the Channings as much as it was in him to feel love for anyone. They'd been the only good thing in his miserable life. They'd bought him the dog for Christmas the second year he was with them. It was the best gift he'd ever had.

The only real grief he'd ever truly felt in his entire life had been on the day Jake died. The death of his dog had opened a hole inside that he'd never been able to fill.

And now here was this little dog, wagging his tail, licking his chin, wanting to play.

The girl could wait. But right now, more than anything, he wanted that little dog.

He unlatched the gate, then locked it behind him. He hoisted Spike under his arm and, taking the steps slowly, one by one in the dark, descended to the ground. He paused long enough to pick up the fallen dog toy before slipping away into the night.

Chapter Twenty-one

Mara stretched her arms over her head like a happily sated cat and sighed sleepily. She'd dozed on and off, each time she awoke reaching a hand out for Aidan to assure herself that she hadn't been dreaming. She now awoke in the pale light from the remains of the fire. The room had chilled as the fire died down, and she tried to rally the strength to get up to add another log.

Next to her, Aidan rested on his side. He reached out for her, his hand gliding through her hair to push it back from her face.

"You alive there?" he asked, his voice husky from sleep.

"Umm-hmm." She snuggled closer.

He tensed. "Do you smell something burning?"

She sniffed at the air. "Oh, my God." She struggled to get up. Grabbing her T-shirt from the edge of the sofa where it had earlier landed, she pulled it over her head and ran to the kitchen. "The pizza."

She opened the oven door, and black smoke poured out. Coughing, she grabbed a mitt and pulled the flat pan out of the oven and all but ran outside, where she placed it on the top rail of the front deck.

"Guess that takes care of our midnight snack." Aidan stepped outside in his bare feet. He'd taken the time to pull on his jeans, but that was all.

"I'm sure we can find something in the freezer after we clear out the smoke and we —" She stopped in midsentence and looked around. "Spike?"

Confused, she walked to the opposite side of the deck, where the shadows were deepest. "Spike?"

"He was here a while ago. . . ." Aidan followed her to the end of the deck.

"Well, he's not here now."

"Maybe he fell off the deck." Aidan unlatched the gate and started down the steps. "Spike! Here, buddy . . ."

"Spike." Mara followed on his heels. "Spike!"

Not a sound, not a rustle.

Mara bit her lip. "He must have seen something and gone after it."

"How could he have gotten off the deck? If he'd jumped, he would almost certainly have been injured, Mara. It's twelve or fifteen feet from the deck to the ground. And he couldn't have gotten out under the gate. At least, I don't think he could have."

Aidan stretched a hand under the gate and measured the height of the X formed by the rails. "You know, he might have been able to squeeze under here, if he'd really wanted to. If he saw something he wanted to investigate badly enough, maybe he could have done it."

"We have to go look for him." She started past him.

"Whoa, whoa, Mara." He grabbed her by the arm.

"My dog is out there, and it's not safe for him."

"If it's not safe for him, is it safe for you? Especially dressed — or not — as you are. In bare feet." He tugged at her hand. "Come on back inside. We'll get dressed, we'll get our shoes on. We'll find some flashlights. Come on, Mara. If we're going to look, we're going to do it right."

"Quickly, though." She ran up the steps. "Quickly."

She struggled into her clothes and tied her old running shoes with trembling fingers. How could Spike have gotten off the deck? He'd never done that before.

"He must have followed something," she said as she ran out the door without waiting for Aidan.

"Hold up, will you?" he called after her.

"Hurry up, please," she begged. "There are bears out there, mountain lions, badgers . . . even raccoons will go after a dog if they think their young are threatened."

"Don't get yourself into a panic." He handed her one of the flashlights he'd found in the garage. He'd lost what she'd considered precious seconds while he looked for replacement batteries when he discovered that neither of them worked. "Which way?"

"Let's start out over the ridge there." She took off, calling the dog's name, shining the light around her with every step.

They searched for almost an hour in the dark, stumbling along, Mara becoming more and more distressed with every minute that passed.

Finally, Aidan suggested they go back to the house and resume the search in the morning.

"I can't leave him out here." She began to cry.

"Sweetheart, we've been looking for him since midnight. It's almost one in the morning. We've called him and called and we haven't heard a sound. Maybe he chased something — maybe another dog came along and he couldn't resist. Maybe he's off in the hills and he'll find his way back when his little adventure is over. He could just be out having a fun time. But I don't think walking all over the hills, stumbling around in the dark, is going to do much good. If he'd heard us, he'd have come running. I think he's out of earshot now, and I think when he's had his fill of whatever it is he's doing, he'll come back on his own."

"Do you really think so?"

"I do." He took her hand and tugged on it. "Come on. Let's head back to the cabin."

They started down the trail, the twin beams lighting the way. Coming down the slope from the rise above the cabin, Mara realized that

Aidan had slowed slightly and his gait had become uneven.

"Are you all right?" she asked.

"Sure."

"No, you're not. Your leg is bothering you, isn't it?"

"Actually, it's my hip."

"I'm so sorry. Here I am, dragging you through the dark, up and down hills, over rocks . . ."

"I'm okay."

"I'm so sorry, Aidan. I wasn't thinking of anything except Spike. . . ."

"Mara, I'll be fine. I just need to sit for a few, maybe with my leg elevated a little. And don't apologize. I want to find him as much as you do."

The lights from the cabin appeared all the more bright in the vast black canvas that surrounded them. Mara and Aidan climbed the steps more slowly than they had earlier descended.

"Aidan," Mara said when they reached the deck. "Aidan, his leash is gone."

Aidan stopped on the top step. "How could his leash be gone?"

"I don't know, but I hung it right here, over the rail, after we came back from that last walk, remember?"

"It probably slipped off the rail and fell to the ground. We'll look for it in the morning. We'll never find it tonight."

He opened the door and coaxed her back inside.

"Leave the door open so that we can hear him if he comes back and barks for us to open the gate," she said, and seeing his hesitation, added, "It's okay. You don't have to worry about someone sneaking around here in the middle of the night. There's no one around for miles except for us."

Aidan went into the kitchen and came back out with the bottle of wine in his hand. He refilled her glass and handed it to her. Then he stoked the fire and built it up with several small logs, hoping to banish the chill that had settled into the room.

"Here, come sit with me here." He sat in the middle of the sofa and held out his hand.

"I don't know what I'll do if I can't find him," she said as she sat down, tears welling in her eyes.

He put an arm around her and drew her to him, snug next to his body.

"We'll find him. Tomorrow. We'll go out first thing, when it's light. Maybe we'll find some trail, some sign of which way he's gone. But we'll find him."

Mara rested against him, taking an occasional sip of wine. His fingers traced from her elbow to her shoulder, and when he realized she had goose bumps, he asked, "How 'bout I find us a few blankets, since we're leaving the door open and the temperature's dropped below fifty?"

"There's a closet right off the hall. We keep extra blankets in there."

He went to the closet and returned with several blankets and a pillow. Making a makeshift bed on the sofa, he lay down and pulled her alongside him, tucking the blankets around them both like a cocoon. They lay awake, watching the shadows from the fire dance around the room.

"I got Spike for Julianne," she told him, her voice weak. "She had wanted a dog so badly, but Jules wouldn't let her have one. He didn't believe in having animals live in the house. After he took her, I got the dog to surprise her, when she came home. . . ."

"We'll find him, Mara. First thing in the morning. We'll find him," he promised, and hoped he was right.

After lying awake for several hours, Mara finally eased herself from Aidan's embrace and stood up quietly. She walked to the window and looked out. The sun had yet to rise.

She debated on whether to wake Aidan, then decided against it. His leg had clearly been bothering him the night before. She couldn't ask him to walk the often steep paths she'd be following in her search for Spike, though she knew he'd not think twice about joining her if she asked him.

Mara went into the bathroom for a quick shower, then dressed, not bothering to dry her hair before heading out the door. She couldn't stand the thought of her little dog out there all night amidst all the dangers that lurked in the woods. And he just didn't have the sense to back down from a threat. He was pretty fearless, even when he was threatened.

She shivered as she thought about all the things that could have threatened him during the night and wondered what had led him away from the cabin in the first place.

The first light of day was just beginning to spread over the hills when she stepped outside and scanned the scenery for movement, but she saw nothing other than a few birds. She decided to start with the ridge that rose behind the cabin and continued on for a half mile to the west. At that point, the trail led down to the waterfall and, beyond that, to a narrow valley.

She took several steps toward the ridge, but as she walked past the mailbox, she noticed the hollow stem of a dandelion wedged between the box and the little door. She opened the box and took out the flower, expecting to find something old and dried, left long ago. But the flower was recently picked, the yellow petals still dropping pollen on the inside of the box, where it had lain.

Confused, she twirled the stem. Annie?

But Annie wasn't there, her car wasn't there. Had she been at the cabin earlier in the day, before Mara and Aidan arrived? If so, why had she left without leaving a note? Why hadn't she waited for them?

Somewhere in the distance, a dog barked once. Twice.

Had it been Spike? And from which direction?

Maybe there, toward the falls . . .

Three-quarters of the way to the falls, she came across bear scat, and her heart dropped. Praying that Spike had not had a run-in with the bear who'd left the droppings, she paused, for the first time considering the wisdom of having gone out alone, unarmed. She was never armed, she reminded herself, and she'd hiked these trails for years by herself or in the company of her sister. She'd never been in danger here before.

She paused to listen, but heard neither bear nor dog. She resumed her search, calling Spike's name as she walked along the trail, hoping he'd hear her voice and bark in response.

On she walked, cautiously, until she reached the head of a ravine.

"Oh, my God . . ." she gasped.

Scrambling down the sloping, rocky sides of the ravine, she reached the car that was hidden there. It was unlocked, but she didn't have to look inside to know whose car it was.

Annie's.

Cold fear wound around her chest and threatened to squeeze the life from her.

Panic set in. Her sister. Her dog . . .

She knew without knowing who was responsible. The realization froze her where she stood as terror invaded every cell in her body.

How could he have found her? How could he have known about the cabin? How . . . ?

Aidan. Aidan would know what to do.

A rustle of leaves behind her, a happy bark. Spike!

She backed away from the car and turned to run in the direction of the sound.

And slammed into the chest of the man who stood behind her, a look of vast amusement on his face. A joyful Spike leapt on the ground at his feet, barking and whining for her attention. She was too stunned to move.

Unaware of his part in leading her into danger, Spike danced his happy dance, begging to be picked up. Keeping her eyes on the man, she lifted the dog and held him as tightly as she could.

"Now, I couldn't have done a better job finding you, could I?" The man smiled pleasantly. "After all this, you come to me. How perfect is that?"

"Where's my sister, Channing?" she asked, even as Spike licked at her face.

"Oh, and isn't she a direct little thing? No games for little Miss Mara, uh-uh. Right to the point."

"Where is she?"

"She's waiting for you to join her."

"Did you hurt her?"

"My, aren't you the good sister? Here you are, trapped in the woods with the likes of me, and your first concern is for your sister. I am impressed."

"Why did you steal my dog?"

"Because I wanted him. I'm keeping him."

"Are you keeping Annie, too?"

"Maybe. At least for now."

"Where is she?"

"I'm going to take you to her."

"How did you find this place?"

"Now, that was strictly a bit of luck on my part." He grinned. "Actually, I'd say my luck's been running pretty damn good lately, wouldn't you? Maybe I should buy some lottery tickets or something. It seems I've got the magic touch these days."

He reached for her arm as if to take it, and she recoiled.

"Oh, no, no, no," he laughed. "You don't have a choice in this. And let's get something straight right off the bat, since you seem to prefer candor. I am going to kill you. And yes, of course, I'm going to kill Annie. And your boyfriend, well, he's disposable. If my luck holds out, I can make it look like he did you both. Wouldn't that be a kick?"

He nodded as he contemplated the ways in which he could do this. "Yes, that's the way to go, I think. I'm sorry. I really am. It's just the way the cards played out."

"I don't understand. I don't even know you.

Why would you want to kill me?" She held the dog closer, afraid to move.

"Like I said, it's the way the cards played out."

"Those other women . . . the Marys . . ."

"Oh, unfortunate for them, wasn't it, that little misunderstanding? Though I must say I didn't mind. The one woman, the older one, she wasn't much fun, particularly, but all the same, it was an evening out."

"An evening out . . ." she repeated softly, horrified.

"And today is a new day." He reached for her arm with one hand. The other brandished a knife, the blade of which was long and wide, the edge of which gleamed. "Today is your day, Mara Douglas. Yours, and mine . . . and Annie's . . ."

Mara's heart began to pound so loudly and so furiously she almost expected it to leap from her chest. Hands shaking, knees weakening, brain fogging . . .

Get a grip! she demanded of herself. If she gave in to the fear, she'd panic, and he'd win. She had one chance, and one chance only, to survive.

Unfortunately, that one chance was still sleeping on the sofa, back at the cabin.

Aidan awoke with the sun in his eyes. He yawned and eased both legs out straight on the sofa. Something in his tired brain sensed that if

Mara had been there, he'd have no room to stretch. He sat up and looked around the room.

"Mara?" he called.

He walked into the hall to the bathroom. The door was open, and the small room empty. He looked into each of the three bedrooms. All empty.

He stepped outside onto the deck and called her, his voice hanging over the clearing like a cloud. Nothing.

He went back inside, into the kitchen, down the steps into the basement, calling her name.

Damn. She'd gone off without him.

Back upstairs, he sat on the sofa while he put on his shoes and wondered how he expected to find her in these unfamiliar hills. Maybe with luck, he could find and follow her trail.

The fancy handle of the pretty handgun he'd been admiring the night before picked up the light that sparkled through the front window. He went into the bedroom and opened the drawer, took out the bullets he'd found there, and fully loaded the chamber. There'd been too much talk about bears and mountain lions. Hopefully, that would be the worst threat that lurked there in the hills.

You never went anyplace without backup.

Once outside, he stopped at the car, unlocked the glove box, and took out his Bureau-issued Sig Sauer, which he slid into the waistband of his jeans at the back. Aidan had no qualms about being a one-man search party, but he wasn't going to be stupid about it. He'd carry the antique handgun, which was too big to fit anywhere but in his jeans pocket, and since he wasn't sure just how tight the trigger was, he didn't think carrying it in his pocket was a good idea.

A glance at his watch told him the sun hadn't been up for long. Mara must have left the cabin at dawn to look for Spike.

Damn. She should have awakened him.

He stood in the clearing in front of the house where the road ended, wondering which way to go.

"Might as well flip a coin," he muttered, and took the opposite path from the one they'd taken the night before.

Aidan hobbled slowly up the sloping ridge to the top and followed the trail through the trees, every once in a while stopping to call her name.

He stopped after twenty minutes, hoping to ease the throb in his leg. His hip was bothering him now, too, the result of climbing over the uneven terrain. It didn't bode well for his chances of ever serving the Bureau in full capacity again. He was wondering if maybe he should think about another line of work, when he reached the topmost portion of the ridge. From the narrow valley below, he heard voices. He crept to the edge of a huge boulder and looked down.

For a moment, he thought his heart had stopped beating.

In the clearing fifteen feet away stood Curtis Channing, holding a knife to the throat of a pale and shaking Mara. Aidan could not make out the words Channing spoke, but the tone was taunting.

"I'd trust you with my life. . . . ," she'd told Aidan.

Kneeling slowly, Aidan swore that Mara would walk away from this alive, even if it cost him his own life.

He transferred the gun into his left hand, cursing himself for not having gotten out to the range to practice, and prayed that he could still hit his mark with his nondominant hand.

"Let her go, Channing."

Curtis Channing looked up calmly, as if Aidan had been expected all along.

"Who are you kidding?" He sneered. "You're not going to fire that pistol. You'll hit your girlfriend before you hit me. I think I have the advantage here, Mr. FBI. I have the girl, and I am — please take notice here — holding a knife to her throat. If you think I won't use it, you'll be terribly, regrettably wrong."

He turned Mara's body abruptly so that the sunlight filtering through the trees bounced off the blade.

"So this is what you're going to do. You're going to slide that gun right down here to me. No, don't throw it, slide it, right down the rock there."

When Aidan hesitated, Channing laughed.

"Please don't think to be a hero. I will kill her. It's not the way I'd planned — I was looking forward to many pleasurable hours in the lady's company. After all I went through to have her, well, I guess you know that I want to make it worth my while. But if I have to kill her here, and quickly, well, I'll do what I have to do. Your choice, Mr. FBI. Your choice."

Aidan stepped to the edge of the ravine and slid the old pistol down the rock, just as he'd been told.

"That was the right choice." Channing nodded and bent to pick up the gun, his eyes never leaving Aidan. "Now, if you'll just stand a little straighter, I'd like to do this cleanly, with one shot —"

In a blink, Aidan had flattened out on the rock, his Sig Sauer in his hand.

"Oh, for crying out loud. Why did you do that?" Channing laughed again. "What's the point? I have a gun and the girl. You don't put the gun down, I shoot her. Then I shoot you. Either way, you lose."

"Not exactly."

"What do you mean?" Channing's eyes narrowed.

"Mine is fully loaded. Yours only has one bullet." Aidan spoke calmly.

Channing frowned. "How do I know you're telling the truth?"

"Well, if you know anything about antique handguns, you'd know that many of them only take one shot at a time." No need to tell him that the gun had been fitted with modern chambers. "Not to mention that they are highly inaccurate, except maybe for a marksman. And we know that you do your best work with a knife, right? So you just go ahead and take your best shot. But if you miss, you're a dead man. So anyway I look at it, I win."

"It'll take only one bullet to kill her. You'd take the chance that I'd shoot her?"

"You'll be dead before she hits the ground."

"Well, then. This is an interesting scenario. . . ." Channing mused.

"Just drop the gun, let the girl go."

"And then what? You'll take me in? Make the big collar? Isn't that what you law enforcement types say?" He shook his head. "I don't think so."

"I don't see that you have a whole lot of options, Channing. You can die here, or I'll take you in and you'll spend the rest of your life in prison. But, hey, maybe you'll get lucky and they'll put you in with your buddy, Vince Giordano."

"Who?"

"Oh, come on, Channing. By the way, how did he get you to do his killing for him? What's in it for you, anyway? What was the deal you made with Vincent Giordano?"

Channing smirked. "Never heard of him."

"Now, we both know you're lying — and not doing a particularly good job of it, I might add.

Why would you be willing to go to prison — for the rest of your natural life or until they execute you — for the sake of slime like Giordano? I'd had you pegged as smarter than that."

Aidan stared down at Channing, saw how the killer's eyes flickered uncertainly.

"And you know, they're gonna love you in prison, Channing. Now, I know you've never served any real time, so you don't know what to expect. I can enlighten you, if you want."

"Don't bother trying to scare me with all that talk of prison rapes and solitary confinement. I can take care of myself. And I'm not afraid of being alone. But I gotta tell you, I admire your chutzpah. I really do. You got balls, Mr. FBI. You sure do."

Channing raised the pistol and placed it to Mara's temple.

"But are you bluffing?" He met Aidan's eyes. "Shall I call your bluff, Mr. FBI?"

"Let her go, Curtis," Aidan said softly.

"I can't do that."

"Channing, you know it's over. There's no way this can end well for you. This time, do the right thing. Let her go."

Channing shook his head, but Aidan noticed that in spite of his bravado, the hand in which Channing held the pistol started to shake almost imperceptibly.

"Oh, hey, I almost forgot. Claire Channing sends her love."

Channing visibly stiffened.

"She's a lovely lady. You got lucky there."

"When . . . when . . ."

"Oh, let's see. Two days ago, was it, Mara?"

Mara nodded, her head jerking nervously.

"And you'll be glad to know that she spoke glowingly of you. Isn't that something? All these years, you haven't kept in touch, but she still spoke so lovingly of you."

Channing began to sweat. "Don't . . ." he whispered.

"Oh, and she asked, if we found you, to let you know that your father died. Mr. Channing. He passed away a few years ago. She'd been hoping that you'd hear about it and come home to be with her. She still considers you her son, you know, but of course, she doesn't really know you, does she? Not like we do. Now, how do you suppose she's going to feel when she finds out you've been murdering women for . . . how many years has it been?"

Channing stood like a statue, Mara gathered close to him in his left arm, the pistol still in his right hand, the barrel to her temple.

"Yeah, she is going to be heartbroken, don't you think? She told us how she and her husband wanted so badly to make things right for you, after you came to live with them. How they did all that they could to help you. They sure did love you, didn't they? They never saw that ugly thing growing inside you. Not that they'd have believed it anyway, you know? Parents are like that. From everything she told us, it sure seems like they tried to be good parents to you. Tried to give you a good home, tried to make up to you for everything that had happened. Guess they didn't try hard enough . . ."

"Don't say that. It wasn't their fault." Channing's voice was strained, gravely. "They did their best. . . ."

"Well, this was just a case of the best not being good enough, right? I mean, look how you turned out. . . ."

Aidan lowered his voice slightly. "You know, maybe this is all their fault. That could be part of your defense, Channing. If they'd tried harder, maybe none of this would have happened. Even in spite of all that your real mother did to you, if the Channings had done a better job, maybe they could have made up for all that."

"Don't say that. Don't . . . say . . . that."

"Well, it hardly matters now, right? I mean, either way, that woman's heart is going to be broken, don't you think? Here, she thinks you've grown up just fine, and you are . . . well, what you are. Going to be real hard for her to deal with that, to know that she failed you. She tried so hard, loved you so much, and all for nothing."

Channing swallowed hard, the gun in his hand wavering.

"Boy, I wouldn't want to be you, Channing. Having to look that wonderful woman in the eye when she finds out what you are. What you've done . . ."

"Don't . . ." Channing licked his lips.

"When she realizes what a coward you are. That you hid behind a woman, even when you knew it was over for you. And it is over, Channing. It ends here." Aidan's eyes never left Channing's. "How do you think she's going to feel? I hope the shock doesn't kill her. That would be real tragic."

"Stop . . ." Channing's voice was all but inaudible.

"How are you going to look her in the eye, Channing? Personally, that would be the toughest thing for me, if she had raised me, thinking she'd done a good job and all, and I'd turned out to be . . . well, what you are. But I guess that's not going to bother you, to look that sweet lady in the eye, knowing that she still loves you so much. She'll blame herself, though, don't you think? Mothers always seem to blame themselves for everything, don't they?"

"It's not her fault. . . ." Channing's voice was quivering.

Aidan kept his eyes on the gun that was still dangerously close to Mara's head, Channing's finger still on the trigger. Who knew what it would take to set it off? But Aidan had no choice. He had to keep talking. It was the only chance Mara had.

I'd trust you with my life. . . .

Aidan took a deep breath and forced his voice to remain calm, not for one second forgetting what was at stake.

"Now, you know what's going to happen here, don't you? You shoot your one bullet off, I can take you out in the blink of a eye. But right now, I'm thinking that the thing to do is to blast your kneecaps off, keep you alive — painful though that will be — so that we can bring you to trial. Shame for Mrs. Channing to have to go through all that, though, isn't it? And you know she'll stand by you. Probably come out here for the trial to be with you. That's the kind of woman she is, don't you agree? She really loved you the way a mother is supposed to love her son." Aidan shook his head sadly. "And you know, this is going to kill her. She's probably going to be called to testify, too, you know. At your trial. How do you think she'll hold up under all that? Hell of a way to repay that good woman for all she tried to do for you."

Channing was staring at him from across the distance of a scant fifteen feet.

"How are you going to explain to her why you put that gun to an innocent woman's head and pulled the trigger?" Aidan's voice dropped. "How will you look her in the eye and explain any of what you've done?"

"Don't . . ."

"Do the right thing, Channing. Be a man. This one time, do the right thing."

"The right thing . . ." Channing mumbled.

"It's your one chance, Channing, your last chance to get out of this with some dignity. Let her know there was still some decency in you, that in the end, when it counted, you had a choice, and you did the right thing."

The two men continued to stare at each other.

Then, in the blink of an eye, Channing's hand twisted and his finger pulled the trigger before anyone had time to react.

Mara screamed as she hit the ground, and Aidan slid down the slope on his good hip. He lifted Mara and turned her away from the body that still jerked, the head of which was partially blown off.

"Ohmygod . . . ohmygod . . ." Mara cried. "He . . . he . . . he . . ."

"Shh, it's over, it's done." Aidan held her and rocked her as one might rock a small child. "It's over."

"No, no, it's not." She sobbed. "Annie . . . he took Annie. . . ."

"What?"

"Annie . . . She must have come to the cabin, he must have found her." She pointed behind him, her words coming in a desperate rush. "Down there, in the ravine . . . her car . . ."

Aidan set her feet on the ground and hurried to the car. Mara scooped up Spike and followed Aidan into the ravine. He opened the front and back doors and made a perfunctory inspection.

"There's no blood. Can you open the trunk without a key?"

She leaned past him into the front seat, opened the console, and hit a red button. The trunk popped open and he looked inside. It was empty except for a bag of books and a shopping bag holding a newly purchased sweatshirt.

"He must have taken her someplace." Mara's face was filled with fear.

"Then there's a good chance she's somewhere close by," he told her. "We'll find her. First, we need to call for help. I guess you don't have your cell phone on you."

"I do." She pulled it out of her back pocket with hands that trembled so badly, the phone dropped to the ground. "What if we can't find her? What if —"

"We'll find her. Right now, we need to get the local police out here. With their help, we'll find Annie." While he dialed for assistance, Aidan kept one arm around her, shielding her from the bloody mess that once had been Curtis Alan Channing.

"You knew he was going to do that, didn't you?" She leaned back against him, still shaking as if desperately cold. "You knew he was going to kill himself."

"I knew it was going to be him or you. It had to be him."

"All that talk about Mrs. Channing . . ."

"She's the only living person he cared about. I wanted him to think about the reality of facing her. Of having her attend the trial, of having to look at her, and see how much pain

411

he caused her. I didn't think he could face that."

"After you planted the idea in his head."

"Like I said, one of you was going to die. I couldn't let it be you. . . ." He held her as tightly against him as he could. "There was no way I was going to let it be you."

"We have to find Annie." Her voice broke. "What if he has her locked up someplace without air? What if he's hurt her and she's bleeding? What if he . . . if he . . ." She couldn't say the words.

"We'll find her, sweetheart." He took her hand and they walked up the hill. Sirens screamed far in the distance. "We'll find her."

Chapter Twenty-two

They stood in the road and watched the state police vehicles fly up the hill in clouds of dust. Aidan left a still-shaking Mara in the company of one of the detectives, who took down all the information she had about Annie's disappearance, while he led the others to the body at the foot of the ravine.

The crime scene crew arrived to begin their process, and the others spread out across the hill to search the caves and crevices and small valleys that dotted the area for Annie.

Mara watched anxiously as the men and women disappeared, one by one, over the ridge or into the woods.

Where was Annie? Was she still alive?

"This your house?" Detective Lenosky asked after he'd gotten all of the information he'd needed from Mara. They were standing in front of the small cabin that stood among the trees on the opposite side of the dirt road.

"No, that belongs to a man who lives out of state. Florida, I think," Mara replied. "Our house is farther down the road."

"We'll be sending a team of crime scene investigators in to dust for prints and other evidence."

Mara nodded. She'd expected as much.

"Excuse me," Lenosky said to Mara, signaling to the second team of investigators as they arrived. "I'll be right back."

Mara watched him point at her cabin. The car began moving slowly in that direction.

Lenosky walked back to where he'd left Mara. As he approached, his attention was drawn back to the small cabin. "Is anyone living there now?"

She shook her head. "My sister said she heard in town last year that the owner was going to put the place up for sale. I don't know if he's done so yet."

They both stared at the cabin.

"Hey, it's worth a look," Lenosky told her.

He started across the road, with Mara close behind, Spike trotting along at the end of the leash.

"No, no. I want you to stay here. Just in case . . ." He softened, choosing his words carefully "We don't know what we're going to find when we go inside."

"If she's in there, I want to be with you when you find her," Mara insisted.

"I can't let you do that. But I'll make a deal with you. I'll go in first, alone. You can wait right outside the door."

Mara made a face.

"Take it or leave it," he said as they neared the cabin.

"I'll take it."

The detective tried the front door, but it was

deadbolted from the inside. They went around to the back, and as soon as they turned the corner, they saw the car.

"I don't think the man who lived here owned a car with Georgia plates on it," Mara said.

Lenosky shined a flashlight inside the car. Fast-food wrappers were tossed on a map of Pennsylvania that lay open on the front passenger seat. Other than that, the car was as neat as a pin. All the doors were locked.

"First things first. Wait here," Lenosky told her as he walked to the back of the cabin and tried the back door.

It swung open easily.

Mara took a step forward, and the detective blocked her way.

"You're not listening to me, so let me put this in terms you might understand," he said a little more forcefully. "If your sister is in here, and if she's been harmed, it may not be a pretty sight. Furthermore, it's a crime scene. I can't have you mucking it up. You just have to wait."

"All right." Mara backed down.

Lenosky entered the cabin with his gun drawn. Anxiously, Mara watched him through the back window until he disappeared into the front room. He came out minutes later, shaking his head.

"I'm sorry. I thought . . . I really thought maybe . . ." He said. "Aw, I guess it would have been too easy, you know?"

Mara began to cry. She sat on the back step,

her head in her hands, and sobbed.

"Hey, I'm sorry. I know you've been through a lot." Lenosky tried to comfort her, but it was obvious that weeping females were beyond his own comfort zone. "Look, you want me to get your boyfriend?"

Mara just continued to sob.

"Oh, jeez, lady . . ." Lenosky ran his hand through his dark hair. "Look, you wait right here. I'll get your boyfriend, okay? You just sit here with your dog . . . where the hell is the dog?"

Lenosky looked around. Spike was at the rear of the car, standing on his hind legs, sniffing at the trunk, gleefully wagging his tail.

"Miss Douglas." The detective touched her shoulder. When Mara looked up, he pointed to Spike. "The dog . . ."

"Spike?" she called. The dog's tail wagged faster.

Lenosky started toward the car.

"Oh, my God . . ." Mara bolted off the step, rushing past him. "Open it. Get it open! Annie? Annie!"

From inside the trunk of the car came the softest moan.

"Open it." Mara turned to the detective. "We've got to get her out!"

"I can't very well shoot the lock off the trunk. You stay here, talk to her. Let her know that she'll be out of there in just a few more minutes." The detective ran for the road.

"Did you hear that, Annie? Just hang on. Just a bit more." Mara was sobbing with anguish and laughing with joy at the same time. "We're going to get you out. . . ."

In minutes, the detective returned with Aidan and two other state troopers, one of whom was holding a key ring.

"Is that the key?" Mara asked anxiously.

"We'll soon find out," the trooper replied as he slid it into the trunk lock. "It was in his pocket, the dead guy's. If this was his car, chances are . . ."

The lid popped, and the detective raised it. Inside, Annie lay facedown, her arms tied behind her back, her ankles tied together. Aidan and Lenosky turned her over gently and removed the gag from her mouth.

"Oh, thank God," she gasped. "Thank God you found me. I don't know how much longer I could have lasted."

They lifted her from the trunk and cut her bindings. Mara was there to hug her, and the two sisters wept in each other's arms.

"Where is he?" Annie wiped the tears from her face. "Channing. Did you get him? Is he in custody? Please tell me he didn't get away."

"He's dead, Annie," Mara told her.

Annie looked up at Aidan. "You . . . ?"

He shook his head. "He shot himself," Aidan told her.

A strangled laugh escaped Annie's throat and her eyes widened. "You have to be kidding."

Aidan shrugged. "I guess he figured since it was all over, he'd save himself the humiliation of an arrest and trial."

"It's not . . . it's not what I'd have expected him to have done." She shook her head slowly, clearly puzzled. "It doesn't fit his profile."

"Well, now, I guess you'd know as well as anyone that profiles aren't always exactly on the money, Annie. Sometimes all the pieces don't really fit the way you think they're going to."

"I guess." Annie flexed her hands. "Boy, does that feel good. Help me stand up here, Aidan. Let me lean on you for a minute or two."

"Take as much time as you need, Annie," he told her. "God knows I've leaned on you plenty over the past year. You just take your time. . . ."

". . . so I checked the prison records, accounted for every goddamn minute that Curtis Channing spent under that roof." Evan Crosby stopped at the red light and switched his phone from his right ear to his left. "Guess what I found?"

"Well, I'm sure it was something really good," Miranda Cahill replied, "or you wouldn't have called me to tell me about it."

"Right. I found that on Monday, the sixteenth of February, a van left the prison with four inmates, a driver, and two deputy sheriffs on board. Want to see if you can guess the names of two of those passengers?"

"Oh, let's see . . . could one have been Curtis Channing?"

"Very good, Agent Cahill. And the other?"

"Hmm, let's see, who could I be thinking of? Starts with a G . . ." She pretended to give it some thought. "Oh, I don't know, could it be . . . Vince Giordano?"

"When she's hot, she's hot." Crosby nodded to the guard at the prison gate, flashed his badge, and was waved through.

"So I guess you're going to ask Vince if he'll fill you in on what they might have chatted about while they were in that van."

"Yeah."

"What?" Miranda frowned, picking up on his hesitation. "What are you thinking?"

"According to the deputies who were with them in the van, they didn't chat at all." Crosby pulled into a parking spot and cut the engine. "Apparently, they didn't even sit near each other. Vince liked to sit in the front, behind the driver. Channing sat in the rear, next to one of the deputies."

"They had to have been alone at some point," Miranda murmured. "I know there's a connection between these two."

"Yeah, my gut's telling me the same thing." Crosby got out of the car and walked up to the prison doors. "I'll call you back and let you know what Giordano tells me."

He stopped at the front desk to chat with the receptionist, then asked her to see if the assistant warden had a few minutes for him.

She placed the call, then buzzed Crosby through. He followed the familiar hall to the administrative offices. He waved to the pretty office assistant as he passed through on his way to Fred McCabe's office. The door was open and McCabe was waiting for the detective to arrive.

"Evan, how've you been?" The beefy ex-wrestler extended an equally beefy paw for Crosby to shake.

"Good. Good, thanks, Fred."

"Have a seat." McCabe closed the door. He nodded at the file that Crosby slid across the desktop. "That help you out any?"

"Helped me connect the dots. Now all I have to do is figure out what picture those dots are making, and we'll be home free. I just need a few minutes with Mr. Giordano —"

"Vince Giordano?" McCabe's brows knit together.

"Yeah, how many Giordanos you got out here?"

"None."

"What?"

"As of two o'clock this afternoon, no prisoners named Giordano."

"But . . ." Crosby felt flustered, deflated. "How . . . ?"

"Court order. Didn't you hear about it?"

"I heard one was in the works, but —"

"Judge Mulvaney signed it this morning, and

by two, the bastard was walking out the front door, smug as could be." McCabe shook his head. "Had his lawyer send someone from the office to pick him up. Laughed all the way from his cell to the car."

"Son of a bitch." Crosby's face flushed and he slammed his fist onto the top of the desk. "Son of a bitch . . ."

"Hey, Crosby, I know how you feel. Believe me, if there'd been any way to hold him, we'd have done it."

"Any idea where he was going?"

"He didn't confide in me. Try his attorney. He might know. Want me to look up his lawyer for you?"

"No, I know who it is. Thanks." Crosby stood, the room suddenly too small to contain him. His anger was growing by leaps and bounds. He had to leave.

"Thanks," he said again, and headed out the door, silently cursing the system that could turn an animal like Vincent Giordano back into society.

Chapter Twenty-three

Aidan sat on the sand, his heels dug in, and watched the woman who lay beside him, her face turned to the sun. He reached out a hand to straighten the old quilt where it had curled back on one end, resisting the urge to lie down and just hold her close to him. They were at the end of a long, perfect weekend at the beach. Mara would be leaving soon to go back to Lyndon, back to her job, her home. Her life before him.

He didn't want her to leave, but he didn't know how to ask her to stay.

Spike trotted across the sand with something in his mouth. The dog ran to within ten feet of the blanket, then shook whatever it was he had to tease Aidan.

"Bring that over here, let me see what you have, you little monkey," Aidan whispered loudly. The dog pawed the sand merrily.

"I'm not asleep," Mara told him without opening her eyes, "so you don't have to whisper. What does he have, anyway?"

"Looks like a crab shell." Aidan rose to take it from Spike, who immediately took off down the beach with it, Aidan in pursuit.

On the blanket, Mara sat up on her elbows to watch the chase. Aidan's gait had improved somewhat thanks to a good physical therapist and a lot of determination on his part. His leg looked stronger and stronger all the time. Not strong enough to allow him to pass the exam to go back on full, regular duty, but enough to get by. Besides, Mancini had called on Friday and asked him to report in on Monday morning. He had another special assignment.

Good for Aidan, Mara thought as she watched him play with the dog. *He needs to work again, needs to know he's still what he always was: a damn good special agent. God knows he's the most special person I've ever met. . . .*

He headed back to where she sat, his feet kicking up little clouds of sand. Spike, sensing the game had run its course, followed, then ran ahead to lie at Mara's side.

"I almost forgot. I have something for you," Aidan told her when he reached the blanket. "I found it before we went to Ohio and forgot to give it to you."

He took something from his pocket as he sat down, and she leaned over to look. A smooth piece of green sea glass lay in his open palm.

"Beautiful," she sighed, touching it tentatively. "For me?"

"It matches your eyes."

"This is perfect." She picked it up and held it up to the sun. "Just perfect. Thank you."

She leaned over to kiss his mouth. "I'll take it to the jeweler back in Lyndon and see if he can drill a hole in it so that I can wear it on a cord.

I love it. Thank you. It's the loveliest present I ever received."

She leaned against him. "I am so happy here," she sighed.

"Well, it is great here in May, but the crowds build up as the summer progresses. You might not enjoy the beach as much then."

"It isn't the beach that makes me happy." She nuzzled the side of his face. "Being with you makes me happy."

"Then you should spend more time here. Come more often, stay longer." He put an arm around her and snuggled her close to his body.

"I fully intend to take you up on that. Whenever you have time for me . . ."

"I will always make time for you."

"May not be so easy. It sounds as if John plans on keeping you busy."

"He knows I have to have a certain amount of time each week with the therapist. I suspect that, whatever this special assignment is, there's going to be some leeway." He rubbed the side of her face with his own. "I can't imagine going back to a life with no you. I feel like I've come back from the dead. I never thought I'd ever feel this way again, that life held . . . *promise*."

"I know that exact feeling." She looped her arm around his. "Isn't it amazing? Isn't it wonderful?"

"Wonderful, yes." He pulled her closer. "Where do we go from here?"

"We go weekend to weekend" — she grinned

up at him — "and we see where it leads."

"That sounds good." He nodded. "That sounds just right."

They sat close together, watching clouds gather and scatter across the afternoon sky.

"There's one thing you need to understand," Mara said solemnly. "I'll never stop looking for her. No matter what, I will search for her until I find her. No matter how long it takes."

"Then I will search with you, every step of the way, until we find her," he promised. "No matter how long it takes . . ."

The road leading out of town was a long one, but Vince Giordano was whistling all the way. Fifteen more miles to go . . .

He lowered the driver's side window of the car he'd borrowed from his attorney — promising its return by evening — on the pretext of visiting his mother. *Right.* He snorted. *Like my mother has had one word for me in the past three years.*

It doesn't matter, he told himself. *None of it matters now.* He was out, and out for good, thanks to the stupid goddamn policeman who couldn't resist shooting off his stupid mouth. And Vince Giordano did thank him most sincerely.

Five more miles, according to the odometer, and he'd be at his destination. Jeez, he hoped that no one had found it while he was gone. His biggest fear was that some kids playing around would have discovered what he'd buried three years ago, on the afternoon he'd gone to the house he'd once shared with his family and . . . well, done what he'd done.

He turned off the main road and onto a country lane that was wide enough to allow one car in each direction. He was close now, and he slowed down, searching for his landmarks. At the stop sign that marked the T-intersection, he looked both ways before pulling straight across and into a clearing. A barely visible drive, once dirt, now overgrown with weeds, lay ahead, and he followed it until he came to a barn that was one bad windstorm away from oblivion. Giordano pulled around the barn to park behind it. He got out of the car and, leaving the door open, stood in the knee-high weeds, his hands on his hips, and studied the back of the barn.

He counted twenty-two boards over from the corner, then knelt at the foundation, where he worked with his bare hands at a large loose rock until he could move it from side to side. He tugged at it, then pried at it with a stick he found a few feet away, waiting for the rock to dislodge and pull away from the foundation to leave a gaping hole. He thrust his hands inside, his fingers searching for cold metal.

Relieved to find the box right where he'd left it, he held his breath while he opened it and found the contents intact. Inside was the large stash of cash that he'd embezzled from his own construction company over the years after his marriage and before his arrest. He liked to think of it as his nest egg, a source of cash that Diane had never known about. After all, hadn't he earned it all with his sweat and blood? A wife didn't need to know everything.

Testing, just to make certain, he reached deeper into the hole and felt around into the farthest crevice. Yes, it was still there. He smiled to himself. The gun he'd used to kill his family, the weapon that had never been found.

And never would be, as long as this old barn stood.

He looked up at the old structure. Might be time for a new hiding place.

For now, this one would have to do. He counted out a large amount of the cash, stuffed the bills into his pockets, and returned the rest to the steel box, which he then shoved into the hole. He slid the rock back into place and stood, dusting off his hands. He looked up into the clear blue sky, watched a few birds settle into a tree off to his right. He took a deep, deep breath, feeling good about the day, about his circumstances, about his life.

He got back into the car and drove out the way he came in, grateful that there'd been no other traffic to see him come and go. He wanted to lie low for a while, enjoy his new-found freedom.

On his way back to town, he made a mental list of things to do. Find a place to live, some-

place cheap and out of the way. And a car —
he'd need wheels. A job was out of the question
— everyone around here knew him. Some
other place, though, he could start up another
carpentry business. He had plenty of cash to
bankroll himself. He could change his name,
start life over again.

And of course, he had a job to do.

After all, if Curtis — that crazy son of a bitch
— could do for him, he was sure enough going
to do for Archer. After all, Vince was as much a
man as Channing had been.

And then when Archer got out, he'd do for
Curtis. Whether he wanted to or not. One way
or another, Vince would see to it that Archer
played out his part, did the deeds for
Channing. After all, Channing had given his
life doing for Giordano. The least he could do
was to make certain that Archer repaid the
debt.

Giordano thought about the kid as he negoti-
ated the narrow bends in the road. The kid had
been green as new grass and dumb as mud.

He'd never killed anyone, he'd said.

Well, he'd probably never made a deal with
the devil before, either, but he was still going
have to ante up. And if Giordano did for Archer as Channing had done for him, well, you
can bet your ass that Archer was going to do
for Channing. Even if Giordano had to stand
behind him every step of the way and tell him
what to do.

It was only supposed to be a game, Giordano mused. Just a game . . .

Then, unexpectedly, Curtis Channing had decided to play it out for real. He'd dropped the gauntlet, and now Vince Giordano was about to pick it up.

In his mind, he ticked off the names that Archer Lowell had whispered as they'd huddled together in the courthouse that icy day in February, names he'd repeated to himself every day, lest he forget.

Amanda Crosby.

Derek England.

Marion O'Connor.

He came to a full stop at the stop sign, and leaned over to raise the volume on the radio. Tapping his fingers on the steering wheel, he headed back to town to return the borrowed car. He had plans to make. Places to go.

People to see . . .

About the Author

Mariah Stewart is the bestselling author of numerous novels and several novellas. A RITA finalist for romantic suspense, she is the recipient of the Award of Excellence for contemporary romance, a RIO (Reviewers International) Award honoring excellence in women's fiction, and a Reviewers' Choice Award from *Romantic Times* magazine. She is also a three-time recipient of the Golden Leaf Award for contemporary romance. A native of Hightstown, New Jersey, she lives with her husband, two daughters, and two rambunctious golden retrievers in a century-old Victorian home. She is a member of the Valley Forge Romance Writers, New Jersey Romance Writers, and the Romance Writers of America.